Vltava River

JUDENSTADT
JEWISH QUARTER

Bath House

Altneu
Synagogue

The Rabbi's
House

Cemetery

Zev the
Shoemaker

STARÉ MĚSTO
OLD TOWN

Market

Powder
Gate

CELETNÁ ST.

Astronomical
Clock

City Gate

Stone Bridge

NOVÉ MĚSTO
NEW TOWN

Print
Shop

Cattle
Market

Václav's
Room

City Gate

Slavonic
Monastery

Oswald's
Barn

Vyšehrad
Old Castle

The Book of Splendor

The Book of Splendor

FRANCES SHERWOOD

W. W. Norton & Company

New York   London

For information about permission to reproduce selections from this book, write to Permissions,
W. W. Norton & Company, Inc., 500 Fifth Avenue, New York, NY 10110

The text of this book is composed in Berling with the display set in Elspeth
Composition by Tom Ernst
Manufacturing by The Haddon Craftsmen, Inc.
Book design by Chris Welch
Production manager: Andrew Marasia

Library of Congress Cataloging-in-Publication Data

Sherwood, Frances, 1940–
The book of splendor / Frances Sherwood.—1st ed.
p. cm.
ISBN 0-393-02138-6 (hardcover)
1. Jewish women—Fiction. 2. Prague (Czech Republic)—Fiction. 3. Judah Loew ben Bezalel,
ca. 1525–1609—Fiction. 4. Rudolf II, Holy Roman Emperor, 1552–1612—Fiction. 5. Brache,
Tycho, 1546–1601—Fiction. I. Title.
PS3569 .H454 B66 2002
813'.54—dc21   2002000520

W. W. Norton & Company, Inc., 500 Fifth Avenue, New York, N.Y. 10110
www.wwnorton.com

W. W. Norton & Company Ltd., Castle House, 75/76 Wells Street, London W1T 3QT

2 3 4 5 6 7 8 9 0

To my son Leander Benjamin Madoo

Part I

CREATING A GOLEM requires patience, brilliance, study, prayer, and fasting. The creator must be worthy in character, close to God, free of sin. Traditionally only rabbis can make such a being, and not any rabbi, but a tzaddik, one of the righteous. Understandably, it is an undertaking filled with presumption and fraught with the possibility of error. Insight into the magical possibilities of the Hebrew alphabet is imperative, as is the ability to use the exalted language of God's various names.

Some say Adam, made of dust, was the first golem, the golem non-pareil. Of gigantic proportions, he lay dormant and crude until God breathed a soul into him. There are those who maintain that Adam's soul, his neshama, came from the earth of Paradise itself, where the trees were angels and a creature, half virgin, half snake, abided. The Kabbalists of the sixteenth century who lived in the high blue city of Safed forbade golem-making, regarding it as a kind of demonology, idolatrous in the extreme. Earlier in the century, the Swiss physician-mystic Paracelsus was said to have made a small man out of blood, urine, and sperm who grew for forty days in a retort. He was called a homunculus, an artificial embryo. But this was not a true golem, rather something like the wax figures pricked by witches for the purposes of inflicting pain on another.

A golem is, at best, a God-send, at worst blasphemy incarnate. Yet, whether apotheosis or apprentice, elemental or ethereal, what is agreed upon is that a golem is something larger than life. In some accounts he is as big as the Titans of Greek myth, and in other narratives he appears the size of the tall man in a market fair. He is also depicted as ugly, indeed, as ugly as a wild man of the woods, as ugly as a grotesque beast or a child's nightmare. Furthermore, he is marked by a lack of intelligence, described frequently and without charity as a doltish slave at his master's command. He is without voice, that is, literally mute. Legends survive of golems brought to life in Poland, Lithuania, and Bohemia. In most of the old tales the creature gets out of hand, runs amok.

In this story, of Prague in 1601, Rabbi Loew creates a golem to protect the Jewish community from certain and dreadful threat. Here as elsewhere, he is larger than those around him and does not possess a tongue, cannot speak. However, our golem has powerful feelings and a complex mind. Thus, it will not be necessary to read between the lines of this simple tale to regard this stranger as brother to us all.

1

THE BRIDE WAS an orphan, and therefore the rabbi's wife was the one to accompany her to the Khuppah. According to custom, the bride walked seven times around her bridegroom to show that he was the center of her existence and that he would receive the light and virtue that marriage brings. Afterward, the rabbi recited a portion of Psalm 118 and a short blessing. He told the bridegroom to be good to his wife, and his wife to be good to her husband. Both the bride and the groom had been outfitted in new clothes, and the wedding feast—kreplach stuffed with cheese and kasha knishes, smoked fish and pickled cucumber, radish salad, kugels of various kinds, and honey cake, days in joyous preparation—stood ready in the Jewish Town Hall, built by their mayor, Maisel. It was all going as should be. Behind the wall in the synagogue separating the women from the men, the women, although not able to see the rabbi or the couple, were smiling. It was the beginning of a new family, who could not be happy?

Solemnly, the groom began to place the token ring on the index finger of his wife. She had large hands, her knuckles were knobby, and although the ring was oversized, as was the custom, he had difficulty pushing it all the way down her finger. He pushed harder. It would not budge. A little harder. Suddenly the ring slipped from the bride's finger and, horror of horrors, clattered to the floor. At the same time, a high-pitched whistling, like a thread of wind caught in a narrow tunnel, reverberated through the aisles of the synagogue. Just as quickly, it hushed. The women behind their barrier looked at each other, terrified. The men began muttering. Quickly Zev scooped up the ring, held it aloft, and, as if nothing had happened, old Rabbi

Loew, his demeanor unruffled, recited the marriage vow. The bride-groom, slipping the ring inside the folds of his shirt, repeated:

"Behold, thou art sanctified to me by this ring according to the laws of Moses and Israel."

The marriage contract was read in which the obligations of the husband in compensation for his bride's virginity were set forth. The bride and groom drank from the second cup of wine. There was a recitation of the seven blessings, and a glass was placed on the floor.

"*Mazel tov,*" all the men chorused.

The groom shattered the glass in remembrance of the destruction of the Temple and all those exiled. Then the couple, as was tradition, were given a moment of privacy. It was permitted because they were now officially husband and wife.

"I thank you, Zev Werner, for marrying me," the bride said, for not only was she an orphan without family, but her very origins were occasion for sorrow and her marriage charity. Indeed, each person had done his and her appointed duty, for in the Jewish community of Prague on the last day in the last month of 1600 in the Christian cal-endar, an unmarried woman was the responsibility of all. Rabbi Loew, as was proper, arranged the match. Perl, the rabbi's wife, helped the orphan bride ready her clothes. The bridegroom, himself a widower, was honoring obligation, for he still loved his first wife of fifteen years who lay buried in Judenstadt's cemetery.

He was persuaded to marry this new wife, whom he had never seen and had no dowry, on the basis of her talent with the needle and thread. She, with her grandmother, three months dead at the time of the wedding, had made fine clothes not only for Mayor Maisel, the one Jew who had to appear at court, but for gentile noblemen and noblewomen who lived in palaces below the Hradčany Castle. A prodigy at her craft, Rochel had already embroidered a fine doublet for none other than Emperor Rudolph II.

True enough, as a Jew and a woman, she could not belong to the Tailors' Guild, and Zev, as a Jew, could not be in the Shoemakers' Guild, but together, using Christian go-betweens such as the tailor, Master Galliano, and Karel, the junkman, they would be able to pay the rent on their one room, which was both shop and home, and also afford, Zev decided, a new bed of fresh straw, a couple of hens, a rooster. They would be able to keep their larder full of cabbages, onions, and turnips. Indulging himself, Zev further dreamed of feeding and clothing children, for despite his great love of his first wife, that marriage had proved barren.

At the wedding party, Zev was put in one chair and his new wife in another and, like a king and queen on their thrones, they were held high aloft, paraded, as all the men and women of the Jewish neighborhood Judenstadt, in their respective sections, followed in procession. Rochel grew giddy with pride. The wine she had drunk during the ceremony rose to her head, making her nose tingle, the room close with warmth and swirling color. Almost swooning with happiness, she realized this was the beginning of her new life. However, when the grand party was over and Zev brought her to his room and shop across from the cemetery, which was to be their home, her heart, which had that very afternoon opened like a flower caressed by the sun, tightened as if struck with frost. The hearth, damp and acrid with soot, was hung with the dingle-dangle of wooden shoe forms, each pair matched to a person's size. Originally from a tree, yes, yet these shapes were not lively or shiny like leaves, but rather resembled pieces of flesh wrenched from within a tree body, remnants of slaughter, to her eyes, a row of mis-shapen puppets. Rochel feared what they would turn into when it got dark.

"When somebody dies, I take down their form from my row," Zev said, going to the cupboard and getting out his flint box to light the candle placed in a pewter dish. It was cold in that room, colder inside than outside.

"Perhaps not a fire tonight," he announced. "We will be going straight to bed. Better not to waste good kindling."

There was only one chair, the table, the bed, and now that he held up the candle Rochel saw the animal skins fixed to the rafters, strips and whole hides dyed blood red, inky black, and brown. The odor was of carnage, and overlaying it all was something sickly sweet, like perfumed wax. I have entered the forest of the dead, she told herself with a shudder.

"The carpenter is making a chair for you, Wife. Two chairs, think of it. We are very fortunate to have a roof over our heads." Zev carried the candle over to the bed. "Blessed to have clothes on our backs and food in our bellies."

The bed, raised from the floor to avoid drafts and vermin, and curtained in fabric yellowed with age, reminded Rochel of a coffin.

"Come, Wife."

She would have to make new curtains, she decided, and in time replace the oilpaper of the one window with real glass, and wash the stones of the fireplace clean, scrape out the ashes. Linen for the bed-curtains would be the least expensive fabric, but wool would be best for winter. Of course, she could not mix both. Silk, of all, was her favorite, the kind with a raised, textured pattern, or a silk velvet, soft and supple with greater luster and warmth than other velvets, or silk taffeta, with its ribbed plain weave, or silk damask, which was a pattern from Damascus, or silk brocade—

"Wife, do not stand their dawdling. I will not hurt you."

She wrapped her cloak more tightly around her.

"We do not need supper tonight, so best to bed."

She wavered. The candle he was holding cast a funnel of light illuminating the webs in the corner, octagonal gossamers, and she imagined the spiders eavesdropping on her marriage bed, climbing up and down their strands bowlegged and hunchbacked, and in the morning gossiping to each other in their little spider language squeaky and fast. At the base of the lit V, Zev's beard was given a point and the rest of his face floated around like a bubble. He had a cat's cheeks, like an old torn tom with tufts of fur, and his round eyes were clover-colored. My husband, she told herself. Thirty-three, he was an old man.

"Do not be frightened, Wife."

Mice skittered around the baseboards of the walls. The rat-catcher man in town, who walked about the streets with a pole topped with a cage hung around with rats tied by their tails, that frightened her.

"Rochel?"

There, he had said her name. Rochel.

"Rochel, your duty is to obey your husband."

Rochel knew that well from the little sessions in the rabbi's wife's kitchen as they sewed Rochel's wedding clothes, the fire warm on their faces, Perl's grandchildren underfoot. Then, duty seemed something almost cozy. Now and here, duty was cold comfort. It meant she would have to make her feet move one by one, take off her clothes. She would have to dutifully get into that gaping grave of a bed, receive her husband in matrimonial embrace.

"Rochel."

After her grandmother had died, the wedding day was fixed to follow at least the thirty days of mourning. The ceremony could not occur on a Sabbath or any holiday and, according to the Law, had to be from the time of Rochel's five unclean days, counting from the first spot of blood on her rag, and the seven days when there had been no sign of her bleeding at all. On that evening, all traces of blood gone, Rochel had taken her ritual purification bath at the mikvah, the bathhouse. As specified and supervised by the rebbetzin, Perl, she was totally immersed, not even her hair floating on the surface. When Rochel disappeared under the water, she kept her eyes open, held herself very still, being for a moment a carp sleeping deep under the ice of the Vltava River, and then, bobbing up to the rush of air, she imagined herself emerging at the spring thaw. At the time, she felt victorious, vindicated. She was to be married, after all, become a mother, if HaShem permitted, a grandmother. Now she wondered how she would survive the night.

"Do not be frightened," Zev said gently.

She wished he would be silent. Then she could do it, move her feet one by one. He was taking his shoes and breeches off now, his yarmulke. His wedding shirt hung loose over his thighs; underneath hung the fringes of his tallit katan, which he placed in the cupboard by the bed holding the bowl of water to wash before his morning prayers. "I am not a monster, believe me, Wife."

She knew about monsters—the water goblin who lived in lakes and rivers, the lady of the wailing wind who cried for her child in chimneys, the fire ghost who was able to turn you into stone, rot fruit, dry grass before harvest, the wild man of the woods with his piercing bray, and men with dog's heads or one foot or feet turned backward, unicorns, griffins who were half lion, half eagle, Hyperboreans who lived a thousand years, giants.

"We need to rise early tomorrow. Come, say your prayers with me."

She felt rooted to the floor.

"Come, come."

Forgive her, but Rochel thought her husband's chin wagged like the junkman's mule, Oswald, when he was chewing oats. Her husband's bushy eyebrows took wing with every word. And the excited catch of anticipation in her chest for her new life that had been pleasurable at the wedding party now sat heavily in her stomach. Her feet hurt. Her head felt like a hive of buzzing bees.

"This is your home, Wife. Take off your cloak." He slid down beneath the ragged quilt. She looked around for rescue, but knew that there was nothing in that room which could save her; no object gave her hope. On the hearth were bundles of herbs tied in dusty, dry, rustling bouquets. In an open cupboard were two sets of blackened pots and two sets of earthen bowls. On the long table, along with strips of leather, were dirty rags, a line of tools. Knives and awl, an instrument for making holes in leather, and needles the size of spoons. She had brought with her, tied up in a cloth bag, needles, her thimble, her pincushion in the shape of an apple, and her grandmother's very sharp scissors. She tried to draw solace from these things and her everyday brown wool skirt, the bodice and shirt she left bundled in her bag by the door, and another skirt of a dark gray. For her wedding, she had been given cloth to make a new white shirt, which she had decorated with a raised pattern of vines in white thread, and enough fabric, an unheard-of luxury, for a skirt and bodice. She had taken it to the dyer, who, using an expensive indigo and fixing the color with alum, fished it out of the boiling water with a long stick, flung it dripping and heavy on the line. The cloth matched the dark blue of the sky in winter just after sundown.

Now she felt silly in her wedding clothes, vain and insubstantial. She wanted to go home to her little room where she had tended her grandmother in her last illness, which, although dirt-floored and bare of any decoration, was clean and cheerful.

"I want you to know that I do not hold your birth against you," Zev said, his head peeping up from the top of his covering.

She knew it would come to that.

"I can see that you have good hands. I noticed them right away, hands used to work."

He was trying to be kind, she knew, but she hated her hands. Thick fingers, stubby tips, large palms, and nails which she did not pare and burn as was the custom, but which she quietly nibbled when her grandmother was not looking. And her knuckles were a cause of embarrassment, more than embarrassment, the bringer of bad luck. Had she been outside when the ring fell off, she would have spit seven times against the Evil Eye.

"Oats and hot water in the morning, and I think there is not a finer dish than lentils simmered with onions, challah for the Sabbath."

Her grandmother had let her roll out the dough from when she was a little girl.

"On the Sabbath, we will always have meat, that I promise you. Roast chicken, lamb."

Rochel did not like meat, or even fish. She did not like to eat anything that had once had a face on it.

"Do you see the leather on the table? Shoes for Rosenberg, the burgrave to the emperor. I sell them to the Christian shoemaker, who sells them to the burgrave. Tomorrow is laying out. Tuesday is cutting. Wednesday is stitching. Thursday is finishing. Friday morning is delivering, shopping, and cooking and cleaning for Sabbath. I do not want you to tire yourself out, wife, but bit by bit we shall do it all." He had placed the candle by the bed. "You have been standing there like a statue in the Square, no? It is your wedding night."

She moved one foot, then the other, inched forward. He waited. She moved closer still.

"Come, come." He gestured with his cupped hand.

She had reached the side of the bed.

"You will have to take off your skirts and petticoats, Wife." Zev took up the candle again in its little pewter dish and held it over his head so he could watch her.

She stepped back into the shadows.

"No, no. Closer," Zev said.

Moving to the very edge of the bed, her heart lodged in her throat, she slowly, with trembling fingers, undid her skirt panels held together with a looped button. Her petticoat had a drawstring. Her bodice had many tiny buttons of wood. Her head covering was tied in a tight knot at the back of her neck. Tonight, her clothes seemed sewed to her skin. Her hair was fixed back by combs with teeth that dug like tiger claws. Each fastening seemed a puzzle resisting solution, and her fingers, so deft with a needle and thread, were tangled with trembling. She took off her shoes, which were old and not the best, the heels cork and the sides held together by a ribbon frayed and dirty with mud. Her stockings were held up on each leg by a little belt hung with ribbons. Putting her legs up one by one on the bed, she undid the knots.

"Now the shirt," Zev said, his voice a little hoarse.

Rochel shivered, but bravely pulled her shirt over her head.

"Let me see you."

Rochel moved within the light.

"Good heavens," her husband exclaimed.

Rochel, at eighteen years old, had been in danger of being a spinster. Nobody had ever really looked at her, the orphan, save one, and he, not a Jew, could not marry her. Her long yellow hair, heretofore hidden by a scarf and now let down, bordered her face like the scrolled ornamentation on a frame surrounding a fine portrait. Her eyes, usually downcast, were large, deep, a rich brown, and slightly slanted the Russian way from long-ago Tartar blood, as were her sharp cheekbones. Her lips were fuller than was the usual of her community and her teeth large, so that her mouth, even at rest, opened a little. Her nose was sharp, distinct. She had a long milky white neck. The breasts, small, had pink nipples puckered in baby creases with large areolas spread over them like late-blooming roses, and her hips were a boy's, straight, while her legs swelled womanly.

"You are a beautiful woman." Zev was truly amazed.

She flinched.

"You are beautiful. You are a gem."

With her narrow face, she had a slightly feral look, and despite her meekness, she frightened Zev. Her beauty was frightening.

"Do not move. Let me look at you."

"Husband?"

"You are . . . beautiful." He felt as if a sharp rock had lodged itself in his left lung. "I cannot believe how beautiful you are." He squeezed his eyes shut, opened them again. "You must cut your hair, cut it all off."

"Cut, Husband?"

"We cannot have you walking about unshorn. It is not enough that your head is covered. Cut, it must be cut. That is all there is to it. Cut, cut, cut."

"Husband?"

"We will get you a good horsehair wig, no?"

She opened her mouth.

"Would you like that, a nice black wig? A roof over your head, food in your belly, a nice horsehair wig. Come, come to me." He said this gently, tenderly, as a father would console a child.

Gaining courage, she raised the quilt, stepped inside. Emerging from the water of her ritual bath before her wedding, she had felt newborn. This time, sinking into her marriage bed, she knew the transformation she was to undergo would awaken her from the dream of childhood. It was to be. Her husband blew out the candle, quickly mumbled a prayer, and immediately moved his body over hers. The flesh of his stomach doubled in a ruffle over the bones of her pelvis; his breath, hot and damp on her cheek, gave off the flavor of wedding food soured in the stomach. She bit her lips, clenched her fists, reminded herself that she was a bride, soon, God willing, a mother. She would make good what was bad, but her husband's weight was great, and when Zev entered her, she felt that she was Jonah devoured and Zev, the Leviathan.

Then, in an instant, it was all over. Zev slid off of her, repeated the Shema Yisrael, and fell asleep.

Rochel lay there, the blood seeping out of her, her legs straight out, her arms stiffly at her sides, as she sucked in the cold air, blew it out. I am married, she mouthed to the ceiling lost to the darkness. Rochel could hear the town crier call from the Stone Bridge.

"Eight and all is well."

Eight and all is well.

"Nine and all is well."

Nine and all is well.

It seemed that shortly after, she heard horse hooves outside the gates of Judenstadt, voices coming from across the cemetery, from the rabbi's house, from the head of the Burial Society's house, from the schoolmaster's house next to Zev's. Doors opened and slammed. Zev slept on. Then the clomping of hooves pounded along the cobblestones once more, and silence spread throughout Judenstadt.

2

ECEMBER 31, 1600, was the worst day of his whole wretched life. Forty-eight years old, his body a daily burden, his mind unsettled, his mood execrable, his temperament that of a peevish child, and without any company to warm the cockles of his wizened heart, the emperor had only a light supper: *Wildschwein* cooked in wine and beer, a platter of fried tripe, plover pie, and a special drink brought from Spain—hot chocolate. Sighing heavily, he signed some documents brought by the lord high clerk and left instructions for the Privy Council and War Council to carry on without him for the morrow. He was indisposed, he explained. The Holy Roman Emperor, Rudolph Habsburg II, like God, needed a rest. Could they understand? Of course they understood. The emperor kissed his supreme burgrave, Vilem Rosenberg, on both cheeks. Then he excused all those waiting on him, the four young pages of the bedchamber brought from the Habsburg castle in Vienna, the ten Slovene guards who stood at attention all night outside his bedchamber, and to his court astronomer and astrologer, Tycho Brahe, he bade a fond good-bye.

"Your Highness," Brahe said with some concern. Too occupied with his new assistant, Johannes Kepler, a scrawny but admittedly brilliant German, the big Dane had not cast Rudolph's horoscope for the day, December 31, 1600. Something must be amiss for the emperor not to request it.

"A little tired, Tycho, is all."

Václav, Rudolph's valet, companion, advisor, and daresay only friend, dutifully trotted behind his Holy Roman Emperor, ready to take up his station at the foot of the imperial bed.

"Can an emperor have some privacy," Rudolph asked Václav, "for once in his life?"

"Pardon me, Your Majesty."

"I do, of all your various sins. Now leave me alone, Václav, begone."

It was Rudolph alone, followed only by his pet lion, Petaka, who entered his bedchamber for the night and with his own hands closed the big double doors.

"At last." The room was huge, and the bed, on its platform, seemed like a galley lost in the ocean, but instead of stiff white sails, it was canopied in soft silk the color of thousands of snail shells crushed to a purple pulp. There was a cupboard with a few books—his Rabelais, his Erasmus, his Castiglione, his *Aeneid*, *Travels of Marco Polo*, no consolation now, philosophy, and writing tools—quill, freshly mixed ink, a dish of sand. No, he did not want to leave a note. There was a small altar with a kneeling stool. Nor did he want to pray. The box with the double eagles looking east and west, with spears in their claws, tongues curling out of their mouths, the Habsburg emblem, held the royal chamber pot, the seat padded with thick velvet tufted with gold buttons. For certain, he was not going to leave evidence to be examined and pondered in the doctor's laboratory. Some five trestle tables held a mere twenty of his famous clock collection. Apparently it was nine or ten minutes after eight, five minutes to eight, two before, one after, thereabouts. After a few minutes, Rudolph could hear the town crier at the Stone Bridge.

"Eight o'clock and all is well."

And the bells from the Capuchin church began to toll. And other bells, all over Prague, one after another, each off by several minutes. At that, the hunting dogs in the imperial kennels set up a mighty howl and the lions in the lion court answered with bloodcurdling roars. The birds in the imperial aviary twittered and fluttered and the horses in the imperial stables whinnied in response. Donkeys heehawed as if they were being led to slaughter.

"Jesus Christ in Mary," the emperor seethed, "can a man not die in peace?"

For here he was at the end of his life, and to the last second everything was irritation. A moment of dignity, please, a slight pause in the world, that was all he was asking for. He made his way across the room, adjusted himself on one of his uncomfortable wooden chairs by the fire, attempted to gather his wits. The lion had taken his station by the fireplace.

"Ah, Petaka, Petaka."

The beast, not old, but tamed, declawed, broken-toothed, was more rug than companion.

"Woe is me." It always came back, this sadness. He could be eating the most delicate of cakes or examining a priceless object in his collection, receiving nuncios from the Papal Court, or even in the midst of lovemaking with his favorite mistress, Anna Marie Strada, when a suffocating horror would descend like the cover of a coffin being shut over him. It was a gray cloud capable of muffling the lovely music of Monteverdi and dimming the brilliance of gold. Sometimes he thought it a curse or spell. Which, given the nature of the world, could come from any quarter. Wandering witches. Distraught Protestants. Turks in disguise.

That very afternoon, after a morning abed, Rudolph had walked in his gardens seeking some solace. Yet the knowledge that in successive waves the tight, hard ground would yield up snowdrops, and then the tiny velvet petals of purple violets and cat-face pansies from England, daffodils and hyacinths from Holland, and priceless tulips of velvety lips smuggled from Turkey in the time of his father cheered him not at all.

Now it was night, the castle gates closed, only the sound of New Year revelers coming from the main ballroom, and Rudolph was in the bedchamber he had chosen for the act. The costly tapestries of saintly scenes hanging on the wall—Saint John's head on a platter, Saint Laurence being roasted alive on a grid, and Saint Agatha getting her breasts cut off—seemed appropriate decor for the occasion, a conspiracy of sorts. No wonder I want to die, Rudolph thought. The one window of the room, unlike the narrow arrow slits in other parts of the castle, was paned with the finest Venetian glass. As he looked out between the latticework at his window, his gaze met the beady eyes of a monk supposedly at his evening prayers.

"Damn you to hell, letch, leech." Rudolph heaved his portly self up out of his chair, hobbled to the window, wrenched the curtains shut. St. Vitus Cathedral overlooked this side of the castle, on higher ground, closer to God, no doubt, and any time of day or night the good brothers felt free to peer at him from their various posts. Indeed, they seemed to be adhering to his castle walls like lichen, attaching themselves, wet slugs, to every conversation and event.

He went to his bed, undressed all by himself, something he could not remember doing for all of his forty-eight years of life.

"What have I come to, Petaka?" he sighed to his lion.

Then the emperor carefully lifted from an oaken chest the attire chosen for this occasion, his cream silk nightshirt, his green woolen trunk hose, a fresh, crisp ruff, which with his beard helped obscure his protruding chin, and a three-quarter cape of ermine, for he was one of those people who were always cold day or night, summer or winter. Setting his new crown by his side, so his last sight could be its eight diamonds, signifying Christ, and the ten rubies and pearls and one magnificent sapphire, he got in bed. One of his relatives, Charles V, Rudolph remembered, had practiced his own funeral service to the extent that he donned his burial clothes and stepped into his coffin, all of his court, as well as wife and children, in attendance. Rudolph felt a bit like that now, or perhaps even more so, for he was preempting, by an act of his own will, destiny's appointed hour. Yes, yes, he had the razor ready, taken surreptitiously from one of the court's barber surgeons. In recent days gazing at it had given him comfort, reminding him that Socrates had taken hemlock, Brutus had fallen on his sword, for were not all things rendered unto dust and ashes?

He supposed he should commend himself to the mercy of God, but faithful Catholic that he was, he did not believe in the flames of hell, although he had seen several times, once dancing to the tune of a pipe on Petřín Hill, Satan. What Rudolph believed in was oblivion, not to feel, not to know, above all not to suffer. Yet when first conceived, it was exactly the idea of suffering which served as obstacle. For the truth of it was that he was afraid of heights, hated water, did not relish ropes, cords of any sort. And the sight of blood, particularly his own, sickened him, which was why he had a Paracelsian physician. No bleeding or leeching for him. Pills, herbs, tonics, that was his medicine. And the battlefield, jousts, tournaments, fencing matches he, as monarch, was required to attend, were graced with his presence only from an imperial distance. When hunting, he averted his eyes from the butchery. He had his meat well cooked. Nevertheless, blood it was to be, quick and certain, for here he was, holding his wrist over a bowl filled with sawdust, razor in the other hand, looking away.

And with one bold stroke, he braceleted his left wrist with a thin line of red.

"Václav," he screamed.

Petaka yawned.

"Your Majesty." Václav, loyal valet, who had been at the doorway lying on the floor between the guards, hoping for a spot of rest, threw open the doors, bounded into the bedchamber.

"What is it, Sire?"

"Do you not see, you knave, I am bleeding to death? Get Dr. Kirakos, only Kirakos."

Václav pulled a sheet from the emperor's bed, clumsily wrapped it around the wound, and then ran, his head bobbing on his thin neck like a top on a stick, out of the room, down the hall.

"The emperor is dying, the emperor is dying."

"That is right," the emperor fumed. "Inform the whole world."

"The emperor?" A guard questioned Václav. "Is what?"

"Fine, fine, just fine," Václav answered, slackening his pace, pretending unconcern; then, turning a corner, he sped down through Vladislav Hall, where jousts were held, raced out through the courtyard across from St. Vitus Cathedral toward the imperial stables adjacent to Rudolph's private picture gallery. That was where Kirakos's apartment was situated. Breathlessly he knocked on Kirakos's heavy wooden door. No answer. Václav pushed it open. The room, dark, empty, the roses on the carpet on the floor like pads floating on a black pond, the pillows on the floor plump shadows, gave Václav a sudden chill.

"Holy Mary," Václav prayed. "Let me find him."

Avoiding the entrance to the lion courts, Václav went toward the Ball-game Hall and Orangery on the other side of the Stag Moat, then, seeing a light in the Powder Tower, crossed back over. Perhaps the physician was at work in the emperor's own alchemical laboratory. But it was only a guard. Kirakos, of various strange habits, was known to stroll on the bitterest of nights in the Gardens of Paradise or along the ramparts.

"Kirakos, Kirakos."

Silence. The air was cold, dense. Václav hoped his wife had a fire going in her room. She was with child, twenty-nine years old, well past her prime. And if the emperor died and he, Václav, had no work . . . "Oh, dear, oh, no." He raced above the kitchens and servants' dining hall, where the myriad cooks and their assistants were boiling all manner of beast, fowl, fish, and vegetable for the midnight meal. There were guards, of course, everywhere, and musicians, ladies, men about court, servants galore, for all had gathered to celebrate the new year, the new century, but Václav could not betray his errand. He circled the two tiers of the imperial ballrooms, only seeing the gorgeously clad guests as tableaux against arched panels of yellow. Václav panicked. Where else could the physician be? Picking up speed, running again, Václav passed the Basilica of St. George, found himself in Golden Lane, the alchemist quarter.

"Who goes there?" a guard called out.

"Only me, out for some evening air."

He was panting now, and pain flamed up his calves and thighs. He limped along the fortification wall, decided to go in the direction of the Singing Fountain and Belvedere, the summer palace. There, on the terrace which ringed the stately marble building, on this cold night stood the astronomer Johannes Kepler, looking up at the sky.

"Have you seen Kirakos, the Armenian?"

"At the Golden Ox playing chess with Brahe."

And indeed, below the castle, in the hole-in-the-wall tavern the Golden Ox, was the Armenian physician Kirakos; his assistant, the good-for-nothing Russian, Sergey, a man of few, if any, words; the portly Danish astronomer Tycho Brahe; and Karel, the legless junkman. They were seated in front of the blazing fire playing chess, drinking plum brandy, and eating slices of ham spread with mustard and gingerbreads unfit for imperial guests and sold from the kitchen door of the castle. Karel agreed to carry them back to the castle in his cart. Brahe stayed behind.

"Where is the sluggard?" the emperor bellowed when he saw Václav carrying Karel in his arms, seconded by the Armenian physician Kirakos, and followed by Sergey. Each of them made careful not to disturb the mangy lion.

"Good heavens," Kirakos exclaimed when he saw his monarch's wrist wrapped in sheets. "How did this happen, Your Majesty?"

"How do you think? I cut myself. What is *he* doing here?" Rudolph pointed to Karel.

"Just in the neighborhood," the junkman replied.

"Well, out, nobody invited you."

Václav carried Karel out to the courtyard, placed him on his little chair built onto his cart, then came back to the emperor's bedchamber.

"Rope, Sergey," Kirakos commanded.

The Russian dug into the depths of the doctor's bag, came up with a thick cord. The doctor tied it around Rudolph's upper arm, pulled tightly.

"No, no, Kirakos, that hurts."

"Do you wish to live, Your Majesty?"

"I am not sure."

"Needle, Sergey," the doctor ordered next.

"Needle?" Rudolph nearly popped out of his hose. He hated needles worse than blood.

Sergey brought out a red velvet case in which were laid all sizes of needles. Needles for blisters. Plague needles, smallpox needles, enema needles, needles for searing and stabbing and sewing, needles so small they could be used to hem lace fit for a princess.

"That one."

Rudolph did not like the look of it. It was one of the bigger ones, a veritable sword, it seemed, and the point glittered like glass.

"Kirakos, be a nice fellow, let me die in peace. I have changed my mind."

"Your Majesty, remain tranquil."

"I am tranquil, Václav. Any more tranquil and I will be dead."

"Clampers," Kirakos commanded.

"Is clampers." Sergey handed the doctor a set of little pincers. They, too, looked deadly—silver, backed by an ornate little crab, points like daggers.

"Ouch," Rudolph said before they were set to hold the skin together.

"I am here, Your Majesty," Václav said.

And indeed Rudolph was gripping his servant's hand with such force, Václav thought he might be the one to fall down dead.

"Do not just stand there, imbecile, fetch some brandy," Rudolph commanded.

Václav was more than happy to disengage himself and obey.

"Brandy for the emperor," he shouted to the Slovenian guards who stood in formation at the door ready to brandish their ungainly and antiquated swords. The harquebuses were locked up in the basement with the barrels of wine and only Václav had the key.

"Brandy," they chorused, and the word echoed down the halls like a general's imperative.

"Now thread needle," Kirakos ordered his Russian assistant.

Rudolph winced. There was a light knock on the door and in came a servant bearing a decanter of brandy, a glass on a silver tray.

"Aqua vitae, love of my life," the emperor moaned.

The servant, in scarlet livery, bowed gracefully, and with studied finesse poured the liquor from the beautifully decorated decanter into a lavender-tinted glass in the shape of a fluted lily.

"Christ's blood, give it over, man." The emperor grabbed the decanter, threw the whole down his throat at once.

"Do not drown yourself, Your Majesty."

"Are you telling me what to do, Václav?"

"Oh, no, Your Majesty."

Meanwhile, humming an ancient Armenian melody, Kirakos set about his sewing.

"Jesus Christ in Mary and all the apostles." Each and every prick was an exquisite pain beyond endurance. Rudolph felt like one of the martyred saints in the tapestries hanging from his wall. "Have mercy on a poor Christian soul."

"Ointment."

"Is ointment." Sergey was said to be a refugee from the havoc Ivan the Terrible had inflicted on Russia. Prague was filled with such people—Jews who had fled inquisitions and indignities, Armenians like Kirakos, whose country had been taken over by Turks, Germans seeking their fortune, honey-haired whores of Viking blood, Italian craftsmen, alchemists of every religion and region, artists of dubious talent, more priests than anybody liked to see in one place, and pesky Protestants, some of old Hussite families, and others who'd followed the Reformation and become the newly minted of Luther's legions. The Jesuits had, of course, made an enclave. And the emperor himself was Austrian, Prague the capital of his empire, which extended over Bohemia, Moravia, Upper and Lower Silesia, the two Lusatias, Austria, of course, Tyrol, Styria, Carinthia, Carniola, the German states, and a piece of Hungary. Often forgotten, the Czechs were in Prague first—the city dwellers who were merchants, tradesmen, members of the many guilds, laborers, workers, and, from the country on market days, free peasants, villagers.

"Linen," Kirakos commanded.

"Is linen."

The physician wrapped the bandage around Rudolph's wrist. There had been no real danger, the cut being shallow. However, Kirakos made good show of it. And Rudolph, now patched up, calmed down. A glass of heated wine was brought in, and additional nourishment—cheese and soft, white bread, a side dish of tenderly stewed rabbit.

"Now, then, Your Highness," Kirakos said gently, "you must tell me what led to this."

3

A CROSS THE RIVER, within the damp walls of Judenstadt, Zev sound asleep beside her, Rochel held herself rigidly still in the hope that her grandmother's voice would not find her. Wispy as smoke, it hovered above, and then, like a bee crawling into the corolla of a flower, the words entered her ear.

"Memory fails me, Rochel, I cannot tie the threads. The best of times holds the seeds of the worst. Trouble is never far away. It may be your wedding night, but God forbid you forget what you come from."

How could Rochel forget?

"First of all feet, many feet beating a fast flurry of escape, and the smell of animals being roasted alive in the barn, their shrieks human as they battered against the wooden slats of their pens. It was the end of hope, Rochel, the end of the world, the face of evil. Your mother and I ran, we ran."

Until the age of thirteen, up to the day of her first bleeding, Rochel had different pictures in mind, childish dreams—for instance, her mother bathing her in a blue bowl, the warm water running down her chest in silver spangles, her mother walking across the Stone Bridge, the sun a shimmering button on a breast of blue, and she, a little girl, trying to hold on to her mother's coarse skirt, her hand so slippery that the cloth was like catching scratchy sheaves of wheat in wind. Rochel even imagined a time when her mother and grand-mother were on the way to the great city of Prague from their small Ukrainian village. Supper, and the two women spreading their cloth, reaching into their basket to pull out a loaf of soft bread, sweet raisins, and a jar of warm, very clean milk, nearby a brook singing merrily as it channeled between stones sitting like freshly washed jewels, lambs frolicking in the meadow. It was only a short walk to Prague, a sum of a few days, and in this dream, her mother and grandmother did not walk, but rode in carts and carriages with doors that snapped shut and window curtains closed against the dust of the road, and at night they slept in large beds framed in heavy wood, many coverlets over them, this after a meal of thick dumplings and braised cabbage. When they arrived at the gates of Judenstadt in Prague, Rabbi Loew, his long robes flying behind him, Maisel, the mayor, the members of the Burial Society, the rabbi's sons-in-law, and all the yeshiva boys spilled out of the gates to greet them. Welcome, welcome.

But it had not been that way.

Indeed, her grandmother's words the day of Rochel's first blood, as she remembered now, had been so harsh, Rochel wanted to put her hands over her ears, cry: No, Bubbe, no.

"You are today a woman." As was custom, her grandmother had slapped Rochel across the cheek when she showed her the bloody underskirt. And that night, hobbling over to light a candle as the evening fell, the one trestle table and lone chair already fading in the dark, the world dropping quietly away behind them, the old woman first of all told Rochel how to keep clean as a woman, and how she must never touch a man when she was unclean, and how after the right number of days she had to go to the bathhouse so she would be clean. Rochel was told she could no longer run or skip, but must walk sedately, head lowered, her eyes to the ground. She must keep her shoes only for certain occasions, such as Shabbat and the High Holy Days. Already, she knew how to use scraps for a coverlet, how to boil the groats over a fire slowly so that the kasha was tender, how to peel an apple, save the shavings to throw into the oats, how to take a portion of the challah from the loaf, how to peel a boiled egg so the shell came off in one piece by tapping it first, then rolling it in your hand, and that she must never, ever eat an egg with a drop of blood in it.

True enough, these prohibitions and injunctions paled alongside what had happened in Russia, did not seem directly connected, yet somehow it all went together, as if it, the tragedy of her mother's village, had been her fault and was to be repeated if she were not observant, truly careful. Indeed, Rochel had always felt particularly susceptible to mishap because she was not like everybody else. From before she could remember, she understood she was an orphan who did not even know for certain if her grandmother was her grandmother, and hearing her grandmother's travails, she realized that it was only through accident of time and place that she had been spared the fate of her ancestral village. Meanwhile, the rest of the world seemed to go along without a backward glance. Children woke up, washed, said their prayers, played their games. Mothers cooked and cleaned. Fathers and boys were swallowed up into the doorway of the shul and, in the streets at twilight, flocked back like dark pigeons to their homes. The round of their lives spun on a wheel of days ordained. They were all so self-assured that Rochel wondered if there was a key she had not been given, another lesson she had missed. For without any lettered guidance, because as a woman she was not taught the Torah, could not read, she worried about her soul, the neshama. Was she born blemished, wayward, and discontented or, according to lore, was she possessed by a dybbuk, another's spirit who could not leave the earth and must enter a body to tease and torment? Could it be that her girl presence alone was unpleasing to God? Although to be a woman, her grandmother told her, was to be close to the Lord, and every Jew, man, woman, and child, lived according to the Law.

"The summer of 1582 was a year of famine, a year of drought, and in Kiev, the Plague bell rang all the nights as they carted away the bodies."

Green onion bulbs in the gray sky was the Ukraine Rochel envisioned. Soldiers on stiff parade thrusting out their booted legs, Russian boyars in peaked hats edged in fur, Polish peasants in embroidered shirts.

"In the Ukraine of 1582, people lived like moles in hovels, ate bark, died of thirst."

Rochel, at thirteen, sitting on the three-legged stool by the warm coals of the hearth, looked down at her sewing. In the dim candlelight, she was embroidering French knots, doing couching and whip stitches on the floppy collar of a courtier's cloak, the wool from Britain, bought in Frankfort, carted to Prague by merchant caravan, the silk thread made in Italy sent north across the alps. Her needle was silver from the Fugger mines in the Tyrol, her thimble wood from the Black Forest. The world was at her fingertips, she told herself, and she wanted it to be a kind world, a generous world.

"Wells were dry that year, Rochel, and we had to buy our water from the water carrier, who carried barrels of it in a cart dragged by a horse so thin that even the poorest person in the village was sorry for it. Water, Rochel, was precious as gold that summer."

There was plenty of water in Prague, several wells in Judenstadt; the rabbi had one right in his own courtyard, and the emperor had water pumped from the Vltava River straight into his scullery at the castle. That was what her friend Václav had told her when she was a little girl. Not only water by pump, but inside the castle there were candelabra hanging from the ceiling and circular stands of candles in every corner, sconces, and, braced against the walls, even glass lamps lit by oil. Rooms in the middle of the night cast a golden afternoon glow. It was glorious, Václav said. And indeed, if you went to the edge of the Vltava River at night and looked across, you could see the castle on top of Hradčany Hill lit up like stars fallen to the ground.

"Your mother was betrothed to a fine boy."

Betrothed, a word soft as feathers, a word meaning father-to-be, her father.

"The boy helped his father collect rents for the landlord and manage the accounts for the vast estate, which was hectares of wheat tended by hundreds of serfs."

Such a countryside belonged to dreams in which horses roamed in tall grass. The idea frightened her. She was fortunate to live in the city of Prague, Prague in Bohemia, the heart of Europe, the capital of the Habsburg Empire.

"Your mother's betrothed was a clever boy. Someday, they said, he would do the accounts himself."

Rochel had never even held a book in her hands, but she could do numbers in her head, sign her name, taking the quill to sketch the pattern in ink as she would use a needle to embroider a flower, for at thirteen years of age, she was an accomplished needle woman. Of course, fancy clothes were not for the women or men of Judenstadt, who wore homespun, homemade, shapeless dresses or long shirts and breeches like peasants; rather, Rochel and her grandmother sewed for the nobles who lived in palaces along the hill below the emperor's castle, which overlooked all of Prague, the spires of St. Vitus Cathedral, within the castle grounds, taller than anything in the city.

Master Galliano, the gentile tailor who brought them their cloth and patterns, threads, the work commissioned by castle and courtiers, said Emperor Rudolph II was prone to tears and frantic declarations, but fortunately for people who sewed for their living, this vain and capricious man insisted his court attend him in suitable attire. To be sure, the nobles and courtiers living on Hradčany Hill, and the emperor in the castle, did not know that many of their gorgeous garments were made and decorated by a mere girl and her feeble grandmother in their one dirt-floored, ill-lit room in Judenstadt, really not even a stadt or much of a neighborhood, but one street, Judenstrasse, flanked by a tangle of tiny alleys, and that the brilliantly colored threads and cloth were trundled under the cover of night across the Stone Bridge in a wheelbarrow from Master Galliano's fine shop near At the House of the Three Ostriches, where hat makers bought their plumes.

"It was so hot that summer of 1582," her grandmother had gone on, "that we could not sleep and, when awake, could not move, and when the sun traveled across the sky, we were afraid that it, too, might stay its course, the relief of night never come to us again. It was so hot that women forgot their modesty and opened their dresses, showing their chemises, and people did not go to the fields to work, all the earth scorched to death."

Until the time of Rochel's first blood, her grandmother's stories had been about important women in the Bible: Esther, who saved her people; Ruth, the daughter-in-law of Naomi; Leah, Jacob's wife, who bore him many sons; or tales about kings and queens who lived in elegant castles.

"I am telling you so you know what has gone before you and can happen again, anywhere, anytime."

Rochel dared to hope her mother experienced joy in her life, if even for a moment. For her own life, now that she was honorably married, Rochel believed that each day would open with promise, close with tenderness. She wanted many children. She wanted to feel rightness fall across her path like sunlight through a canopy of leaves in the forest. Indeed, now that she was a person among people, she wanted to learn to read, to be able to read the Torah, to cipher out the word *Baruch*—blessed.

"First it was young men coming out from the town, mischief-makers, a few rocks, the usual insults. Then came the scoundrels and beggars who were always ready for a fight. The dangerous ones were the ones on horses. Peasants joined in. They were angry at the landlord who kept them serfs and employed many of us, not only to keep accounts, manage the estate, but our women who tended his children and served as maids. Then it was the shopkeepers who did not want us to have our little shops, what was the harm, some threads, a ribbon. A little lick of flame, Rochel, was enough because the thatched straw of our roofs was already crackling in the heat of the day, and the houses were old wood, brittle as kindling."

At another time, her grandmother told her of winter wolves who roamed the steppes and chased after sleighs. Once there was the bridal party, members of nobility, chattering happily in their sleighs when the wolves appeared out of the forest, blue icy eyes, ghostly white fur. People were thrown to the wolves, first the servants, one by one, and then the relatives, cousins, uncles, aunts, mother, father, and finally the groom threw the bride herself.

"The entire village burned down to the ground. All the men were massacred."

"My father, was my father killed?"

"You have no father."

You have no father: ah, ah, ah.

Your mother is a whore: ja, ja, ja.

That was the taunt from the children in her neighborhood.

"But the betrothed, Grandmother?"

"Not your father."

Even now, five years later, in her marriage bed, staring up at Zev's cobwebbed ceiling, Rochel could remember the exact tone of her grandmother's voice when she said it. *Not your father.* In her dream, her father was like the horses wandering in tall grass, or the Israelites, forty years in the desert. He was lost and looking for her.

"We had to stop in Kraków for three nights, for your mother was with child, just a child herself, and could hardly walk."

Rochel had lived her whole life within the moldy, cracked walls encircling the Jewish community, and when permitted to accompany her grandmother on her errands about town, she loved best of all the Vltava River, also the woods on Petřín Hill where big, leathery mushrooms could be picked. Rochel liked going to market in Old Town Square, first crossing the Jewish Cemetery where all their dead rested many feet deep, next passing the Jewish Town Hall built by Mayor Mordechai Maisel, a rich and influential man, court Jew to the emperor. Mayor Maisel had bestowed a chair for Rabbi Loew in the Altneu Synagogue. Rochel, who had to sit with the women behind the wall during the service, had never seen the chair, but she knew it was near the ark where the sacred scrolls of the Torah were kept, the holiest place in the synagogue.

The Christian Church of the Holy Ghost she did not like at all, with its high windows like long, sad eyes, but emerging from the crush of buildings at the Old Town Square predominated by the City Town Hall, which had double doors with lion heads on them, heavy gold rings held in their mouths, Rochel's heart would lift. In the Town Hall Tower, from within the Astronomical Clock, puppets came out at the stroke of the hour, twelve old men with hoops of gold around their heads.

The one man her grandmother talked to besides Master Galliano and the rabbi was Karel, the junkman. A Christian like Master Galliano, he had no legs and thus had to either be lifted up onto a little chair fastened to his cart with a bell over it, a string to pull, or he was placed on a board with tiny wheels. Rochel's grandmother had made him special breeches that looked more like a skirted doublet, and a glover had fashioned him leather gloves so strong they did not tear when he pushed himself about on his board. A mule pulled his cart. All day, Karel Vojtech dealt in garbage, cast-offs, junk.

"Oswald, say hey-ho to little Rochel."

Oswald would shake his shaggy old head slowly up and down, flick flies off his rump with his black tail with the same swishing movement her grandmother used to sweep the floor. On rainy days, Oswald wore a felt hat with holes for his long ears. Karel would call out from his perch as he went through Judenstadt, "Rags, rags and bones, sell me your rags and bones." Once, Karel had taken her and her grandmother for a long ride in his cart. When night arrived, they were far down the river, nowhere near home.

"Careful of thieves," Karel had said.

Thieves? Rochel had been worried about the Night Hag flying above them on her broom, swooping her up with one grab, eating her in one gulp, or the Erl King, who traveled on a horse, brought death to sick little children, or a merman who would rise up from the river, swallow you whole, or wood sprites. There were so many things that could happen to you when you ventured out at night. Even in bright sunlight, without the walls of Judenstadt, there were the Christian children who could run her down, press her head to the ground, forcing her to "kiss the cross, kiss the cross." She wanted Karel to make Oswald take them back right now. But no, they traveled as far as the old castle, Vyšehrad, where the first queen, Lubice, had reigned, and was now tumbledown rocks looming on a cliff behind them like a giant mountain lion set to leap. When they finally stopped, Karel brought out his jar of beer and pointed:

"Look, that is the Whale, the Phoenix, the Crane, the Goat, the Eagle, the Bull and Ram."

As much as Rochel had wanted to see the animals floating in the sky, all she saw was a dense black cloth with many pinpricks showing the light beyond. Or perhaps the little bits of light were islands, like Kampa Island in the Vltava River, where women who lived by the mill brought their clothes to wash and bleach white.

"Mind me well, Rochel. After a long, hard journey, me and your mother, we get to Prague."

Although Rochel was in her own house now, a married woman that day, her grandmother two months buried, her mother long dead, she could picture them as if alive, placed right there in that room.

"When your mother's time came, we sent for Rabbi Loew's wife, Perl."

Perl, a very busy person indeed, small and bent, alert as a ferret, with spectacles at the end of her nose attached around her ears with metal hooks, never appeared without her blue linen babushka tightly tied about her head and tidy apron cinched about her waist.

"I called for Perl because it was a difficult birth." The rabbi's wife, midwife to the women of Judenstadt, could be imagined fingering the sheets on the bed, peering into the water in the bowl, touching the table, is there dust anywhere, for she could not abide dirt in her own home, and had a duster made of black rooster feathers tied to a short stick which she brandished like a scepter against invading disorder. Her birthing bag contained many clean rags and balls of dried spongy moss, sacks of shredded rosemary and thyme, mugwort, wormwood, sage. In its depths was a large, sharp pair of scissors, a suspiciously long pair of tongs, a little stoppered bottle of aqua vitae which was distilled wine, called brandy by some, some valerian root, and crushed, caked poppy pulp.

The candle, melted down now, just a feeble flame, sputtered, wavered, and was extinguished in a pool of wax. Her grandmother, duty done, got up to wash her hands, say her prayers, make ready for her night's rest. Her granddaughter had been prepared for her womanhood, told what she needed to know, given enough for the time being. However, Rochel, who at the beginning of the story had wanted her grandmother to stop at every word, now wanted to know: Did the rabbi of the burning village rescue the Torah scroll, carrying it like a baby out of harm's way, leaving behind the scorched earth and acrid ashes, coming in time to a place safe from flames and hate? And her mother, when and how did she die? Was it the Plague, the pox, the flux, the bite of a rabid dog?

Rochel at eighteen, awake on her wedding night, thought she could hear the river, small waves lapping the shore, and the muffled *clop-clop* of horse hooves going across the bridge to the castle as the snow accumulated as softly as petals fell from fruit trees in the spring. She believed she could hear whispers coming from the rabbi's house, one of his daughters getting up to see about a child, somebody tossing in her bed. Her grandmother never told her where her father was, how her mother died, if her mother bathed her in a blue bowl of warm water, as she liked to remember, and walked across the bridge in the bright sun of the afternoon. Her mother's Hebrew name was Chava, Eve, from *chai*, for life, that she knew, but there was no marker, nothing to tell her mother's yahrtzeit, the year after her death. Was the day of her death a sunny or a cold day, the snow packed high against the walls, icicles hanging on the eaves of the houses?

Rochel, at thirteen, in her grandmother's dark room, took the warm wax left over from the puddled candle, shaped it into little animals —a cat, a fish, two lambs. She understood then that stars clustered into outlines of animals were not real animals, and that the puppets which came out of the Astronomical Clock were Christian apostles, that glass windows in the Church of the Holy Ghost were not eyes of a ghost, but she still must be wary, that the emperor who lived in the castle on the hill was the Holy Roman Emperor, not merely haughty and fickle, but he who must be obeyed, that to walk from Kiev to Prague took three months, that Karel, the rag and bone man, lost his legs with great pain, that other girls her age were already betrothed, but that no family would want her married to their son.

Yet, her grandmother's room had a window which opened out so that on warm days Rochel could see the leaves of a tree outside the walls of Judenstadt. Birds sat among the branches. She pretended they were larks, birds of joy, and nightingales, peacocks, and phoenixes, why not, which were born of ashes and lived forever.

On the river, ducks floated out, their heads feathered in green as bright as emeralds. She could say emeralds because she knew the gems from embroidery threads. Emerald green, sapphire blue, ruby red, amber yellow. Swans white as snow. And her grandmother was old as Moses, and slow as thick syrup dripping from a ladle, and Oswald, the mule, sweet as honey.

At eighteen, married after all, with flying fingers and a silver needle, she would make finery so resplendent it would fetch a high price. Zev, her husband, a kindly man, a good man, with his larger needles, rougher material, stronger hands, would shod the feet of the people who must trod the road day in, day out. Together, they would make a life, have children, and she, as a mother, would be honored among women. She would be a good wife to Zev, she promised HaShem.

The town crier called: Twelve and all is well.

Quickly Rochel repeated the blessing of thanksgiving. "Blessed are You, Ruler of the Universe, You have kept us alive, and sustained us, and enabled us to reach this moment."

4

T HE EMPEROR WAS just about to tell his trusted physician why it was that he had decided to live after all when there was the sound of shuffling feet and voices in the hallway. Then, quick as a snake, the mayor of all of Prague slithered into the sickroom with his retinue of councilmen. They were all wearing furs, Rudolph noted. Close on the burghers' well-heeled heels was the head of the Butchers' Guild. Jesus in Mary, the emperor wondered, did the butcher think he was called for? A further discord in the hallway was a clamor of monks and nuns. No doubt spies at St. Vitus spread the news far and wide among the holy minions. And who notified the Joiners and the Carpenters? Rudolph wanted to know. Was it their emperor's coffin they planned to ply? Of course there was the rotund Tycho Brahe, wearing his silver nose tied to his face with strings around his ears, replacing the real nose he once had, one of the very few men Rudolph could abide, but with him was his infernal dwarf, Jepp, and that scarecrow, Kepler, who at the best of times looked worried and now was a wreck, for what would happen to his position as assistant court mathematician and astronomer if his emperor succumbed? All the guests who had come for the New Year's revels in their conspicuous finery, chamberlains and burgraves, let them bow down and scrape the floor with their slavish manners, along with the lord high steward, lord high marshal, master of the horse, and the chamber orchestra and singers, which struck up Diego Ortiz's "Recercada Doulce Memoire."

"Stop, stop. Have mercy."

"The emperor says stop," Rosenberg, the lord high burgrave, announced.

The trio of trumpeters put their golden instruments to their mouths, sounded the volley.

"Václav," the emperor gasped, "save me from them all. I am in a weakened condition."

Yet they continued to file in. Imperial bakers and chandlers, a plethora of confectioners, goldsmiths, lion tamers, armor makers, the artist Spranger, painter of Venus and Adonis, Mars and Venus, and also Hoefnagel, who did close observations of nature, replications of beetles and butterflies. Ottavio Strada, the antiquarian, no less, and his daughter, Rudolph's mistress, in hastily thrown on robe, her pregnant belly protruding.

"Rudie, Rudie," the sweet Anna Marie squealed. "What have you done to yourself?" She heaved her sizable body up over him, nearly achieving success where the razor had failed.

"Anna Marie, I am going to live another day, my love, my nightingale, my little pet. Let me breathe, my precious sweetheart, my little starling."

Václav and two other servants had to lift her away.

The omnipresent castrato, Pucci, who had once been a pretty boy and was now plump as a strutting pigeon, was there. And then who did Rudolph see, of all people, but some Jews, not just the court Jew, Maisel, to whom Rudolph was indebted in more ways than he liked to remember, but also the ancient rabbi of Prague, the tall Rabbi Loew, adorned in a caftan with the requisite yellow circle, who must, bird that he was, have arrived on wings straight from Judenstadt.

"Where is Petaka when you need him?" Rudolph cried out.

Petaka, on his leash, had been taken out by a page for a breath of air.

"What is the meaning of this?" Rudolph asked. "Why are all of you here?"

"They have heard."

"Heard what?"

"That you are indisposed, and they fear for your health," Válcav answered.

Casting a cynical eye around and about, the emperor muttered, "Fear for my health? Unlikely."

But he sat up straighter in his bed. Václav made smooth the sheets. Rosenberg placed the crown on his emperor's head. And the volley of trumpets pealed forth again.

"Now hear this," the emperor began, his voice strong and stern.

A hush descended on the raucous throng.

"A false report, an unknown source, do not presume to know, life is a voyage, God sends us forth, His infinite wisdom, the stars above, and all that seems unwell is in the light of truth revealed to be in most excellent order. What is above is below and what is below is above. Set the mirror to your own sins. Those are my words."

"They do not understand what it is you wish them to do, Your Majesty," Václav dared to say.

Rosenberg gave the trumpeters the signal again. The trio sounded their notes. Quiet descended.

"Go home to your ugly wives," the emperor spat. "And should anybody so much as make whisper of any sickness, anything amiss at the castle, which word might wind its serpentlike way to the ear of one nefariously ambitious younger brother mine, greedy for crown and glory, one general and archduke Matthias, botching our war with the Turks, conniving with the Protestant princes, yes, should our enemy Matthias get so much as hint wafting like a breeze from Prague down to the borders of our southern states, you, you treacherous tale-teller, I will find you out, wherever, whoever, whyever you be, and you may thus look forward to the parting of head from neck, so give heed, understand it well, this emperor is fighting fit."

With that, Rudolph handed Rosenberg his crown, pulled his coverlet over his head, and scrunched far down out of sight. The multitude looked at each other in puzzlement. The man was mad. Definitely mad. A mad, melancholy man. If he feared for his throne, did not want his avaricious brother, Matthias, to inherit, why had he tried to do away with himself in the first place? Yet he was their emperor and they, as well as the royal executioner, were his loyal subjects. So they bowed ceremoniously and, one by one, backed out of the room.

"Are they gone yet?" the emperor asked, his voice muffled by the covers.

"Yes, Your Majesty, you can come out now."

Rudolph peeked, saw Václav hovering over the bed, Kirakos still seated beside it, some Slovenian guards in the shadows; Petaka, licking his paws, was back from his walk, and Sergey, the Russian, was sitting in the corner by the fire warming his toes. Rosenberg was gone. The large room, save for the tapestries, seemed cavernous.

"Kirakos, you have saved my life." Rudolph's voice was small as a child's now.

"At your service, Your Majesty."

Kirakos, as physician-in-chief, was given free rein of the castle. With his black eyes and heavy brows, he looked like an Egyptian and did not wear doublet and hose, but dressed in woolen robes, a cloth twisted around his head, his hair long and face shaved, a young man out of fashion. Nobody quite knew how he had found his way to Prague and become a trusted member of the court, or where he learned his art and skill, yet his talents were beyond reproach. He had attended the emperor's mistress in a childbirth so difficult all midwives had relinquished hope, the astrologer had been dismissed, and the coffin maker sent for. He had cured the French pox rampant in the court with carefully administered doses of mercury—a night of Venus, it could be said, meant a lifetime with mercury—and he did not disdain to do the work of barber surgeons, setting and stitching, even delousing, for he claimed, on his own authority, that the Plague was brought by fleas which traveled on the back of black rats. Thus, cats were brought in, let to roam the castle, pounce at liberty, annoying Petaka to no end.

"What a night," the emperor said, throwing off the top cover, which, a carpet of red foxes, one sewed to another, nose to nose, tail to tail, rippled and glistened.

"A night," Kirakos echoed. He sorely regretted being parted from his chess game.

"Yes, Your Highness, a night." Václav was standing first on one foot, then the other.

"Hold still, Václav, for God's sake. You make me want to shake you." The emperor's wrist hurt as if he were tightly shackled to himself, as well he was. Václav, faithful servant, would, had not the emperor tried to kill himself, be on his way home, to an earth-floored room in a tall wood house on the hill above the Slavonic Monastery, near the cattle market.

"What now, Kirakos?" the emperor asked.

"Sleep, Your Majesty," Kirakos replied, and the sooner the better, he thought.

At the word *sleep*, Václav gratefully took up his post at the foot of the bed, balling himself into the shape of a nautilus so as not to interfere with the emperor's legs, for if he could not go to see his wife and five-year-old son, Jiří, second best was to sleep on the job.

"I cannot get to sleep," the emperor moaned dramatically. "Sleep no more."

"Come, now, is that a way to talk?"

"I cannot help it." The emperor pouted out his lower lip.

"So tell me," Kirakos sighed, understanding that he would be indefinitely detained.

The emperor looked askance, then brightened, then groaned.

"To cause such grief, you take a razor to your wrists, Your Majesty?" Kirakos prompted.

"All but Kirakos and Václav leave," the emperor commanded.

"Let him stay, Your Majesty. He understands little, says nothing." Because the Russian, if not permitted to stay by the fire, would have to go down the hill across the Stone Bridge to his lodgings in New Town, a hovel of wattle and thatch. The fine crust of snow on the ground would seep through the cloth soles of his pathetic boots and he had no cloak.

"So," said Kirakos, "tell me how you can be so mournful. Tomorrow is the New Year, a new century. We live in a golden age."

"I came this close, Kirakos." The emperor held up his fingers in a tight pinch.

"This close." Kirakos held up his fingers in a wide two inches.

"Certainly close enough, pray tell."

"Yes, Your Majesty. When the black bile comes up and the moon is full and the stars align themselves in certain pattern."

"I thought you did not believe in humors, Kirakos." Rudolph did not like any references to the moon, for lunatics were governed by her cycles.

"I do not believe in humors, but still one cannot rule out what one does not believe in."

The emperor bit his lip. He blinked away a tear. "I never want to die again."

"You tried to die, yet you never want to die, Your Majesty?"

"I saw it. I saw death in all its ramifications."

Kirakos seriously doubted that the emperor had ever truly seen anything more profound than the bottom of his plate.

"To die is to live eternally." Kirakos wondered if a priest should be brought in. Paracelsus believed in treating the whole man, yet even though he was a follower of that thinker and healer, Kirakos had not the temperament to hear confessions. He preferred the strategy of chess, the certainty of prescribed moves, the boundary of clear-cut rules, a self-contained world.

"To die is to live eternally? The devil be with you, too, Kirakos."

"Are you not a Christian, Your Majesty?"

Václav, who was not asleep and was always attentive, also had little sympathy for his emperor's quandary. Having lost a child to the Plague, he prayed for a heaven, and for himself, at the time of his child's death, feared not death, but that he must continue to live.

"In all honesty, Your Majesty, you should enjoy life." A game of chess, a glass of wine.

"How can I enjoy anything, knowing that all will come to a swift and definite end?"

"Some say that brevity adds to appreciation. Or why not cultivate new pleasures?"

"I am emperor—what new pleasures? That close proximity, and I am not talking of the heat of flame and all that folderol . . . when I saw that I would be nothing . . . " The emperor would have hopped out of bed if he did not think that would be bad for his wound. He had to take care of himself now. "Because," he continued, "even if I were to be a galley slave to the Turkish fleet, chained to my oar, or as a deaf-mute, my tongue split and ears deafened with hot oil, I would want to live . . . forever."

Kirakos seriously doubted that. "Perhaps you must find new meaning to your life. A family, an heir."

"Family . . . you say family, Kirakos? Brahe predicted I would be killed by my son. Do you think I want to raise my own murderer? The king is dead, long live the king. I am not old."

"Brahe is not Nostradamus, Sire."

"Would that he were. Family is replacement, Kirakos. My castle, my crown, nothing is mine. I merely fill a space for this time in a long line of Habsburgs, Rudolph the Second. There was a First, will be a Third. With an heir, I will be nothing in myself."

Ivan the Terrible had killed his own son, Kirakos knew; Philip II of Spain, no doubt, let his son, Don Carlos, die; and Suleiman, the Turk, had his firstborn strangled. Pigs ate their young.

"May I take leave?" Válcav had raised his head. "My bowels are boiling, Your Majesty."

"Leave, leave, and come back, Václav, promptly. No dawdling at the garderobe."

Václav stumbled out.

"They are animals, you know, the Czechs. I only keep Václav with me because of his excellent German, and he speaks Spanish, too. His father was a pure Austrian."

"You were saying, Your Majesty . . ."

"If only I could live forever, Kirakos. That would be a remedy to all my ills."

Kirakos walked over to the window. The moon, full, pale yellow, shone like a wheel of cheese.

"If you could make me immortal, I would make you rich."

Kirakos warmed his hands at the fire, took caution not to step near Petaka. "Impossible, Your Majesty."

Václav reappeared at the door.

"You took long enough," the emperor said. "Two whole minutes."

Václav climbed back abed.

"It came to me in the midst of despair, as when St. Paul was on his way to Damascus." Here the emperor took a deep breath. "If I found my way back from death to life, why should I live only to die a certain death shortly? I want to live, Kirakos; ergo, I wish to live forever."

"But in your other melancholies, Your Highness, last week, last year, the many times before, did you want to live forever then?"

"What other melancholies? Are you insinuating that I am of a saturnine temperament? And I suppose you do not want to live as long as possible, Kirakos?"

"Man cannot live forever on this earth, Your Majesty. It is wrong, unnatural, against God's will."

"How can I be wrong? I am the emperor. I do not speak of any man living forever, ordinary man. Magellan sailed around the world, Kirakos; Copernicus, it is said by some, put the sun in its rightful place. Did not Montaigne declare that man is the measure of all things? Good God, the New World was discovered some one hundred years ago."

"I thought you hated all that, that . . . new stuff." Kirakos flung his hands about. "Anyway, Ponce de Leon did not find the Fountain of Youth." That this emperor, for all his distaste of humanist learning, was now prating progress, Kirakos found ironic. I am old, I am not old. I want to die, I do not want to die. Give me eternity, give me oblivion. Place me within the engine of the future, take me back to the womb of time. The emperor in the grip of an idea was like a stubborn dog with a rag in his jaws. How tired Kirakos was of all of this, yet this was his mission, to become indispensable, pass on his observations.

"Do not contradict me, Kirakos. The best treatment for death is life. Have you not successfully cured the French pox? Pray tell, why? Why do we wish to do away with the Plague? Is that against God and nature? Reprehensible to prolong life? A little bit? Why not longer, and longer still? Unnatural to cure sickness? I am first in the land, why not the first in forever? Come, come, we are in the seventeenth century. It behooves us."

"Within an hour of the seventeenth century." The emperor was not a complete fool, Kirakos noted.

"Think on it."

"I am thinking on it, Your Majesty." When Kirakos was a shepherd in the mountains with his herd of goats, there had been a man in the village who was said to be one hundred and twenty years old, the age of Moses. His diet was sour milk; he had outlived five wives.

"Perhaps with the right food, sparing of meat, sufficient exercise, frequent bathing—"

"Do not be stupid, man. Frequent bathing?"

The fire in the hearth, which had been blazing, was now dying out. Soon the many church bells in Prague would toll twelve, ushering in the New Year, 1601. All the clocks on the trestle table were ticking in discordant rhythm, driving Kirakos to intense irritation. One needed a clear mind for chess.

"I will think on it tomorrow, Your Majesty, after you are rested."

"Now."

"But I cannot think of anything now, Your Majesty."

When Kirakos was taken as slave to Constantinople from Azerbaijan, he had not been able to read in any language, but they said that he was intelligent, could learn to serve the sultan. The stronger slave boys became janissaries, protectors of the sultan. I am intelligent, he reminded himself, as he began to pace. Then he stopped, spun on his heels.

"Shall I tell you what I think, Your Majesty?"

"By all means."

Kirakos sat down by the emperor again and hoped that intent and appearance would lead him to discover a solution, that is, one word would lead to another. He had to rely on intuition, mere pawns.

"I will have to tell you, Your Majesty: All your alchemists, all your magi, they—"

"I have yet to see any gold come out of any fevered action on Alchemist Row."

"An alchemist's worth is not gold. Their real quest is the philosophers' stone." Kirakos was on new ground here, and from what he had seen, all alchemy was fraud, and yet there were those who thought of themselves as kind of priests involved in not only the transmutation of metals, but transformation of the self.

"I have always wondered what the philosophers' stone was, Kirakos, and felt like an imbecile for asking."

"It is more substance than stone, I believe. I am not entirely certain, Your Majesty, except that with it they can create gold and the elixir of eternal life."

"They can? The elixir of eternal life?"

"Perhaps."

"Against nature and God, you said, eternal life, Kirakos."

"I now say: Can we know God's intent?"

"'The Bible, Christ . . .'" The emperor was confused. Was Kirakos saying yes to no or no to yes?

"We read Him through all His works, Your Majesty, do we not, the Book of Nature? Are not God and nature one?" Now he found himself prating the rhetoric of the day. "Furthermore, if one thinks of the Bible, the patriarchs lived hundreds of years, and that was back at the beginning of time. So in our modern age, think of what we can do now."

The emperor's eyes were smarting and his head ached. It had been a long and eventful night, yet he could feel his blood coursing eagerly through his veins. The patriarchs, he had forgotten exactly who they were. Abraham, Isaac, Jacob, and the twelve tribes, but were not ten of them lost?

Kirakos began pacing again, head down, hands knotted behind his back. "If I may be so bold, the alchemists you have now are slackers and hobnobbers, late to work, early to leave, who make their dinner their nap and their nap, supper, and on to sport with their wives. We must find among their kind not only a man of virtue and insight, but a man whose quest is the essence of essence, that which is within, behind, under, above, all around. . . ." Inspiration was his. Befuddling talk was all the rage.

"Michael Maier? Do you think he can create the elixir of eternal life?"

"That necromancer. Well-meaning, Your Majesty, but lacking in all but inflated reputation."

"Bruno."

"Another peripatetic thinker of the Neoplatonic school, Your Majesty, one who believes all religions are one, that there is harmony in the universe, thoughts inimical to the Church, and, by the way, was just burned at the stake in Rome, green wood they used."

"He should be burned for such heresy, although I liked him when he was here. Sendivogius?"

"None that are here in Bohemia, Your Majesty, is up to the task."

"Who, then? Where?"

"Britain."

"That race of pirates and tavern brawlers?"

"Edward Kelley and John Dee."

"Kelley is a common criminal who had his ears cut off for fraud, and Dee, a sniveling spy, was enemy of Spain, our dear departed uncle, Philip II."

"Perhaps politically they are suspect." Here Kirakos paused. He was venturing forth, perhaps treading too far. He did not know why those two were at the tip of his tongue. However, Dee was a translator of Euclid, a learned man, which seemed adequate recommendation, despite his reputation as an agent in the queen's secret service, and Kelley was his partner. Supposedly the two communicated with Merlin, Arthur's magician, and had their own fleet of angels— Enochian angels, they called them.

"Why is it you recommend them?"

Kirakos was happily contemplating the end of this long evening. "John Dee is famous for many things, Your Majesty. A noted scholar, a cartographer, a cryptologist." Not to mention a favorite of Queen Elizabeth. Dee served her well as spy, had had a hand, it was rumored, in the defeat of the Spanish Armada. Kirakos had heard that Dee's code name was Double 0, for the spectacles he wore, 00, with an overhanging seven, 7, the magic number. 007. "And Kelley has communed with the dead in Dee's crystal ball."

"I do not wish to commune with the dead, Kirakos. On the contrary, it is with the living I wish conversation." The emperor folded his arms, kicked off his covers. He was deliciously alert. Two pages came in and pulled out the trundle bed under the emperor's bed.

The fire was poked anew. A flame sprouted up, spread, leapt, and climbed up the chimney in a sail of red.

"There are a few difficulties, Kirakos." The emperor had difficulty holding a thought for more than a minute or so, and now he was getting muddled again.

"Difficulties, Your Majesty?" Kirakos blinked. "Dee is a powerful magi, Kelley his able assistant."

"What if they cannot find the secret to eternal life?"

"How do you customarily deal with failure, Your Majesty?"

"Do not be impertinent. Malefactors are put in the Dalibor Tower, executed."

"Well, then."

"Yes, but how will I be able to tell when the elixir is efficacious, that is, how will I know that I will live forever? What if I live and then I die? What then?"

"Your Majesty, any undertaking worth undertaking is fraught with trials and tribulations."

"You speak the truth, Kirakos, you speak God's truth."

And although it was winter, and the room tall and drafty, the floor made of cold flagstone, warmth spread through the chamber like melted gold. The pages, asleep in the trundle bed, glowed in their youthful goodness. Petaka looked healthy as a stallion. In the hallways the changing of the guard resounded with thumps and heavy clattering. Two of the Slovenes came into the room and stood at the double door, as was customary, with axes in their hands crossed in an X.

"Then there is the cost of it all. If the alchemists I now have make no gold, how am I to pay?"

"Fuggers and Maisel, Your Majesty."

"The silver mines, the Jew?"

"Is it not tradition, Your Highness, to make the Jews pay?"

"They have a powerful rabbi, I have heard, that is, for a Jew, and Maisel built the Altneu Synagogue, a Town Hall for the Jews, a bathhouse, cobblestoned the street of Judenstadt," the emperor mused. "Yes, the Jews are powerful, rich, too powerful, too rich. Maisel is the one."

"He pays for the war against the infidel Turk, does he not?"

"That, Kirakos, is a malicious rumor. No one is as good to the Jews as I am."

"Quite."

There was a drumroll. The emperor inched down in his bed.

"But I must look young and as handsome as I am now in the forever."

"Without doubt, Your Highness."

Suddenly there was the sound of loud popping in rapid succession.

Václav, rushing to the window, exclaimed, "The fireworks for the New Year."

From his bed, the emperor could see the sky filled with the burst of rockets making great streaks and fountains of magenta and puce, chartreuse, crimson, royal purple, glittering silver, and a gold so brilliant that the very stars were rivaled.

"Look, Kirakos."

But the good doctor had already bowed low, backed out of the room, and was making his way down the hallway, his cloak billowing behind him like the wings of some great angel.

5

WITH THE EXCEPTION of an occasional book-burning, the frequent raising of taxes, threats of expulsions, repressive restrictions, and the requirement of the wearing of yellow circles to distinguish them from Christians, the Jews of Judenstadt had been relatively secure for the last fifty years. However, one recent event marked a change. Not everybody in Judenstadt was aware of it, but the rabbi, naturally, knew, as did his wife, Perl. Mayor Maisel, as mayor of Judenstadt, was informed, Rochel's grandmother was involved, and it had been Rochel who had stumbled upon it.

That year, 1600, which was to be Rochel's grandmother's last, a few days before Passover—a time when houses were cleaned top to bottom, clothes washed, hope reborn—Rochel was outside Judenstadt's walls feeding the birds some crumbs. Ordinarily, her grandmother did not believe in this kind of waste, for crumbs could be rolled up, used to bread fish, thicken gravy, sprinkle over kugel, crushed into a paste and fried, mixed with raisins and baked. At the very least, you could lick crumbs from your fingers wet by your own spit. But for Passover, there was not to be a trace of leavened bread. Furthermore, Rochel was supposed to burn the crumbs, not scatter them. It was the Law.

For the Passover Seder, Rochel and her grandmother were, as always, invited to be guests of the rabbi's family. Rochel loved this joyous meal and most particularly how each food meant something other than itself, that the unleavened bread, matzah, was not baked more than eighteen minutes as a symbol of how quickly the Hebrews had to make the bread for their escape for freedom from the pharaoh's slavery. How the karpas, greens dipped in salt on the Seder plate, represented the coming season, spring. How the horseradish showed the bitterness of slavery, and charoset, a mixture of fruits and nuts, recalled the bricks the Israelites had to build for the pharoah. The shank bone of a lamb signified what the Israelites ate in Egypt, and a roasted egg was token of ancient sacrifice, a hard-boiled egg a reminder of new life, and salt water stood for the tears of slavery. When they were all seated and ready, it was the task of the youngest child to ask the four questions, beginning with, "Why is this night different than all other nights?" The air itself seemed different on that night, lighter, and while nothing was really changed in the next day, Rochel was able for that moment to imagine bundling her belongings together in order to flee slavery for freedom. And when the door during the ceremony was opened to invite the prophet Elijah, Rochel always felt a little tingling, not that she believed a real ghost entered, but rather, each year, she felt at that moment the possibility of a new world filled with love.

That year, Rochel feeding the birds crumbs by the back gates and making little bird movements by holding her elbows up like wings and shuffling in a tight circle, she noticed something in the wall. Stuck and poking out, a patch of pink. It was in the very hole where Václav, her former playmate, had put little treats and bits and pieces of finery for their games. Moving closer, Rochel thought it was a doll fashioned by a master puppeteer, for it had the perfect form of a baby, each fold pleated like real flesh, with a boy pouch and uncircumcised penis. She crept up on it, and saw the tiny clenched fists held up before its face in protection, the delicate toes curled back, eyes squeezed shut, closed mouth—as if it were holding in an angry cry. Dear God, Rochel gasped, it was a real baby, a dead baby. For a moment she could not move, for she thought HaShem was punishing her for not burning the crumbs. But the next moment her feet started moving. She ran for her grandmother.

Her grandmother only needed one glance, immediately turned ashen, and sent Rochel, fast as she could go, to fetch the rabbi.

The rabbi, followed by his wife and Mayor Maisel, arrived, breathless from their running.

The mayor pulled the infant from the wall, put his ear to its mouth and chest, looked up at the rabbi.

"He has been dead awhile," Maisel announced.

With care, as if the child were still alive, the rabbi lifted him from Maisel's arms and, using Perl's apron, wrapped him up, cradled him close to his breast.

"How did he die? Why did they not bury him? Whose baby is it?" Rochel's mind was in a tumult. "What are you going to do with him? Where is his mother? Was he old enough to be circumcised?"

"Get her inside," the rabbi insisted. "Get the girl inside."

"Go home, Rochel, this is not your business," her grandmother said.

Rochel, head hung low, obediently scooted through the back gates, but instead of returning to her room like a good girl, she crept behind the wall, positioned herself so that she could hear every word said about this strange and horrible occurrence.

"I think I know whose handiwork this is," Mayor Maisel said. "The child was probably left on his church doorstep by a desperate mother."

"Unwed," Perl added.

"We know nothing about the mother," the rabbi corrected her sternly. "So best say nothing."

Rochel held her breath.

"Father Thaddaeus is a clever one." Mayor Maisel was always one to measure his words, yet he could not restrain himself on this subject.

"Clever and diabolical. How will we get it back on his doorstep?" Perl asked.

"Perl, regard yourself."

"He is not a good man, or kind, Judah."

"So we must be the same, dear Wife?"

"Karel, the junkman," Mayor Maisel suggested. "He will help us."

Rochel had heard that Maisel had been a junkman himself once, one who gathered and sold secondhand clothes. Now she and her grandmother made him fine clothes for court—black velvet doublets with silk braiding and fasteners of ebony and ivory, puffy black trousers which came above the knee, white linen ruffs for his neck and wrists, hose spun of so fine a silk, they were like a second skin.

"Do not chide me for telling the truth, and, given our predicament, best be blunt. Maybe the baby is one of the emperor's bastards." Perl, as always, was undaunted by her husband's criticism. "The city is rife with children cursed with his blood."

Rochel always pictured the emperor seated on his throne, his scepter and orb in his hand, commanding people to do this and that. Fetch me my slippers. Cut off his head.

"So a royal burial, Perl, is that what you are saying?"

"On the contrary, Judah." Maisel softened his voice so that Rochel could barely hear. "Less notice if he is the emperor's. First we need Karel to get the body to Father Thaddaeus's doorstep from whence it came, and then we need a witness other than that villainous priest to spot it. Somebody from the castle is best, so that he cannot turn the story around and accuse us. We must be as wise in our rectification as he was in his original deception, although, sadly, the child is dead and beyond our efforts."

"Maybe it is not the emperor's but the priest's," Perl thought out loud.

"Perl," the rabbi warned.

Rochel had never heard of this priest before. Thaddaeus? Father Thaddaeus?

"Whomever fathered or mothered this innocent being, his death is a commentary on the state of the world, my friends," Maisel said, "and the blame has been assigned to us. Left on the doorstep of the church, had he lived, he would have been taken in, become an acolyte, a monk, or a priest, who knows, perhaps a good man. Dead, he serves the aims of those who mean us harm, a means to discredit, hurt."

"Why does Father Thaddaeus wish our destruction?" Perl asked.

Rochel was wondering the same thing.

"Frustration born of ambition, is my conjecture," Maisel reflected. "Without much power, he wields what little he has over the most defenseless, obtains ready support from other discontented sorts. It is, no doubt, simpler to attack those who are not already held in high esteem. And, as we know, he is most jealous of our venerated rabbi."

"Why would anybody be jealous of me, pray tell?"

"You are revered for your wisdom and goodness, Rabbi," Maisel said. "And winning the debate."

Rochel knew that the rabbi occasionally left Judenstadt on behalf of them all; indeed, he wrote books and sometimes gave talks in Christian places, not to mention the warm welcome he received in synagogues all over Bohemia and Moravia, Poland, the German states.

"It has to be Václav," Perl interrupted, "who finds the baby."

Rochel's heart stopped, and if she were not eavesdropping, she would have called out: No, not him.

"Himself a bastard of royal issue, he is the logical choice, Judah."

"Perl, please. How you assume, and if true, not necessarily the logical choice."

"Everybody knows, Judah, except him."

"We will sneak the baby back through Karel on his evening rounds. Later, Václav beside him will say, 'What is that?' 'I do declare, but it looks like a baby.'" This was Rochel's grandmother, who had been silent until that point. "Václav will hop down off Karel's cart, knock on the priest's door. 'Who is that at the door?' "

"The old drunkard will stumble forth, irritated at the interruption from his ablutions."

"Absolutions, Perl," Maisel corrected.

"Maybe both," the rabbi concluded.

As the little group bade each other fond farewell, Rochel ducked down the alleyway, doubled back at the entrance of Judenstadt, hopped between the gravestones of the cemetery, pushed open the door, and with one leap jumped into the bed, pulling the covers over her head and letting out breathy snores.

"I know you are awake," her grandmother said when she entered the room. "You cannot fool me, Fräulein Rochel."

Rochel poked her head up. "Why would somebody want to tell lies on us, Grandmama?"

"Rochel, Rochel." Her grandmother lowered herself to the side of the bed with difficulty. "We are different, that is all."

Rochel knew different, knew how that was regarded. But when she looked at little birds, their differences were a joy and the many colors of threads she used in her work created beauty. The bright orange sun, the pale moon, the blue water gave meaning to the day. In her heart of hearts, what she longed for was more variation, not less.

"But Grandmama, putting a dead child in our walls instead of burying it properly?"

"My dear." Her grandmother sighed and reluctantly explained that it was the custom among those who despised Jews to bring ignominy and infamy on them by putting recently dead children within the walls of the Jewish neighborhood so that the Jews could be accused of murder. As outrageous as that idea was, her grandmother continued, it was even worse that the Jews, who did not taste blood of any kind, were reputed to kill Christian children in order to use their blood for their Passover matzah.

Rochel could barely believe it, except she knew all too well that her mother's village had been burned to the ground for no reason and great malice.

"Karel would not do such a thing, Master Galliano helps us."

"True, true. There are good people of every religion."

"And bad people?"

"Yes, there are those who are misguided, but it is best not to speak of them, Rochel."

Her grandmother put her fingers to her lips, cautioned her grand-daughter against speaking ill of anyone or telling lies or being, in any way, less than honest. Rochel, while realizing that she could not completely trust her impulses—for had she not just broken the Law by feeding the birds?—resolved thenceforth to always be good. In truth, she prayed every day to keep the mitzvot. And now, she began to cry over her own weaknesses, and for the poor dead baby, and for the whole wide world, which seemed fraught with evil.

Smoothing Rochel's hair from her face, trying to console her and distract her, her grandmother told her the story of King Solomon and the Queen of Sheba. King Solomon had once been kind to a bee, spared its life. Then, when the Queen of Sheba was visiting, she wanted to trick her friend, King Solomon, about the difference between real flowers and the artificial flowers her craftsman had made. King Solomon, not one to be fooled, summoned his bee friend, who buzzed over the real flowers, thereby saving the king's pride. That made Rochel laugh. And there was the tale of the mid-wife who switched babies at birth, replacing the dying baby of a woman who had no living child with the healthy newborn boy of a woman who had many strong children. The son who was the only child fell in love with a girl from the other family. Only at the wedding, when the ghost of the midwife was summoned, did everybody find out that the bride and bridegroom were brother and sister. Rabbi Loew had been officiating, and it was through his powers, his goodness of soul, that he detected something amiss and was able to summon the midwife from the kingdom of the dead to tell the truth.

While her grandmother was lulling Rochel with these stories of gentle mistakes and well-meaning tricks, at the other end of the city, in New Town, Father Thaddaeus was napping in his favorite spot, his stuffy study with vermilion windows latticed in dark wood. The dark red light spread a warm glow like brandy or blood throughout the chamber. On a carved dais, pride of place, sat the Good Book, bound in the softest of calfskin. Costly crucifixes studded with rubies from Spain and Portugal attested to the power and the glory of the Church Supreme. Indeed, as a young seminary student, Thaddaeus had studied in Rome and been privileged to serve in Spain, where he was witness to many a public burning. They knew what to do with heretics and nonbelievers in those God-fearing countries, he boasted to his Bohemian flock in his broken German. Secretly, once upon a time, he had entertained hopes of gaining a position on the Inquisitorial staff itself. Not to be, alas—for, doing God's work on earth, selflessly unaware of time passing, he found himself old, addled by wine, and instead of being promoted was shipped to the backwater of Eastern Europe, where he had to administer rites to the residents of a city where Protestants could practice their blasphemous rituals, or should he say lack of rituals, and Jews walked freely about the street protected by the law of the land. This abomination had been going on, the pious priest realized, far too long, and regrettably the present emperor, Rudolph II, had other things on his mind. Furthermore, most of Thaddaeus's fellow churchmen did not give ear to his urgent concerns. Not that he had high regard for them, either. The nuns kept pet dogs and cheetahs, trained tropical birds in their convents, and he knew of priests and monks who took celibacy as a vow to be broken, if not daily, then weekly.

"Who is at the door, Marta?" Father Thaddaeus called to his housekeeper.

"Father, it is Václav from the castle. He has found a dead baby on the doorstep of Our Lady of Sorrows."

"A Jewish bastard, no doubt. Not ours."

"He is not circumcised," Václav called out, "and more than ten days old."

"Oh, bother and bluster." Father Thaddaeus, bleary with sleep, sallied forth awkwardly, and when he saw it was the same damned baby he had placed in the walls of Judenstadt shortly after finding it alive on his doorstep, he was furious. He had no idea if it had been baptized; probably not, which meant burial in the Pest graveyard outside the town gates near the dump, not even a cross to mark the spot. He hated to go out there, with its smell of sewer and rot; and with all those children scampering about the hills of garbage poking for food like hungry rats, could anything be more disgusting? And the Jews, by hook or by crook, he would get them, not only out of fidelity to principle, but because he hated their little alleyways, their drooping side curls hanging like pigs' tails about their narrow faces, and their skullcaps, the smell of garlic on their breath, Judases one and all, who must be punished, purged, wiped from city of Prague. It was the least he could do, his sanctified duty.

Part II

6

WHEN VÁCLAV WAS ten years old and not yet working
in the castle confectionery kitchen alongside his mother,
all of Prague was his playing ground, and each new thing
he encountered appeared both strange and wonderful—the pigman
who sold bristles for brushes, the harlots in petticoats red as cockscomb,
monks marching in a line, peasants from the country pushing wheel-
barrels full of turnips and cabbages, the rowing boats of the fisherman
mysteriously afloat in the middle of the river like birds in the air, par-
rots from the New World with their curved beaks and bright green
feathers. So that when he went through the high gates with the six-
pointed star and saw the skullcapped, long-bearded men with fringes
at their waists, bearing yellow circles on their breasts, it was for him
just another adventure in his beloved city, and he was in no way
frightened. The women in that section of town, unlike his mother,
who only bathed on Christmas Eve and Easter morning, had no
smell. And while the houses were crowded together, the alleyways
were clean of garbage and excrement. There were no pigs snuffling
through rotten vegetables, no herds of goats scrounging through piles
of refuge, no dogs trailing the intestines of butchered animals.

But where were the children? Around the town square, Václav
had made friends with ragamuffin children who lived in huts by the
town dump, children who worked with their parents at market, children who could balance on a rope stretched between two ladders or
jump flips for crowns, children who cleaned latrines wearing cloth
tied over their noses, thin linen over their eyes against flies, children
employed to carry water from the river or wells in two buckets suspended on a board across their small shoulders, children who fetched

kindling, bearing it on their backs in great humps, children who herded sheep. The children of this place must go to school, for coming from a large building was the sound of young voices in a unified chant. *Baruch ata Adonai,* a language Václav did not understand. Then he heard a small voice singing *"Meine Liebschen,"* an old German lullaby. The child was not within the walls, but by the back gate, in a patch of earth under a large tree, a small girl, maybe eight or nine, sloe-eyed, and her hair was the yellow of custard his mother made in the confectionary from an exotic fruit called a lemon. She was constructing a city of mud, dolls of sticks, and since he had been in many places she had not, he took it upon himself to advise her. The emperor's kitchens are filled with ovens, he told her, as they made a trench for the Vltava River, a hill behind it, and the serrated walls surrounding the castle. The Vyšehrad Castle has a graveyard, he instructed, making crosses of pieces of straw, fixing them in a row. "So they can go to heaven."

"Rochel, where are you, what are you doing?" An old face appeared around the corner. The woman was shriveled, and like Václav's nanny goat grandmother, Mutti, her hands shook. "What is this?" She looked at Václav, stared at the little straw crosses he had made. "What is this I see before me?"

"So the dead people can go to heaven, Grandmama," Rochel said.

The woman put her hand to her chest, stared at Václav with horrified eyes. "Who are you? What do you want with us? Go, go. Go home." She shooed him away, motioning her hands as if swatting a fly. "You are not to come here, do you hear, ever again. This is not your place."

She grabbed Rochel's arm, hoisted her up, but as the little girl was dragged back inside the walls of Judenstadt, she turned around, gazed at Václav, with those eyes.

Thus, behind her grandmother's back, he played with Rochel, all day, every day, the whole summer long, placing offerings early in the morning in the hollow of the wall where the bricks were missing. An apple. A clump of soft bread. A bag of chestnuts. Not only food, but he was able to steal scraps of silk and braid, tiny feathers, cotton stuffing, buttons and loops, glitter and glue, bits of wood, broken crockery, polished rocks, all discards from the castle. Little by little, Rochel's castle, which had only been one part of the mud city before, became the main construction, built with Václav's direction along authentic lines. There were the emperor's apartments, his Kunstkammer, the stables, the lion house, the rest of the zoo, the gardens and orchards, the courtyards, Golden Lane where the alchemists worked. The stick dolls, too, were made as replicas of the royal family—the emperor himself, the emperor's lady, Anna Marie, and their illegitimate children, including Don Julius Caesar. A bad boy, he came into the castle kitchen to boil live frogs, tie the tails of the cats, and to torment Václav, giving him jabs and pokes, twisting his arm so it burned, and kicking him hard in his shins.

Rochel made Don Julius Caesar's eyes of tiny apple seeds, a bulbous nose of red apple skin, the stem into the downturned mouth, ears as big as a bat's of black velvet. Václav got her cuttings of horsetail for his hair, coarse and stiff, so that it stuck up straight from Don Julius Caesar's round head as if startled by some frightful vision, and the two children filled the doll's body, sausage legs, and arms with pine needles which pricked him inside out. Sometimes Václav would throttle the doll or take him by the leg, swing him about, fling him against a tree. Rochel, in a spirit of cooperation, tightened the knot of his cape, squeezed his neck. Mercy, mercy, Václav would speak for him. Or she would stick a bone needle straight through his belly, impaling him to the spongy soft earth at the base of the tree. Once, they set his feet afire with a candle Rochel had carried out from her house. They watched with fascination the toes turning up in singed curls, and would have toasted him to a fine crisp except that Václav was afraid that the fire would spread, igniting the tree, the wall, all the houses. Quickly they threw water in his face. Sorry, no supper for you today, Don Julius. Straight to your bed, Don Julius, thirty lashes on the morrow. Don Julius, you cannot go outside to play. Don Julius, hold out your hand, this hurts me more than it hurts you. Once Václav said, You must die, Don Julius, I will cut off your head and stick it on a pole outside the city gates.

Rochel at eight years old was not quite sure what that meant. True enough, her mother was dead, and the little girl had been to funerals, so she knew what it was to sit the seven days of shiva. Furthermore, in Judenstadt, because the Jews were not permitted to live or be buried outside its walls, people had to live in close proximity to those already underground. But she had never seen a head on a pole. She had never seen a dead body pulled up from the river. She had never even seen a pig hung up and cut from belly to throat, all its guts spilling out still steaming from its body, or a deer carcass dripping over the shoulders of a hunter, the open eyes glazed with a viscous film.

"Killing is a sin," Václav said, realizing that his pretend torture of Don Julius Caesar, the emperor's illegitimate and wayward son, trespassed even play. "I do not really want him to die. I just want him to suffer. Suffer as much as a Jew."

Rochel, who had been crouching over her little city, shifted a little, stood up.

"I have to go now," she said evenly.

"But it is not even dark."

She stood up, brushed her apron with her hand, as if cleaning herself of all their play.

He waited for her to come out again, but she did not appear the next day or the next. In the days afterward, he would see her going about with her grandmother, but if she saw him, she gave no indication. Later, when he was working in the confectionery kitchen of the castle alongside his mother, earning a wage, the games of sticks and mud he had played with Rochel seemed babyish and too girlish. Soon he began to go about with boys his age to taverns, where they talked about women's breasts and hips, bragging and swaggering, carrying on in manly fashion. But, unlike his comrades, Václav never maligned Jews, for he understood, in his maturity, that nobody deserved to suffer, least of all Rochel. Furthermore, he realized that as a Slav in a country ruled by an Austrian, he, too, was regarded a lesser person.

Yet for all Václav's keen awareness, there was one thing that remained a mystery to him, and that was who his father was. His mother, tall as a man, handsome in her old age, taciturn, speaking only a kitchen *platdeutsch* and gruff Czech, offered no clues. His mother's brother conjectured that Václav's father was a silver miner who had worked for the Fuggers and died in a peasant war resisting the tyranny of landowners everywhere. His mother's mother, Mutti, with her narrow forehead and white-bearded chin, denied that story, asserting that his father was a latter-day Hussite burned at the stake because he had paraded in the street in a priest's vestment, insisting that Christ was not in the Eucharist. Other accounts included a brigand, a ne'er-do-well, a fool who should be dressed in motley or bound in jacket straight and tight, a player. In one tale, his father had begged his way across Europe as a poor student, ensconced himself finally in the Habsburg court as a tutor for the lesser cousins, where his mother fell prey to his unbidden craven lust. Václav doubted this last story as much as the others, because he was not born until after the Habsburg court had moved to Prague with Rudolph in 1576, yet there was something to the idea that his father had been educated, because he, Václav Kola, was quick-witted and could read and write Czech, German, picked up Italian from the people who made plumed hats At the House of the Three Ostriches. Spanish, much spoken at court, was easy after that. With a good ear, nice manners, he was destined to rise high in the castle kitchens, when one day he captured the emperor's attention. That occasion was the feast day of St. Bartholomew. Václav helped serve because he was a comely lad, with his well-defined chin, copper-colored hair, pleasant manner.

"Come here," the emperor said to him from his place high on the dais, a table separate from all the others, his plates gold, his goblet glass, a cloth to wipe his face called a napkin, and that new instrument at the table, a fork, although there were some who said its use was sacrilegious, for otherwise why would God give us fingers?

Václav was frightened, but bowing low, he approached the emperor.

"Answer me this, young man: What relation to you is your father's mother-in-law's only daughter's only child?"

"Myself, Sire."

"A king who loves chess decides to give up his throne to the son who can answer this question: If I give up my throne to you, you must spend exactly half of your remaining days playing chess. How many days would that be?"

"Every other day until he dies, Your Majesty."

"Move this fellow," Rudolph commanded, "out of the kitchen straight to the imperial bedchamber."

"But Sire, the pages of the bedchamber are members of nobility."

"Bosh. I like the boy. He will serve me personally."

7

THERE WAS ONLY one garden in Judenstadt, and that was
the garden of the dead. The Jewish graves were layered one on
top of another so close together they toppled and overlapped
each other like crooked teeth crowded into a tiny mouth. Rather than
flowers, small pebbles were placed on the stone slabs to mark respect
and grief. That was the tradition marking the many years the forefa-
thers had spent wandering in the wilderness. Most graves, in addition
to the names and dates of birth and death in the Jewish calendar, had
small carvings which indicated the calling of its occupant or, for a
woman, the words *"ha-ishah ha-tz'nuah,"* the modest women. Although
forbidden in generations before Emperor Rudolph's time, the people of
the ghetto had professions among themselves. Thus, a tailor had scissors
on his gravestone, tweezers for a doctor, pestle and mortar for an apothecary, a jug a symbol of the Levi family.

Rabbi Judah Loew's name, last and first, meant lion, the lion of
Judah. He was a large man, and his house, except for Mayor Maisel's,
was the finest in Judenstadt. He had two whole floors for himself and
Perl and their three daughters and two of their husbands. The rabbi's
floor was wood, not dirt, and in the summer these floors were strewn
with flowers and sweet-smelling herbs, and in the winter, straw. The
front door led to a passageway that opened onto a courtyard flanked
by the kitchen and the reception room. The second floor was where
they had the bedrooms and the rabbi's study facing over the walls of
Judenstadt.

Rochel's grandmother had one room with a single table, a chair
made from a barrel half, and a stool for Rochel. On the hearth was a
cauldron always kept full of hot water, a long-handled frying pan. In

the rabbi's house the hearth had a hood, and stone seats were set under it and a long bench in front of it, so that all could sit by the fire. In the reception room there were chests with drawers in them, several chairs that folded up, could be moved easily about, a chair with arms and a cushioned seat for the rabbi, and other chairs of newfangled design—rush-seated, high backed. The windows of their house were glass of small circles with casements that could be opened. And in the kitchen, there was a row of copper pots, pewter drinking vessels, iron candlesticks, and a menorah of pure silver.

For Rochel, disapproval, palpable in the street, was particularly thick in the air at the rabbi's. Not from the rabbi, of course, who was a dear, kind, holy man, and not from his wife, Perl, who was generally fussy but in no ways mean. It was the daughters. Leah, Miriam, and Zelda. When she was a child, to make herself feel better in their presence, Rochel would repeat in her mind: I have my Bubbe, I have my sewing, I have the birds outside our window, I have Oswald to pet, I have challah on the Sabbath and sometimes a bowl of warm milk brought by Karel from the country. Once she had even eaten ruge-lah, a tart made of soft buttered dough with honey, chopped nuts, and raisins inside. Was there anything more tasty?

Two days after her wedding, considering herself a person among people, Rochel, with her husband, confidently crossed the cemetery to the rabbi's house. Without hesitation, she sat herself down on a chair nearest the kitchen fire, smiled at all, took little Fiegel, the old-est daughter's youngest, on her lap. Fiegel had orange curls, gray eyes, and did not merely walk her toddler's tripping step, but ran, rolled, jumped, skipped, danced. Rochel told herself, Someday I, too, will have a beautiful little girl, as she smoothed the child's hair with her hand. Rochel had braided her own hair for this visit, knotted the two tails at the end with bright blue threads, and, of course, wore a scarf.

"I will leave you ladies," Zev said. "Go to the butcher's."

"Yes, Husband." Rochel liked that word in her mouth. *Husband.* My husband. My kitchen. That morning Zev had discussed the sea-soning of a nice brisket for the Sabbath meal. Although she did not eat meat, she listened attentively. Yes, she would soak it in vinegar and bay leaves overnight, then cover it in thyme, salt, and stick it with gloves of garlic, roast it slowly, turn the spit as she worked on her sewing. Already she had cleaned their little room top to bottom, lining up the cooking utensils in a neat row, and she scoured all the pots with sand and potash so they shone in the brittle winter light like family treasures. The next thing she would see about was the bedcurtains.

"Take off your head covering, child," Perl said, as soon as Zev stepped out the door.

Rochel looked at Perl, then at Leah. The youngest daughter, Zelda, had a pair of big scissors in her hand.

"No," Rochel said, sliding Fiegel off her lap and putting her hands over her head.

"Behave yourself, Rochel."

"Please do not cut my hair. I wear my head covered all the time, every day. It does not have to be cut, it is not seen."

"It is seen, Rochel."

"Nobody sees."

"It is seen, Rochel, and not by man alone."

Rochel began to weep. Her hair was the only thing about her appearance she liked. True, not many people had her unusual gold color, but it was her prized possession. Every night her grandmother had brushed and combed it in the way she, Rochel, petted Oswald's neck and mane, with tenderness and appreciation.

"Leave me something that is my own, I beg of you, Frau Loew."

The children looked up from their play on the floor. Little Fiegel ran back to her lap.

"Put the child down," Perl commanded.

"I want my hair, Frau Loew."

"For what do you need hair?" Leah, the oldest daughter, asked. "You are married, we are Jews."

"Where do you think you live?" the next daughter down, Miriam, asked. "In the castle?" Miriam, only a year younger than Leah, followed her older sister in everything.

"It is clear that you wish to incite lust." Leah, who had a long jaw, a furrowed forehead, and an undistinguished nose, wore her own hair so severely shorn that under her scarf the scalp glistened.

Zelda, unmarried, had hair the color of copper and so thick it sprang from her head like a forest afire. Her large, dark eyes were full of worry.

"It is my hair," Rochel protested piteously. She cowered, covering her head in her apron. When Zev had said on their wedding night that she must cut her hair, she had not wanted to believe him. She knew some women cut their hair out of modesty, but she did not understand why her own long hair should offend HaShem.

"Do you think you belong to yourself alone?" Leah's hands on her narrow hips were balled into fists.

The old mother, Perl, sighed, sat down across from Rochel, put her hands on her shoulders. "Listen, Rochel, it is for your own good, for our common good."

"That is right," Miriam concurred. "Since the time when Christian noblemen took the right of the first night with the bride, it has been the custom among the most devout to shear our hair so they do not find us appealing and so do not force us to lay with them and so we belong to our husbands, our own husbands, so all in all, it is well and good."

"Miriam," Leah said. "That is not why."

"Why, then?"

"Before their wedding, my daughters had their hair cropped," Perl explained to Rochel.

"My mother of blessed memory, did my mother?"

"Ah, the mother." Leah shook her head sadly. "Of the mother, best we say nothing."

"Was my mother's hair cut on her wedding night?" Rochel insisted.

"Your mother, Rochel, she was not a bride, God help her." Leah seemed happy to impart this.

Rochel stood up, turned her back to them, went to the window. The rabbi and the other men were in the shul praying, studying. If she were born a man, she would be able to talk to God. If she were a bird, she could fly away. If she were a bear, she could scratch. She stopped that bad thought. Not a bride—therefore, her mother had sinned. Rochel had fathomed that many years ago. So her mother knew her betrothed before the wedding. It was, yes, a shame. And her father, he had sinned, too. In the Ukraine, over the hills where the summers were so harsh, there was no water, and wolves roamed the streets in the winter, they had sinned. So they had sinned. Her mother had died, her father was lost. She tried to think of her parents in the way that she and Zev were at night, she flat on her back, spread-eagled, he arching above. She imagined her father, he who held the quill and kept the accounts, laying his baby finger across her mother's hand, shyly, tentatively.

"Nobody will see me, Frau Rabbi Loew," Rochel said slowly so there was no mistake. "I promise."

"Do you think you are being responsible for yourself and to your people and to God when you cherish your vanity above all?" Miriam resembled her older sister so closely that when they were girls, people took them for twins.

"Do you live alone, that you can put yourself in danger and not endanger us?" Leah added.

Zelda, the youngest, said nothing. She was a quiet, good girl. Loud voices scared her. When she had been little, Leah had told her that because she was not born a boy, the rabbi, her father, did not want her. Now tears were welling in her eyes. She was not sure why she was crying, if it was for herself or Rochel.

"You have always been selfish, Rochel, selfish, selfish." Miriam stamped her foot for emphasis.

"And you must atone for that."

"For having hair, Leah?" Rochel wanted a cup of hot water flavored with specially gathered leaves. Perl's brews included drinks that could sooth the nerves, make one sleepy, give courage. The morning spread before her like parched land.

"On Rosh Hashana, it is written, on Yom Kippur, it is sealed," Leah continued, victory in her voice, " 'How many shall pass on, how many shall come to be, who shall live and who shall die, who shall perish by fire and who by water; who by sword and who by beast; who by hunger and who by thirst; who by plague, and who by stoning—' "

"By stoning?" Rochel asked softly.

"I am not a rabbi's daughter for nothing."

"Hush, Leah," Perl admonished. "You are too much a rabbi's daughter and not enough your father's child. Those harsh words are not meant to be taken in the way you say them."

"Adultery is close to idolatry. Adulteresses were stoned in the olden days."

"Jews do not stone people, Leah," Rochel insisted.

"Maybe not Jews. But other people garrote and torture and draw and quarter. . . . The Inquisition, the emperor, and indeed the townspeople are known to just about do anything—"

"*Genug*, Leah, " Perl shouted. "Enough."

"I must say this, Mother. Even as a child, she thought she was better than anybody else."

"You have it wrong, Leah, I have always thought myself worse." At that a heat rose in Rochel's chest, up her neck, scorching her cheeks red. Sweat beaded her forehead, and her tears blurred all together. She was underwater, in the mikvah, in the waters of Eden, in the Vltava River, floating away somewhere far, far away, yet she could hear them conferring, their whispers snipping the air—the bad blood, the Cossack in her, no mother, the grandmother too clever by far, she thinks she is pretty, she is fortunate somebody took pity on her and married her, what can you expect, mark my words, she will come to a bad end.

"What is that? What is that you say? I can hear every word, and it is evil talk. Frau Loew, tell them who my father was. Tell them the truth. My father kept accounts."

Perl did not say anything.

"Everybody knows, Rochel Werner, that your father was a Cossack."

"My father is looking for me, Leah. He is looking for me right now."

"Looking for you? Do not be silly," Leah scoffed openly.

" 'Our men were butchered like animals before our eyes,' that was what my grandmother told me, but my father escaped."

"Escaped? Looking for you? Your father was one of the butchers. That is the truth."

"He kept accounts for the master of the estate, Leah. He was not a butcher." The Jewish butcher, the shochet, had to be licensed by the rabbi, and the mode of killing by humane law was a quick thrust of the knife through a major artery. It was an honorable calling, but her father did not dirty his hands with blood. Why were they saying such things?

"Your father was a butcherer of Jews, Rochel, a rapist, that is what you come from."

"It cannot be, Leah."

"Look at the slant of your eyes, the color of your hair, your cheeks. You are marked by your mother's betrayer. You wear her disgrace daily."

"You want to find your father?" Miriam added. "Look in the mirror."

"No, no. It is a lie." Rochel put her hands over her ears.

All the children began crying. Zelda was biting her lip, pulling at her springy hair.

"Shush," Perl shouted. "Rape is rape. The only dishonor is to the rapist. Dinah, in the Bible, was raped. Jewish women during Roman times were raped, our men crucified. Pity the wounded and tortured." Perl drew Rochel to her. "Listen to me, Rochela, according to Law, you are a Jew anyway, it is that common. You must not think that, because your father raped your mother, you are at fault."

"I have my own scissors," Rochel said, backing away. She felt like stabbing herself in the heart, but instead, when she pulled her grandmother's scissors from her basket, she held them to the back of her neck. "I can cut off my own hair." So saying, she cut off her two braids. She did this dry-eyed, which later, after everything was said and done, would be construed as haughtiness. Then, head high, scissors in one hand, braids in another, she crossed the graveyard, sidestepping tombstones and wading through the tall snow in between. Inside her little room, she went over to the chest, opened the doors with a little key from her basket, took some more blue thread, and tenderly tied the other ends of the poor dead braids. Then she flung herself on her bed, buried her head in the coverlet, and like a little child, she began to cry piteously, not for her mother or her grandmother or the loss of her father, but for mercy, for God to have mercy on her. She cried until her eyes were red, and her throat sore, and she was too worn out to cry anymore. Then she lay still on the bed, and in the silence of the winter afternoon, the snow cocooning Judenstadt from the tumult of the marketplace and all the busy people hawking their wares in the surrounding streets, she realized that she had known about her origins before Leah and Miriam told her. In a way, her fanciful belief in her father was like her vision of her mother coming from Kiev in a coach, eating soft white bread. Just a story, just another fairy tale she told herself in which virtue was rewarded and everybody wore nice clothes. Such a fool. Perhaps she had known at the time of her first blood, at the very same time she knew about the stars in the sky and the tragedy of Karel's legs and that the yellow circle she had to wear on her clothes was not a badge of privilege. Not your father, her grandmother had said. Maybe she always knew.

Then she sat up, looked about the room. The supper had not been started. The hearth was cold. It was getting dark. Zev had not come home. She lit the candle and she went over to Zev's rusty-looking glass, looked at her image. Her short hair was ruffled and standing up all over her head. She lifted her upper lip, inspected her teeth. She turned her face to the right and to the left, ran her finger along her cheekbones. Heartened, using the scissors artfully, she trimmed and shaped her hair. Surveying her work, she was not displeased, for what she resembled was not a Cossack. In truth, she looked like a grown woman, a married woman. Then she realized that she had left her sewing basket in Perl's kitchen. She had begun the morning thinking that she would sit by Perl's fire, do some embroidery. Not bothering to slip scarf or cloak on, she hurried through the cemetery and breathlessly opened the door to Perl's house, went down the hallway.

The rabbi was home, sitting by the hearth, reading. He peered at her uncovered hair, her flushed face, her expectant mouth, her wide eyes, and without meaning to, he let his gaze move to her smooth neck, down her body, taking in the soft curve of her breasts, the neatness of her waist.

"I . . . I just came for my basket," Rochel said.

"Yes, yes, take your basket," he said angrily. "Go."

She snatched her basket, ran out of the room. She had never seen the rabbi so perturbed. Surely she had not done anything further to hurt her people, not since the morning, not since her birth, not since her conception. If she was beyond redemption, was there any sin she could commit? For a moment, she hated not only herself, but the rabbi, too, and everybody else, for that matter. For shame, her grandmother's voice admonished. I do not care, Rochel replied peevishly. But, nonetheless, she spit seven times to shoo away the Evil Eye, and set about making herself useful, so that by the time Zev came home, she was wearing her scarf, stirring the pot of lentils, and singing a little song.

"You are not to sing, Wife," he said. "A man may be passing by, hear you."

"The window and door are closed, Husband."

"Still, it is not decent."

"Forgive me." She hung her head, but the same heat she had felt that morning rising from her chest to her neck and overtaking her tongue came upon her. She had been able to cheer herself up, do her duties, act like a wife. She had cut her hair. She was making supper. What more was required of her? In another moment, she would scream or run.

"No matter," he said gently. "Look, look what I bought you," and he unwrapped the net bag he had under his arm, showing her a big chunk of meat for the Sabbath meal. "Lamb," he declared. "And look." He pulled out some knotted bags, undid their strings, and set them out on the table. "Pepper." He wet his finger, touched the black grains, put the finger to her mouth. "Go ahead, taste it. Yes, yes. Now taste this." He put his finger in what seemed to be red dust, a warm red like the leaves of fall, brought it to her mouth. "Paprika from Hungary." He clapped his hands excitedly. "Is it not wonderful? And lamb. People were lined up at the butcher's from early this morning. I intended to get in line, but after I left you at the rebbetzin's, I saw Karel coming down our street. He says that the alchemists will be here in March, the ones to make the emperor immortal. Hah, I said to him, that will be the day, a man living as long as God. Karel said the emperor is going to Venice for Carnival and that His Highness is so anxious for immortality that he cannot sleep. Why does he need to sleep? I asked. He does not work for a living. So I went with Karel all day buying and selling. Do you know that the linen clothes he cannot sell to people, he sells to the paper factory for paper, and the old bones he collects to be ground for glue at the book bindery, and at the end of the day, he goes out of the city gates to the dump to dispose of what he cannot sell? Wife, only then, I remembered the butcher. Karel rushed Oswald back, and what do you know, the butcher had some lamb left."

He stopped. "What? What is it, my little one? You look so downcast."

"My mother died in childbirth, did she not?" It was the first time she gave voice to this fear.

"Your mother died in childbirth, yes, blessed be her memory." He reached out, tried to draw her to him, but she fended him off.

"My father raped my mother, and then I killed her." It was a terrible thought. Two terrible thoughts.

"That is not the way to think of it, Rochel, my dear." He shook his head, his eyes soft as Oswald the mule's.

"How else am I to think of it?" She tried hard to remember something real, not the made-up parts such as being bathed in a blue bowl or her mother walking across the bridge in the bright sunshine. Concentrating, she conjured the smell of her mother's cheek and her mother's body. Her mother's breast, her mother's neck, her sweat, yet as the night wore on after Perl left with her midwife bag and the city folded back into silence, Rochel smelled something sour. And she felt moisture seeping around her baby cloth; it spread to her back and head, covered her limbs, then it began cooling, became a chill, clammy, dripping cold. Rochel remembered waking up in a bath of blood, her mother dead beside her.

"My dear, my precious, it is not your fault," her husband comforted, reaching again for her, but she would have none of him. "You must put it out of your mind, Rochel, for we are a family."

"You married me," she accused.

"Indeed I did."

Rochel dragged herself over to the bed, sank down onto the straw mattress. It was held in its frame by strung ropes, which were now sagging. She would have to tighten them tomorrow with the crank on the side of the bed. Crank the bed, yes. She would take the soaking lamb in the morning, prepare it well, turn it on the spit all day as she worked. The lamb. Crank the bed, turn the lamb, sew the cloth. She was a needlewoman who could make beautiful things, earn her keep. She reminded herself of the threads Master Galliano had brought for the Emperor's new doublet. A rich red like paprika, a color she had seen only once before on that new fruit from the New World, the tomato, and the gold thread was a burnished yellow like old gold. She tried. She tried to remember all her duties, the objects which held up her life.

"I cannot stand it," she moaned.

"We must be strong, Rochel, you and I must be strong." He knelt on the floor by her side.

"I hate everything."

"No, no, Rochel, God forbid. Do not cry, my dear, do not cry, for if you cry, I will cry."

Rochel laughed at the thought of Zev crying. "Would you truly cry?"

"I would. I promise I would."

"You married me despite everything," Rochel stated, staring up at the ceiling. "How could you bring yourself to do it?"

"I married you," he repeated. "How did I stumble upon such a prize? Did God look down at me from the stars, see me in all my loneliness, and, taking infinite pity, bless me? Look at me."

Rochel looked at her husband.

"What do you see?"

A mouth lost in a beard, bushy eyebrows, big ears sticking out under his yarmulka.

"I see a man."

"A man who loves you, Rochel."

"A man who married me out of charity."

"Perhaps. But now I love you."

"In two days?"

"From the moment you entered my home."

"Because I am your wife."

"Because you are Rochel, my dearly beloved wife. Do you not think you can learn to love me? It should not be so hard. Remember Moses telling the Israelites, 'Cut away, therefore, the thickening about your hearts'?"

"I do want to be good, Zev. I truly do. I want to be a good woman."

"You are."

"I want to be a good wife, Zev."

"You are."

"I promise to do everything right, Zev."

"You will, then."

That night, prayers said, Zev raised the candle to see her shorn hair. "Now it is time for me to look at you."

She reached up with her hands to cover the back of her neck.

"Come, come, Wife. Let me see."

She let her hands drop. Her neck felt naked and cold.

8

B Y THE TIME Václav was fourteen, he had become a favorite, by eighteen, he was first valet.

He married that year, as a matter of course, a helper in the kitchen some years older than himself who had no dowry, but was of sturdy stock, willing, and, indeed, their children were born both strong and well formed. Nonetheless, their first child, Katrina, died of Pest when she was four. Václav's wife did not want any more babies after that, cried piteously when he came to her, but then Jiří was born, a fat, happy baby.

On the market days, free of castle duties, Václav would carry Jiří, on his shoulders, take him to see plays in church courtyards, or to puppet shows in the Square performed on planks across two barrels, featuring Kasparek, the hero; a red devil with a wooden leg; the yellow-haired farmer, Skhola; a young knight, an older knight, a young lady, a country girl, robbers. These wooden characters, known to every Czech, traveled with their human masters through towns and country in horse-drawn carts, barrel-shaped caravans with curtained backs. Václav boiled carp on Christmas, and he enjoyed the Christmas tree decorated with nuts and fruits and candles at the castle. He ate goose on Martinmas. On Twelfth Night he had roast pork at the gala in the castle, bringing some home for his family. On Corpus Christi, he watched the processions and pageants. But Carnival was the most wonderful. Carnival in Prague meant meat and pancakes, drinking and dancing in the street, horned hats; sausages were swallowed whole, flour flung, chickens and hounds rained with stones. The spirit of Carnival was represented by a big, fat man hung with fowl, rabbits, sausages, and Lent was a lean, old woman bereft of decoration.

Other people dressed as devils, fools, clerics, and wild animals. It was an upside down world—birds walking, fish flying, a horse trotting backward, rabbits as big as men hunting the hunters in green motley, and there, look, the husband helping the baby.

The year of 1601, Václav, as always, looked forward to Carnival, but the emperor was convinced that a trip to Venice would provide good distraction from the wearisome wait on the famous British alchemists. Too nervous to sit still, too restless to concentrate on affairs of state, too eager for eternity, each night the impatient monarch could not get to sleep, had to be brought glass after glass of water. Only Venice, the floating city, each house a port, would suffice to quench his anxiety.

At the time of departure, the emperor and Václav were in the main courtyard of the castle, the last chests being boarded into the carts while a knifing wind tinkled the icy branches of the trees like glass chandeliers. Václav had left his home near the Slavonic Monastery and cattle market early in the morning when it was still dark, piling several logs on the fire, tucking the end of the coverlet tightly about his wife's and son's feet as they lay in the bed sleeping. On the way to the castle, he saw some crows. It was a Czech superstition that cranes brought boy children and crows girls. His wife was pregnant again, and despite the habits of his countrymen, Václav was happy to see crows.

"I will not miss being in Prague for Carnival, Václav, not one bit," the emperor noted as they lingered in the courtyard while pages were running out with still more packages for the journey. "No cacophony of banging pans, no shrill whistles blowing, no straggling parade of raggedy peasants. No Butchers' Guild marching first and foremost, followed by the Potters with their banner of Adam and Eve, Weavers to the back, the tail of beggars and aged whores with sagging cheeks stained in berry juice and withered lips pressed with lard and blood to give lively color, stuffing themselves with fistfuls of intestines, roasts and rumps, legs and kidneys, men and women like beasts brought to the trough, fornicating despite the winter weather under every tree and bush, bush and tree, all restraint thrown to the winds, skirt over head, head over heels."

The emperor, Václav noted, was talking rather much these days, and making less sense.

"In Venice, Italians dress for Carnival as characters from commedia dell'arte. They have taste, imagination, manners."

Václav did not know what commedia dell'arte was. He did not care. He wanted to stay in Prague, his wife needed him, but now that the time had arrived to depart, the next best thing was to get out of the cold and into the imperial carriage. He was privileged to ride with the emperor in a coach made of the finest Afric mahogany and embellished with silver scrolls shaped in pattern of vines and dripping grapes, a little bejeweled crown set on top, ready bait for any footpads or bandits in the vicinity, although supposedly the four footmen front and back and the phalanx of Slovene guards, all on black stallions, should deter any untoward action. Behind the imperial carriage were the carriages of the nobles, and behind them the carts of food and supplies.

"Do you know, Václav, that the ice in the lands fronting the North Sea is so thick that whole carcasses of animals are frozen in waves like insects in amber?"

Václav did not doubt it for a second. Nostradamus had predicted disastrous weather for 1601 and there was a run on almanacs already this year.

Rudolph wore boots of heavy leather with thick soles of wood, and his doublet and breaches were of padded velvet, his hose of a close knit Merino wool. His cloak, with matching hat, was red fox, and his pigskin gloves were lined with soft rabbit fur. Václav's livery, lively red with gold thread embroidery forming the double Habsburg eagles with tongues and claws extended, was of the thinnest silk, ill suited to the temperature of winter both inside and out. His shoes were cloth. He could not remember when he last felt warm.

Finally, Rudolph climbed aboard the royal carriage upholstered in Moroccan leather and carpeted with leopard skin. Václav, following most eagerly, settled the fur blanket around the emperor's knees and another servant reached in, lit the coals in the two earthen braziers on the velvet floor. The royal chamber pot was placed under the seat, a small table set to the side, a basket of fruit, jugs of wine, the emperor's travel chess set. All was accounted for.

"Are we ready, Your Highness?" Václav asked.

Just then, Anna Marie, the emperor's devoted mistress, rushed out. "Rudie, kiss me good-bye."

She squeezed in, her stiff skirt shaped like a hobby horse taking up all the space, her bosoms pushed up to her neck spilling out of their bodice like aspic from its mold. His pregnant belly brushed against Václav hard and round as a bowling ball.

"I told you, Anna Marie, I will be back as soon as I can. An emperor has duties."

"Do not forget me, Rudie."

"How could I forget you, my pigeon?"

Two Slovene guards pulled her off, dragging her back into the castle.

The emperor settled himself again. "It is good to get away from the castle once in a while, do you not agree?"

"And Kirakos, Sire?"

"Kirakos will tend to all the preparations for the alchemists, Václav."

Václav thought it was Kirakos who needed tending.

"Well, then, I think we may begin our journey, Václav."

And with a volley of trumpets, off they went in grand procession down Hradčany Hill toward the Stone Bridge. Despite the cold, the streets of Prague were crowded. With its uncobbled, fetid little alleys, people of all class and opinion defecating where they paused, Prague had an odor reputed foul enough to keep the Turks away. Despite that, the city was a center of papermaking, book printing, silk and spice, imports from the East. Prague had a glassworks, the emperor's brewery, Krusovice, many monasteries, Charles University, bakeries, a horse market, and a pig business unmatched in Eastern Europe. Powered by the big water wheel on the Vltava River was an iron-works. Judenstadt, with its Rabbi Loew, was a center for Jewish learning. Maisel, their Mayor, had built them a bathhouse, a Town Hall. The Altneu Synagogue was one of the oldest synagogues in that part of the world. According to a count for tax purposes, the emperor told Václav, there were many more than a hundred thousand people who lived in the city of Prague. This, the emperor said, compared well with Naples, which was reported to be of almost three hundred thousand people, nearly as many as Amsterdam and Paris. Istanbul, unfortunately, was reputed to have about seven hundred thousand people. That, the emperor made note of, counted all the slaves. All in all, it was reckoned, the emperor stated, that there were a hundred million people in Europe now that the worst of the

Plague years had passed—a hundred million, an unimaginable number, which made Václav think of people having to stand side by side, one against the other like trees in the forest, yet, in truth, it was not like that, for bordering every town and village was the real forest, dark and dense, the home of hungry beasts—wolves, bears, mountain lions—and wild men half human, half animal. Václav hoped they would not meet any such beings on their trip to Venice.

"I remember Venice in 1575, Václav." They had gone through the city gates. "I was young, or rather younger, a fine figure of a man, in my prime, my first prime. Carnival in Venice, and to be received by a lady, a court courtesy, a court-courtier, a courtesan, who was listed in the Catologo of Courtesans, none other than Veronica Franco, the most famous courtesan of her time, an honest courtesan, God be praised."

The emperor dug into his food basket, pulled out a drumstick of a new fowl brought back from the New World. "When I live forever, I will have plenty of this turkey."

"Pardon me, Your Majesty, but what if the alchemists are unable to make you live forever?" Václav had heard that one of them was a charlatan who had his ears cut off as penalty for forgery.

"They would have to or be executed, plain and simple."

Indeed, the alchemists, Dee and Kelley from London with two servants, had already started their treacherous journey to Prague, which would involve crossing the Channel by boat, Europe by horseback, cart, rickety coach, trudging their way along roads as old as the Romans, some worn down by foot and mule hoof alone and others wider but rutted to the bone by great European engines of war—catapults, cavalry, and, more lately, cannons. The traveling party would be wise to keep as much as possible to valleys and lowlands, but sometimes would have to scale mountains used only by the most intrepid merchant caravans going between Antwerp in the Spanish Netherlands through Frankfurt am Main, on through Saxony to Pilsen, finally to the capital of Bohemia, seat of the Habsburg Empire, Prague.

"Ah, but once they make the elixir," Václav said in hopeful tone, "you will make them knights?"

"Once they do, they will be executed post haste. Do you think I want people running about who know the secret to eternal life? In *Portrait of Veronica Franco* by Jacopo Tintoretto, Václav"—the emperor waved his drumstick like a conductor's baton—"the courtesan Franco has a pink nipple peeking above the lace of her bodice, a heart-shaped face, deeply set brown eyes, red hair, a small mouth, bee-stung lips, a cleft in her chin, long earlobes, a slight point to top of ears, shadows under eyes."

Václav had piled up enough wood for the whole winter for his wife. Karel, the junkman, helped him in the dark of night to transport the logs in his cart from the emperor's woodpile.

"Not only a lady of the senses, but also a lady of sense. Exceptional among her sex, she could read, and not only read, but to herself, and not only to herself, but without moving her lips, and not only read and to herself without moving her lips, but write, and not only her name and lists for the market and to copy out words from sacred texts, but write poetry. A most honest courtesan, Veronica Franco."

Big wet drops of snow softly pelted the windows of the carriage, which were made of thin Venetian glass. Václav wondered if wolves could break through. The Russian, Kirakos's ready slave, had told Václav a story about wolves. A bridal party in Russia set out after the wedding in a sleigh of pure white, bells on its sides. Soon they were pursued by a pack of wolves. One by one people were thrown out of the sleigh to appease the hungry wolves. Servants went first, of course, then parents, finally the bride herself. At the end, it did not do the groom any good, for the voracious animals tipped over the sleigh, ate him, too. "Served him right," Václav had said. The Russian shrugged. "I could tell you about the Ivan the Terrible, do not let me start. I come from the Novgorod."

"Veronica Franco's palazzo was on the Grand Canal, Václav." The emperor sighed, rummaged in his food basket again, brought out a nice hunk of fig cake. "Her building bore the red flags of St. Mark, the golden-winged lion, and she had those arched windows in the Turkish style, *sgraffito*, pictures, decorations made right on the facade of the building. Can you picture it, Václav?"

Václav tried to remember when he had eaten. The night before? The day before? Was it porridge he had eaten last? A crust of bread?

"She loved me, Václav, they always do." The emperor waved his turkey leg about with one hand and squeezed the cake with the other, alternating bites—cake, turkey, cake, turkey—and, finally surfeited, threw the bone out of the window, used his chamber pot to loud effect and disgusting smell, and began to regale Václav with fond memories of chubby buttocks and bouncing breasts, jellylike thighs and long, sinuous calves, mounds like forests of soft spongy moss, necks for the nuzzling, breath in his ears with the warmth and moisture of steam rising from a hot bath, tickle toes on his belly, and pink pillowy folds rolling open like subjects bowing before him in absolute and reverent obedience. He planned to ravish many a maid, break many a heart in the Venetian Republic.

9

K AREL, THE LEGLESS rag and bone man, was in his habitual place by the hearth at the Golden Ox when he heard the
word *Judenstadt*. They were conferring in low tones, the three
brothers who owned the barn where Oswald was quartered, and
Thaddaeus, the priest of Our Lady of Sorrows, who had lost a public
debate with Rabbi Loew, the subject being: What did Abraham mean
when he said to his companions, "Abide ye here with the ass; and I
and the lad will go yonder to worship and come again to you"? The
group thought him asleep. In truth, Karel was on the verge of sleep,
the first delirious dive under the day to where all was possible, a
place where he had legs, back in his village on his own farm. He was
teetering there, on the verge of freedom.

Judenstadt.

It always happened. Without the presence of the emperor, if
somebody lost his purse, became ill with the ague, hurt his toe, or a
cow came down with something, a baby got colic, if a branch fell off
a tree or a chicken was crushed by the wheel of a coach, if a child
had gone missing or a wife run away, some poor Jew would pay with
his life. But on this night, Karel heard words that made him so upset
he wanted to leave the Golden Ox immediately, go straight to Rabbi
Loew. However, the gates to Judenstadt would be locked at this
hour. Even if they were not closed, he would have to ask somebody
to carry him out to his cart. Then the three brothers and Father
Thaddaeus would realize he had not been asleep all along. Karel kept
his eyes tightly shut.

The next morning, as soon as the tavern maid came to sweep out
the bar, he dragged himself to the door, had her help him up on his

cart, and instead of going through the streets of Hradčany first, he urged Oswald on across the Stone Bridge to Old Town, then to Judenstadt.

"Rabbi," he called out in front of Rabbi Loew's house, ringing the bell he had by his seat. "It is only me, Karel, and Oswald. Rabbi, come get me."

"Ah, Karel, so early in the day you arrive at my door." Rabbi Loew stuck his head out of an upper window. "We have no rags, but a good day to you nonetheless. Shall I get the rebbetzin to bring you some warm milk?" The rabbi had said his morning prayers when there had been light enough to tell a blue thread from a white thread, and had washed his hands from a bowl of water by his bed so he would not have to walk a step before praising God.

"No, I have something to tell you, Rabbi." Karel looked around, behind, and forward.

"All right, all right. I am coming, Karel. I am coming."

Karel's head was flat as a board and his hair grew straight up. He had a small beak nose, round yellowish eyes; he resembled an owl, and his arms, from moving himself about on his little cart, were as strong as a woodchopper's. Even if he were whole, he would not have been a heavy man, but as it was, he was all torso and most adults could carry his weight. The strong rabbi lifted the legless man up the stairs.

"Are you well, Karel?" the rabbi asked, putting him by the stove on a chair of Italian design, a *sgabello*. The rabbi lowered himself into an austere ladder-back.

"Rabbi, something terrible has happened, is to happen," Karel sputtered.

By now more members of the family were rising, the rabbi's daughters and the grandchildren. Hands were being washed, prayers said. Soon breakfast would be under way. Afterward, the men were to head to the shul, the women to the kitchen. It was only seven o'clock by the spring clock the rabbi kept in his study, five minutes after seven by the Týn Church clock, and one minute to seven by the Astronomical Clock in the town square.

"Your troubles, my friend, tell me."

Karel took a deep breath, shook his head back and forth, held his arms together while his eyebrows lifted in mournful arches into the deep furrows of his brow.

"Begin at the beginning, Karel, go to the end."

"It is all beginning, and there is no end, no end in sight, no end to it, Rabbi." Karel started crying.

"Zelda," the rabbi called down. "Bring some water for washing, please, my darling, and something for Karel to eat."

"Coming, Papa."

Zelda came up the stairs with a bowl of water, a pitcher. She was a comely young woman and arrangements had long ago been made with the family of a noted scholar in Posen, a rabbi's daughter could expect no less for a husband. She poured water over Karel's hands, holding the bowl. He washed, dried his hands on the towel she had ready. Then she returned downstairs, came up with a plate of prune tarts, a pitcher of warm milk, and a mug.

"Eat, refresh yourself, then slowly, Karel, word by word."

Karel did not look at Zelda in the eyes, but fastened on her feet, and then, feeling embarrassed, looked at her middle, and then his eyes traveled to her breasts. He did not know where to look.

"Thank you, Zelda," the rabbi said.

Karel, without shame, guzzled the tarts, gulped down the milk, wiped his mouth on his sleeve, then proceeded.

"You know I love Oswald. Your mayor, Maisel, saved him from being killed, gave him to me. He was all skin and bones. Now I even go across the Stone Bridge to buy from the castle. Everybody knows me. I am on good terms with all. I am a respected man."

"Yes, Karel, you are."

"It was a Jewish doctor who saved my life when my legs were cut off in the field by my father when he did not see me in the tall wheat. I never mean to harm Jew or Christian."

"You are a rare man, Karel."

In Karel's village, the day after a wedding, the bride and groom paraded dressed as each other, he in skirts, she in breeches. There were performances, medicinal shows, jugglers, and horse trainers, followed by a parade of people costumed as clowns and bears, chimney sweeps, and one portrayed as a Jew in a coat of many different-colored rags, a hat with bird wings, and a staff with bells on it to warn others of his approach. The Jew was spit upon. Thinking of that now, Karel was ashamed.

"You are a good man, Karel."

"My devoted mother, may she rest in peace, taught me to say no evil of any man."

"She did well, Karel."

"I have worked hard all my life."

"In truth, you have, Karel. But have you hastened to my house so early on this morning on this cold winter day to tell me how hard you work? " Rabbi Loew could smell the buckwheat groats being boiled on the kitchen hearth. His stomach gurgled. He heard steps, and then Perl appeared in the study.

"Good morning, Karel, would you like to share some breakfast with us?"

"No thank you, Frau Rabbi."

"How can you live in this mess, Judah?"

Karel looked about. Other than books in piles, the room was tidy. In fact, the rabbi's house was less soiled than any other place he had been, including the castle. There, for all its magnificence, little piles of excrement—dog, lion, human—could be found on stairways and in corners. Bones and offal were tossed out of the doorway of the kitchen, and flies from the stables and zoo settled on all. Centuries of dirt and waste were encrusted on every sill and floor despite the battalions of maids and scrubbers.

"You may dust just a little," the rabbi said indulgently, "when Karel goes."

"So good to me, Judah."

"Light of my life, Perl."

"So tell me," the rabbi said, sitting forward when Perl went down the stairs.

"You know, I stable Oswald in a barn in New Town, not too far from the Vyšehrad Castle in some farmlands. These brothers let me out a stall. At a considerable cost, I must say."

"Go on."

"Oswald and I can look up at night from his stall, which has its own door, up to the dark shadow of the old castle. That is where the Czech kings held court, and our first regent, Queen Lubice, reigned."

The rabbi knew of the legendary Lubice, the daughter of Cech, the first settler. It was said that Queen Lubice had a dream about a group of people who would seek refuge in her country. If the Czechs welcomed them, prosperity would be granted to the land. Thus, her grandson opened the city gates to the first Jews, who had wandered for twelve years after being driven from Lithuania and Moscovy.

"Yes, Karel, the old castle is lovely." Vyšehrad, across the river from the emperor's newer castle, had a drawbridge flanked by two great towers, and fortification walls in broken formation. Built to protect long before cannons could break through walls, Vyšehrad evoked soldier-knights who handled the sword not just for sport, and a nobility who were not merely idle courtiers in sumptuous clothes.

"The brothers do not know I sleep there beside Oswald when I am not by the hearth at the Golden Ox. But tell me, where would I sleep? Do they think I would float to a room somewhere else all on my own after I stable Oswald?"

"No, of course not, Karel." The rabbi stretched out his legs before him, quickly drew them back, remembering how rude it must seem to Karel, who had no legs.

"When I pull myself to the door, I pretend to see way down the river to the emperor's castle, Hradčany. When I was a little boy, I heard about Prague, but I never thought I would live here."

"It is a privilege, is it not, to be in a city so rich with history. But you were saying something about the castle. Is your news to do with the emperor and the elixir of eternal life, the alchemists who are coming? Is that what you wish to tell me?"

The rabbi knew full well no alchemist, magician, or wizard could prolong life beyond its natural course. The emperor, having to face this fact, could fall into a deep despair and loosen the reigns of government, thereby giving the Protestant princes, his greedy brother Matthias, the landless peasants, the Inquisitorial force of Rome propitious time for attack. Rudolph, and more particularly his father, Maximilian, had continued to grant the Jews permission to stay in Prague without harassment, and the community had flourished, with its printing press, yeshiva, and synagogue, a butcher, baker, cobbler, and Maisel's business ventures. Now, the rabbi feared for his children, his grandchildren, and all his people.

"Sometimes I believe I can hear music from the castle and they have all the candles lit so it is like a city on that hill, a starlit city."

"You wish to tell me something about the castle, Karel? Have the alchemists arrived?"

"No, Rabbi, not the castle, the barn."

"The barn."

"I am not sure I should be telling you all this, Rabbi."

"Perhaps, then, you should not."

"I have many coverlets, and Oswald, too, he also has a cover, and all in all, except for the coldest nights of winter, we are very cozy, Oswald and me, very cozy indeed."

"Good, Karel, good for you."

The rabbi had regrettably, in his old age, developed a need for napping in the afternoon. It was such a delight to hear the city go on about him, the criers selling their wares, the commerce of life, children's voices at play, while he lay sheltered in his room, the closed window shutters emitting thin stripes of light across the floor, warmth radiating from the Kochenhofen, a large, earthenware stove. He had just wakened, but he was already looking forward to his nap.

"It was late at night. I know it was late, for I was almost asleep. I heard some voices."

"Voices?"

"The brothers who own the barn and another voice. They were plotting, Rabbi."

"Against the emperor?"

"No, Rabbi."

"You were at the barn?"

"No, at the Golden Ox, sleeping on the hearth."

"I thought you said the barn."

"I know, but it was the Golden Ox, for it was a night I could not go to the barn, I was so tired, where I heard them talking, the owners of the barn were drinking at the Golden Ox, and the priest, Thaddaeus."

"Are you certain? Father Thaddaeus?"

"As certain as I do not have legs."

"Maybe it was a dream."

"Would that it were."

"Maybe the drink."

"No, it was clear."

"What was clear?"

"The voices, and then I peek a little."

"And?"

"They were plotting, Rabbi, with Thaddaeus."

The rabbi got very still and was suddenly very awake.

"Against us, Karel?"

"Yes, Rabbi." Karel hung his head.

"When, Karel?" the Rabbi asked in a whisper.

"Right before your, what do you call it, when you pass over? A fire it is to be."

"An attack before Passover." The rabbi closed his eyes. "Why now, Karel?"

"Because, Thaddaeus said, that the people know that the emperor is letting the Jews take on trades in the town, that they can be furriers. Maisel is a furrier, is he not? And some Jews are silversmiths who work for the Italians, tanners, too, and that the emperor permits your merchants licenses to buy and sell goods like the Christians. Because, Thaddaeus said, no place is better for Jews than Prague. He says the emperor tolerates the Jews because he has borrowed money from Maisel for his alchemists, therefore Jews will be granted more favors when the alchemists come. Thaddaeus says that you won the debate two years ago by unfair means, that the judges were bribed by Jewish money. He says that Prague is too full of Jews, that Jews have too many children, that still more come from Spain and Portugal, all the way from England and France since they have been expelled, from German states since the Crusades because they are protected here. Thaddaeus says the next thing will be that Jews will not have to wear your yellow badges and nobody will know who you are and you will be able to ruin good, Christian daughters. Jews will grow rich while the Christians are taxed beyond endurance with the Turkish Wars."

"Enough, Karel."

"Thaddaeus says he will be able to rouse all good Christians to burn down your houses, kill the men outright, sell your children into slavery, cut open your women, put cats inside them as they have in other cities."

"No more." The rabbi stood up, went to the top of the stairs. "Perl, Perl, come up, I need you."

Perl, who had been seasoning a chicken for the Sabbath meal that night, put it down, wiped her hands on her apron, and quickly bounded up the stairs. "Judah," she said, studying his face, "dear Husband, you look stricken."

If Karel had not been there, the rabbi would have enfolded his wife in his arms.

"I have always kept you safe, have I not?"

"Oh, Judah, you have, you have."

"What are you doing now, my wife?"

"I am preparing the Sabbath meal, Judah."

"Good, good. Do not let me distract you."

Perl gave her husband a searching look, then turned and went back downstairs.

"What will you do, Rabbi?"

"Pray, Karel. Pray and fast."

"Pardon me, Rabbi, is that all?"

"Karel, all we want to do is live in peace. We do not own weapons, are not permitted to." The rabbi got up, began to pace the room.

"I am just a poor peddler, I have no legs, beg pardon, Rabbi, but your books, the Kabbalah, are there not spells?"

The rabbi put his finger to his lips. "Be quiet, Karel. The Kabbalah must not be spoken about lightly in the giddy give and take of casual conversation. It is not for dabblers or outsiders."

"The letters of your alphabet, Rabbi, the manipulations of numbers, magic incantations, I have heard—"

"Dear friend—the Torah first, always the Torah, and then for students the Talmud, if a page a year." The rabbi stopped, squinted his eyes. "After many, many years of study with a righteous man, maybe the works of the Kabbalah for contemplation, meditation. The Torah forbids magic, absolutely." The rabbi raised his finger skyward. "The Kabbalah means 'to receive' and 'the tradition.' It is a private and sacred journey few are qualified to take. It is a path to the unknowable, a way of beginning to see, nay, feel the mystery that is called God. Not for the uninitiated, mind you, and to tamper with it is to invite disaster. Men have been made mad by this quest."

"I am sorry," Karel muttered, "for mentioning it."

"My friend, history is estrangement from God; we are not created in His final perfection, but each man must realize His perfection himself, and the Kabbalah is a path. We must work all our lives to repair the world, and always in partnership with God."

The rabbi collapsed back in his chair, exhausted.

"I will go now, tend to Oswald," Karel said softly.

"Do, do." The rabbi shook his head as if ridding his brain of a thought.

"Help me, please, and I will be gone." Karel lifted his arms, and the rabbi crossed the room, picked him up, carried him back down the stairs, set him on his little perch on his cart.

"I did not mean to be sharp with you. It is just that the news you bring tangles my mind, twists my heart. I am grateful for your courage, we all are."

Despite his harsh talk, it occurred to the rabbi that the humble junkman, in his inept way, may have happened upon, if not the solution, an approach. He, Rabbi Loew, although he had never been through the mystical gates of knowledge or entered the garden of bliss or crossed the final threshold, and never, ever experienced ecstatic union with God, was nonetheless no mere novice at reading the supposedly simple examples and tales that made up the *Zohar,* one of the books of the Kabbalah.

"You are very good to us, Karel, and I thank you."

"A Jew saved my life when my father accidentally cut off my legs with the scythe, Maisel gave me Oswald. I am indebted."

The rabbi smiled ruefully. Would that a Jew could give him back his legs, a fine horse, all that this good man deserved.

"Good-bye, my dear friend," the rabbi said, grasping Karel's hand.

Slowly, holding his robe up so he wouldn't trip on it, Rabbi Loew made his way back to his study, sat down, put his head in his hands.

"I have some groats for you, Judah," Perl called up.

The rabbi descended the stairs again, looked at his family. Little Fiegel was seated at the end of the bench, her curls nicely combed, a smile on her face, happy as a lark, her mother Leah on one side, and Zelda the youngest on the other, Miriam across the table. His three daughters, the two husbands, and the grandchildren. This was his family, his home, the sum of his life.

"Tomorrow I may go to have a talk with Maisel," the rabbi said after the blessing, "for the emperor will be back from Venice soon, will he not, and I will be fasting for the next two days."

The rabbi began the meal praising God, but could only pick at his food.

"You will have to do better than that," Perl said, "if you are not going to eat for a while."

10

UNLIKE THEIR EXTRAVAGANT departure, the entrance into Prague of the imperial coach, the coaches of the nobles, the supply carts, and the troop of guards was less than splendid. After rattling along over dirt roads through Italy, Austria, and on up through Bohemia, some of the carriages were returning with mismatched wheels; windows were broken so those inside had to huddle in furs, the silverwork along the sides and tops was tarnished, and gold and mother-of-pearl inlay was spattered with mud. The horses were no longer prancing, the donkeys pulling the carts were bedraggled, the guards were tired, cold, and hungry, and a group of raggedy whores, picked up along the way, carrying pots in their hands and bags on their backs, had attached themselves to the end of the party. Yet when the procession entered the town gates, the royal volley of trumpets announced their presence as if they were returning from triumphant war in glorious condition.

"Who goes there?" the gatekeeper asked in ceremonial parlance.

"It is the Holy Roman Emperor, Rudolph II," answered the captain of the Slovene guards.

The city gates, fiercely spiked and high as a house, marking the beginning of the royal route, and closed at troubled times, such as Plague, were opened. After the gates, they rode along Celentná Street. First came the mint where the money was made, Václav counted, then the House of the Black Madonna, the Blue Stork, At the Golden Well, the Golden Unicorn, the Golden Keys, House of the Golden Ship, House on the Golden Corner, Charles University, House of the Two Golden Bears, House of the Golden Jug—gold, gold, gold, as if God had rained gold leaf on Prague as generously as those that fell from trees in autumn. Many of the houses of the rich and members of the city council, and in some cases taverns and shops were trimmed, topknotted or even completely roofed with golden flakes. In summer, Prague gleamed, gem of Eastern Europe.

Dear God, but Václav was frittered and frayed. They had stayed in Venice, after the arduous trip, only two days, and then it was time to pack, turn around. Indeed, the emperor had not been able to leave the city fast enough, worrying afresh over the alchemists. What if they arrived while he was gone? What if something had happened to them? Also, Václav suspected, it had not gone as well with the courtesans as expected. And although it was not snowing in Venice, it rained continuously, and the dark waters of the canals lapped over the docks, threatened the gondolas. The emperor could not swim.

"How different it was when I was in Venice for Carnival years ago," the emperor continued to reminisce at this last stage of the journey. "The elegance of Franco's abode bespoke volumes. She had heard of my dislike of cold, had a roaring fire going. Not only that, but bedsheets were been warmed top to bottom with hot stones from the fire and long-handled covered pans of coal. On top of her coverlets she had many little dogs, forming a living, breathing blanket of fur. Her silken skin, softened by olive oil, the honeycomb color of her hair, her limbs rounded smooth, you can imagine, Václav, my pleasure was diffuse, mellow as summer, spun out as if I were swimming in Bohemian beer flavored subtly with rosemary and thyme. The moment became embedded in my memory like a delicious morsel of tender fat."

Václav was anxious to see his wife, see how tall Jiří must have grown in the time he was gone.

"Franco controlled the night, no mean feat with a new emperor. Our coupling was *gaillarde*, a pavane, *musica noster amor.*" The emperor had not a worry in her presence, so he did not ask for submissive surrender. All she had to do was say it, just say she loved him, too. Say it and then agree to come back with him, live in the castle, a wing of her own with all the privileges of an official mistress. Could any woman ask for more? She was a citizen of Venice, she explained, a free person, whatever that was. Rudolph was still in a quandary over her reaction. It did not make sense. He an emperor, she a mere courtesan. How could any woman anywhere refuse him? These troubling memories he did not confide.

"Afterward, Václav, " the emperor went on as if all had gone well those years ago, "the serving maid brought us pitchers of the strong red wine, and sitting at a small round table of black and white marble inlay, we supped on steaming, heavy soup made of white beans, hocks of ham, followed by a bowl of long strands of boiled flour flavored with a delicate sauce of crushed garlic, pine nuts and olive oil, followed by a salad of little black octopi so fresh they hung onto my teeth. She wanted, you know, to come back with me, become first mistress, for she loved me so. I could not have it."

"Interesting, Your Majesty." He and Jiří had pushed rags all along the seams where the walls met the floor before he left his home. He hoped the room had kept cozy and dry. He had filched fish and venison from the castle smokehouse, several breads from the bakery, a basket of dried apples, five heads of cabbage, a bag of flour—enough, he hoped. His wife needed to eat well in her condition, and, of course, Jiří was a growing boy.

Nobody knew, but it had taken Rudolph six months to get over Veronica Franco, the first few of agony he did not think existed, to forget their one night of love. Had Venice belonged to his Empire, he would have forced her to return with him, but as it was, he had no jurisdiction, could not bend her to his will. Every morning of those six months, he had awakened exhausted and empty with the awareness that he did not have her, his Empire counting for nothing. Vainly, he tried to assuage his hurt by fornicating with all and sundry, high and low.

"Years later, Václav, she appealed to me for help, for she was accused of being a witch, invoking the devil using a wedding ring, a blessed olive branch, holy water in a basin, and blessed candles. I was sorry to send word that I could do nothing for her. After all, what was one night of love? But having other powerful connections, she was acquitted and lived to a ripe old age of forty-five."

After the Prague city gates, Celentná Street emptied out into the Square, where the Town Hall stood with its great and famous Astronomical Clock. Below the wheel of time rimmed in gold were small statues of Greed personified by a figure of a Jew, a turbaned Turk was Lust, Death, the skeleton. And within the bowels of the clock tower was the centerpiece of the twelve beautifully painted Apostles, which, placed on a flat disk, at the hour when their little window opened, were put in motion by a rope pulled by the figure of Death. Along the royal route through Old Town, the returning emperor was greeted by the mayor of Prague, his councilmen, members of the Merchants' Guild, the Rope Makers, the Tanners, the Ironworkers, the Brewers, the journeymen and apprentices, merchants, priests and monks, beggars, all on bended knee, their hats off. Last in line, at the beginning of the Stone Bridge, stood the Jews in dark, somber clothes, yellow patches affixed to their chests. They inclined a little.

"They are stiff-necked, are they not?" the emperor said to Václav.

"It is out of respect for their God," Václav answered.

"What about the respect of their emperor?" Rudolph, despite his constant chatter, had been in a sour mood since Venice. No famous courtesans this time. Furthermore, there was dysentery among the guards and twenty new cases of the French pox, which did not surprise the emperor one bit, not to mention all the bad weather they had encountered, and the troupe of shoeless whores, who now would settle in Prague, spread their disease and needs. Thank God he had not gotten the French pox, but he had acquired a bad case of crabs. For more days than he liked to count, he had wanted to be in his own bed, in his own castle, the door closed, the fire roaring. And he could not remember when last he'd had wild boar in a savory mushroom sauce, a decent dumpling, *Lammbraten, Henne stuffed mit Brot*. As soon as he got home, he would have some oysters and some partridge, maybe turtledove, plover. Yes, he was in a mood for fowl. Then, just as the thought was cheering and the castle spires came in sight, the carriage lurched, came to an abrupt stop.

"What is this?" The emperor pulled the curtains aside, pressed his face to the glass window.

"Sire." One of his guards knocked on the door of the carriage.

"I did not give the order to stop."

"Your Majesty, the Rabbi Loew is standing in front of the carriage."

"So keep going."

"He is standing in front of the coach."

"Run him down, man."

"The horses will not move. They are as if transfixed."

"Transfixed, my arse."

The emperor flung open his door. The guard pulled out the step, helped the emperor. There, surrounding the horsed guards was a great throng of people, and in front of the carriage was the rabbi of the Altneu Synagogue. Rudolph remembered him vaguely from the night at the castle when the multitudes had crowded into his room. He was a large man with a white beard, long hair, a forehead lined with creases, an impressive man, and yet, still and all, a Jew, and as that, as anybody else in his Empire so bold as to stop the royal progress, deserved no better than to be trampled to bits.

"Move aside, I command you." The emperor said this with all the authority of his position, but there was something he noticed about the rabbi, an aura which defied the idea of earthly station.

"I respectfully request an audience with Your Majesty," the rabbi said.

"Begone. I do Jewish business only with Maisel, the court Jew."

"It is a matter of immediate and grave concern." The rabbi was not so much obstinate as gravely peaceful in his stance. His planted feet and folded arms demonstrated most visibly the responsibility of an emperor to his subjects, not the opposite. The fate of cities and peoples, his presence seemed to imply, hung on a thread of mutual consensus.

"Bosh, do not distract me with trivialities. Make way for the imperial entourage."

The emperor got back into his carriage. "Remove him. Whip the horses, to death if need be."

But the guards could not move their arms and the whips in their hands lay limp as snakes.

"Do I have to destroy this blight myself?" the emperor fumed.

Townspeople on the sidelines began to gather stones. One person threw one. It pelted the rabbi's back. Another stone was thrown, and shortly a rain of stones landed on the rabbi.

"That is right," the emperor said. "Stone the Jew." He closed the curtains of his carriage. "You know how I feel about blood," he said to Václav.

The carriage did not move. Shortly there was another knock on the door.

"What does it take to get home, I ask you?"

"Your Majesty?"

"What is it now?"

"Look."

The emperor opened his door, stepped out. The stones that had been hurled at the rabbi had turned midair into roses the color of gold and lay in a lush, buttery carpet about the rabbi, scenting the air like a spring day.

"By Mary and all the Saints," the emperor gasped. "What is the meaning of this? Stones into roses?" He quickly got back in his carriage, slamming the door. "The devil is here in our midst, Václav. Can you smell the sulfur?"

"We could go around him," Václav suggested.

"But he must be arrested, punished. How can stones turn into roses? Are you not puzzled?"

"Just for now we could go around him, get home to the castle, Your Majesty. You must be tired." Václav, of course, knew of the rabbi. It was said that he was a powerful magi.

"Right you are right, Václav. I am very tired, very tired, and to be accosted like this, it is the last straw, but for now, yes, let us go around and on." The emperor was trembling. He was uncertain, perturbed. "Yes, yes." He leaned out of the carriage window. "Go around— around, I say."

The imperial convoy, including the many carriages carrying the nobles and the supply carts and phalanx of guards, the marching, barefoot prostitutes, cut a wide swath, avoiding the rabbi standing in the midst of roses.

"You see, Václav, it is not easy being emperor," the emperor explained, relieved, as they left the rabbi behind on the Stone Bridge, climbed the hill to the castle. "Every day brings a new trial."

"When you live forever, Your Majesty?"

"That will be different, much different. Do you think God is confronted by problems? Recalcitrant subjects, holes in the road, French pox, bad food and diarrhea, rotten teeth, ungrateful brothers, rabbis who can turn stones into roses? The thing you have to remember about eternity, Václav, is that it is . . . well, eternity is eternity, therefore eternity." The emperor stopped talking for a moment, pondered. "Curious. If he can turn stones into roses, there is no telling what he is capable of. I mean . . ."

"He is a man of God, Your Majesty."

"He is a Jew, plain and simple, but talented, I must give him that. He may yet put his abilities to good use. Stones into roses."

11

MADE FROM MUD of the right bank of the Vltava before the first light of day, you could say he was born yesterday. Given arms that stretched to his knees, legs longer than any man's, hands the size of three hands, and the strength of twelve men, you could say he was a giant. Since there was no book of generations for his origins, no Adam who begat Seth who begat Enos and none who walked with God among his ancestors, no history to his blood, no choice to his direction, you could say he was a mere robot. Having no tongue, lacking the power of speech, you could say he had no neshama, no soul. He was, in all aspects, a golem.

To make this creature, the rabbi, a righteous man, a tzaddik adored by his congregation, prayed and fasted for seven days, recited parts of the Torah to evoke its secret code, and studied *The Book of Splendor* to discover the profound meaning hidden within its seemingly accessible exemplar, and far into night he sang Psalm 139, "when I was made in secret *and* curiously wrought in the lowest parts of earth," until the words became a meditation ingrained in heart and mind. Furthermore, Rabbi Loew was a mature man, indeed old, a father and grandfather, and thus ready to see with his heart and mind the wisdom that lay in formless matter. He had learned how, by using the incantation *abra-kadabra*, which meant "I will create as I speak," he could make a manlike thing. He knew that a golem's body must be imbued with the power of certain combinations of numbers, which corresponded with the letters forming God's divine name. He understood, as he knelt before sunrise on the bank of the Vltava River, how to shape each member of the golem body in careful proportion. Slowly, he fashioned arms with the dimensions of branches and the fingers of clay he made as big as joiner's tools. Like mounding a gigantic sand castle, the rabbi pyramided the expansive chest. The legs were constructed in style, size, and power along the lines of pillars to hold up a roof. The feet were paddles. The torso had the girth of a bear. Each part was fitted larger than life, yet was complete in all the humanly attributes—save a tongue.

On its forehead, the rabbi traced the Hebrew letters EMETH. This word meant Truth, one of God's names. However, if the first letter were to be removed, the Hebrew letters would spell Death. Then, the mud man flat on his back on the bank of the river, the Rabbi walked seven times around him, right to left, then seven times the other way. Using *The Book of Creation, The Yetsirah*, the Rabbi recited combinations of the twenty-two letters of the Hebrew alphabet leading through Awe, Love, and Yearning to the Throne itself. These were the holy circles formed by letters with groups of two consonants through which streamed the creative power of the universe. That was how both the cosmos and man were formed, because all things lived through the secret names inside them. God said, Let there be light, and there was light, God called the firmament Heaven. Moses also, using the many secret names of He Who Is Completely Unknowable, the Hidden of Hidden, had parted the seas.

Most importantly in this whole process, the rabbi assured God that he, Rabbi Judah Loew, was using his knowledge only for this one time and in no way was he trying to assume powers inappropriate to his humble lot. Meticulously, judiciously, reverently, sweetly, the rabbi intoned two hundred twenty-one more combinations of the letters of the name of He Who Shall Remain Nameless, which had the thirty-two ways of wisdom of the ten original numbers. Then, holding the scrolls of the Torah, he bowed to the four corners of the world chanting blessings. And he said to the golem, "You are not man, you do not have a soul. You are not an idol." Then the rabbi went down to the waters of the river to wash his hands, offer a final prayer. It had gone well.

However, the moment the rabbi's back was turned, something occurred which was in no way part of his strenuous calculations and meticulous recitation. Faint as a whiff of turned milk, brief as one slightly discordant note in a long melody, like a slight sagging of the hem of an otherwise finely stitched garment, or a bad taste in the mouth, or just a touch of fever, something untoward, disturbing, malevolent crept up to the inert figure. A cloud passed over the

newly risen sun, in an instant casting all that was familiar into ominous shadow. Was it a dybbuk, a witch, a restless gilgul, the Evil Eye
itself? Whatever, it planted its gruesome kiss on the newly made
man's lips. Immediately, a shiver went through the rabbi, and the
hairs on the back of his hands stood up, and, suddenly weary and out
of sorts, he turned around quickly. But it was nothing. Indeed, the
sun, a golden ball ascending the sky, so to speak, was soon to reach
the tip of the turrets of the castle, soar above the spires of the St.
Vitus Cathedral and shine down on Prague, proclaiming that all and
all alike merited the beneficence of warmth and light.

Assured that his uneasiness was only tiredness, the rabbi knelt
again beside his creation, and this time blew into the mouth the
words, "You have been made of earth and water, been given breath."

Tremors passed through the mass of mud, and the features of the
face and details of the fingers, the tendons of the neck, the collarbone, the elbows and knees, all of which a moment before had been
mere sculpture, and crudely melded at that, transformed, gained
distinction.

"I name you Yossel."

To cover his monster's nakedness, the rabbi bunched together
blankets, improvised a sort of cloak and breeches for him.

"You will live as a man."

Like bubbles rising to the surface of a boiling pot, life rippled in
the golem's chest, spread to his groin, infused his limbs. His flesh
took on the hue of a person with blood coursing underneath a skim
of skin. It was as if his various parts spoke to each other in silent conversation, so that they could act in harmony. His legs would hold up
his body, his feet would show the direction for his legs, his arms
could stretch, his hands grab, hold, handle. A long sigh escaped his
lips, and then steadily Yossel began to breathe.

"You are alive."

The golem's huge hands twitched as if he had been tickled on his
palms.

"Rise, golem."

His huge knees knocked together.

"Rise."

The golem blinked his eyes, opened them widely, closed them
again, and turned his head away.

"Rise, I said."

Sleepily, Yossel roused himself, sat up, stretched his long, long arms, looked about. The river was sparkling like cut glass. The seven mountains of Prague rose around him in caring embrace. He could hear birds singing, and on the Stone Bridge, he saw people bringing their wares to market, women with baskets of onions on their heads, men pulling carts. What a merry conglomeration of color and sound.

"You are in my power, golem. Stand up."

Prone, the golem had been bigger than any man in Judenstadt. Upright, he was a Goliath.

"Dear God, what have I done?" The rabbi tottered back, resisted the impulse to run and hide.

Like a baby learning to walk, the huge thing tried one foot, then the other.

"Stay, stay," the rabbi ordered, flustered, frightened.

The golem wavered, took another step.

"Stop. Halt. Do not move."

The mud man easily had the girth of the heaviest set, and was certainly the strongest muscled, yet for all his size, the rabbi reminded himself, Yossel was created with meager understanding. In truth, he was made to follow only the simplest of commands. Come. Go. Do this. Do that. Nor was it intended that the golem have feelings, not even the small gratitudes and satisfactions of a dumb animal. The golem was fashioned from the mud of the banks of the Vltava River for one purpose and one purpose alone, and that was to stand guard at the gates, patrol the walls, to protect Judenstadt against the newly planned violence. He was a puppet, a watchman, a bulwark against the hateful tide of the season's threat.

But unbeknownst to the rabbi, the artificial man could actually feel and think. Indeed, as his creation and birth was an act of faith beyond the reach of reason, miracle of miracle, this creature had the knowledge and perception of an intelligent, educated man. And emotions? Manifold. No matter that he was mute. By breathing into his mouth, the rabbi had, in effect, imprinted the blank pages of his mud-made son with his own learning and yearning. Or perhaps these human attributes had been the gift bestowed by the unwelcome and malevolent presence hovering so patiently on the banks of the river.

Either way, blessed or cursed, innocent or wise, Yossel, towering above his creator, a sight to behold, following his father into town, silently marveled at the beauty of the world—the stinking streets and pox-marked people, a dog walking on three legs, lepers and hungry children, beggars galore, and whores still plying their trade from the night before in the early hours of the morning.

"My God," good wives said to husbands when they saw the mountainous figure approaching. "What is that? Is it real?"

"Maybe that is the way the Jews are formed who come from Silesia."

"A race of giants? He is ten heads taller than the rabbi."

"Only three heads higher."

"Over two meters, this monster."

"All in all, he is the biggest man I have ever seen, save none."

"Do not stay in the street when you see him, children. He may trample you."

"Somebody must tell the emperor, so the guards can tie him down, put him in prison."

"Maybe he is the devil himself."

Yossel was enthralled by everything. Utterly fascinated, he drew in through his large nostrils the delicious smell of the river, rank and rotten. The snaggletoothed fishermen near shore had already stretched their nets on poles for mending, and others had already pushed off from shore in their boats, making hardly a ripple in the stinky, stagnant river. Yossel would have liked to embrace them, these brave cullers of the watery depths, and pet the brown ducks, with featherless backs where their comrades had pecked them. Good day, pretty birds. Scrawny chickens in the street stepped gingerly between puddles of old urine and blackened snow, searching for squashed bugs and grubs. How dainty they were. Near the Square, market stalls were being set up of scrap and string, and carts, makeshift and worn, were wobbling in from the country with heaps of worm-eaten cabbages and sprouted onions, turnips slimy with cellar mold. Beautiful, beautiful. Yossel inhaled stale bread, steamy pig intestines, layers of sweat-soaked wool, fat being boiled for soap and candles, diseased whores, night water. Ah, how rich it all was. He was alive. The city was coming alive.

On this morning, the emperor had arisen from the warm bed of his mistress, Anna Marie, breakfasted on pottage, a thick fishy broth, red deer, and manchet bread, butter, and eggs. Václav was at home with his wife, who had only two days before given birth, a beautiful baby girl. Brahe was just now tucking into his bed next to his wife in his house below the Strahov Monastery. In a few minutes all his children would pile in beside him. Kepler, whose wife was a virago, a harpy, a shrew, a hellion on two legs, did not go home after a night of stargazing, but had begun his daily ramblings. He had noticed something interesting the night before, very interesting. Mars seemed to be zigzagging in its path across the sky, backing up. Was this impression due to the motion of the earth, which went twice as fast as Mars around the sun, or was it an idiosyncrasy of Mars? Karel, the junkman, was on his perch above his loyal Oswald, who was tripping down the street like a young filly on the way to the races. The church bells were ringing in all their discordant times. The town crier was calling, "Eight and all is well."

On they went, the rabbi first, Yossel behind, one street so narrow they had to walk in the middle so that Yossel would not bump his head on hanging signs, and in the alleyways he had to be careful not to hit his body against the sides of buildings. He watched his feet very carefully, for he did not want to tread upon some small animal or harm a living thing. Turning a corner, having gone through the gates of Judenstadt, they heard a female voice singing a German folk song in a high, pure voice, using the familiar you, *du*, not the formal *Sie*. Yossel turned his head, as did the rabbi, who immediately cast his eyes down, but Yossel, knowing much, but not this, continued to gaze, for at an open door, sitting on a chair trying to catch the first sun of the day, was a young woman, her head without wig or kerchief, her yellow hair cropped short as a peasant boy's. She was holding her chin up, her eyes closed as she let the sun melt down her face, spread along her bare neck.

"Rochel," hissed the rabbi, "cover yourself, woman."

The shoemaker's wife quickly ducked back into her dark room, but not before Yossel could see her eyes, which were the color of fresh earth. And not before she could note that Yossel's eyes were the color of the sky on a rainy day, a gray-blue, like the rabbi's. And not before Yossel could absorb her small, foxlike face, full, pert lips. And not before Rochel could wonder at his fleshiness and glossy hair, black as ink, and his generous nose, his rich, tawny skin. He had, in his massive face, little creases in his cheeks, as if some grandmother had given him two little tweaks. Dimples! Rochel could not help it, oh, no, it was not possible that she was doing this. But yes, her mouth, over which she suddenly had no dominion, was smiling at him. She lifted her head, smiled straight into his face. Yossel felt something pierce his groin, and an exquisitely sharp pain spread down his thighs.

"Come along, golem," the rabbi said, grabbing Yossel's fingers.

Then they were there, at the rabbi's house. Yossel had to bend low not to hit the top of the door.

"Perl," the rabbi called up from the hallway.

Perl was in her apron, and as usual, her babushka. On her side, perched at her waist, was a grandchild. In her right hand was her cleaning rag.

"Judah, where have you been?"

She stopped short, took a good look at Yossel. The child began to cry. "Gracious, Judah."

"Do not be afraid. He is a Jew." Here the rabbi paused, thought twice. Was a golem a Jew? If the creature was made by a Jew, was he a Jew? He could not say the golem was his son. "A sort of a Jew."

"His mother, who was she?"

"He has no mother, Perl, and no father, either, but he will not hurt you. He will fetch wood, cut it, pump water, run errands, sweep and scrub out the house for you, and most importantly, wife, he is here to protect the homes of our neighborhood. He will be our night watch-man. He cannot talk, he has no tongue, nor can he understand much. A schlemiel, Perl. Just a schlemiel, so do not trouble yourself about who he is."

"He does not look like a schlemiel, a dummkopf." Her appraising eyes, behind her thick spectacles, took in the black hair, the dimples. Except for the greater height, several heads above her husband, and darker skin, this big man could have been her Judah when he was a young, handsome husband.

"He is a relative, perhaps?"

"Distant."

"Ah, I see." She suspected, for what woman on this earth would not?

"His name?"

"Yossel."

"Are you hungry, husband, hungry, Yossel?"

"No. I will see you later. Good-bye." And with that, the rabbi prac-tically ran out of the house.

"Hello, good-bye," Perl said, "that is his way. Oh, well." She turned to Yossel. "I will make you some kasha." She put the child she was carrying down. "Do you like kasha? Of course you like kasha."

Already a pot of water was boiling. Pearl threw in some buckwheat groats, a pinch of salt. Taking some dried apple slices from the wall, she minced them into fine flakes. She got a wooden bowl, a spoon, placed them on the rough table.

"He does not have a tongue, Grandmother," little Fiegel said, for when the golem sat down on the floor, she had opened his mouth with her two hands, felt his teeth, peered deep inside.

"But you have everything else, do you not?" Perl turned to her guest, looked him in the eye.

He nodded.

"And you are a Jew?"

Yossel nodded.

"Well, that is the important thing. Let us go out in the courtyard for a minute. Fiegel, be a good girl and get grandmother a little twig." The three of them went out into the courtyard. The ground was clear of snow and Perl took the twig, used it to scratch in the mud: "Can you write?" Then she handed Yossel the twig.

"Yes," he wrote back in German.

She wrote in Hebrew. He wrote back in Hebrew.

She wrote in Czech. He wrote back in Czech.

"Well, well," she said. Then she wrote, "Where do you come from?"

"I come from dust and unto dust will I return."

"I see, I see. This is very interesting."

When they got back into the warm kitchen, little Fiegel asked, "Why does he wear those funny clothes, Grandmother?"

"Ah, now, that we can do something about. Those horse blankets, Oswald would wear."

Fiegel laughed to think of the mule.

Perl handed Yossel a piece of unleavened bread. He turned it over, examined it.

"This was the food the ancient Hebrews ate on the night of Passover, when we were escaping Egypt. We did not have time to let the bread rise."

"Are you going to make him a suit of matzah, Grandmother?"

"That is an idea, Fiegel."

The child crawled into Yossel's lap.

"We will have to go to the shoemaker; Zev will make your shoes, and Rochel, his wife, will make some breeches and a nice doublet, good hose. That Rochel is deft with the needle. If you have no tongue, can you taste? But you can smell. You will have to sleep on the floor, for we have no bed big enough. We will put some straw down. A kippah, gracious me, nothing to cover your head." She went to the shelf by the door, took down one of the many yarmulkes, picked the largest one knitted in blue with white letters of Hebrew in a border all about. It sat on his head like a tiny patch. "You will find that we live simply, but we are not without enough to eat and to wear. All my girls have learned to read and write. I go to market once a day. Of course, my husband being the rabbi, there are a lot of people coming in and out, so you will not be bored. There is always something. Weddings. Zev and Rochel were the last couple to marry. Hold out your hands." She held a basin of water under his hands with one of her hands, and with the other poured a pitcher of water over them. Then she handed him a towel. "Let us praise God, my friend."

They prayed, she standing, he silently sitting. When she served him the kasha, he had never smelled anything so wonderful, and the soft grains and bits of apple went down his throat, settled nicely in his stomach.

"Eat, eat."

Yossel examined the old lady. A face wrinkled as a weathered map, penetrating eyes behind her spectacles, the gray hair beneath her kerchief stiff as straw, and a mouth so restless that Yossel wondered if she talked aloud in her dreams at night.

"You are a good boy," Perl said after they ate, and thanked God for the meal.

"He is too big to be a boy," Fiegel said.

"He knows what I mean, Fiegel, and you, little miss, mind your manners."

"Grandmother, who will be his wife?"

Perl was startled by the question. "A wife?"

"To take care of him."

"I will take care of him, Fiegel, we will. He will have all he wants with us. Yom Kippur, Passover, all the holidays. So do not worry about Yossel."

However, as she spoke, there was a loud clamor at the door, and at the opened window, a collection of women were trying to peer in.

"Did he come from out of the river?"

"Are you not frightened to death?"

"Is it alive?"

Perl went up to them, spat out, "Mind your own business. You have nothing to do but gawk? You do not know a golem when you see one? He walks like a golem, does not talk like a golem, what do you think? Busybodies, be gone," and she slammed the window shut and bolted the door.

Mother, Yossel thought.

12

I T WAS NOT apparent the alchemist had had his ears cut off, the
wounds so cleverly hidden by a mop of unruly red hair.
Furthermore, the rapscallion seemed to hear as clearly as any
man. In fact, there was nothing subdued or repentant about Edward
Kelley. The fellow had a rakish, impudent look, a victorious gleam in
his protruding eyes. My God, Rudolph sighed, into whose hands have
I delivered myself?

About thirty members of the court had gathered for the occasion.
Pistorius, Rudolph's confessor; Crato, his second best physician;
lawyers galore; Rosenberg, Rudolph's burgrave; and, of course,
Kirakos, author of the daring plan and physician extraordinaire, with
his surly assistant, the silent Russian. Václav, as ever, was on the
emperor's right hand. The day of the meeting had been fixed with
Brahe's assurance that the stars were propitious, and who knew
when, during the course of a meeting, his services as court astrologer
would not be called upon, and Brahe did not stir from bed without
Jepp, the dwarf. The dreamy-eyed Johannes Kepler was dragged
along, too. Rudolph wished the bone-thin mathematician would see
to his wardrobe. He looked like a scarecrow with his raggedy cloak.
Maybe he should pay him. Maisel, court Jew and financier, on the
other hand, was handsomely attired, as well he might be. Even his
requisite patch of yellow was fixed to his doublet like an expensive
jewel. The meeting with Maisel when Rudolph had gotten back from
Venice had yielded nothing more serious than the usual Jewish plea
for protection. What the emperor wanted to know was about the
powers of the rabbi. Maisel was mute on the subject, referred to
God, as they always did in such situations. Well, the emperor con-

cluded, if the Jews were so close to God, they did not need the protection of an emperor, did they?

At present Maisel was standing with the other courtiers, smiling
his curious smile signifying neither mirth nor good humor, which the
emperor felt he could wipe off his face. But the man was too rich to
be made into an enemy, and that alone accounted for the fact that
the emperor did not arrest the rabbi. Perhaps he could turn the
rabbi's powers to his own advantage, although he did not understand
the Jews. For instance, how had Maisel acquired his wealth? The
Fuggers you could see. Silver lay in the ground. You dig it, sell it,
become rich, and the richer you become, the richer you are. Plain
and simple. From rags to paper was Maisel's story, for linen rags
beaten, raked with water, pressed into sheets made it possible, with
the new printing, for everyman to have his almanac. Heretofore,
parchment was made of expensive sheepskin, a book requiring a
herd. Maisel also owned the Jewish printing press, Prague the center
of Jewish publishing. Rudolph did not inquire too closely. He did not
believe rags were the whole story. No matter, for what was Maisel's
wealth but his to "borrow" and eventually take away? Indeed, Maisel
had come up with all the crowns, kopeks, doubloons, francs, shillings,
lire, and crusadoes necessary to finance the elixir of eternal life.

In the corner were the lord high juticar and the lord high marshal,
the royal prosecutor. Pucci was nowhere to be seen, but it was still
morning. The castrato said early hours ruined his voice, something
about fresh air. But, bailiffs! Thick as fleas on the backs of rats. And
the official advisor, Wolf Rumpf, whom Rudolph increasingly suspected of high treason, was almost positive he might be a spy for his
brother, Matthias Habsburg, or even, and this was not entirely impossible, the Turkish sultan. If these were his so-called friends, his court,
let God save the king.

"We extend the royal welcome to our guests from the British Isles
here in Vladislav Hall."

With its great vaulted ceiling and hanging circles of iron candelabra, Vladislav Hall was a room large enough for jousts, with an
adjoining hallway of stone steps used by the horsemen thundering
up. Yet, for all its tradition, it resembled nothing so much as a big,
drafty barn. The tapestries on the high walls featured a series on the
three Hebrews who in Babylonian captivity walked through fire—
Shadrach, Meshach, and Abednego—in silvery white tunics. Rushes

tipped in fire and carried on long poles were a further attempt at pomp and gave some semblance of warmth, as did ten small braziers of coal set by the emperor's chair, which, raised on a red-carpeted dais, was topped by a ledge of heavy gold. Nobody could stand higher than the emperor.

"We are most delighted you are here and we are delighted to be here." The emperor smiled beneficently at them all. However, most of the court in attendance wished they were someplace else, any-place else.

Tycho Brahe, court astronomer and mathematician, wanted to be at the Golden Ox, sitting with a mug of beer in front of him, the good fellowship of fellow patrons around him. He adjusted the bridge of his nose, the silver piece kept tight on his face with two strings tied around his head. He had recently lost two chess matches to Kirakos, a trou-bling coincidence—Kirakos, a physician who in practice was not that removed from an apothecary or a barber surgeon or a damn midwife. It was humiliating enough that Kepler had come from Germany to be his assistant. Young Kepler, at the beginning of his career, the author of *De admirabili porportione coelestium orbium*, an audacious and mistaken Copernican, had theories of his own. Theories. Brahe was wary of the-ory, save that of the venerable ancients. This meant Aristotle, Ptolemy, not Plato, nor any pre-Socratic. For that matter, anybody could have a theory. The moon is made of cheese, a man lives in it, planets have tones and sing in harmonic chorus. Was it Bruno, poor soul, burned at the stake in Rome last year, who postulated that points and circles were God and all religions one? He, Tycho Brahe, imperial mathemati-cus, if you please, knew that close, consistent observation, accurate recording of what one sees, the organization of long-standing records were what guided one to truth. And here was this upstart Kepler, who fancied his job to think. Think? I did not hire you to think; Brahe wanted to shake that idea, and all others, right out of his narrow box of a head, keep the presumptuous puppet in his place. Be all that as it may, Brahe had given him a real job, a job which just might take a life-time. Chart the orbit of Mars? Kepler had said in his Simple Simon way. At the most, seven days. After seven days, ten . . . years, if it came to that. Keep him busy, busy as a blasted bee, that was the key.

The alchemists, worn out from their long trek east, would have liked to be in their beds. They had traveled along potholed, icy roads, spent nights at inns filled with the riffraff who wandered the highways and byways of Europe—students who had to beg to pay for their lessons, the lower class of merchants, musicians, tinkers, play-ers—all vying for their place near the fire. In residence now in com-modious accommodations at the Rosenberg mansion, the two, in addition to their duties for the emperor, were to be employed on the burgrave's behalf, for despite four wives, Rosenberg had no children. Bull testicles, everybody said, washed down with buckets of raw oys-ters. But that and other remedies had not proved effective.

"We share, I hear, a passion for mechanical toys. Roger Bacon, the philosopher, had his talking head, did he not, which declared: Time is. Time flies. Time is no more. And who was it with an iron man? Albertus Magnus?" The emperor was working toward his point, start-ing with little flourishes of flattery, and affecting a disarming inno-cence. "I am most particularly interested in inventions to do with the abolition of time."

"Nice clocks," Kelley said, agog over the collection on display. They had been brought out and placed on trestle tables flanking the throne, for Rudolph could not long be without the proximity of some treasure or another. Gems, in particular, which could light up any room, anytime, Rudolph believed had an innate life of their own, their glow the very breath of God.

"Yes, I like clocks," Rudolph admitted. Not only did this Kelley inter-rupt him, the emperor noted, and omit the polite "Your Majesty" in his speech, but the ogling wretch held within the core of his distasteful being, it seemed, a fistful of rebellious disrespect. The man's broad face shone with a greasy luster, as if he, for all his reputed spiritual abilities, was an imbiber of meats laced with fat and thick, foamy beers. He seemed intent on stealing a clock. "It is known, Dr. Dee and Master Kelley," the emperor continued, "that you are in possession of an ancient Egyptian manuscript which holds the secrets of eternal life."

"An unfortunate rumor, Most Glorious One," Dee replied.

"We have no Egyptian manuscript," Kelley confirmed.

"Oh, bosh. It's as true as this leg," and the emperor raised his foot, kicked Brahe's dwarf, Jepp.

The emperor noticed that Kelley was edging toward a timepiece with a blackamoor made of onyx and ebony, the turban a brilliant band of gold studded with tiny pearls.

Oh, dear, Brahe thought, his bladder paining him mightily, too much small beer for breakfast.

"This Egyptian manuscript, which you have found with the secrets of eternal life, is written in an unknown language," the emperor said, honing in. "I want you to translate it, adapt its formula."

Dee's own book, *Monas Hieroglyphica*, was in English, yet nobody could understand that, either, Kepler knew. The Egyptian book he had never heard of.

"What I am interested in is a kind of perpetual motion machine, eternal substance, elixir of immortality, time no more, plain and simple."

Kelley had assumed that they were summoned to make gold and that the rest of their time would be spent in court prattle. He envisioned looking into the scrying glass at Rudolph's request, perceiving love, good fortune, balmy weather. The emperor's letter to Dee had said, "We would be honored if you could grace us with your presence," then mentioned a princely sum, which they could well use. Kelley certainly did not like the sound of "time no more." More to the point was the blackamoor. One object in that room, one object alone of those casually spread for display—the silver clock in the shape of a cannon with sapphires up and down, the gold clock in the shape of a ship with a little gold crew and a captain, a king encrusted with jewels, a pendant in the shape of a cross, no doubt a reliquary, a saint's toenail, a bottle of Mary's tears, Christ's something or other (Catholics had a rich trade and barter in these fakeries and trinkets, even purchased their way to heaven, what a pretty penny those circling nymphs would fetch)—one object alone would provide sufficient pounds to last his life, keep him in ginger cake and juniper-berry pancakes, casks of wine.

Dee cleared his throat. "Your Majesty, please pardon me, but Master Kelley and I must confer." Dee pulled Kelley over to a corner. Outside the window, snow had started to fall.

"Do you want to have your hands cut off, as well as your ears? Take care not to pinch anything," Dee hissed into Kelley's hair. "The emperor wishes us to make a perpetual motion machine."

"Surely he would get tired on such a mount," Kelley whispered back.

"No, Edward. Will you pay attention? He wants to be in motion in perpetuum."

"As I suggested, he may become tired."

"He means"—Dee grabbed Kelley's arm—"he wants to live forever."

In point of fact, Kelley was the greater magician of the two, the one gifted in sight, the one who "saw" the spirits in the convex mirror and peered into the small, cloudy scrying glass, and it was his guardian angel, Madami, who led the explorations to the world of the occult, the Enochian angels his angels.

Václav's legs ached. He wished to be home, his wife rubbing his tired calves with lard. Furthermore, he did not like talk of the supernatural. Next to wolves, he hated ghosts. The alleyways behind the Týn Church in the Old Town Square were already haunted with the spirits of those who had been mercilessly murdered. The Rabbi Loew, it was said, could present phantoms of the posthumus prophets, Elijah being a favorite, and other wonder workers made puffs of smoke appear before your very eyes, pulled scarves from the cuffs of coats, rabbits out of hats, put swords down their throats, breathed fire. Once, when Václav was wandering about at night, he came upon a house in the Old Town all lit up. The door was open. There were many people at a long table. A woman in mannish clothes came up to him, said, "Golden Prague." Was she a witch, an unholy, upstart Lilith, first wife of Adam? Was he being tempted to sign the Book?

Kirakos needed just a sip, that was all, one sip. The emperor hoarded those wonderful beans common in Turkish lands and parts of Hungary which worked miracles on headaches. His head felt as if in a vise. He, as imperial physician, could get the chief steward to unlock the spicery, have a kitchen maid grind some into powder, and brew a nice, hot bowl of it. Coffee. Elixir of sultans.

A trainer came in to take Petaka away on a golden chain for his morning stroll around the castle. A brace was wound about the beast's belly so that it would not drag on the floor.

"Look," Kelley whispered, still huddled in a corner with Dee. "The lion wears a corset."

"You want the emperor to throw you to the lions, Edward?" Dee suggested softly but pointedly. "You are playing the fool with me."

"I may be playing the fool, Dr. Dee, because I am wisely frightened. Gold comes from fire, silver from air, copper from water, and we are dust. We have the power to kill each other and, through our loins alone, create. We can plant the seed . . . but make it live forever? Did I tell you we should not come? Do you remember, just before we left, the very night before we left, that warning I had from Madami?"

Before Kelley was permitted "sight" of Madami in the scrying glass, he had to fast for thirteen days, have a repast of mushroom stew at every sundown, followed by seven heads of Turkish poppy mashed and mixed with honey and cardamom. That was one recipe. Another was seven ounces of pounded hemp seed strained through a cloth woven by a virgin and stirred thoroughly in a liter of wine.

"Gentlemen," Rudolph said brusquely, "if you are ready. It is an elixir of eternal life, I wish you to—"

"Beg pardon, Your Majesty." Dee turned. "We feel we cannot presume to do God's work."

Kirakos stepped forward. "If you would let me speak for you, Your Highness."

Rudolph nodded assent.

"We are not saying anything against the rules of God, Dr. Dee, Master Kelley, for that would be blasphemy, heretical; but surely you, Dr. Dee, you who have made nautical instruments, plotted maps, translated Euclid into English, drink water that is pumped with a water wheel, are cognizant of the advances of our world today." The clocks all ticking in discordant time, and loudly, too, seemed located right in his head. Oh, dear, how long the morning seemed and how Kirakos could do with, if not coffee, some soothing broth, a bracing tonic, a compress for his eyes, a poultice on his feet to draw out the poisons in his blood. Too much wine last night. "Indeed, regarding cannons, harquebuses, the art of Dürer, Leonardo da Vinci, Raphael, all that is part of our world within the short period of the last century, you, of all people, must understand our quest. Columbus did not fall off the horizon, now, did he? Before Magellan did we know of other oceans? Daily we grow in knowledge. Has God revealed the end of what we must know?"

"Thank you, Dr. Kirakos, for your concise history. But one other consideration . . ." Dee paused. "It may not be a matter of will not."

"If not will not, what not, Dr. Dee?"

"Cannot."

Now Kepler felt a little apprehensive. This talk was going down an uncharted path; unlike the movements of the planets, which were to be discovered and predicted, this was like the trail of a comet. He wished it were already night, or at the very least, that he was settled in a chair, his notebook on his lap. Undisturbed.

"Tsk, tsk, cannot?" Now the emperor shook his finger. "Dr. Dee, if it pleases you or no, God's will is my will and my will is God's will. All correspondences converge in the person of the ruler."

"As you so correctly point out, Your Most Exalted Highness, this is a most spiritual mission. An alchemist who sets about a task such as this, to find the elixir of eternal life, whether through the philosophers' stone or by a recipe already in a book, as you seem to think, or something he must discover in his laboratory, such a searcher must at once be in tune with the universe and pure of heart—and unfortunately, we, as British subjects, Your Highness, are not even members of your Church."

"I care nothing of your religion," the emperor said. "It does not matter one whit."

"In that case, Your Highness, in Prague you have a most learned Jew, the Rabbi Loew, who knows the combinations of the letters of the Hebrew alphabet and their numerical equivalents. I have heard he is capable of making a homunculus."

"Homunculus? What is that?"

"A tiny man spawned in an alembic, a man to do his bidding."

Václav looked at Maisel. Maisel looked at Kepler. Kepler looked out the window.

"As little as Jepp?" The emperor pointed to the dwarf.

"Smaller," Dee replied.

"The rabbi has made a large man, a giant." Brahe had seen it once walking along the river.

"Small, big, I am perfect in myself. It is forever we are speaking of, not size, gentlemen, and my very own laboratory in the Powder Tower is to be your laboratory."

"How good of you, Your Majesty." Dee's eyes looked like two bowled fish behind his glasses. "An important undertaking of this nature will take a very many years."

"Seven months, your magic number. Seven angels, seven trumpets, Double-O-Seven."

Kelley knew seven was a sacred number made up of four, as in the four corners of his room, four winds, four elements—and the number three, as the three sons in a story, the trinity, the three questions and Hermes Trismegistus, the thrice-born Egyptian magi, a favorite of alchemists. Seven was also the seven electors who chose the Holy Roman Emperor, the Seven Hills of Rome, the seven seals, seven days of the week, but now and forever after, for him, it would be a most unlucky number.

"Seven months, Your Majesty?" Dr. Dee gasped.

"Seven months. And what you concoct will be tried first on butterflies in the sixth month."

"Butterflies? But they only live for a day, Your Majesty."

"Not if they are fed the elixir of eternal life, Dr. Dee."

A sigh went through the crowd. Maisel could already feel the brunt of misfortune across his back.

13

R OCHEL WONDERED IF she was the only one in the world who did not like Shabbat. It was irreverent of her—wicked, even—but except for the dinner, which meant the best food of the week, the twenty-four hours of rest always seemed to her like an ordeal to be endured rather than a well-deserved respite from work. She could not sew on the Sabbath, could do nothing with her hands, indeed, had to sit on them to keep from biting her nails. And a morning at shul? She and her grandmother were so privileged as to be permitted in the women's section upstairs behind the mechitza, hearing chanting and droning she could not understand from below, in the men's section, which went on for hours on end; the only part she paid attention to was the cantor's haunting melodies. She did not have a siddur of her own, and the only Hebrew she had mastered was by rote, repeated household prayers like the blessing before eating, the Ha-Motzi, the Model Ani upon rising, the Keriat Shema before going to sleep. Having never studied the Torah, she did not know God's words on a firsthand basis. She did not know that there were really six hundred and thirteen commandments corresponding to the bones in the body, nor did she know who Hillel was, Rashi, Moses Maimonides, or even where Safed and Israel were located. Kept within the constraints of home and hearth, as clever as she might be, as attuned to the natural world or sensitive to her craft, she was an innocent. Her relationship to God was as child to father, and in her community she did not truly hold the rights of citizen, and as for her husband, she was his wife and must demure to him in all matters. She could only compare her own struggles to the unequivocal and fanciful framework of her childhood fairy tales, fables, Bible stories.

Even her daily examples were restricted, for whom did she know besides the handful who peopled her life—Zev, the rabbi and Perl, their daughters, Karel, his mule, and Master Galliano.

Her grandmother had never seemed perturbed by the fact that the women entered the synagogue through their own hall, were kept well away from the rabbi, the Torah scrolls, and all that was truly holy. Her grandmother professed to love Shabbat, and she tried patiently to explain to Rochel that HaShem had intended the world to be a Paradise on Shabbos, that it was a day of redemption, a chance to live the dream of perfection. If Shabbos was a little piece of Eden, Rochel thought, there would be a garden, animals, the kinship of creatures. If in Eden, she would be outside. If in Eden, there would be clapping and dancing, a wedding, or it would be like Purim, a celebration with noise and revelry, costumes, little children running about, or like Sukkot, the harvest festival, when she got to eat outside in a sukkah under the sky.

Instead, on Shabbat they had to stay inside, she on the bed, her grandmother on her chair, facing each other, the fire cold in the hearth, the cholent, prepared the day before, sticky and thick, a gelatinous mixture of vegetables and dumplings because they could not light a fire on the Sabbath. Supposedly the Sabbath was a time to be a person among people. But in the winter, she and her grandmother just crawled into bed, spent the day under the covers in their good clothes, which, worn for years, were in Rochel's case too little, her skirt high above her petticoats and her bodice tight as a corset, and for her grandmother, as her body shrunk with age, hanging like sheets on twigs. Shabbat itself—Good Shabbos, everybody greeted each other—was to her grandmother the day one needed nothing, asked nothing. It was the one day without grief. But what better day to feel sad? Rochel silently asked. Judenstadt would get so quiet, so still, that she could scream. She could not wait for the first stars to appear on the second night, marking the end of the day of rest, the last cup of wine of the Shabbat, the braided candle, the shaking of the spice box.

"Be praised, Lord our God, Ruler of the Universe, who creates the lights and fires."

Then, with a jump, Rochel was all about the room, lifting things up, putting them down, moving from here to there, tossing her thimble to the ceiling, catching it. She could separate threads, tie knots, untie knots, spin, card, sew. The fire could be built up again, flour

sifted, bread made, the paper-thin brown skins of onion peeled, cabbage chopped. She might even dance and, God forbid, sing. And the
whole week would start up. Karel might visit, letting her pet Oswald.
Master Galliano would drop by with new orders to sew. Grandmama
would begin one night with, "Have I ever told you the story of the
wife who turned her husband into a werewolf?" And Rochel could go
outside in the day, which meant birds to watch and imitate, and in the
spring and summer, trips to Petřín Woods for strawberries and blackberries, and, wonder of wonders, mushroom picking. Sometimes she
got a glimpse of trees clipped in the shapes of animals and forms
through the Royal Garden Gates. As a little girl, before she began to
sew well enough to stitch his doublet, she thought all the emperor's
clothes were made of gold threads. He did have a carriage of ebony
and silver, and royal pets—lions, no less—walked freely about the castle. That was what Master Galliano told them. Every night the
emperor supped on food fit for seraphim, sweet fruits of colors
unseen before in Prague, from places so far away it took caravans and
ships to get them to the table, the meat so tender a baby could chew
it, and pastry the consistency of clouds of spun sugar. Rochel was
amazed, delighted, would clap her hands in glee. Then, suddenly in
the round of workaday, it was the night before Shabbat again, and the
two challah had to rise so that in the morning they could be rushed to
the bakery ovens to be baked, along with the cholent.

Rochel and her grandmother had often been invited over to the
rabbi's house for the Sabbath dinner. It was a mitzvah for the rabbi
and rebbetzin to have them, the orphan and her old grandmother, and
even after Rochel and Zev married, the habit continued. However,
the evening after Rochel had seen the golem in the street, as she
touched the mezuzah nailed in the rabbi's doorway, marking it a
Jewish household, and then kissed her fingers, a tightness gripped her
stomach and foreboding clouded her vision. She remembered well
and regretted terribly her immodesty, her smile, for now she would
have to face him again.

Rochel knew that Yossel was created by the rabbi to be their night
watchman. Zev, with all of the men in the community, had been told
by the rabbi about it in a meeting, after which all the men rushed
home to tell their wives, who knew already anyway from those who
had peeked into Perl's kitchen, and soon everybody—man, woman,
child—knew about Yossel. Nobody in Judenstadt was afraid of him,

for he was under the rabbi's control, and during the day he was the rebbetzin's helper, the one to fetch and go, bring and carry.

They hastened to take their seats at the Sabbath table. Before the candles were lit, coins were collected for the poor, tzedakah, then "L'cha do-di" was sung. Perl lit the candles and Rabbi Loew said in honor of Perl, his wife, the mother of his children, "A woman of valor, who can find? For her price is far above rubies." The children were all blessed and the children blessed their parents and grandparents. Other blessings were said: the blessing of the wine, the blessing and breaking of the challah, pieces torn from the loaf. Perl was wearing her wig, which sat on her head like a nesting bird, and Leah and Miriam, self-important in their Sabbath apparel, preened like princesses. Zelda, trying to think no less of herself than her sisters, also carried herself with a regal and disdainful air. The husbands seemed happy at the sight of the food. All the grandchildren were lined up at the end of the table, giggling and gurgling like happy little pigeons. Rochel was in her wedding clothes, her kerchief over her shorn hair. Meanwhile, Yossel, the golem, dressed in shabby coverlets wrapped clumsily around his waist and shoulders, went back and forth between the hearth and the cupboard, the table and the boiling pots, bringing the fish, the chicken soup, the squash and turnips, the chopped liver, carrots. He moved about the kitchen as if to efface himself, being careful not to knock over a chair, bump into a person, disturb the peace. Yet his face shone; indeed, he glowed like the real bridegroom welcoming the Sabbath, his bride, with pious joy.

Rochel was touched and, being served by him, humbled. For she, too, was a servant. Her husband's servant. God's. Although she may have felt at times as if her heart were the home of rich possibility, she had never felt entitled to sit with the assurance of a Leah or a Miriam. Despite her short-lived pride at being married, she had realized afresh, in their presence, that she was what she had always been—a guest, a foreigner, an orphan bastard, a charity bride, and, of course, what everybody else had known all along and she had lately come to acknowledge, the child of rape. In Zev's room, it was already dark, the leather strips casting vertical shadows like trees in a melancholy forest. Here at the rabbi's the fire in the hearth cast each face in a warm yellow and the silver candlesticks gleamed, and when Perl waved the Sabbath flames toward her with her hands, all was light and right.

When Rochel was a little girl, before she knew the truth of things, she believed if you lay down and held still enough, grass could grow like sharp hair through your clothes and skin, so that when you stood up, the sun would pour through the little holes like a sieve. When her eyes met Yossel's the few minutes before the sun went down on that Sabbath, she recalled that magical belief and she remembered herself as daydreamer and stargazer. Yossel's eyes glancing at her hands made her think her stubby, thick-knuckled fingers could flutter up like winged doves, feather his cheeks, which were smooth as a boy's, unlike all the bearded faces of Judenstadt's men. Horses from the royal stable she had seen through the grill gate of the emperor's garden had smooth, polished rumps, and that is what Yossel's backside looked like when he bent down to fetch the food from the fireplace. Zev, who dropped his breeches in a pool at his feet every night, had the shanks of a billy goat.

"Have some more fish," Perl said. Her tidy head moving up and down over her food made her seem like the trio of chickens on a wooden Russian toy who peck-pecked-pecked when you whirled it around.

Yossel, this golem, Rochel pondered, was engaged, as she was, in ordinary life, but was also mysterious. He was like an unsaid story, for indeed he could not talk. He was a beginning, unfinished. She could make up anything about him, put words in his mouth. Rochel, she had him say. Are you a bird, Rochel? Can you fly?

"Have some chicken." The rabbi's son-in-law was generous with what was not his. Rochel saw him hiding in his beard as in a thicket of brambles, his eyes shining like flint, hard and cruel. How could he have rabbinical aspirations? His wife, Leah, had a damp smell of drains and dishes soaking in a pan of old water, milk spoiling in a jug.

Miriam, the other married sister, trying to outdo her sister in haughtiness, kvetched to no end. The streets were mud up to her waist, she nearly slipped on the ice, the prices were high, herring, you would not believe, the baker rude, who does he think he is. Yet for all her nasty temper and sour outlook, her husband, with his hand between her knees, adored her and acted as if every word which passed from her mouth was a babka.

"It is the Sabbath. Peace, Miriam," the rabbi declared.

Yossel looked at Rochel. She looked back from beneath lowered lids. A delicious tingle started at her heels, spread upward, and the tips of her fingers sizzled like a water bubble in a frying pan.

"The emperor is so afraid of dying, he tried to get it over by killing himself," a son-in-law said.

There was laughter all around the table and the children banged their spoons.

"Do not laugh at another's pain," the rabbi insisted.

"Not even the emperor's?" Miriam asked mockingly.

"Especially not the emperor," Perl replied, a frown furrowing her forehead. "When the emperor sneezes, we must take to our beds."

The children looked anxiously at their mothers. Zelda, the youngest daughter, laughed.

"I tremble to think of what will happen to us if he dies," the other son-in-law said. "As bad as he is, it is better he does not die."

"Must I remind you," the rabbi intoned, "it is the Sabbath?" The rabbi had written a treatise on how the congregation should not talk while the service was going on in the synagogue. While he did not indulge in pilpul, Talmudic casuistry, he frowned on breaking the Law and rudeness was positively hurtful to him. Shabbat was Shabbat. Did anybody heed his word? "We must talk only of cheerful things, not mourn, not fear. Give the world a chance," the rabbi pleaded. "On this one day, it is perfect."

Not mourn, not fear. On the Sabbath, Rochel mused, nobody was dead. In nearly a year, at the yahrtzeit, her grandmother's tombstone would be placed at her grave. And someday she, too, would be in the cemetery. Zev's first wife was there and Rochel wondered if she would be put beside her. Just then, the thought of death making her shiver, Yossel, bending over to put a bowl of turnips on the table, brushed against her. HaShem, help me, she prayed, for not only was that not permitted, a man to touch a woman, for she may be unclean with her montly, but she felt temptation grow around her heart. She had heard, and she did not remember where or when, that Adam's first wife was not a good wife. For her sins, Lilith was condemned to wander the world as a witch, visit men in their dreams. She appeared in a dress of gold shiny scales and nobody survived her embrace. Could the evil thought of death on the Sabbath summon Lilith? With the sun down, night demons came out. They did not care if it was the Sabbath or a day of work. Dybbuks, the Evil Eye.

"Are you well, Rochel?"

This was her husband, Zev, she noted, he who had married her out of the goodness of his heart, and now coveted her youth, for surely that was all it was, her beauty, as he called it. She was young, he was old. We all have our day, Zev, she wanted to tell him. This is mine, and soon enough it will be over. She felt herself tremble all over, as if her body were being plucked like a lute. The rabbi, across the table, ordinarily a gentle soul, looked at her sternly.

"You are well, are you not, Wife?" Zev laughed nervously, turned to the others.

The three sisters lowered their lids, cleared their throats. Rochel could imagine the haircutting episode in their eyes, how she had disgraced herself. They were waiting, Rochel believed, for her to fail in a grand way. Zev's glance hopped from one person to another. She cast her eyes down, looked at her lap. The night before, Zev had put his ear on her stomach as if listening for a child, and then, hearing nothing, kissed her forehead. They rarely kissed on the mouth, and when they did, it was the chaste kiss of relatives. Was that not what in the stories woke the princess up, the kiss of life? Yossel had no tongue, she knew, but his mouth was large and she thought of how her lips would be overlapped, lost in his.

"So I say to her," Miriam resumed, " 'I am the rabbi's daughter.' "

"For shame, daughter, that you use a position granted by God to have power over others."

"Yossel, more beets."

"Yossel, get the carrots."

"Yossel, bring the fish."

"Yossel, onions."

"Rochel," Zev said. He looked at his wife with some concern. Everybody else looked at her, too. As a newlywed, she may be pregnant, prone to moods and sleepiness. No doubt that was it. Allowance could be made for a woman in her first pregnancy. Why, Perl could remember when she was pregnant with Leah, she must have raisins day and night, and sleep? Did she sleep? Could you call it sleep when your head hit the pillow, but your stomach could find no room to settle?

14

THE TWO ALCHEMISTS had been quickly ushered out after their audience with the emperor. Through Vladislav Hall, down the stone steps, into the courtyard, out the castle gates, into the street. The sky was as gray and bitter as the crypt. Snow tumbled down in thick, vengeful clumps. Kelley's stomach felt as if a cannonball had been shot through it. His throat was dry and his eyes burned. Where his ears used to be ached with cold. Something was wrong with his nose, and the ends of his fingers tingled with a temporary palsy. His cloak was worn and thin and the cloth of his shoe bottoms was barely patched with scraps and held to his feet with string. Dee, albeit better dressed, was just as miserable.

"John," Kelley gasped as they made their way down the hill from the castle into the Malá Strana, the little quarter below the castle. "What is this book he talks of, the Egyptian book? Not Trismesgistus? Do we have to write hieroglyphics? Did you notice Brahe's silver nose strung to his ears?"

The church bells began to peal one by one out of pace with each other.

"You would think that if the emperor can request eternal life, he could get the damned clocks fixed around here," Kelley continued. "Columbus, Magellan, for Christ's sake, all the advances of the modern world."

They passed some smithies, a gaming house, a grocer, a draper, a cock pit, a house selling drinks, a monastery. They saw a row of monks sitting in their basement refectory about to eat their noonday meal. Down by the Vltava River, huge billows of smoke rose from the glassworks. A tinker called out, "Pots, mend your pots," and a bunch of street lepers, with red hats and gray cloaks, were out with their begging bowls.

"I need a drink," Kelley said. "Urgently." And it had been some hours since last he had eaten.

Near At the House of the Three Ostriches, they found a tavern and eating house—the Golden Ox. They went in, sat on a rough bench at long table, said not another word until the maid brought their brew in pewter mugs.

"We have to leave this place hard and fast." Kelley took a slow swallow of his beer, the only kind available, Krusovice, from the emperor's brewery. As much as he hated the man, he did not care if it was the emperor's own brewed piss as long as it was fermented. He just wanted to be good and drunk that moment, but, as it happens in these circumstances, although he was drinking with all his might and on an empty stomach, he had never felt more sober in his whole wretched life.

"This is the end of us, John. It is one thing to make gold out of a piece of iron, boiled to its essence, a little mercury, poof, lo and behold, but, my friend . . ." He downed his last swallow, tipping his head way back. "Eternal life is beyond my reach."

"You are most correct, Master Edward. We can cure the stomach ague with shaved ginger root, fever with comfrey, the French pox with small doses of mercury, vomitus, flux, unnatural voiding, all that is within our grasp, but in the stars above, therein we all have our appointed time no matter what we do."

"Some appointments are later than others, John. Ours is hastened to seven months hence."

"Woe is me, why did we ever come?"

"For money, John, for money. We have no money. Despite your service to the queen, you are almost a pauper. Can I have another drink? Do you think I can get drunk and stay drunk and be a drunk and live a drunk and die a drunk? Oh, God, have mercy."

"Hush. Be a man."

"To be a mouse, John, if only to be a mouse."

"'I saw what appeared to be a sea of glass mingled with fire as he spoke."

"You see pictures in the Bible, John, whereas I see a hangman's noose. Money and Neck went to town. Money did not come back, and poor Neck fell down."

"'Tis true, 'tis true, my dear Edward. Without one, we do not have the other."

By now, the tavern was filling with men come to eat their noonday meal. Some unappealing prostitutes in their red petticoats hovered by the door. To Kelley they were queens in court finery. Women, the joy of his life. The smell of bread frying in fat, poultry boiling in the large cauldrons, and hunks of mutton turning on the spits nearly overpowered him. How could he leave this glorious world behind?

"My hose for some quail on toast, John."

Dee leaned forward, spoke softly. "We will depart in the dead of the night."

"I think not. Look." Kelley pointed to the back table.

"Oh, dear." Dee bowed his head. "Scurvy spies." A pair of Slovene guards glared at them.

Kelley began to blubber. Dee put his head down, muttered, "All is lost."

"Good day. Johannes Kepler here." A beanpole of a man stood beside them.

Kelley turned, looked up. "It is a terrible day."

"Assistant astronomer at your service."

"We do not need any astronomical assistance," Kelley said, his face tear-stained.

"But please, do sit down," Dee invited more kindly.

Close up, Kepler had the aspect of one of the marionettes the Czechs were so fond of, Kelley observed; an upturned nose, big bright eyes, and a mouth that curved high and low at the slightest tug.

"We are soon to die," Kelley informed the fellow. "It might be catching."

"Ah, ja." Kepler nodded sympathetically, sitting down on the bench beside Kelley.

Then a bell was heard in the street.

"What is that?" Kelley asked.

"It is Karel. Will you excuse me?" Kepler said.

In a minute Kepler came in carrying a man without legs. He set him down on the bench.

"Karel Vojtech the junkman, at your service," Karel said brightly.

Kelley looked at the stunted man through narrowed eyes. "Soon you will have us to cart away."

"Do not be so glum." Karel gestured to the barmaid. She came over, but she was no maid, although not yet a crone.

"What is your name, lovely lady?" Kelley asked in German. All the Czechs spoke German, he found. They hated to, but had to.

"How can you think of women at a time like this?" Dee whispered.

"Until the end, John, until the end."

Kepler and Karel ordered sausage and cabbage, apple fritters. Dee and Kelley concentrated on their empty mugs. When food was brought on wooden boards with knives, Dee and Kelley looked away.

"Lost appetite on the road to town." Kelley thought he might faint at the smell of it.

Kepler reached in his purse hanging on his belt, took out a coin, held it up, passed it over to Dee.

"The emperor paid me today, a rare occasion, which must, with all due respect, be celebrated."

Dee looked down at the rough wood of the table. Somebody had carved initials "D.K."

"I am of the Lutheran faith," Kepler said, "and thus interpret the Bible for myself. Let me pass on some of the knowledge I have obtained. God said we must eat and drink."

"Well, if God says," Kelley acquiesced.

"Edward," Dee warned, giving Kelley a swift kick under the table.

"John," Kelley insisted, "we cannot go against God."

"I am Catholic," Karel announced, "and I agree. If I knew Latin, I could cite verse and line."

"If you knew Latin, you would be a monk or priest." Kepler called over the barmaid, and Kelley and Dee ordered sausages and cabbage.

"Nobody in this town envies your task," Karel said as they were stuffing themselves.

"So you know Rabbi Loew?" Kepler asked of Dee. "You mentioned him in court."

"By reputation only," Dee answered. "I am interested in the Kabbalah."

"My view," Kelley said, "is that all mysticism in all religions comes together."

"I would keep that under your hat, because for that very idea they burned Bruno at the stake."

"Do not speak of fire. Another round?" Karel suggested cheerfully.

"Oh, woe is me," Kelley moaned. "Poor Bruno, and we are doomed as well."

"Do not give up the task so soon," Kepler said. "You have yet to start."

"I am but a mere junkman," Karel said, "but Oswald and I will help."

"Who is Oswald?" Kelley asked.

"A most noble creature."

"Oswald is a mule," Kepler explained.

"Made by God," Karel added.

"Why does Tycho Brahe have a silver nose?" Kelley asked Kepler.

"It was cut off in a duel over who was the best mathematician when he was a schoolboy."

"He won, of course."

"No, as a matter of fact. But this is what I was musing upon. Perhaps the rabbi can help you in your plight."

"I think the rabbi has enough problems, Johannes," Karel pointed out, "although it is said he once tricked the Angel of Death."

"My friend Edward, here," Dee said proudly, "sees angels, too."

"Only once in a while," Kelley said modestly. Actually, Kelley had to admit to himself that his visions were not quite like seeing angels. He could say he almost saw Madami, his guardian angel. She was a mere girl in his mind's eye, lithe and, of course, angelic, and there were other shapes and colors swirling in the scrying glass which could at certain angles approximate shapes, but there were many times when he had not partaken of his weeds and had to say his angels were present, for the benefit of his clients, when they were not there at all. Then he used his other powers—for instance, throwing his voice, so that, sitting at a table without his lips moving, he was able to make the sound of the spirit from the netherworld. There were also techniques of affecting a hazy cloud, dusts which produced miraculous explosions. Ointments of aconite, nightshade, juice of hemlock gave visions of flying. You will travel on a long journey, he would intone, putting a pinch on a client's tongue, lightening him first of excess baggage, namely his purse of coins.

"So," Kelley said, patting his full belly and thinking that maybe, just maybe, things were not as hopeless as he had felt at first, "this talented rabbi who evaded the Angel of Death is a friend of yours?"

"No, no, of course not," Kepler answered quickly. "What gave you that idea?"

"He is not my friend, either," Karel said.

"We cannot enter Judenstadt. It is verboten. They cannot come into our taverns. That is verboten. They cannot marry us or have us as friends. That is verboten."

"All forbidden?"

In fact, the only Jew Kelley had ever known was Shylock in *The Merchant of Venice*. It was Kelley's belief, however, that had not Portia, as judge, ruled against him, Shylock would never have insisted on his pound of flesh, that it was merely a ploy on the part of the playwright to show how much Shylock was a foreigner to Venetian city life—that, daily deprived of his humanity, he was forced by the perception of others to a villain's role. Shakespeare was no fool. Kelley hoped not, particularly now.

But"—Kepler shrugged—"although it is forbidden to be friends, once in a great while I see him—in passing, that is."

"Sometimes I see him, too, when I am passing in my cart through Judenstadt."

"In passing?" Kelley inquired.

"As we go to and fro about the earth, and from walking up and down on it, understand, *verstehen*?" Kepler smiled.

"When you are passing him next, Johannes," Kelley said slowly, "could you ask him if he knows anything about butterflies?"

Part III

15

"The emperor is due at any time, is he not?"

Kelley, in great agitation, was pacing from one end of the laboratory to another.

"We can show him the powder, Edward, do not upset yourself." Dee, experienced as a spy, was not rattled by subterfuge if it was in good cause. He stood at the stove, stirring a pot of thick goop.

"If he were to smell it, he would know it is not an eternal elixir. Elderly elephant hoof power, musty and fusty, that is all it is."

Hugging one wall was a waist-high brick stove fed constantly with logs at both ends. The young boys who were employed to work the bellows, keeping the flame going high and hot, were outside fetching kindling. On a shelf on the opposite wall stood a series of vessels— clay, milky glass with golden Latin inscriptions, some like pitchers and others with rows of spouts along both sides; others had apertures at the base. There were apothecary jars filled with nostrums and cures for every ailment under the sky—pills for overcoming drowsiness, tablets of crushed oyster shell for virility, salves that smelled nasty to repel the bloodthirsty mosquito, liniments to mend broken skin, unguents for aches and pains, and soothing herbs to quell the heart beating fast with love.

"No matter what it is, when we have sufficient amount, we will feed the butterflies."

They had devised a strategy which would fool the emperor, delay their punishment.

"Are you sure you wish to hasten the feeding?" Kelley was, above all, a practical man.

"It is not hastening anything. Think of the chain of command—traders, trackers, hunters, marksmen, haulers, merchants."

"And the poor elephants of Afric and India."

"If you are to regret anything, Edward, pray think on your neck."

The rough trestle table was littered with instruments of the profession: funnels, braziers, scales, mortars and pestles, stirring spoons, alembics strong enough to be placed directly on the flame with long beaks at their end through which condensed substances could travel to another vessel, pans for coals, baskets, retorts, much like the alembic for purifying, pots of all sizes. Alchemical symbols marked specific components on a row of boxes—the snake swallowing his mouth, the old Gnostic sign for the universe, a hermaphrodite signifying conjunction, kings with suns for heads, queens bearing moons, men rising from coffins, griffins and chimeras, symbols for silver, copper, ginger, potash, gold, and on one box the most startling allegorical creature of them all, that which served as symbol for mercury, a squat dragon resembling a chicken in shape and posture but with a bearded human head, wings as ears, human legs in winged boots, and three scaly tails sprouting from its head knotted with a long tail snaking out of its back. The verse beneath it said, "Raising myself from death, I kill death—which kills me."

In the midst of all this equipment, Karel, the legless rag and bone man, seated by the stove, was snoozing. Kelley, for the occasion of the emperor's visit, had replaced his rakish garb with a dun-colored scholar's gown thrown over his shoulders, and he had discarded his velvet feathered hat for a serious woolen cap. Dee, too, dressing the part, had exchanged his somber skullcap and court attire for a twisted turban, which, loosely tied, draped down his neck, and magisterial robes. Indeed, he appeared the bona fide wizard.

Books provided by the emperor for their endeavor included *Egyptian Secrets or White and Black Magic for Man and Beast*, compiled by none other than the peripatetic physician Paracelsus himself. On a reading dais in the middle of the room, place of honor, was Hermes Trismegistus's *The Emerald Tablet*, the alchemist's bible, written by a third-century Egyptian and translated from the original Arabic into Greek, then Latin, finally English. It was not in the new Gutenberg print, but a manuscript of the old style, with gold-flaked illuminated letters at the head of each chapter, so that a *B*, as in *Beware*, held a hive of bees and *D*, as in *Dead*, contained within its curling script the deadly curlicue of nightshade. Feigning assiduous concentration over his reading, Kelley scraped the illuminated letters filled with gold leaf with his fingernails, pocketed the rubbings. Dee stirred the pot.

"You realize it was not the rabbi who helped us with our scheme, but his wife, Perl."

"The ploy of a rabbi's wife told to a penniless astronomer by a kitchen fire on a cold winter day? An old wives' tale if I ever heard one," Kelley scoffed.

Perl, eavesdropping on her husband's guest, as usual, dusting cloth in hand, had said to Kepler:

"There may be butterflies who live more than a day, for what we take as truth is often hearsay, gossip, lies. Do all butterflies live but a day? Only one well versed in the ways of butterflies can tell you true or false. If there are those who are long-lived, it behooves the alchemists to find them. Giving the appearance of invincibility, if not immortality, these butterflies will convince the emperor that they wake up each morning through benefit of elixir alone."

"The butterflies will live as long as they naturally do, no more, no less, John. The 'elixir' we feed them will not make one whit of difference. Be wary of believing our own lie."

"Think of what we do not as falsehood, Edward, but as preservation, if not the emperor's, our own. The elixir of life is an act of faith, a work of art, demonstration of science. The butterflies, as taster-testers, will prove without a doubt the veracity of our formula while we devise escape."

A loud banging of drum announced the emperor's presence on the drawbridge. Kelley ran to the window of the tower, peered out of its narrow frame.

"They are coming, they are coming."

Dee returned to his book, Kelley to his pot. The helpers ran in, dumped the kindling, started to press the bellows fanning the flames of the fire. Even Karel roused himself from sleep, tried to look attentive.

First came the servants, followed by nobles of the court; officials; the trumpeters; Kirakos; the Russian, Sergey; Rumpf, the imperial advisor; Pistorius, the confessor; Pucci, the castrato; priests; various other hangers-on; and, of course, Václav.

"Our sovereign, the gracious High Emperor Rudolphus," Dee said in his most obsequious tone, bowing low. "We are honored."

"It is hot as hell in here, and I am never hot," the emperor said. He was wearing a cloak of the finest Persian silver lamé brocaded in gold and polychrome silk. Beneath, his doublet was of violet silk damask brocaded in large leaf shapes with decorative bands. His breeches, made by Rochel to match the cloak he had worn for his first audience with the alchemists, were royal purple. His hose were tasseled in red thread. On his head was a velvet cap in the style of the British Henry VIII; broached with a giant emerald, it made him look like a baker.

"We must keep it hot here, Your Majesty," Kelley replied. "To attain heaven, the fires must be kept burning frantically."

"Humph," the emperor replied. "It is nearing May."

"Yes," Kelley trilled, "it is spring."

"What about the butterflies?"

"We are seeing to the butterflies, Your Majesty. Only the most noble, if you will, or rather royal, nay, imperial of the butterfly kind will do for our examination," Kelley said shrilly.

"We need more elephant powder, Your Most August Highness," Dee mentioned. Their recipe included elephant powder, tortoise toenails, and the sap of long-lived oaks.

"Elephants do not come cheap," the emperor said.

"Life is precious," Kelley replied. "Your life, that is, is precious."

Pushed into corners of the alchemy laboratory were containers of all sorts of repulsive animals, alive and dead.

"The snakes, what are they for?"

"We use the blood, Your Highness." Kelley warmed to his words. "You see, the blood of a snake is cold, does not heat up unless warmed by the sun."

"I do not like blood."

"Nor do I, but in the interest of eternity, your eternity, I have taught myself to love that which will be beneficial to our brew."

"I can understand the salamanders and sliced newts, but the dried bats?" The emperor pointed to one opened box. They looked like a pile of black gloves, save for their hoary faces and fanged teeth.

"Bats are best, my lord, for various things. Bats and snakes, toads, hemlock, foxglove, arsenic, mercury. To contradict death, we turn it back on itself," Dee waxed on.

"Ah, I see. I see." The emperor hated to be confronted with riddles, but what they said seemed obvious enough, and a touch of metaphysics, well, that was like spice to banal fare.

"To describe the alchemical process, most honorable sir," Dee spoke in ponderous tones befitting their task. "A transmutation. You see, that which turns base metals into gold is not merely heat, but rather the addition or application of what is called the philosophers' stone, the great quintessence."

"We will, of course, be trying this elixir on butterflies first," the emperor replied, "and then Václav."

"I do not want to live forever, Your Majesty," Václav interposed hastily. He had been standing by, careful not to be too close to the snakes.

"You want to die, Václav?" his emperor asked.

"Not immediately, Your Majesty." Václav, of course, would not mind living forever, if, in fact, his wife and children could live with him forever, and everybody he knew and everybody he did not know and so on unto the whole wide world, although would there be enough room, he wondered, for all the new babies to come? But not under any circumstances did he want to outlive his children. That he had already done for his first daughter, Katrina, and when she had sickened and died, he had prayed to be taken instead of her. Sometimes Václav feared that God was actually the Evil One or the Erl King or the Night Hag who lurked around corners, lived at the bottom of wells, came in the dead of night to take children.

"We will try it on the butterflies, then Václav, tasters, several in a row."

"You wish to waste the priceless elixir on mere me, Your Highness?"

"Just enough to make sure it does not kill anybody, Václav."

"Not to worry," Kelley said with a smile.

"Yes, and you, too, will taste of your own elixir," the emperor confirmed.

"But of course. We will be lifting the spoon to the mouth often, like any good cook."

"What is he doing here?" the emperor asked, pointing at Karel scrunched on the floor. "Should he not be out ragging and boning?" He went over, kicked Karel, the poor fellow, in the crotch. "Václav, carry the crippled idler and miscreant down to his wretched cart posthaste."

"Your Majesty," Karel protested, "it is my supper break."

"Get him out of my sight."

Karel held out his arms to be lifted. Václav picked him up, carried him down the stairs of the Powder Tower.

"It does not do to bait the emperor," Václav admonished.

"Václav," Karel whispered in the servant's ear, "I am glad we have this chance. Father Thaddaeus and the three drunken brothers who own Oswald's barn are going to incite a crowd to burn down Judenstadt. We must stop them."

Václav suddenly lost his strength, nearly dropping Karel on the hard stone stairs. "It cannot be."

"In truth. I heard them conspiring at the Golden Ox."

"Does the rabbi know?"

"He knows. Have you seen the golem he made? But he will not be enough."

"Ah, a brilliant day," Václav said, quite loudly, when he saw the guards. "And Oswald looks in fine form. Hey-ho, old Oswald."

"Yes, yes," Karel readily agreed. "A fine day."

"God be with you, my friend," Václav said.

"And you, my good man."

Václav waved Karel off, returned, and with a worried air ascended the Powder Tower.

"And the butterflies, Your Excellency," Dee was saying, "must be of the strongest cocoons, the fattest, and the honey we feed them needs be the very best."

"I am strong," the emperor said, putting one foot forward and baring his teeth, revealed his few remaining stumps.

"Indeed you are." Kelley wondered that this man who was so fond of contraptions, vain of body, and rich in pocket had not had some new teeth made for him.

"It will be hard to keep them alive for the trip, the butterflies," the emperor said.

"If silkworms were smuggled out of China concealed in bamboo staves, surely we can transfer mere butterfly grubs openly," Dee said. "However, what we require, Your Majesty, is a home for them both secure and warm."

"We have seen to it. Surely your crystal ball has showed you that?"

"A detail, Your Majesty, and I have been far too busy to consult with my angels as of late."

Since he arrived in Prague, deprived of inspiration, the only visions

Kelley garnered from the crystal ball were cloudy at best, murky at worst. A clogged pond, a churning sky, earth riddled with worms.

Dee made note that the emperor, despite his rotten teeth and bandy legs, was bursting with robust good health. The pallor he had observed on their first meeting was replaced with a rosy glow, and the man's big belly looked solid as a boulder. God help him, but Dee wished Rudolph II would just fall down, break his head on the stone steps, die of a lion bite from that insufferable Petaka, or choke on a piece of hastily swallowed meat.

The message sent to Queen Elizabeth via secret sources, beseeching her to intercede on their behalf, had gone out several weeks before, and there was no telling of its course and the return. Their other plan was to talk loudly of their predicament in their bedchambers at night, speak so that all servants in the Rosenberg household, where they were staying, became privy to their plight, would tell their friends. From Dee's considerable experience with code and secret, he knew nothing traveled faster than gossip. From the maids to the cooks, from the cooks to the marketplace, from the marketplace to the traveling merchants, from the traveling merchants to the courts. "Do not tell anybody," and instantly the most private of information was as if it were written in the almanac or posted on the churchyard door or announced at the pulpit:

Citizens of the British Realm:
Hear ye, hear ye, do not tell anybody, one Doctor Dee,
court astrologer for the Queen Herself, and the medium
Edward Kelley, are being held prisoners by the Habsburg Emperor,
nephew and brother-in-law to Philip II, he who ordered the Armada.
Remember the Armada.

"Yes, yes, all is made ready for the butterflies." The emperor was strutting about the laboratory now like a trained dog on his hind legs. Oh, he was in fine form this morning. "Vladislav Hall is transformed with gauzy netting strung up on thin spires made of twigs. We have a dozen tables with trays for the cocoons. Turkish braziers are installed. Indeed, the former site of jousts and book fairs is already banked with earth, and many, many bushes of sweet-smelling flowers have been transferred from the greenhouse. Kirakos is in charge."

For today's tour, Kirakos had a pounding headache. However, he had to admit to himself that the alchemists put on a good show, desperation apparent only in their eyes. Where were they going to get the butterflies? He knew that their queen would soon be getting word of their predicament, if she had not already heard. Spies in Prague were more numerous than rats. Spies for the queens and kings, Turkish spies, spies for Rudolph's brother, Matthias. Spies, lies, supposition, assumption, misconstrued belief, uneducated guess, farfetched possibility; a dense, smothering cloud of misinformation hung over the city ready to break and drowned them all in a rain of words. But he seriously doubted that fickle Elizabeth, enamored of pets, poets, and playwrights, although good at statecraft and for a woman extremely clever, would raise a beringed finger to rescue Dee, a minor and unpaid member of her court, and his cohort of questionable character and no known patriotism.

This game of deceit required constant vigilance, Kirakos understood, although on this day—on all days, as a matter of fact—he would rather be sleeping. Drowsily, he remembered the chill air of his childhood, the amazing blue of the sky, the goats, an occasional rude cart drawn by a mule along the one rugged road out of town. This pristine scene was pierced one day by the sound of the bell in the white stucco church with the crude wooden cross. Everybody started to run. Kirakos remembered his mother grabbing him, hiding him with the other children under straw piled up in the barn. Peeking out through the open door, they saw the men in the village lined up, their hands on their heads, later to be found with their testicles stuffed in their mouths, his father among them, blood as dark as roses between his legs. His mother's silence when she was raped and killed still lived in his bones. His little brother and sister died in ways he did not want to remember, and then he was taken with the able-bodied boys and girls as a slave to Istanbul.

"We do not want to detain you from your work," the emperor said to Kelley and Dee, arching his little fingers in mannered glee.

"Always happy for a royal visit, Your Highness," Kelley, ever the gracious host, said, and then he abruptly turned. "Bring up some more wood," he commanded with authority to the wood carriers, "but first go to the shop. We need some lizards, some comfry, some pennyroyal, make haste."

"Another visit," the emperor said, "in three days hence. I am well pleased."

"We can hardly wait," Kelley replied daintily.

As the emperor and retinue could be seen crossing the Stag Moat, Dee hissed to his partner, "Are you going mad? 'We can hardly wait'? And then sending the assistants on errand for such hodgepodge. We do not need any of those ingredients."

"You are the officious one, John, and speaking of ingredients, we need poison, that is what we really need." Kelley began pacing. " 'It is nearing May,' " he repeated in falsetto. "I am glad he came, because now I know we must kill the beast."

Dee looked around. "Hush."

"Is there any other way out of this, John? The butterfly scheme will only postpone the inevitable. How can we escape?" Kelley peered out of the window, saw the guards posted below. "Your fairy queen is not going to fly to our rescue, it seems."

"What about your guardian angel, Madami? Seems that she has not appeared in the magic crystal for some time now."

"That is not fair, John, and you know it."

"I am sorry, Edward. We must have faith."

"Many a faithful man has gone to the gallows, and although I am no atheist like poor Marlowe was reputed to be—"

"He was a Catholic, fancied boys."

"No matter. I must wonder sometimes at the attention of the Almighty." Kelley drew closer to Dee, spoke in a quiet tone, kept his eyes focused out the window. "The poison I was thinking of is not any old kind, nor any substance which might induce visions or alteration of mind, nor anything with unpredictable results, nor detectable by tasters. If the emperor were so obviously poisoned, who would be the immediate suspects, pray tell? Have you noticed anything strange about that Kirakos?"

"Ah, a curious and cold man," Dee agreed. "Shifty."

"Sleepy," Kelley suggested, "yet he is strangely alert."

"He likes his wine," Dee observed.

"More than wine, I daresay."

"You, of all people, should know, Kelley."

"Yes, the poppy—rather a lot of it, is my conjecture. No crime in the poppy. One can get it at the apothecary for every malady under the sun, and that is what we must put our minds to, my friend, maladies. Listen to me, John. Syphilis, the French pox, is slow, far too slow. Some say the emperor already has it and it is what makes him mad. Then there are all types of ague, coughs and cramping, chills, fevers he could catch, a pinch of hemlock would do the trick, glass ground so fine it would seem like salt to have him bleed inside out, and then it struck me, the most convenient sickness of them all. I was simpleminded not to consider it before. Listen to me, I am coming back around to my intended point."

Dee, although he, too, was considering afflicting the emperor, did not like the sound of this. It made him distinctly nervous. "Killing is a sin," he cautioned.

"Do not the English wish to kill the Spanish?" Kelley inquired. "And have you not been instrumental in such an endeavor?"

"That is war."

"Ah, war, you call it. And the French, too," Kelley added, "in the Hundred Years War."

"We had right to that land," Dee said.

"And Queen Mary, who killed the Protestants, and Queen Elizabeth the Catholics, and Henry VIII, who dispatched Thomas More as well as his numerous wives."

"They are kings and queens," Dee protested.

"The emperor, do you think, should have the right to kill us because he is emperor? Does that make you want to die more, live less, my venerable colleague?"

"No," Dee admitted.

"If somebody were to attack you, Dr. John Dee, would you not defend yourself? Is not your life of equal importance to you as that of any emperor who stoops to imprisonment and murder for his selfish gain?"

"It is the way of the world."

"The way of the world, dear friend, is the way the strong take over, torment, and decimate the weak. I may be a mere forger, a fraud, a man without ears, but I do have eyes in my head. I have had enough of the way of who gets what, when, and how. Anyway, what I am thinking of is a poison which would not be poison."

"Is this a conundrum, Master Kelley? A poison which would not be a poison?"

"What is that which he already enjoys, which in moderation he employs, leads to dreams of triumph, pain be gone, yet in excess fells an elephant?" Kelley clapped his hands in glee.

"Opium, the poppy? Is that what you are talking about?" Dee smiled and began to quote, " 'I possess a secret remedy which I call laudanum and which is superior to all other heroic remedies.' " Dee was getting in the spirit of the thing. "Paracelsus used the word *arcanun*. Here is his recipe: 'opium mixed with henbane, crushed pearls and coral, mummy, an Arabic, tarlike drug, dezoar stone, which is made of cow intestine, amber, musk, other oils, the bone from the heart of a stag, and unicorn.' The sage could not think of practicing medicine without opium."

"So if we leave off the unicorn, not worry with the stag, and make it thirty grams, that would be a powerful poison—rather, medicine—indeed," Kelley agreed.

"I believe the Turks take twelve grains day," Dee said. "That is what I have heard."

"Four grains is already a lot. I am sure Kirakos takes more than that in a day."

"We cannot get it from Kirakos," Kelley said. "Definitely not, nor the apothecary. The emperor would know of it straightaway, would wonder, suspect something amiss. And the kitchen garden variety used by every midwife, witch, and who-have-you across the land to make a soothing tea, mild soporific, something to quell the crying babe—not that cozy, weak-kneed kind of seed. For our purpose, dear friend, we need the poppy of the serious and habitual partaker, the potent juice of the cultivated flower, squeezed of its nectar, drained and dried, caked, indeed professionally prepared. I am talking, John, of the very best of this poisonous ambrosia, the kind that is imported, smuggled, indeed, forbidden and beyond the reach of those in this city except for the very rich or the dissolute few who dare defy the rules. We must obtain the *crème de la crème*. Only Turkish opium will do."

"It will show up in his urine," Dee pointed out, for it was well-known that the emperor's urine was examined in an alembic every morning by court physicians.

"He will not have chance for urine. Mixed with wine, it will be too fast, his sorry state will be taken as a consequence of imbibing."

"But the taster, Edward?"

"The taster will not be drinking the whole goblet, will he? The taster sips."

"The taster sips," Dee repeated.

"The taster sips," Kelley prated, marching in a circle, clapping his hands.

"I almost feel sorry for the emperor," Dee said, "that his demise is to be so soon, after all."

"Do not waste your tears on such as he unless you love the axe that fells you."

"To have obtained a throne, only to be cast down into a grave. To pursue forever at the cost of never. Once, Edward, he was a mere babe."

"Quiet, the boys are coming back. Look downcast. Spies and lies."

And the snakes in their cages coiled and uncoiled.

16

RUDOLPH II STARTED his life in Vienna on a sultry July 18, 1552. In attendance at his birth were seven midwives, a priest, and the court astrologer. His mother refused myrrh and valerian root, Turkish poppy, did not even take a drink of water, but bore her pain, which she thought her Christian obligation, although no woman was ever sainted for giving birth, save Mary. The ladies-in-waiting, clustered like crows at feed, whispered in alcoves and corners, along hallways and within antechambers. The baby, very small, was not expected to live. And who had not lost a child or two or three? Even queens. Among the poor, the weak and misshapen were put out to die. But the priest baptized baby Rudolph, the astrologer cast his horoscope. Cancer, the Crab, element water, characteristics including ambition, stubbornness, yet one who likes his shell, scuttles sideways—in other words, a born emperor, and despite the sweltering day, the sickly child was immediately plunged into the body of a freshly killed lamb. When the cavity of the carcass cooled, another newly slaughtered sheep was rushed from the butchery, one animal after another. It was only after the second day that the future emperor could be set to suckle at the wet nurse. Consequently, all his life Rudolph suffered from cold, and wore, even in the high heat of August in Prague, heavy furs from Russia. For this, his mistress and mother of eight of his children, Anna Marie Strada, called him Bear. Indeed, he visited her bed in hose, a cascading cape of ermine, and in lieu of crown kept on a special copulatory cap with flaps reaching down around his ears.

Rudolph's wet nurse at the Hofburg Castle for those first years was a strong, healthy girl who had smothered her own baby through overlaying. Her sweet milk, mixed with the salt of her tears, determined in Rudolph a taste for the mixture of sweet and savory. Of course, there was no danger of having anybody roll over on him. First son of Maximilian II, Holy Roman Emperor, he slept in a cradle of gold shaped like a swan, inlaid with pearls, the top a little baby crown with the Habsburg double eagle looking east and west and from which gauzy curtains fell in a haze of white.

When he was seven, Rudolph's lessons began. He and his younger brother, Ernst, were given over to the care of one Master Bergamo, a tutor with a body like a tuber set right atop two strands of straw. They learned their Latin alphabet using books with sheets of transparent horn protecting the page of letters, hornbooks rightly called, and similarly, they learned their numbers. Civility was taught from the beginning, first from Erasmus's *Manners for Children*, later his *Education of a Christian Prince*, and the German *Hof und Tischzuchtern* and French books of courtesy and table manners.

Always attired in the hues of the poor, an indistinct gray or candlestick tallow, Master Bergamo was soon dubbed by the errant boys Master Onion Bulb. And although Rudolph would be emperor or at the very least king of some country or other, Master Onion Bulb did not believe in sparing the rod and spoiling the child. Indeed, while the boys studied their lessons, Master Bergamo sharpened and tested his weapons by whip-whapping the air, stabbing cushions, poking the ancient beagle, Schatzi, who slept in the nursery, and by frequently parrying and thrusting at innocent curtains. At readiness were birch for back, willow for calves, a nice long pine branch for boyish buttocks. Then in the evening, lessons over, the spent scholar at the brothels near the abattoirs, young Rudolph and his brother, Ernst, would make their stealthy way into their schoolmaster's filthy chambers to piss upon the hearthstones of his fireplace and to sneak-read how Rabelais' giant, Gargantua, ate twenty Frenchmen for his salad, how he was born out of his mother's ear, and how he used a goose neck to wipe his dirty bum. Ernst and Rudolph spoke German, of course, their father's tongue, and Spanish, their mother's language, although she grudgingly used German on occasion. They could read French also without benefit of book or birch, simply from being at court and attending to conversation. Latin was what Master Onion Bulb was engaged to teach the boys, as well as arithmetic, logic, music, astronomy, geometry, rhetoric, and theology.

With other teachers, they learned etiquette, clothing, and elegant speech, all required of royalty, as well as falconry, hawking, fencing, riding, jousting, and dancing. In the spring when they walked with their servants in the Hofburg gardens and reached a gate which went up to the sky, Rudolph's nurse told him that the world was beyond it and that someday he would rule it, for although the Holy Roman Emperor was supposedly elected by electors, the position had, by Rudolph's time, become, for all practical purposes, hereditary. He was not interested in ruling the world, although he laid claim to the nursery and would not let his brothers, especially spoiled baby Matthias, who was a whole six years younger, touch his bladder ball, his *Book of Saints*, his stories of Hercules, his game of stones, his whistle, his marbles, or toy animals.

In addition to court entertainments, itinerate puppet masters put on shows, for example the one about the mermaid who sold her voice to the witch for legs. Rudolph's sisters favored *Aschenputtel*, about a poor girl who must sweep ashes from the fireplace, only to be saved by a prince, and they just adored the story of the fair maiden who, blind, recovered her sight by the return of her lover. The tender-hearted Ernst wept over the bad wizard who wanted eternal ice on earth and tried to stop the sun from rising. Matthias, too young to understand much, broke into giggles at the appearance of the wolf puppet in the story of an old man who rescues a she-wolf who then eats him all up. The girls sighed over Patient Griselda, who remained meek and mild to her husband despite the cruel tests he put her through, including taking away and almost marrying their daughter. Dr. Faustus and the devil put all the children into frenzy so that nobody wanted to go to bed that night. Later, as a grown-up, Rudolph heard stories that Dr. Faustus had once been a real man, a necromancer and drunkard, a schoolmaster who was driven out of town for molesting his young pupils and was finally strangled by the devil in Wittenberg. To Rudolph's mind, Marlowe's play, which he saw in his own court in Prague, granted the conjurer too much sympathy by far.

As was the custom, Rudolph and Ernst, at twelve and eleven, were sent for further education to the court of a relative. Thus the boys traveled to Spain to be with Philip II, their mother's brother and soon to be sister's husband. Their uncle Philip did not drink the Leipzig beer Rudolph had learned to love in Vienna as fit accompaniment for all his meals, and the only theater permitted at that staid court were old, creaky morality plays and devotional works in which saints ascended to their heavenly home. Flagellation was the fashion, and for that purpose Rudolph was given his very own little child's scourge with an elegant silver handle, four braided tails.

Outside the walls of Philip's palace, El Prado, in Madrid, the dusty streets were no less religious. Penitents in cowls and robes marked with red crosses went in dire procession, droning their repentance in mournful dirge, dragging, like grotesque tails behind them, Goliath-sized crosses. Crosses were also used to truss up Jews for burning, crypto-Jews, Jews forced into Christianity, called Marranos, and the Moors, the Moriscos, Muslims converted to Christianity, heretical Protestants, and sundry witches, any and all who were slow to recite the Credo, Pater Noster, Hail Mary full of Grace.

More frightening to Rudolph, however, and that which remained within his mind for life, was the notorious Don Carlos, Philip's son, seven years older than Rudolph. Don Carlos's birth, sad to say, in 1545, was attended by only one inexperienced midwife. The ladies-in-waiting had gone for an afternoon's sport, a small burning of twenty-four, an auto-da-fé. The baby, costing his mother's life, was reluctant to emerge, did not breathe immediately, had a large, ungainly head, one shoulder higher than the other. A sunken chest did little to give him royal presence. A lump, which probably was meant for his back, sat on his waist, and one leg was longer than the other. He had a withered hand. Don Carlos was slow to talk and stammered when he finally did, could not ever read well, was dull-witted, sullen-tempered, a glutton, had an unremitting attachment to violence, spurred horses so hard they bled to death, sliced the paws of hapless cats, lashed dogs with more than penitential scourges, whipped young maids.

Understandably, when Rudolph and Ernst heard the approach of their older cousin's limping gait, they sped well away. Although it was luck to touch a hunchback's hump, Rudolph never wished to be in contact with any part of Don Carlos's detestable body. Don Carlos's shriveled hand resembled an animal's paw to him, the large, lopsided head, wobbling on the thin neck, looked as if it might fall off and spill its eyes. Then one night on amorous quest, as if not already a horrible enough example, Don Carlos fell down the stairs, enlarging his head to three times its size. Doctors were sent for from all over Spain. He was blooded, an incision made in his scalp. Trepanning was discussed. Philip brought Vesalius, other noted surgeons, the wound dressed with powdered iris and birthwort, an unguent of turpentine and egg yolk. Then, secretly, a Moorish doctor, who had not yet been burned, was smuggled in from Valencia. Too weak to be blooded once again, Don Carlos was cupped and purged. Prayers were said, relics offered. Finally, no longer knowing what else to do, his distraught father brought the embalmed body of a holy friar, Fra Diego, to set beside the poor boy in his bed. At that, the young prince, like Lazarus risen, recovered. It was a miracle, and Don Carlos, all proclaimed, was a better person for his ordeal.

Rudolph, for his part, did not detect any appreciable difference in the temperament of his miserable cousin, as he lurked about the palace grounds muttering rude and indecipherable imprecations, lopping the blooms off jacaranda trees, slicing hibiscus, and thrashing bougainvillea with his cane. Yet life at court returned to normal, as if Don Carlos were not a monster in their midst. Philip once again assumed his imperial duties, spending each day composing missives, making pronouncements, giving out official orders, issuing declarations, declaring decrees, deciding verdicts, administering Spain and Portugal, New Spain and most of South America, consigning infidels to rack and mortal ruin.

The last installment in Don Carlos's short and detestable life was the plot he hatched to murder his father, articulated in the confines of holy confession. Thereafter, Rudolph and Ernst could hear their cousin, imprisoned in his bedchamber, sing a wordless, almost tuneless lament, and sometimes the ill-fated creature would wail a beseeching "Forgive me, father, I have sinned." In his last days, Don Carlos was altogether silent and the cicadas in the tall grass around the room, as if detecting death, sang an eerie, deafening melody. He was twenty-three, Rudolph sixteen, and Ernst fifteen, shivering in their beds despite the desperate heat. On Don Carlos's last night, Rudolph almost felt sorry for the miscreant. Fingering his rosary, he whispered to Ernst, "Are you asleep yet?"

"No, are you?"

They got up to play primero by the light of a single candle. Rudolph won two games with hands of kings and queens. Ernst could only draw low numbers, this determined by Rudolph, who shuffled the deck with practiced dexterity.

The boys stayed at the Spanish court for seven years, coming to manhood in the royal gardens amid the hairy-trunked palms and tall tubular cacti. During siesta, they tied the bandy legs of their white-feathered friends, bagged the pecking heads. Increasing in imagination, the lusty boys turned their energies to more noble species. Around and around the terrified beasts would run, down the airy hallways of the many deserted courtyards, stirring the dust of the well-trod paths, darting under leaves as slippery as candle wax, resting finally beneath bushes of sticky-sweet madrona. Ambushed. Caught. Pinned. Pushed down against the cool mosaic tiles of fountain fonts left by the Moors. Cats scratched and yowled. More docile were the sheep. Calves, the occasional goat, matted fur and thrashing legs. Need it be said that the many descendants of Noah's Ark would begin to tremble with fear when romance was in the air?

Rudolph's first woman was his nursemaid, the very same who had salted his milk with tears, her breasts long gone dry, but buoyant still and very to his liking. Had she not tweaked his penis when he was a mere babe? On to the assistant of a silk spinster, the little one who set out the cocoons on trays of mesh, a glover's helper after that, girdler fetch-and-go, a haberdasher's girl, a cap maker's maid. When he was sixteen he actually fancied a lady in the Spanish court. Her hair, parted in the middle, flat and severe in a little knot at her neck, looked like it had been painted on her tiny skull. Her eyes, snapping-turtle black, were almost audible, and on her belt hung a little prayer book bound in blood-red calfskin.

Before he left the Spanish court, his uncle Philip and father, Maximilian, did arrange his engagement with his cousin Isabelle, and Ernst was engaged to another of Philip's daughters. Isabelle was thirteen then, Rudolph nearly twenty, and twenty years were to pass before one of Rudolph's younger brothers, Albrecht, married her out from under him, which he could not forgive. Other marital arrangements also fell by the wayside. When Tycho Brahe made his dire prediction that one of Rudolph's legitimate sons would murder him, Rudolph felt justified in resisting conjugal bliss. This despite the entreaties of his family, for his ancestors, mere lower knights in a tumbledown castle called Habichtsburg or the Falcon's Castle on the Rhine, had married themselves across Europe. It was said that the Habsburgs acquired through Venus what was usually obtained by Mars.

Not that he practiced celibacy as a regent bachelor. Indeed, many of the crinkly haired, jut-chinned bastards running around in the alleyways below the Hradčany Castle carried royal blood, and he favored the women whose job it was to serve his every need and whim—his maids and laundress, his confectionary cook, a tall, blond Czech virgin.

17

ONLY THE HUSBAND would officially know when the wife
went to the mikvah, the husband and the bath attendant,
with whom the woman would have to make the appointment. From the beginning of a woman's menstruation and for seven
days after its end, and until she immersed herself in the purifying
water of the mikvah, the husband had to refrain from touching his
wife. That was the Law. Rochel examined herself daily during the
"white period" right after the flow to be certain there was no spot of
blood, and then, on the seventh day, after nightfall, walking quickly,
her head down, she would make the necessary trip across Judenstadt
to the back gates.

The mikvah in Judenstadt, built according to Halachah specifica-
tions, financed by Maisel, was in a rather elegant building of brick on
the outside, tile on the inside, the roof of tin. As ruled, the pools
themselves were dug into the ground, one for storage containing a
minimum of two hundred gallons of stored rainwater, which fed into
the other pool, the mikvah, by a hole of at least a two-inch radius.
The water was chest-high and kept warm by a system of tunnels
heated by one great fire at the entrance, tended by the beggar who
cleaned the synagogue and did odd jobs, Judesnstadt's schnorrer.

Unfortunately, what had not been accounted for in the construction of the mikvah, and unbeknownst to everybody in Judenstadt,
was a flaw. In the wall of the bathhouse which abutted the back wall
of Judenstadt, and in exactly the place where the two bricks in the
ghetto wall were not securely cemented and could be removed, the
very same place where the dead baby had been placed by the jealous
and hateful Thaddaeus when Rochel's grandmother was alive, and

where Václav had hidden treats for Rochel when she was a little girl, there were two small cracks. The cracks had been craftily chiseled into two small, eye-sized apertures tunneling straight through the inner wall and tile. Kirakos was the one responsible for this breach of decency, and through those peepholes he had for several years lecherously watched all the men of Judenstadt cleanse themselves before services and the women prepare themselves for holy reunion with their husbands after their obligatory abstinence.

Rochel welcomed those days of rest from conjugal duties. It was as if her own lack of desire was sanctioned, for although she wanted a child more than anything else, when her blood came and she must fix a rag about her waist fore and aft, she was filled with relief. For her, this most feminine event was a blessing, not a curse, even though in the olden days the women would be sequestered during their monthlies, and there were those even in her day so afraid of a woman's uncleanliness they thought of them as soiled in heart and soul.

Not one to get headaches or stomach pains, and knowing that, according to Law, Zev could not touch her, she was all the more ready during the time of her "visitor" to be sweet to her husband, singing merrily, skipping and hopping about the room, waiting on him hand and foot, and listening closely when he recounted every tiny thing that happened to him or how she must fix the food. He was cherished and dear to her then, and she would long to pat him on the head, assure him that indeed they were good friends, well fitted workmates, and that their marriage would prove fruitful. True, he was older than she was by many years, but not tottering or feeble, not so old as her grandmother, and although, like her grandmother, he did all the talking, she found her husband companionable, and their struggle to put food on the table seemed ordained.

However, when her monthly was over, coming back from the mikvah, trudging reluctantly across the cemetery, skirting the rabbi's house, the shul, the baker's, the shochet's, dread would enter her heart. Opening the door to their room, all would be different. The air itself would have shifted, as if there were a sudden spill or lopsidedness to the earth beneath. Zev would act like somebody who had pepper on his skin, for his hands trembled at their ordinary tasks, and a smarting flush would rise above his beard, across his forehead, and a hard, glittering look would come into his usually soft eyes, and later that night, as Rochel held herself steady, clutching the sides of the bed while he rocked above her, she would have the strange premonition that she was sliding off the edge of the world into a swirling dust, would be lost forever, never known.

Before immersing in the sacred water at the bathhouse, Rochel had to wash her hair, her nails, each and every part of her, all the crevices with soap, including her teeth and tongue with a clean cloth. The attendant, whose skin had turned, from the constant dampness, into jellylike flesh, freckled with splotches of brown, would rub her back. At the last stage, buckets of fresh, clean water nicely heated would be thrown over her like a heavy shower of rain. Only at that point was Rochel deemed ready for the mikvah.

From the little Rochel knew, the tiles of the mikvah appeared Moorish, for there were little designs on them of a bright blue and green, and altogether they gave you the impression you were in an arbor, a garden with a fountain, or, when night came and the candles were lit, a grotto, ancient and enchanted. The water made a lighted moving shadow against the ceiling then, and within the enclosure each sound echoed with the rich history of tradition. Rochel, who liked things that stood for other things, knew she was symbolically immersing herself in the four mystical rivers that had emanated from Eden. Jewish women had purified themselves since biblical times. Bathing, Rochel was in the company of Sarah, Rebecca, Miriam, Hannah, Deborah. Rachel, mother of Joseph, of course, was her favorite ancestor. She could not forgive Rachel's sister Leah's trickery of disguising herself, marrying Jacob first, and she did not know what to make of Joseph's brothers selling him into slavery. In her humble opinion, woman that she was, she did not consider even God above reproach, for did He not pretend to demand the supreme sacrifice of Abraham? Job suffered. Jonah was swallowed by a whale, the world flooded, Lot's wife became a pillar of salt for only looking back. Why was the price of disobedience so high? Not that she ever had or would have any occasion to try His patience, yet His retribution seemed excessive, and even the innocent paid dearly.

Under the watchful eye of the attendant, least she slip or fall, Rochel, after her thorough cleansing, would go from the preliminary room to the mikvah itself, descend the few steps, then submerge herself completely. She liked to stay under the water, hold her breath as long as she could, and then, with a push from the bath floor, jump up with a great splash. She was inclined to throw herself immediately back in, kick, shoot water from her mouth. But no. She composed herself, davened, submerged herself twice more.

Kirakos, the emperor's conniving physician, had figured out her cycle. Every month, he waited for her with anxious anticipation at his point in the wall, his hands between his robe. He was standing thus one evening when he heard footsteps, great, huge footsteps, come toward him. Quickly he ran for cover. Cowering behind some bushes, he saw, lo and behold, a huge man, a man far bigger than any man he had ever seen. He was amazed, and had to restrain himself from gasping out loud or running away. This was the creature mentioned in court, the mud man the rabbi had made. Kirakos did not see the face very clearly in the dark, but he could take in the measure of the creature's wide shoulders, the long arms hanging well below his waist, the waist the span of several men, and the thickness increasing up through his chest. Then the thing, whatever it was, lumbered up to where Kirakos had been poised, saw the light coming from the little holes in the wall, and, bending on his knees, he pressed his huge plate of a face to them, peered.

Rochel had not gotten into the bath yet and was still soaping her breasts and parting her legs, creating a lather of white foam on her womanly crest. Yossel held his breath. She placed a handful of foam on the attendant's forehead, who laughed, clapping her webby fingers like a child. God forgive me, Yossel prayed. Unrestricted by skirts, the young woman took masterful strides around the room. She was like a young boy glorying in his limbs as he grew into the strength of manhood, or a warrior long trained for battle testing his body in the solitude of evening, thrusting his sword here and there, parrying forward, slighting back. Her whole form glowed in the candlelight, and unlike the way she had held herself at the Shabbat dinner, slumped, head down, eyes demurely lowered, she stood straight up in the bathhouse, shoulders squared, her feet planted on the floor, her buttocks thrust out. Her breasts were much fuller than they had appeared in her clothes. She was both regal and playful at once, elegant. Occasionally the attendant, clearly charmed and ministering to Rochel, would obscure the view. Move, move, Yossel thought.

Rinsing off before her immersion, Rochel threw the bucket of fresh, clean water over her own head, letting it drench her. She splashed more bucketfuls against her sides and legs, making certain all parts were thoroughly clear of soap, and even rather immodestly parting her buttocks. Then she shook like an animal ridding excess water from its fur. The attendant wrapped her in a cloth. Rochel disappeared into the next room, stepped down into the sanctified water. Yossel turned away, rested his back against the wall of the ghetto, amazed at what he had just seen. His body ached with longing, yet at the same time he castigated himself, was full of remorse.

After a little while, he saw her come out of the bathhouse, now in her drab clothes and scarf, her head once again lowered. She seemed to linger as she walked through Judenstadt, pressing herself into the sides of buildings, and her tread, unlike her little dance in the bathhouse, was weighted with hesitation. She looked as if she wanted the ground to swallow her or the night to lift her away. However, the patch of sky over Judenstadt, opaque now, bordered by the rickety buildings housing generations of Jews, was indifferent, cold as a knife. Compressing her lips, she went in to her room. Yossel, for his part, felt his chest contract, as if squeezed by a hand bigger than his own. He leaned his head against the trunk of a tree, banged it steadily, as to flatten and reduce to chaff what was in there. Dr. Kirakos, observing not far away, nodded to himself knowingly. So the monster feels, he thought.

18

THE MAN WHO knew most about the natural world in Prague was not a scholar at Charles University, did not in the least resemble a professor of syntax or professor of superior and inferior grammar, did not teach courses in philosophy, poetry, and rhetoric. He was neither officious in his bearing nor erudite in his references. Indeed, he had never read a book in his life about butterflies or anything else, for he was illiterate. Easily taken for an ignoramus, the butterfly man was knurled as an oak root, had only one eye, and that rheumy with age. This font of knowledge wore a cloak made of sacking, not out of religious conviction, but because the junkman had bestowed this garment on him out of pity. He lived in a stick hut at the edge of the emperor's garden with five malodorous dogs and two ancient, incontinent six-toed cats. He was an assistant-assistant gardener who had the ability to sit still in field or forest for hours and train his one bad eye on butterflies, crickets, ants, worms, anything that crawled, flew, crept, or buzzed.

"Ah, yes, the butterflies," he told Kelley as he boiled mint leaves in a big pot suspended from three iron legs. His fire, unlike those in most homes, was not built into the wall, but free standing in the middle of the circular hut, vented through a hole in the middle of the roof. His mangy dogs were restless, some kicking and scratching in their sleep, others wheezing, one audibly farting.

"My beauties," the old man explained.

"The butterflies," Kelley reminded him. He had eluded the guards who watched him night and day and was impatient to return to the main road, for other guards, posted all about, would be looking for him.

"Ah, yes, the butterflies."

He handed Kelley an earthen mug of the mint water sweetened with honey.

"This is delicious." At first Kelley had sipped politely, wondering how anybody could eat in such a stench, and he then drank boldly because the hot, tangy liquid was a delight to the taste and cut through his mind, which was saturated with ale and wearied with worry. It had taken him two nights of foraging among taverns, inns, and marketplace to locate this supposed gem. Each person he encountered knew of a man who might, perhaps, maybe have heard of a somebody who had learned the lore of all that lived in forests and fields, which brought to mind scenes of childhood innocence and dillydallying among dells and glens and bowers, and would you care for another mug, we are all children of God, are we not, under the roof of heaven. It was finally Karel, the rag and bone man, who directed him to the butterfly man.

"Such boiled drinks, methinks, can be good for the ague, shingles, digestion, a woman's monthlies, what have you. Peppermint leaf—"

"Butterflies," Kelley reminded him yet again. He and Dee had divided their mission threefold. Kelley's tasks were to gather information on butterflies and discover a source for the major quantity of opium they needed; Dee's job was to ascertain the position, power, and personality of Kirakos. Thus armed with long-lived butterflies, adequate opium, and a thorough understanding of their enemy, the two alchemists believed they could outwit what seemed their inevitable fate—execution.

"Ah, yes, you say these butterflies must live longer than a day, the longest-lived, you pray. Well, there are the Moroccan Orange Tip." The butterfly man raised the head of one of his dogs, fed the smelly beast from his own cup. "Anjelica is old, not her fault, must soon be put safely in the vault."

"Morocco?" Kelley did not fancy travel that did not point to the British Isles.

"Morocco? Not far, no, no. Any field has them, my dear fellow. They are in the garden grounds, in Petřín Woods, all around." One of the dogs yawned, vomited. "Žižka is a peska. Pardon her—"

"We can gather these butterflies easily?"

"Pause, if you please, while I pluck Teta's fleas."

"These Morrocan Orange live nearby? Tell me, man, and be quick about it."

"Ah, butterflies, but exactly why the butterflies, do not tell me lies. I lend an ear to your affair, will not breathe of it, far or near, and in truth, you are welcome as my guest, yet, new stranger, I must know your quest."

"Please, no more rhyming." Kelley, trying to be patient, wondered how candid he should be, decided to tell the old man everything. "The butterflies are to be fed the elixir of eternal life, that which we are making for the emperor. We are the alchemists, my friend John Dee and I."

"Ah, I see, I see. . . ."

"If our butterflies live longer after being fed the elixir, the emperor will see fit to drink it himself."

"Ah, I see, I see. There once was a Portuguese Jew who the Inquisition he did flew, and now a respected lawyer in Yemen has grown a giant grove of lemons."

"The butterflies."

"Ah, the butterflies. Yes, yes. Yellow wings with orange tip for the male, and a hidden underside suffused in bold green with yellow marks. The female is plainer. You will find their cocoons fastened to tall grasses and mustard plants. They feed on ordinary flowers. They are everywhere."

"And you can help us find the cocoons?"

"To be sure, only . . ." the old man held up his feet, bound in rags.

"We will get you some shoes."

The old man coughed.

"And a cloak." Kelly nodded.

"And just one small thing more, I do implore. A drop of the elixir, just a drop. I have a son, who ran away to become a scholar, begs for his lessons town to town, and I would like to see him one more time, and I would like to be with a woman one more time, too, and there are foods I have not tasted, and more than anything I would like to sample the medicinal water at Karlsbad."

"Is that all? Your each and every wish?"

"I am but a humble assistant-assistant gardener, but while we are at it, I would like . . ."

Hunched over, Kelley backed quickly out of the hut, did not turn back, made straight for the rose garden to the little green gate in the wall. To think, the butterflies were close at hand. To think they did not have to import the creatures, tend them on their journey, to

think he did not have to be involved with merchants, ships, and caravans. Before him, in his mind's eye, Kelley saw the tall houses on
London Bridge, the rounded walls of the Globe, British bawdy
women, British pubs, and Yorkshire puddings made with the rich
drippings from roast beef. If he never tasted a Czech dumpling again,
he would be happy indeed.

KELLEY HOPED HIS next mission would be as easily accomplished. True enough, every apothecary carried opium, for it was
used for sundry ailments—love sickness, sleepwalking, to make soldiers ready for surgery, to lull babies to silence, but he could not be
conspicuous in his purchase, with Slovene guards always over their
shoulders and medicines and supplies signed for on the emperor's
account. The merchant Kelley had to ferret out would have to belong
to the silent legion of eaters and sellers, men of disrepute, who, buying poppy in secret quantities, would not attract attention acquiring
more—in short, those who lived on the underside, friends and keep-
ers of prostitutes, the sort who made little forays into Austria and
Hungary, fearless men who would not shun unusual requests, men
who frequented less-known inns and disdained tariffs and taxes, kept
no accounts, were familiar with the comings and goings of caravans
and ships, men who knew who was docking at Naples when and with
what, members of a vast conspiracy, spreading tendrils like a giant
jellyfish, silent, slimy, undermining in secret sabotage the underpin-
nings of the Empire.

Again, Karel, the junkman, fixed at his usual spot by the hearth at
the Golden Ox, proved indispensable.

"There is a door," he conveyed in conspiratorial tones. "On the door
is a brass knocker in the shape of a woman's hand holding a small
globe. You let the knocker fall three times, stop, and four more times.
Then the door will open. The petitioner utters, 'Golden Prague.'"

Kelley chose early morning for this errand. Fortunately, the
Rosenbergs, exhausted from a night of dutiful heir-begetting, were
both snoring in their bed like grunting warthogs. Evading the guards,
who were not at their best at early morn, either, Kelley doubled back
several times, headed for the river, slipped down behind some fishermen mending their nets, and, making his way along the shore,
emerged near the Slavonic Monastery. Then, satisfied he was quite

alone for the sum of a few minutes, he found his way through Old Town to one of the dark and twisty alleyways close to the Square and Astronomical Clock, near the bordellos and behind Týn Church.

The person who opened the door on the seventh knock, trim and beardless as a boy, appeared to be more apprentice than master.

"Golden Prague." Kelley uttered the code words in a whisper.

The room was austere, dimly lit with one candle, without ornament, in truth, painfully neat. The narrow, uncurtained bed, one table, a chair attested to an austere life. There were many books, however—printed books on cheaply made paper.

"You are a student?" Kelley asked.

"Of philosophy," he answered.

"Your other occupation?"

"One must live," he explained.

"Why did you not become a monk or a Lutheran priest?" Kelley, who was nominally Church of England, knew that while most were not, there were some highly educated clerics.

"I am not religious," the young man said.

"Ah, you are a doubter." There were some such, even within the ranks of the clergy.

"My opinions do not concern you, sir."

And so, without further ado, the two worked out the details of their transaction, the sufficient amount that would be acquired over the course of a few weeks. At the end of their short conversation, they shook hands as would any two reasonable men consummating a business arrangement.

"And what did you say your name was?" Kelley asked.

"I did not say."

DR. DEE WAS not a physician, although he had studied medicine along with law. A mercer's son in the court of Henry VIII, he had attended Cambridge with distinction, lectured at his former school, on the continent. Mathematics was his passion, Euclid his devotion, the occult a kind of sideline, which in his time was part and parcel of a scholar's general concern. He possessed the largest library in England, was a court intellectual, a lover of puzzles and codes, and dabbler in magic. He was reputed to be the one who found out that the Spanish had intended to burn down Alden Forest, the very tim-

ber the British were going to use to build their naval fleet. His quick
work in getting word back to the queen saved the forest that saved
the boards that saved the fleet, which went on to defeat the great
Spanish Armada. Furthermore, in his astrological capacity, he predicted the bad weather on the day the Spanish were swept away by
winds. Thus, it could be said without much exaggeration that Dee
saved the day. And while he was not of a swashbuckling nature, he
had garnered much respect in the cloak and dagger business, anything to be of service.

Now, deserted by his monarch, far from home, trapped in the
Powder Tower laboratory as the chief alchemist involved in the
longevity elixir, this august gentleman had to use all his ingenuity
and cunning to simply save his own life. Fortunately, the Powder
Tower attracted talkers. Everybody who was anybody in the fair city
of Prague must stop by, take a gander, offer advice, and pass the time
of day in desultory conversation about the brewing tubs. Karel was
regularly ensconced in the warmest corner and had beer sent up
from the Golden Ox. Kepler and Brahe stopped of a morning after a
night of stargazing. Kepler, especially, who was not happy with his
wife and was known to doze off in various places, made the tower his
second home. Pistorius, the confessor; Crato, the second-in-com-
mand physician; Rumpf, the advisor—all liked to grace the laboratory with their illustrious selves. Even Rosenberg, the alchemists'
host, was wont to drop by when things got slow at court—every
morning, it turned out—to keep them posted on the virility liniment
they had prescribed. Václav, too, a friendly sort, brought his son, Jiří,
a child of much promise, to meet the alchemists, get their signatures
in his chapbook in which he wrote down quotations from his read-
ings, thoughts of the day, things of note.

"What is Kirakos's chess game like?" Dee asked Brahe casually one
day as he bent his lean torso over a boiling pot. There was nothing in it
but water and a hunk of pyrite. This was supposedly calcinato, the
third step in the alchemical process—the heating to a high temperature to effect changes, that is, purgation of stone. Brahe, Jepp, and
Kepler were ringed around a large bowl of water, a large stone in the
middle, the lodestone. Having already had a few mugs rushed up from
the Golden Ox, they were wagering on its weight, did not care about
its properties or magical potential. Wood carriers, as always, were

busily running wood into the place to feed the ever-blazing fire. Kelley, poseur extraordinaire, was reading Ramon Llull's *Book of the Lover* at the desk, could not be disturbed. Quarters, frankly, were crowded.

"The physician Kirakos plays like an Arab," Brahe said from an X-chair, one that could be folded and moved around. He reached into the pouch of his codpiece, where valuables, the family jewels, were often carried, brought out a little gold box, snapped it open with proud display, and pinched some of the Indian leaf, minced into something you could snuffle up your nostrils. How Brahe did this with half a nose was a puzzle to Dee. Furthermore, he sounded like a pig rooting for truffles. Kelley had agreed that tobacco was quite the rage among those who could afford it. Brahe insisted it cleared the mind like nothing else.

Dee threw some copper into his pot of boiling pyrite to blacken the brew. Copper belonged to Venus. From a lidded jar with a picture of a man with a lion's head, he took a spoonful of rosemary.

"What is that you are adding?" Brahe asked. "It looks like rosemary. Turnip soup?"

"Ground rhino horn," Dee answered. "Very efficacious."

"For what?" Kepler asked skeptically.

"Anything you can think of," Dee answered.

"I have heard say," Brahe said, "that rhino horn is good for husbandly duties."

"Perhaps," Kepler said, "if you are a husbandly rhinoceros."

"So what is Kirakos's style of play, did you say?" Dee pressed.

"He keeps his queen as zealously as the king, uses his horses until there is sweat on their flanks, sacrifices his pawns easily. Too easily. He does not know what to do with his bishops, whereas with his rooks he is a bold master, making them bravely guard the fort."

Dee went over to check the alembics, vessels with round, bulbous bottom and swan necks, used for distilling. In these, he and Kelley had poured their own urine.

"But of course, Kirakos is an Arab," he casually added.

"Not really, Dr. Dee," Brahe said. "He was taken as a slave to Istanbul. They conquered his country, his people, and he hates them like the very devil."

"How do you know?"

"How could he not?" Brahe reasoned.

Dee feared for the legs of the chair Brahe was sitting on. Jepp was nosing around. Kepler stood at the window. Even when stars were not out, he could not help but study the sky.

"He says if there is one thing he hates, it is the Turks."

"Perhaps he protests too loudly."

Brahe sniffed the air. "It smells terribly of urine around here."

"Eternal life," Kelley said, looking up from his book, "often has a moldy smell."

Jepp was rummaging among the containers kept low on the floor. He opened one lid, stuck his finger in, tasted.

"Careful, Jepp," Dee said. "There are many poisons and potions and powerful substances all around. You have just opened the arsenic jar."

"It tastes like flour," Jepp said.

"It may very well taste like flour," Dee said.

"Jepp," Brahe admonished.

"Kirakos does not like to visit us here in the laboratory, I have noticed that, only in official capacity with the emperor, it seems."

"In the morning, Dr. Dee," Brahe said, "Dr. Kirakos is indisposed; tired from the night before, he rests. Like Noah, his Armenian forefather, he is fond of wine."

"The Muslims cannot drink."

"Well, he is in Prague, how can you not drink in Prague? Besides, he is of Christian blood and thus can drink himself under the table if he so likes."

"Kirakos is a wizard, I have heard," Karel said. "One of the devil's minions. In his bedchamber, he has a magic wand."

"Really," Kelley responded. "How interesting."

"And he has a magic carpet, a special lamp, which, filled with oil, creates visions."

Kirakos also had a special bed brought from Egypt, more like a long chair with a headrest than a bed, upholstered in a fine velvet the color of dried blood. He reclined on it whenever he had the time, and on this day he could think of absolutely nothing better to do—certainly not go outside. Spring in Prague was always colder than you would think it should be, and the air had a shrill, sharp edge to it. It amazed him that people would point out, as if they were gracious feats, the beginnings of buds of snowbells, forsythia, daffodils, and tulips in the castle gardens. Well, in the case of tulips, Kirakos made an exception. They came, as did many things, from Persia or Turkey, and were appropriated by the Europeans, as were so many things, for their pleasure and palate. Under Suleiman the Magnificent at the Topkapi, the royal gardener was the royal executioner, the *bostanci-basha*, and anybody caught stealing a bulb was executed. Busbecq, an imperial botanist of Rudolph's father, Maximilian II, supposedly smuggled some bulbs out when he was in Turkey, but Kirakos believed they were in the West earlier. At the Battle of Kosovo in 1389, the chopped heads of the Turks in their turbans were said to look like a field of tulips. The Dutch loved the tulip as much as money, he had heard, and he did not blame them one little bit, for what else did they have in their cold, flat, soggy, gray country?

"You must ask Maisel, if you want to know about Kirakos. Maisel knows everything," Brahe suggested.

Maisel had not visited the laboratory yet, but the following day he appeared late in the afternoon.

"Mayor Maisel," Dee said, bowing low. "Welcome to our laboratory."

"Brahe said you wished to talk to me?"

"Indeed. I do. I do. Please come in."

Maisel was a very handsome man, Dee noted, meticulous to a fault, with a carefully clipped black beard, elegantly made clothes in subtle dark colors, and he appeared in every way the courtier, except, of course, for the yellow circle he wore on his doublet breast. Dee tried not to stare at it, be distracted by it, for it made him think, as it was no doubt designed to do, that there was something different about this gentleman.

"And how are you coming along?" Maisel asked. He was a man in his prime, but he carried a walking stick, as a Christian courtier would have a rapier at his belt. The Jews were not permitted weapons, Dee knew.

"As well as can be expected," Dee said.

"Hello, Herr Vojtech," Maisel said.

Karel was in his usual spot, had become a fixture of the place.

"How is Oswald?" Oswald was installed on the first floor, where there was a small, sheltered space for horses.

"Oswald is quite well, thank you, Herr Maisel."

Kelley was reading a book about people called Zoroastrians who worshiped fire and could walk on coals. The other habitués were thankfully absent on this day.

"And so how is it at castle," Dee asked his guest, "these days?"

"The emperor is having trouble sleeping." Maisel's voice was somewhat quiet. One had to lean forward to catch his words. "He is not feeling well."

"Ah, that is unfortunate. His limbs, his stomach?"

"His head, his eyes. His ears. He sees and hears things which are not always there."

"Distressing." Dee shook his head. "He sees things like what?"

"Like somebody in the curtains with a dagger in his hand. Little animals running around. Sometimes he believes he is under the water with the fishes." Maisel pointed to a glass vessel. "What is this?"

"That is an alembic. We use it for the sublimato. You see, Herr Maisel, we take a solid, heat it, and it passes directly to the vapor state, and then we condense it back to the solid form?"

"Why?"

"All of our seven stages involve transformation, or you could look at it like a kind of cooking. In cooking, you combine the ingredients, the parts to make the whole, the dish."

"But it is still the same, is it not, in another form?"

Kelley looked up from his book, signaled Dee with his eyebrows to proceed cautiously.

"It is a mixture composed of several things, but yes, they, through the process of heating substances, are transformed," Dee continued in elevated tone. "Very complicated. Earth, wind, fire, and water. Alchemy is not for the uninitiated. We have our secrets, we keep our secrets. So tell me, sir, you have known Kirakos a long time?"

"Not long." Maisel smiled.

"Kirakos is from Armenia, I hear," Dee pressed on.

"He is Armenian from Azerbaijan, a small country north of Persia and west of the Caspian, really part of Persia. The Turks conquered it and Kirakos was brought to Istanbul as a slave. Actually, their system of slavery is unique." Maisel did not like gossip, disdained it, yet he spoke openly with Dee because he and the rabbi had concurred that the fate of Judenstadt and the alchemists were closely linked. "The foreign slave boys, if they are hearty, are trained for the army and, if bright, educated for the government. In the Turkish society, each man proves himself by merit, not birth, and great favorites and advisors from the corps of slaves have fared well. The sultans' elite bodyguards, the janissaries, loyal to the death, are slaves, and in the Ottoman Empire, better to be a foreign slave than a second or third son of a sultan, for competition for the suzerainty is taken care of by specially trained executioners, who are mute and use cords for gar-roting, red silk for royalty."

"So Kirakos was one of the gifted slaves."

Maisel shrugged. "Still is, I would think."

"But he has run away from the Turks, sought asylum here, is that not the case?"

Maisel narrowed his eyes. "Yes, that is what the emperor likes to believe."

"Is Kirakos a Turkish spy?"

"I think so," Maisel answered.

"But his country was devastated by the Turks."

"He was a young boy."

"And has forgotten?"

"I do not think that Kirakos forgets a thing, Dr. Dee." Maisel put his hand on his chin, stroked his beard, and walked about pensively. "If you will let me indulge myself in a little philosophizing? Do I have your permission?"

"Of course, of course."

"Kirakos was educated by the Turks. Education can be persuasive, and it is very human when you are in a situation from which you cannot escape to identify with the strong."

Kelley, who was feigning concentration on his book, paid close attention to this talk. Maisel hit his left palm with the knob of his walking stick as he pondered aloud, paced the floor.

"I have heard of prisoners, Dr. Dee, who come to love their prisons and, given the opportunity to leave, cannot."

"It is apparent that you have given some thought to this, Mayor Maisel," Dee said.

"I have indeed. Kirakos interests me."

"Because he is evil?"

"Evil? Is he evil?" Maisel paused. "Kirakos is cynical, and perhaps that is a kind of evil, a failure of the heart, as our rabbi would say, an undue elevation of mind. Perhaps all of us have the opportunity to choose evil, and some more opportunities than others. Kirakos has not truly been tested. I believe our emperor could be called evil."

"The emperor is stupid," Kelley retorted.

"He is mad, yes, his thinking clouded from time to time. The emperor has his visions, his manias, his great sadness, which he cannot control—but stupid? No, he is not stupid. He is cruel, selfish, a man obsessed with an idea that he wants to make real no matter the cost to anybody. And since he is emperor, the cost can be considerable."

"I find him kind of a buffoon," Kelley went on.

"A dangerous one, Master Kelley. Do not laugh at or take him lightly. Although the emperor may be more mad every day, do not underestimate his capacity for harm. He is not a holy fool. Far from it. If killed by a man not in his right mind, you are nonetheless dead."

"So Kirakos?" Dee wanted to know more about him.

"No mother, no father, Dr. Dee. And the Turks, no doubt, treated him well. You know the story about Suleiman the Magnificent?"

Dee shook his head.

"He took a Hungarian, or maybe she was Romanian, slave named Roxelana for his harem. She became a favorite concubine in the seraglio, had the sultan so much in her thrall that he married her. As queen, she convinced Suleiman that his firstborn son by his Turkish wife was plotting against him; Suleiman had him strangled even as the young man called out Father. Roxelana's own son was next in line. Which goes to show."

"Goes to show what?"

"Many things, Dee, but mostly the nature of power. The decisions are life and death."

"And what do you think is Kirakos's intention?"

"Dr. Dee and Master Kelley, the Ottoman Turks want to bring down the Habsburg Empire."

"Why do you not tell the emperor that Kirakos is a spy?"

"I like my head. And there are other heads I like, too."

19

I T WAS RAINING that morning, a dull, incessant rain. The sky at nine was still dark, and even though their room was on the bottom floor of a three-story building, the walls were streaked with water seeping through the overhanging eaves. They had ale for breakfast, a heel of bread. Everything gave off a damp, rotting smell.

"Well, wife, no work for us," Zev said. "And nothing for dinner save hot cider."

There was a tap at the door.

"Who can that be?" Zev rolled his eyes heavenward, went to the door, then bowed low. "Ah, come in, do come in."

It was Perl, the rabbi's wife, and looming behind her like an uprooted tree was the golem. By now the Jewish community was accustomed to the big man in their midst.

"Yossel needs outfitting. Maisel will pay for the clothes, the shoes," Perl said.

Yossel dared not sit in the chair for fear he would break it. He stood, trying to make himself small, yet the room was filled with him. He tried not to look at Rochel, yet he was aware of her in all his parts.

"So good to see you, Perl," Zev said. "I was just telling my wife how busy our day was to be, but we always have time for our friends, do we not? Rochel, bring the cloth so they can dry the rain off themselves."

"Yossel requires breeches, an undershirt, a doublet of parchment, boots of buckskin." Perl wanted to get this over with. "Unlike the rest of us, he is to be clothed in leather. The suit of a warrior."

"Yes, I can see the big fellow needs some new clothes."

Yossel was still in his crude suit of blankets, his breeches more skirt than pants, his doublet more tunic than bodice. At night his clothes served as blanket. The first night in residence at the Loews', he stayed awake on his bed of straw by the fire so as not to lose a minute of life. From the kitchen, he listened to cats pouncing on rats, the wind whistling through the bare branches of the trees, unhappy spirits in the graveyard, and from one of the rabbi's daughters' rooms he could hear the sounds of her and her husband pleasuring each other. The other son-in-law slept with loud snores. Some of the children whimpered like dogs in their sleep. The rabbi tossed and turned. Perl said words like "Look out," "Help." Yossel wished he could talk to his family, greet them in the morning with: "Nice weather we are having today, and how are you? Please, some more kasha," and "Yes, thank you," and "Come here, little Fiegel, give your uncle a kiss."

"A suit of sheepskin and boots," Zev was saying, "the shirt you are thinking, Perl, at the size you are thinking, to be good, expensive."

"To be sure," Perl said dryly. She looked over at Rochel, who was looking at the floor.

Yossel wished the lovely woman would look at him.

Zev had, of course, his own ideas about Yossel. Passover, near Easter, was a favorite time for violence against Jews, true enough, but what was the exact nature of the threat this year? He had gone to the meeting, but instead of being specific, the rabbi reminded them that Spain and Portugal were home of Inquisitorial tribunals. Long ago, the Crusaders, on their way to redeem the Holy Land from the infidel Moslems, had killed all German and Italian Jews in their wake. Even in Prague, the Christian year 1389, there had been a rampage in which three thousand Jews were hanged, and as recently as the middle of the sixteenth century, the town councils had tried to get them expelled from the city. In the 1500s, all their books were banned and gathered, taken at great expense to Vienna, where they were burned. The rabbi pointed out that they, in Judenstadt, were so accustomed to persecution that they thought Prague was a haven for Jews, a good place to be Jewish, yet, he countered, to step out of the walled confines of their neighborhood was a serious risk. One could be pushed down, trampled, stabbed, all without recourse. Do we not try to live in peace and harmony with our neighbors? the rabbi asked. We do, we do, the meeting of all the men answered. Have we done anything to deserve death by their hands? No, no, they all replied. People had heard of a golem made in the Polish city of Posen. If Posen could have a golem, Prague could, too.

Other than the persistent precariousness of Judenstadt, Zev saw no need of the golem, had not heard of any definite threat, and living right across the graveyard there was little he did not know about what went on in the rabbi's household. For instance, he could tell you that the rabbi's two daughters had married lazy men who ate much, studied little, that Perl cleaned the house in a frenzy every Friday top to bottom, no help from her daughters, that the rabbi when he could not sleep at night spent many hours with the candle burning in his study.

If she looked at him just once, Yossel bargained with God, he would not look back again for the whole day.

"For the undershirt," Zev said with delicacy, "what I recommend is silk for its warmth in the winter, coolness in the summer. It is just the thing, Perl, and it just so happens we have some excellent blue. Wife, bring the bolt."

Rochel went to the cupboard, and with her ordinarily nimble fingers betraying her, she managed, finally, to unlock the doors. There was only one bolt of cloth, the blue-gray silk, the tone of the sky in the early morning of a winter day. Rochel had gotten it at a considerable discount from Master Galliano as a wedding present. It was the color of Yossel's eyes.

"The color of Judah's eyes," Perl asserted. "How nice."

"A fine color. Wife, let the rebbetzin feel it."

Perl looked over her glasses, pinched the fabric, as if sampling a fruit for softness.

"Maisel will surely want the golem to wear the best," Zev added.

"Yossel," Perl asked, "what do you think?"

Yossel straightened himself a little, looked down into Rochel's eyes. Rochel stood fixed to her spot.

"Wife," Zev reprimanded, "be cordial to our guests."

Rochel, embarrassed to be treated like a child in front of Yossel, hated Zev at that moment. Her neck went lobster red, and the color traveled up to her cheeks.

"And how is the rabbi, Perl?" Zev asked politely.

"He is alive."

"The rest of the family?"

"They are alive." Perl knew better than to brag of the accomplishments of her husband and children, praise their good health, their many fine attributes, for that would attract the attention of the Evil Eye.

"So you must stretch out on the floor, Mr. Golem," Zev said. "Wife, get the string."

Rochel got the measuring string from the hook on the wall, trembling all the while.

"Women, if you please . . ."

For modesty's sake, the women had to go outside, wait under the eave.

"The crops need the rain," Perl said to Rochel.

Rochel nodded, clutching her cloak about her, as if cloth on her body could hide what was in her mind.

"Soon it will be Passover," Perl said.

Rochel nodded, tongue-tied.

"You have been married, now, how long?"

Rochel without thinking put her hands to her stomach. What she felt was not a baby, but she could not say it was not the beginning of life. She was cold and hot and cold again.

While the women were standing outside, Zev was getting the measure of the man.

"Now, Mr. Golem, just lie down." Zev knelt by Yossel's shoulders. "You hold the string for me." Zev pulled the string taunt down to Yossel's waist and put a little knot that he marked with red wax, and then he took it across Yossel's chest and made two little knots, which he marked. Zev did the same from waist to knees and across Yossel's stomach and hips. The giant was not ugly by any means, Zev realized. In truth, with his broad face and brow, unusual nose, expressive lips, Yossel was a fine-looking, well-proportioned man. He was just big. A shirt for him would take up the whole bolt, and the jacket and breeches would empty Zev's supply of sheepskin, and for the doublet he would have to buy from the trader who went to Frankfort once a year, and then to shod the man, indeed, Zev gloated, to outfit the golem entirely would keep him and Rochel in food for a month. Further, they would be able to repair the roof where the water was streaming in, get new shingles, and replace their needles, for the old ones were becoming blunt. He was a giant, this man, almost seven feet, but well formed. Did he have a member commensurate with the rest of him? Zed, wondered. And, of course, he must be circumcised.

"You can come in now," Zev called to the women.

The two women came back into the room.

"We must outline the feet." Zev had Yossel stand on a piece of leather and he outlined his feet with the same red candle wax. "You know, to be sure," he said to Perl as he crouched there, "we will need to be paid half in advance, for we must buy more leather, thread . . ."

"Yes, yes, to be sure." Perl took her purse, which was hanging on her belt, loosened the drawstring, and emptied it on the table.

"So good of you," Zev said.

"So when will the clothes and shoes be ready?"

"Well, if he comes tomorrow, Perl, I can do a fitting. We will have to stay up all night, Rochel and I, but for you Perl, nothing is too hard."

Perl took some coins from her purse, pressed them in Zev's hand.

"To get started," she said.

As soon as Perl closed the door behind her, Zev threw up his arms, did a little dance. "Wonderful," he exclaimed, clapping his hands in joy. "Do you realize, Wife, what this means for us? Clothing him? Oh, happiness, you are mine; monster, you are close to my heart."

"Monster?"

"He is very large."

"He is not that large. He is just somewhat larger than the rabbi."

"He is large enough to be in a fair. Ah, but tender lamb for the Sabbath, Wife." Zev came up to her, put his hand on her stomach.

"Husband, not yet."

"So, not yet." He seemed chastened a moment, then brightened. "But maybe soon, no? You must eat well, be strong so that next time . . . as it is meant to be. But let us not dawdle. We must set to work. First I must see about buying more leather. Can you cut the shirt today? Give me a tiny piece so I can match the thread. Can you imagine? We were sitting here worrying about our next meal, our roof leaking, and a silk shirt, a most expensive suit, and pair of boots, they just walk in off the street. This is the job of our lives, Wife, this will set us up comfortably."

"Are you not first going to make wooden forms for the feet size, husband?"

"There is no point in that, Wife."

"No point?"

"He will probably just have these one shoes, Wife. They do not live long, you know."

"What?" It felt like a stick was thrust in her left breast.

"They live short lives, like butterflies."

"What?"

"They are made to serve a special need, his breed. I do not know what the rabbi has in mind, but yes, he will have life taken from him when he has been of use."

"Why would Maisel spend so much money on his clothes if he were to die soon?" Rochel did not know why she was so upset.

"Yes, that is strange, but I know about these things, Wife; I am your husband."

"But it is not right." She was floundering here.

"The rabbi gave him life. He will take it away when the time comes."

A tear rolled down her cheek.

"I know how you mourn the fallen bird and every little creature." He bent close to her, letting his beard touch her face, which sent shivers through her body. She moved away quickly. "He has no soul, poor thing. I must inquire about the leather." He put on his cloak, pulled the hood over his head, opened the door. "Good-bye, Wife."

Zev closed the door. Rochel, hugging herself, went to Zev's rusty-looking glass, looked at herself. What I am doing? she asked the reflection. She then crossed the room, picked up the bolt of silk, held it to her cheek. Then the door opened. She jumped back.

"Ah, good, you are beginning. Forgot my money. Lentils for dinner sound good to you?"

"We always have lentils, Husband."

"Which are far more than what we anticipated this morning. Karel may drop by. Tell him to come back this afternoon. He and that mule of his; he talks to it, you know. Someday it may talk back, and I do not think Karel would be one bit surprised if it did. Lentils and onions will warm our bellies. The sooner we finish the clothes, the sooner we will be paid; the sooner we get paid, the sooner we eat better; the sooner we eat better, you eat better, Wife. . . ." Zev wiggled his winged eyebrows meaningfully. "Maisel, he is prompt, unlike the emperor, who does not pay his astronomers, Brahe and Kepler. Brahe is, of course, rich, but Kepler has not received wages in months. I have heard with my own ears that sometimes they have nothing in the kitchen to cook at the castle. Other than for the emperor himself. This morning, nothing. Tonight, lentils. Speak up, Wife."

"Husband, you are my husband." Whom, God help her, she could not abide at the moment.

"Of course I am your husband, who else would be your husband?

You came to me with only your hands. I did not require a dowry. Good-bye, again."

Only her hands. Grateful not to go into the workhouse, on the one hand, on the other hand . . . She suddenly forgot what Yossel looked like. In a flutter, she tried to recollect. Gray-blue eyes, tawny skin, black hair, and despite the rags he wore there was something sleek about him, and despite the circumstances of his fashioning he was perfect in his way, a way different from everybody else. She was different, too. And to think there was a man who held his tongue, had no tongue, did not constantly prattle at her, what a prize.

She went over to the spot where he had lain on the floor. His outline was visible in the dust, in fact, as clear as a paper cutout. Careful not to tread too heavily, not to erase the shape of his body with her skirts, she stepped over into his marks. She could fit in nicely. She let herself stretch out like a cat inside the outline of his body, stayed that way for some time, deriving both comfort and excitement at her boldness. However, by the time Zev returned from his errands, she was sitting like a properly married woman in her chair. She had severely swept the floor, boiled fresh washing water, and now she was staring at the fire, willing it to speak to her. If HaShem had appeared to Moses burning in a bush, surely He could make Himself known from within her fireplace. She did not like fire since her grandmother had told her about the massacre. Fire was her enemy, yet on this night the embers glowed like rubies. A virtuous woman is beyond the price of rubies, was that the message? A virtuous woman is a pearl beyond compare. In the time of the ancient Hebrews, immodest women had been stoned. Had not Leah reminded her?

"And look what I have brought you, Wife."

Honey and raisins? A blue dish? A pretty apron, a silver thimble, a dreidel of carved wood? Something beautiful?

He held up a chicken. It had been beautifully alive once, she would give him that. Its tiny, beady eyes were slit shut, as if it did not want to witness its own death. Zev had yet to realize she did not eat meat.

"And we get our leather tomorrow. It is to be soft, pliable, a dream to work with, butter in our hands, yielding to the needle like a child to his mother. As for the boots, let me tell you, that was not easy. I had to go to four stalls and then to a shop on the other side of the bridge. Calfskin, they had, doeskin, buckskin—but sheepskin? That took some doing, let me tell you. I saw Karel, by the way. He has a little awning over his seat to keep the rain off, and that stupid Oswald wearing that old hat, his ears stuck out, how silly he looked. Karel is going to help me fix the roof. He is very handy, hah, hah, hah. I bought some pitch." He leaned forward as if imparting some very important information. "This is what I was thinking: glue and pitch for fixing the roof, a few new shingles for the overhang. You said something about replacing the curtains over the bed. Of course, we have to wait until we finish the clothes. Karel already saw him, the golem, that is. Everybody on that side of the bridge knows about him, too. Except the alchemists. They are not permitted out of the Powder Tower except to go to Rosenberg's house. They say Rosenberg's wife is pregnant. Kepler and Brahe are quarreling again. Who gets to use the sextant, that sort of thing."

"Sextant?" If only he would stop talking, she prayed.

He took off his cloak, hung it on the hook, and came over to the fire, held his fingers out to warm them. He kept his gloves on, but there were no fingers in them, so he could wear them while working.

"Made of two bars, Wife, with an arc, it measures the position of the stars in relation to the horizon, other stars. That is how they chart the sky; it is one of those modern inventions. Kepler and Brahe are going to find all the stars, some say, talk to God."

"Ah." She used a geometer's compass sometimes to sketch on a gusset pattern under a sleeve or to figure how wide a skirt's waist and hem must be.

"All the instruments are Brahe's and he is very stingy and Kepler is very poor. Brahe is the one with the numbers, Kepler the one with the ideas. They need each other, but they cannot stand each other, how is that for a partnership? The alchemists, they say, get along nicely. And look, look what else." Zev drew out a bag.

Buttons, she thought.

"Lentils, as I promised. Now reach in, they are slippery."

She reached in and in the bottom of the cloth bag of slippery beans she felt a thin strip of cloth. She pulled it up. It was a ribbon, a green ribbon.

"For you." He smiled, sat down on the stones of the hearth, very pleased with himself. "It was quite a day, Wife, I must tell you. I saw people who had no shelter from the rain and must live in the mud of the streets, people who have no family or friends. We are lucky to have food in our bellies and a roof over our heads."

She looked at the streaks of rainwater forming patterns on the wall. They had pushed rags to the edge where the wall met the floor, which she had to wring out every hour. Even sitting by the fire, she had to wear all her clothes, her brown and gray skirt and wedding skirt, too. She recalled her wedding night, and how no object in the room gave her solace. But now they were her life. There were her scissors on the table, her silver needle, her wooden thimble blackened with use. The candle in the pewter holder illuminated the bolt of blue silk that needed to be covered against the dust when she put it away. She had arranged their few plates and jugs nicely on their shelf, and the bunches of herbs were fixed like bouquets in earthen jars all across the mantel. The string of wooden shoe forms, which had appeared grotesque to her, were now friendly shapes—people's faces and bodies, tiny trees, bridges, and horses. It was as if their room were a whole city in itself with a little forest behind it. The long looking glass multiplied it, made it two, as the two sides of Prague on either side of the river. In the spring, she would go with the women to pick mushrooms in Petřín Woods. They would see the tulips through the gates of the castle. Everything was going to be fine. Nothing untoward had happened. A pearl beyond compare. The rebbetzin, Perl, she would help her become the good wife she was destined to be, one who cleaned the pots, roasted the lamb, patched the clothes, honored her husband above all.

20

ISCUSSIONS WITH VÁCLAV, no matter the topic, were formal, emperor to servant, with Rudolph seated on one of his many thrones and Václav standing upright staring straight ahead as if listening to the wall across the room. And although Václav slept in the same bed with the emperor, bundled at the bottom, and was subject during the night to his kicks and fits, all the emperor's vagaries—his bad dreams, could I have another glass of water—Václav had never sat across from His Highness at a table. He knew the times Rudolph visited his mistress, Anna Marie, and attended him, both in disguise, on prowls around the Malá Strana looking for other sport. He had watched the emperor wager on chicken fights, roll the dice, play bowls, lose at cards, trip on his feet at tennis. He knew the music he liked, the old songs of troubadours—"When I see the lark against the sun/ Moving its wings for sheer joy"—his taste in books—bawdy Chaucer and Rabelais, wise Montaigne, Erasmus, supreme Catholic, whom Václav read aloud to the emperor seated in a straight-backed chair by the imperial bed. But the emperor had never inquired about Václav's health, Václav's home or family whom he visited whenever he could—on the nights the emperor was with his mistress or when Rudolph met with his confessor or insisted on being alone.

"Do you promise the elixir will work, Václav, do you promise in your heart of hearts?"

Václav sighed. "I am certain it will work."

"On your mother's—" The emperor did not even know whether Václav loved or hated him.

Václav's mother had been very old when she died, over forty, yet it had not been easy for him. He had loved her dearly. As he stood against the wall when she drew her last breath, his legs buckled and he slid right down to the floor, could not get up until his wife bade him rise, close his mother's eyes.

"I am certain, Your Majesty."

Václav could always recognize the signs of the emperor's bad moods. First, no sleep, no sitting still. He must have the full orchestra playing full volume day and night, chamber singers warbling their hearts out. Thoinot Arbeau. Jacob Handl Gallus. Tielman Susato. Bring on Pucci. Send for cook. New clothes. Then, exhausted, he would begin to slow down, spend more time with his collections, repeat how his prized picture, Dürer's *Garland of the Roses*, had been transported across the Alps, hand to hand in relay. In such condition, the slightest mishap proved beyond the emperor's ability to rebuff, so that a friendly growl from Petaka meant the animal wanted to bite his head off, an ambassador who did not bow low enough was too rude to endure. Numbers too complex to reckon, taxes would go uncounted. The utter weariness of life would keep him bedded in the morning; the descent of night would hurl him into a paroxysm of tears.

"Sometimes, Václav, I feel what is the use? Why live another day, let alone forever?"

"We all feel that way from time to time, Your Majesty."

"Do you? And then what do you do?"

Václav was not used to asking himself questions like that or noting his own state of mind.

"Well, I have a family, and then my job, Your Majesty." Here Václav had to laugh. "Sometimes I take a boat out on the river, row until I am tired." That was what he did when his baby daughter died. He rowed out to the middle of the Vltava. On one side was the castle and the glassworks, the brewery, the big water mill on Kampa Island, and on the other side Old Town, the spires of Týn Church, Vyšehrad. He had stilled the oars, hung his head, cried. His wife had stayed home making bread to take to the big ovens of the bakery, each loaf salted by her copious tears. His mother had swept in a fast fury, wielding the brush broom like a weapon against despair.

"Row a boat?" The emperor perked up for a minute, but then, in a second, fell back into his ill mood. "I should have another plan at reserve if the alchemists fail, should I not?"

"As soon as they finish the elixir, you will be able to travel, Your Majesty."

"Travel to stay in some uncomfortable castle, drafty and damp, Václav?"

"And go hunting, Your Majesty. Falconing."

"Hunting?" the emperor repeated dully. "Falcons." It was not even a question.

"And have a great feast. Invite all your friends."

"My stomach aches at the thought. What friends?"

"You and Petaka will be celebrating your birthdays soon."

Rudolph's birth date was July 18, 1552; Petaka was born on July 18, 1590. Brahe, the court astrologist, predicted that when the lion died, so would the emperor. Assiduously attended by the court physicians, the pampered beast risked, if anything, a bout of gout.

"Petaka does not bite me only because I feed him."

"And never forget you are rich, Your Majesty. Land covered in wheat and hops and barley and oats and rye, forests full of timber and game, rivers stocked with all the fish of creation, silver and gem mines. . . ."

Recently affairs of state were in a sore state of neglect. Foreign emissaries were ignored, and daily the Empire, already rough at the edges with the Turks hardly held at bay, was, at center, if not rotting, certainly souring with Protestant discontent.

"He who is rich pays the piper," the emperor continued to moan.

"The size of your court."

"The Turkish sultan has four thousand in his court."

"And handsome."

"But my handsomeness has not done me any good. The only woman I ever loved did not love me, and now she is dead." The emperor, too distraught for charade, had revealed the truth.

"Anne Marie, Your Majesty?"

"She does not count."

"You are revered far and wide for your sanguine temperament."

On the contrary, Rudolph's abiding gloom and frenetic extravagances were hardly secrets. Talk of it had spread to the far reaches of his Empire—throughout Bohemia, Moravia, Silesia, parts of Hungary, the Austrian lands, Tyrol, Saxony, Croatia. Traditional and close-by enemies, the intransigent Transylvanian counts, the Hungarian independents, and Polish soldiers, were always happy to hear of Austria's bad luck. Beyond the borders, the doge of Venice smiled in his soup and the courts of

France and Elizabeth in England were hotbeds of conjecture concerning the blighted Habsburg. Did you know? Is it true? Mad, you say?

"Then your collection, Your Majesty, not to be surpassed in any kingdom."

"Are you familiar with the count in Transylvania who has the secret of eternal life?"

"He is infamous, Your Majesty."

"Because he is a friend of the Turks, this count?"

"Not only because of that."

"I sent a letter to him a while ago, before Kelley and Dee arrived. And he has written back an invitation to stay with him in his castle."

"The roads are icy this time of year, Your Majesty."

"In May? I doubt it. Let us get another opinion on this matter. Bring Kirakos to the Kunstkammer, we will see what he says."

Kirakos was in his bedchamber trying to get some sleep. He had stayed up the night before, drinking and playing chess, and now, after some tossing about, he was just beginning to dream. He was back in Istanbul. It was warm, the air full of the scent of sandalwood. He could see the palms, the domed roof of the Blue Mosque. He could hear the muezzin call out, "God is great." He was slipping into a sweet sleep . . . when his nostrils twitched and he smelled with a start Václav, that lackey, standing by his bed. Although he himself had been born a Christian, Kirakos thought that on the whole they were very stinky people; they did not wash their hands before praying or eating, indeed, hardly bathed at all. And they were not very clever. For instance, they liked to burn books at the drop of a cardinal's hat, not just Savaronala's bonfire of vanities. During the Dark Ages, rightly called, they had burned Aristotle and Plato, the pre-Socratic Greeks, because they were not Christian thinkers.

"Wake up, Kirakos."

No love lost here, Kirakos thought, not opening his eyes.

"The emperor wants to see you."

"Am I not allowed a well-deserved nap? Cannot a man rest his head in the afternoon?" Kirakos opened one eye, then the other, sat up, stood up, kicked his Russian servant, who was asleep on the floor, downed a glass of wine, rinsed his mouth with another glass of wine, grabbed his bag. Following Václav, the three made their way to the other end of the castle, entered the gallery.

"Emperor," Kirakos exclaimed, rubbing his hands together, bowing his head, as if pleased at being roused from his slumbers. Whatever use made of the tidbits he gathered from the emperor's court and sent on to the caliph, or why the sultan wished him to go forth with the plan involving Kelley and Dee, for which he was congratulated in an official communication, Kirakos was not told. In the chain of command, he was only an underling who put missives in other hands, hand upon hand, until it reached Istanbul. All in all, it was a tedious enterprise.

"We are having a discussion," the emperor said, "and need your opinion."

Kirakos told himself to pay close attention, for he could not forget, always and everywhere, that if he failed the sultan, an official executioner, one who had become deaf with hot wax poured down his ear and made mute with having his tongue pulled out, would be dispatched to choke him with a chord. It was tradition.

"At your service, Your Majesty."

"Yes, yes, now tell me, what is your opinion of Transylvania?"

"A godforsaken terrain inhabited by barbarians."

"Come, now, Kirakos. Every place cannot be civilized Prague."

Kirakos looked at Václav. The count was not a friend to the Turks. On the contrary. Yet was not the death of the emperor the end of the chain? Was that not behind all his instructions from Istanbul? Must he obey to the letter or in essence?

"Whose idea is it, this scheme?"

"Mine, Kirakos," the emperor said. "Mine alone, for what if Kelley and Dee fail? I could not stand not to live forever."

"They will not fail. Furthermore, nobody pays Count Dracula a visit, Your Majesty."

"And why not?"

"He is bloodthirsty, Your Majesty, literally."

The emperor stroked his chin. Despite his hatred of blood, there was one exception. He liked pudding made of the blood of a hog, taken while still warm and steeped in oatmeal grouts. After three days of soaking, the groats would be mixed with cream, thyme, parsley, spinage, endive, sorrel, and strawberry leaves. Pepper, cloves, mace, salt, and a great store of finely shredded suet was added. His mouth watered at the thought.

"Like the woman who killed all those virgins and bathed in their blood to be young and beautiful forever."

"She died in prison, Your Majesty, an old hag."

"Perhaps because she stopped her beauty treatment. How old is this Count Dracula?"

"He cannot go out in the daylight."

"There are some that favor the night," the emperor countered.

"Rogues and villains," Václav put in. "Fiends and demons."

"You best stay right here, that is my advice," Kirakos said. "Consider how, on a long journey, you will expose yourself to your enemies." Here Kirakos paused. "Though I know well that Kelley and Dee will succeed, there is something closer than the count."

"Yes?" The emperor was very interested.

"I was going to tell you sooner, but . . ." Kirakos paused for effect. "It concerns the Rabbi Loew."

"The Jew who made stones into roses? Yes, yes, I have been thinking on him myself."

"He has made a man. I have seen him."

"What do you mean? The rabbi has a new son?"

"Not of his seed. He has created a complete man with his hands."

"The homunculus, a small man in an alembic?" The emperor jumped up, raised his finger. "Ah-hah, that is why the rabbi wanted to see me."

"Not a small man. He made a big man."

"Yes. I have heard that, too. Do you think he is to be set against me?"

"No, Your Majesty. Because of rumor that Judenstadt is to be destroyed, burned to the ground by townspeople," Václav interrupted. "That is why the golem was made."

"Do not be impertinent, Václav."

"Plans are afoot to kill all the Jews," Václav pressed.

"Just think of it," the emperor ruminated. "If the rabbi can create life, if that is possible, it should be a small matter to extend life."

"Stands to reason," Kirakos confirmed. "Although, of course, Dee and Kelley are coming along quite nicely with their elixir, I must say."

"It would be quite sad to let Judenstadt be destroyed, people who serve you—"

"Hush, Václav. I believe I would like a little bite to eat." The emperor pulled the rope that connected to a bell in the kitchen. "And new clothes. You know the breeches that matched the cloak I recently acquired with rich embroidery on it; send for the tailor who made that."

"Your Majesty." A servant from the kitchen appeared, bowed low.

"Yes, I am in the mood for something sweet. A light refreshment. Sweet pies."

"It will take some time, Your Majesty, the baking."

"Well, do not tarry. You have nothing on hand? Fry up some apple fritters, blueberry pancakes, honey cakes, quinces boiled in sugar and rose water, preserved violets and primrose, cowslips and gillyflowers, any sugared flower, or something with honey in it."

"Your Majesty," Václav said, "the Jews—"

"To make a man," Rudolph said, "no mean accomplishment. Not a mechanical toy?"

"Mud and mud," Václav answered.

"He walks and talks?"

"Walks, Sire, cannot talk. He is very strong, I have heard, worth twelve soldiers."

"What? Twelve soldiers? Jews do not fight." The emperor flushed red in the cheeks. "Send for this man-made man, I must see him for myself, and the rabbi, too, the rabbi, of course."

"And the two alchemists, Your Majesty?" Kirakos ventured to mention.

"Let them keep working. I want everybody in this city engaged in my eternity, and yes, get the tailor who made my vest of late. The fires, too, must be stoked for some serious baking."

"The tailor is really the Jewish shoemaker."

"What are you telling me, Václav, the shoemaker who is a tailor is really a Jew?"

"It is not the shoemaker, either," Kirakos corrected, "it is his beautiful wife."

"The Jew shoemaker's wife is the tailor who is the seamstress who sewed my vest? Where does it all end? Are the Jews taking over?"

"She is the most beautiful woman in Prague," Kirakos continued.

"A beautiful woman right in this city whom I have not laid eyes on? Most beautiful? I will be the judge of beautiful. Bring her to me, and the rabbi, and this . . . this golem thing. To think this is all happening under my nose. Where has my court been? What are they doing? And the council, has it met today? Where is that abominable Rumpf, he is supposed to be managing things, and Rosenberg, pry him from his wife." The emperor was not only up and out of his chair, but he was skipping about. "The seamstress, this Jewess, what is her most favored part, Kirakos?"

"Nobody has seen much of any part of her, Your Majesty," Václav answered.

"Her face," Kirakos said, "and her body."

"Well, that just about covers it, does it not? I must see her. I must have her."

"She goes nowhere without her husband. Their customs—"

"Be damned, Václav. How did you chance upon her, Kirakos?"

"Kirakos hides out behind their bathhouse, Your Majesty."

"I most certainly do not."

"How did you see her, Václav, if I may ask?"

"I have known Rochel since she was a little girl, Your Majesty."

"Rochel it is," Kirakos sneered.

"It all comes clear to me," the emperor said. "A vast conspiracy to keep me in the dark. And where is that execrable page? There must be something I can eat immediately. Some jam, a piece of bread. And fetch Pucci, singers first of all, have them do Monteverdi's *First Book of Madrigals*. The recorders, the curved serpents, my full orchestra. Hot spiced wine. Hurry."

"Your Majesty, would you like to take a little rest? Let me help you to your bed."

"Bed, Václav? I do not want to go to bed. It is day and I am to meet the most beautiful woman in Prague. Indeed, I must meet the golem man and the Jewess, and you dare to suggest I go to bed? I will bed her. She is married? All the better. What of the right of the first night, which always goes to the nobleman, the king, good God, the emperor, before the husband?"

"That old practice, Your Majesty, is out of fashion."

"Not with me, Václav."

21

YOSSEL, THE GOLEM, with the strength of twelve men, did women's work. He stirred the porridge, cleaned the chickens and fish for the Sabbath meal. He swept out the rabbi's house with the broom made of twigs, and with rags scrubbed the floor on his hands and knees. He scoured the pots with sand, cleaned the fireplace of ashes, taking them out to the compost pile, which he overturned every week, carried the slops to the river, washed them out with a residue of the ashes, brought the chamber pots back to be placed under the beds. He hauled water in buckets from the well in the courtyard to be used for the dishes, washed the dishes, dried them, put them back where they belonged in the cupboard. He chopped wood, stacked it, and gathered kindling in the forest. He watched the children, played games with them—bones and stones, bowling ninepins, hobbyhorse, he the horse. He accompanied the women to the synagogue, waited to escort them home, for even though he was considered a kind of eunuch, he was not permitted in the women's section of the synagogue, nor, of course, with the men.

That particular Monday he was in the courtyard washing clothes in a cauldron of water over an open fire when he heard the ruckus. At first Yossel thought the hooligans had come to burn down Judenstadt. He ran to the gates of the Jewish neighborhood.

First came a man in a motley of patched-together rags fluttering from his hips like a circlet of bright feathers. He carried a branch on which jangled cowbells, and chanted:

"Louts and cripples, vagabonds, I merrily bring.
Indeed, I preen and boast, nay, sing

Of our daily lot, for who wants what he is not
The whole world's vision he would blot.

"The fools," the children from their doorways cawed, and clapped. Women leaned from second-story windows where they were shaking their coverlets and throwing out their slops; men of the town streamed out from taverns, watching, arms folded, both bemused and somewhat taken aback.

The man in motley acted as herald for the parade; behind him came a sundry lot, misshapen, some lepers, those feeble in bone and mind, all in all grotesques on display marching to the rhythm of tabor and fife, and singing outrageous hymns.

"Lord God, who made us thus,
Beware we begin to lust."

The women of the town gasped at that. The men snickered.

"Ho, ho, pay our way
Lest we deem to stay.
We are the fools, the fools."

The line of freaks laughed, their tongues lolled out, they shuffled forward, sashayed back, twirled, and hobbled in rude dance. One woman, knock-kneed and humpbacked, played a haunting tune on her pipe. Another woman scuttled sideways on all fours like a crab. A man with carbuncles on his neck the size and shine of apples and twisted legs, limp hand, loped along sneering, teeth bared. A man with no nose shook a jug filled with pebbles. Two children with seal flippers for arms flapped hurray. A woman who thought she was a wolf growled and rolled on the street. A beautiful young girl whose hair was matted, clothes in tatters, her hands clasped in prayer, sang praises to the Virgin.

Yossel stood there, dumbfounded. Who were these people? The crab woman sidled next to Yossel, looked up from the ground.

"So what say, do you pay? Master Magnanimous, are you one of us?"

Yossel pulled back, opened his mouth, let out a groan.

"No tongue, no tone, no voice to speak." The woman cackled. She skidded around Yossel, pinched his calves. "Are you related to me, so weak?"

Yossel let out another groan.

"He cannot speak." The dog woman groveled on the ground next to his newly made boots.

A woman who had much hair on her face scurried in a circle, performed a double roll.

"Join us, join us, join the buffoons, the fools, feed us, feed us."

People from balconies threw down bread and bits of cheese, little bags of flour, cabbage leaves, turnips and toadstools, onions and apples, coins. Others threw dirty water and slops, and some women chased the begging folk with brooms, and men from the taverns undid their codpieces and made water in their faces, while little boys tried to chase the wretched group down the street and well away. They loped and scuttled their mad dance in a final flourish, then were gone.

Yossel's mind was tumbling. Join us, join us, the fools had said, and even if it terrified him to be one of them, to have the mirror held so close, the likeness seemed beyond refute. It would be so simple, would it not, to merely leave town, be on his way with them, not only acknowledge, but parade his difference, band together with his kind, not Jew or Christian, Bohemian or German, man or animal, lack or sufficient, but among a family of flawed? Yet his legs stayed rooted, duty-bound. Had he voice, he would have said, I am a fool, that is true, but fool that I am, I stay here. Then he realized somebody was standing in front of him. He looked down and remembered with a rush why he stayed, why he lived.

"For a moment I thought you were leaving and going with that band of beggars." She spoke quickly, adding more words, as if to cover up her preceding words. "You must pity them, for they have no roof over their head, no food in their bellies. But then, you must envy them for that, too. It is tempting. For them, difference is so visible, so straightforward; it must be a relief not to have to try to fit in all the time."

Yossel, of course, did not say anything.

"What I mean is that they are free to be completely themselves." She flapped her arms as if they were flippers or wings. "They can go anywhere, no doubt have been everywhere. Think of it. Today Bohemia, tomorrow Silesia. They escape, they see the world."

Yossel smiled his close-mouthed smile, shuffled his big feet.

"Your new suit and boots are nice, are they not? The silk was like handling a brook of clear water, and the leather was as soft as flower petals. First I made patterns, laid them on the cloth stretched straight on the table. I took chalk and traced lightly all around, and then with my grandmother's scissors, which I have inherited, I cut out first the shirt and then the breeches." She reddened at this, recalling how she had smiled at him once, and how she had tucked herself into his outline on the floor like a bird going to its nest. All of that was girlish play, nothing to take seriously, and, fortunately, was contained in the confines of her own mind. Now if only she could halt the flow of words tripping off her tongue. It seemed that they had all been waiting for an opportunity to come out of her mouth.

"Zev is at the market. I do not get out much." She explained this rather merrily, as if it were a matter of her choice. "So . . ." And she took a big breath, for she was really not accustomed to saying so much. Truly, the many words made her feel delirious, almost powerful, for at home Zev did the talking, she the listening. Sometimes she thought of herself as Oswald, the ragman's mule, Mr. Big Ears who had only hee-haw to answer with. Indeed, she was very much like Yossel, himself mute. "Making a piece of clothing is no easy matter. I had to pin the parts together. My scissors and pins, they are made of brass; I have a needle of silver. Next to my grandmother's scissors, it is the most precious thing I have, other than my wedding ring, of course." She twittered away, but saying *wedding ring*, and remembering how her wedding ring fell on her wedding day, she got a sick feeling in her stomach. The feeling disappeared like chaff in the wind in a moment and all was well again. Mainly, it was so wonderful to be speaking to somebody. She wondered at the number of things she had to say, for there was more, she knew, waiting to spill out, as if she were a kind of living book and should she roll up her sleeves and lift her skirts, she would discover letters printed all over her. While she pronounced, declared, stated, began to tell him the story of her life, she was so taken away with the ability of her tongue that, not thinking of other things, that is, what her feet were doing, she walked with Yossel toward the river.

"Last year there was a baby put in our walls, a dead one, when my Bubbe was alive, of blessed memory. Somehow the parade reminded me of that time. The baby was an orphan, like me. I had a friend once who had no father, or rather he did not know who his father was, although everybody else knew. "

He had to lean down to hear her. She noted his attention. She felt like a little child again, cared for, protected, or rather, she had never felt that way and now did.

"Look at the river, Yossel." It was greasy gray, roiling and inhospitable, with chunks of dirty ice lining the shore. "Is it not beautiful?"

He had measured his gait to hers, one of his steps to her every three or four.

"Then, after the garment is all pinned together, I do a rough stitching. It sounds contrary, for we cut the cloth into pieces and then sew them back together again. It is kind of a puzzle and takes much thinking. Do you think of yourself as an orphan? I know you must."

Across the river, the morning mist was lifting from the castle. First the ramparts with their terraced gardens were revealed, slits in the battlements only wide enough for arrows, and then the towers at the ends, one of them the Dalibor Tower, where a nobleman who led the peasants in revolt was imprisoned. He had asked for a violin, and his haunting melodies, played until his execution, moved all to tears. Then the Powder Tower where the alchemists worked came into view, gradually the spires of St. Vitus Cathedral.

"The closest I have been to the castle is to take a peek through the gates on the way to gather mushrooms. They say there is a stag in the Stag Moat who has golden horns. It lives in the Stag Moat, which in long-ago times was a real moat. Now fine ladies sit on the moat bridge, watch the nobles shoot deer from the windows when the deer are run through. It does not seem fair, does it? I know you agree. They say there are so many clocks in the emperor's collection that there is a clock for every minute of the day and night and that they are all made of gold and silver and gems. Master Galliano told us the emperor has toys that can move on their own, dolls whose eyes blink and puppets who, without strings, can march, and little wheels with animals that go up and down and 'round and 'round, and delicate birds with ruby eyes in golden cages who can sing. . . ." She stooped down, held up her skirt, and dipped her fingers in the water of the river. "It is cold. Do you know that there are fish under there frozen in the mud and in the spring thaw they will come loose. Can you just picture it? I know you can. Stiff as a board one minute, and then softening, and with a little bend, a little shake, there you are, off again down the river, like the parade of fools just walking on out of town. I once saw a carnival, which of course I should not have, but I was a little girl and my friend took me. There was a man riding backward on a donkey; they say he was a cuckold, which I am not sure what that is, and a bear on a leash from Russia. Do you know that my mother and grandmother came here from Russia?" Rochel could not help it; she was talking more than she ever had in her entire life. "Yes. You see, I have sympathy for the fools, those without arms or legs, the young girl who was talking to their Virgin Mary? She was mad, poor lady." She swallowed, looked over at him. He nodded. "It is more common than you think, madness. I have heard"—this she whispered—"that the emperor is mad."

She stepped out on a rock a little ways out from the bank, balanced.

"I am a bird," she cried out. "I can fly."

Then she hopped to another rock.

He shook his head no. No, she should not be skipping from rock to rock.

"Look at me, Yossel." She stretched her arms out, jumped to another rock.

She looked straight at him, smiled, wobbled a moment. In the next moment, she lost her balance, slipped, and with a sudden splash fell into the river. The dark water closed over her.

Yossel groaned and with four large steps he waded out, reached into the icy churn, feeling first a bundle of cloth, her skirts, then her leg; he found her waist, shoulders, and, grabbing her shoulders, lifting her up, he hauled her out. She sputtered, flipping in his arms like a caught fish, and then began to shiver so hard her teeth clattered together.

Dear God, he prayed. Dear God. He quickly carried her to the banks, looked about for help, but there was nobody about except some fishermen in their boats far out in the river. Rochel's lips were turning blue. Not thinking of anything, clutching her to his chest, he started to run. He ran as fast as he could, not seeing anything before him. He ran along the banks of the river, up the street to Judenstadt, through the gates of Judenstadt, and with one mighty kick he knocked open the door to Zev's house.

"My God," Zev cried out, "what has happened?"

Yossel quickly lay Rochel by the fire, began to rip off her wet, freezing clothes. He ripped off her top skirt first, which was caked in mud, then her underskirts, which clung to her legs. Zev ran to the bed, stripped the coverlets, dragged them over. Yossel wiped Rochel's legs dry. He tried to avert his eyes, but he caught a glimpse, saw again, as in the bathhouse, the meadow of broom flowers. Quickly the two men wrapped Rochel's legs with the dry bedclothes.

"I am going for the doctor," Zev said. "And to get some aqua vitae to warm her blood."

The women, who had seen Yossel running through Judenstadt and were not able to keep up with his frantic pace, arrived.

"Go, go," Zev told them, pushing them back. "Go home." He slammed the door, rushed out, leaving Yossel and Rochel alone.

Yossel undid her cloak, which was still tied at her neck with a cord, undid the laces holding her bodice together, and unfastened the sleeves. All she had on was her chemise, and he quickly lifted that soggy garment over her head. Her breasts were small when she was lying flat, but her nipples were like late summer roses, separate beings. As he gazed at them, Rochel sighed, and they changed in front of him from soft flat flowers to spring buds. Rochel opened her eyes, blinked, looked about. She was home, she could see, lying on the floor. She and Yossel were all alone.

"Yossel."

He had her head in his lap. And he held her up, covered her shoulders with the coverlet, turned her around to face him. Firmly, he started to work a dry cloth over her hair, which was caked in mud. He spit into the end of the cloth, rubbed it into the strands of her hair, which, shorter than his, stood up in little licks.

"When I was under the water, I thought I saw a fish." And she recalled the water of the mikvah, the water in the blue bowl she imagined her mother bathed her in, all the tears of her life. Her life was a blur. She was floundering under the water. The surface seemed far overhead. Without considering what she was doing, she let the coverlet drop from her chest. He could not help but stare. She took one of his hands, guided it to her. "This way," she said, showing him how to touch her. She closed her eyes, dropped her head back. His mouth followed his fingers. He kissed her neck, her shoulders, her breasts, and then her mouth.

"Do not stop, do not ever stop."

Then suddenly he threw the coverlet over her chest, nearly jumped across the room.

"You have revived her. I have brought the doctor," Zev boomed, throwing open the door. "And look." He held up a jug of brandy. "Ah, you are feeling better already, Wife; here is the rabbi."

Indeed, Zev was followed by not only the Jewish doctor, Rabbi Loew, and Perl, but held in the arms of Kepler was Karel. Oswald poked open the window with his head. Behind Oswald, crowding to see, hovered the group of women who seemed to lurk at every opened door and window.

"She looks quite well to me," Perl pronounced, observing Rochel's flushed cheeks.

"Cover your head, Wife," Zev demanded.

Perl brusquely took the edge of the coverlet, put it over Rochel's head. The doctor knelt on the floor beside his patient with his bag of tools. He put a trumpet-shaped instrument to her chest, listened on the other end. He put his hand on her neck, lifted her eyelids, had her open her mouth and stick out her tongue.

"I do not know how long she was under the water, Doctor," Zev explained, wringing his hands. " It is like ice, is ice, pure ice. Oh, wife of mine. Rabbi, only this morning I said to her, 'We are so fortunate to have a warm room.' Rochel, drink, drink, Wife. I, too, need a little sip. To think you almost drowned."

Zev lifted the jug to his mouth, took a long swallow, wiped his mouth with his arm.

"Once Oswald took a bad fall from a loose cobblestone on the Square," Karel began, "and everybody told me to shoot him. I nursed him day and night, night and day."

"Karel, your mule we do not want to hear about. " Perl did not like what she saw in that room. Rochel was uncovered beneath the bed-clothes, and Zev, the imbecile, had left her alone with Yossel. True, he was a golem. But Zev should be more careful. And now all the nosy neighbors. Where was everybody's sense of propriety?

"Everybody leave," Perl directed, "and get that animal out of the window."

"That is not an animal," Karel insisted. "He is my family."

"Close the window. All of you, go home, stir your own mush."

"Oswald is one of God's creatures, Frau Rabbi Loew."

"And we are to have dominion over them," Perl replied. "Not the other way around."

"We have all felt death's breath on our cheek," Kepler put in.

"What are you doing here, Herr Kepler?" Perl asked. "There are no stars in this room."

"Sshh," Zev shushed. "We do not want to give my wife a headache.

She has been through a terrible ordeal. Why were you out of the house, Rochel? When I came home and saw the house empty, I did not know what to think. You could have died."

The doctor closed his bag, stood up. "I do not think she has been injured. She is strong, young."

The rabbi, like his wife, studied Rochel closely. When they came into the room, she had gone from rosy pink to ivory white, and now her cheeks flamed. The giant had taken some clothes and made them into a little pillow for her head. Rochel was not saying anything, which, of course, given that Zev said so much, was not unusual. God help him, but the rabbi could not restrain himself from considering the lovely woman underneath all her blankets. Her naked arms were sticking out. Thin and firm. Lovely arms, they were. Perl's arms had long gone to pale flesh hanging like chicken skin, a loose fringe on bone. And the young woman had been without her scarf when they came in, her short hair framing her face like curly lace. Nearly in his grave, and still lusting. The rabbi was so ashamed he looked away.

"Let the men leave her to the care of the women," he commanded abruptly, harshly. He then called for his daughters, who had been peering in, to come inside, then he closed the window on Oswald's face. "That is better," the rabbi said. "Perl, bring her over some of the cabbage soup you made yesterday. Do you agree, Doctor?"

"Just the thing, Rabbi Loew. Excellent idea."

"I will not stint," Zev announced. "Anything, the most modern medicine to make my dear wife better. Please, Rochel, talk to me, and tell me, how do you feel?"

People, unused to the sound of her voice, held their breath.

"I feel better than I ever have in my whole life." Rochel said this with an extraordinarily immodest smile.

"She means she is happy to be alive," Zev interpreted.

Beneath lowered lids, Rochel stole a glance at Yossel, who was standing, hunch-shouldered, by the door.

"I have heard it happen, seen it happen," the doctor said. "The proximity to death gives us renewed pleasure in life, has been known, in fact, to enhance our sense of life, make us want to live all the more."

"Look at the emperor," Karel said.

"A fine example," Perl countered.

The rabbi peered over at Yossel. Yossel was not looking at anybody and he had moved to the background, kept his large hands folded in front of him.

"Did I not ask all the men to leave?" the rabbi asked, realizing with a start that he considered Yossel a man. "And the women to help?" The rabbi's daughters now crowded in, not knowing what they were supposed to do, and looked about, wondering how anybody could live in such dreariness.

"I want to thank all of you," Zev said.

"Get her some warm clothes," the rabbi instructed. One of his daughters, Zelda, the youngest, ran out. "And she needs fresh sheets and coverlets, Leah. Miriam, you go with your sister, bring some dry clothes." The rabbi, spent and perturbed, turned around. "Now, would the men please depart?"

Finally, the men filed out, but they stood in the street, huddling together against the cold. Yossel, however, crossed the graveyard, his head down, returning to the laundry in the rabbi's courtyard. Inside the kitchen, the daughters Leah and Miriam dipped a small pan into the large kettle of soup warming over the coals. Zelda grabbed a bundle of clothes and coverlets. Then the sisters, filled with self-importance over their good deed, marched through the cemetery back to Zev's room.

"Zelda brought you dry clothes you can borrow," Leah announced, acting as if they were the finest clothes in the world, and not garments from the rag bag ready to be sold to Karel. "And Miriam has some soup." The cabbage and carrots, the tasty onions—all the vegetables had been culled from the soup. So what was left was only a watery broth.

Rochel, who was still sitting on the floor, stood up, let the coverlet fall.

"For shame, Rochel," Perl gasped, for even at the bathhouse, women held a cloth in their hand at all times.

"You are shamefully skinny," Leah said. "No flesh on your bones."

"We are all women," Rochel countered, "just women." Rochel was confused at her actions, but happy nonetheless. She could not remember feeling this way, except perhaps when she was held high overhead the night of her wedding and was dizzy with wine.

"We may be women"—Perl detected something different about Rochel; quickly she spit on the floor to ward away the Evil Eye, for who knew what bad luck such beauty would attract?—"yet we owe it to ourselves, Rochel Werner, to remember from whence we came and where we will go."

"Dust," Miriam added.

Rochel slipped on the oversized petticoat, the undershirt, the skirt and bodice. Then she covered her head with a big loose scarf.

"That is better." Perl ladled some liquid into a bowl for Rochel, who, before she ate, washed her hands, said her prayer.

"Eat, and be strong," Perl said.

"Yossel?" Rochel asked. "Where did he go?"

"He left," Perl replied.

"He saved my life."

"He was there, I grant him that. And he has big arms—would he let you drown? But what were you doing by the water, Rochel, without your husband, if I may ask?"

"The parade of fools," Rochel explained to Perl.

"Oh, I see, so you have to be foolish, too?"

"I will have to make him some special dish to thank him."

"Yossel has enough to eat," Perl said.

"As a gesture."

"Gestures, Rochel, he can do without. Come, daughters. Mind yourself, Rochel."

Later that evening, with the people gone and all put to order, the room seemed very quiet. Rochel, now seated in her chair, stared at the flames of the fire. Zev, across from her, finished the cabbage soup. Except for her large clothes and the wet river garments hanging on a string near the fire, there was no trace of what had happened. But within Rochel's mind, the room was still filled with Yossel, and most clearly she could hear her own voice: Do not stop, do not ever stop. How could she say that, do that? Who was she, that she knew herself no more? And yet, and yet, she was exquisitely, gloriously alert, as if her whole life previous to that day had been a muffled sleep, her hands mittened, her blood stilled, her eyes closed, her breath shallow, her heart slowed. She had been one of the fishes frozen in the river and the spring thaw had arrived.

"Soon it will be Passover," Zev said.

She thought of the Vltava River, this time not frozen or running freely, but rather like the Red Sea with the waves parting, each side curling away, Moses walking on the dry seabed, leaving Egypt behind him. Yet her direction, while toward freedom, was a turning away from God's law. As a child and young woman she had not felt right in the world. Now that she was grown up and no longer merely her mother's disgrace and her father's sin, instead of redeeming herself she had, of her own efforts, within an afternoon's time, made everything even worse. How could she do what she did? Do not stop, do not ever stop. Struggle as she might, she could not call herself back to her former self, her sleeping, half-alive self.

"Do not cry, Wife. All will be well." Zev got up, put his head in his wife's lap, wrapped his arms around her waist. "Oh, Rochel, what would I do without you? If anything ever happened to you, I could not go on. I would die. You are my wife, my life."

"My hands, Zev, you say I only came to you with my hands." In another moment she would ask his forgiveness, tell him from the first moment when she had smiled at Yossel in the doorway. She would tell him everything.

"Do not say anything." Zev put his hands gently on her lips. "Say nothing. When I saw that golem carrying you, I thought you were dead."

"Zev." When she closed her eyes, she saw herself not married, or, in some mysterious way, more than married, somebody beyond childhood and the concerns of family, as though, through contact with Yossel, she had taken on some of his stature, become bigger, less invisible. Yossel made her feel like a grown woman. Yet he also gave her, she who had only the dreamiest sense of childhood, a chance to have a father, her only possible father. She could see Yossel holding her hand, huge by her side, leading her down the road, Egypt far behind.

Zev, her husband, she reflected, had been kind enough to marry her. He was generous and loving to her, but he had not chosen her on his own for her own particular sake. She had nothing to do with it, and in a sense, he had nothing to do with her. She was his wife. She could not help it, but her body felt no longing for him. Quite the contrary. And if he were to any extent father, he was the father who would fulfill his familial obligation to the letter.

"Zev."

"Hear me out, Rochel. You are more precious to me that anything. If you could believe that, you would be happy."

Yossel in the rabbi's courtyard relit the fire under his washing kettle, bringing the water to boil, dipping the clothes, which had been scrubbed—the babies' cloths, the daughters' skirts, breeches and jackets of the sons-in-law, Fiegel's little gowns. Gently, he rinsed them in the cauldron of clear water sitting nearby, stirring each garment with a stick. He rinsed them in the boiling water again, wrung them out, and straightened them carefully to dry on the walls, clouds of steam rising from them, as if they were hot pieces of meat dredged from the cooking stew. After the washing was done, he sat in the doorway some hours staring out at Perl's brown skirt, aprons, all that his family covered themselves in, yet what he was seeing was Rochel, her alabaster breasts, and the slope of her stomach. Without a tongue, he had not tasted her skin, but he could smell her on his hands despite all the dunking and scrubbing and water of the day.

Part IV

22

THE EMPEROR WAS surprised when he saw the golem. Not at his size, for he was expecting a behemoth, a man larger than usual, but he had envisioned something unformed, misshapen, and ill proportioned, a moving lump of clay. The man was not that ugly. He was not ugly at all. And although he wore the skullcap on his head as they all did, he was darker than the pale inhabitants of the narrow alleyways of Judenstadt who never saw the sun, and he was not narrow of face nor clouded of eye from studying a book all day. There was peasant broadness to his face that spoke of open spaces, the country, wind, and rain. His nose was wide at the bridge and at the nostrils, his lips full, and his eyes, set deep within his tawny face, were startling, a color very much like the rabbi's eyes, a gray-blue. His hair was very straight, very black, and covered his forehead in bangs like house shingles. He was Gargantua, the giant of Rudolph's schoolboy days when he and his dearly departed brother Ernst would sneak-read parts of Rabelais while Master Onion Bulb was absent from his squalid room.

"Your Majesty," Rabbi Loew said, bowing low. "You honor us."

Václav had seen Yossel in and about Prague before, yet something recently seemed to have softened his features. He moved with greater grace. Kirakos, who had seen Yossel that one time behind the bathhouse, was still at a loss to explain him. He was not a big, clumsy puppet who walked stiffly, each step a mechanical feat. He seemed in every way a man.

For this audience, the emperor had chosen a drawing room overlooking the ramparts. Petaka was asleep in the corner, sprawled on all fours like a dead turtle. In addition to the emperor's tall chair decorated in gold leaf and cushioned in velvet, there were a few chairs on the periphery of the room, the ones in the shape of X's which could be folded and transported, the Italian chairs called *sgabello* or Savanorola chairs, after the great judge or heretic, however one may choose, a large chest of lacquer finish with inlaid shell, a long table which held the usual array of clocks and gems, and, in a corner, a small desk. Tapestries made in Belgium depicted scenes of summer and spring in Arcadia. Although the rooms of the castle still held a chill and a fire was going, the grounds were turning from the oppressive gray of winter to the brackish green of spring. The butterfly cocoons were in place in the many drawer tables in Vladislav Hall. The furnaces in the Powder Tower laboratory were going day and night as great batches of elixir were being prepared for the first phase of the tasting.

Rochel had hastily put on her wedding clothes for the meeting, the blue skirt and bodice, her white shirt embroidered at the neck, but she felt shabby. Accustomed to the low ceiling and cramped darkness of her room in Judenstadt, the castle walls soared, and it was so bright in the room, it hurt her eyes. Instead of an open hearth, there was an oven, which pyramided to the ceiling, every part of the square tiles painted—white with blue drawings of baskets of fruit and windmills, wooden shoes, ships. Furthermore, the floor of the room was not wood, but of huge, flat stones, all evenly placed and polished and not strewn with herbs, but in some places carpeted with thick cloth woven into designs of flowers. In the corner was a throw made of a whole lion. The tapestries, she could tell, had been embroidered with the finest of silk threads, for the faces of the people—the shepherds and women garlanded in flowers—were so carefully stitched, they looked alive. I am in a fairy tale, Rochel thought, for the splendor of the castle was more lavish than Václav had explained to her when they both were children. Indeed, there was Václav himself, all grown up, tall as a thistle, in red silk livery, with a small crinkly beard. He smiled at her appreciatively. She inclined her head in a little nod.

Yet, the emperor, sitting very close to the stove, did not match his magnificent surroundings. True enough, he was in pure purple, the royal color. The sleeves of his doublet, of a purple so dark as to be almost black, were richly slashed to reveal a rippling silk shirt the color of white clouds on a summer day. The front of his doublet was not merely embroidered, but garnished with looped and braided cord, tassels and bows, complicated twists and turns. But for all this dressing-up, his chin was at such a point, it looked like the tip of a sharp shovel, and when he opened his mouth, Rochel saw that he had not many teeth, and the few he did have were stained brown.

"So this is the golem," the emperor said.

"Yes, Your Majesty. He is called Yossel."

Yossel bowed.

"And who is that hovering? Step forth."

Zev took a few steps, bowed; Rochel stayed well behind. Václav had told Zev that they were to be summoned to the castle for an employment and not to be frightened, yet Zev did not like this, not at all.

"The needlewoman, I want to see the needlewoman."

Zev took hold of Rochel's hand, drew her forward.

"Raise your head, woman, I am your emperor."

Rochel lifted her head, and as she did so her scarf slipped to her neck.

"Good God in heaven," the emperor declared.

"My wife," Zev said quickly, "Frau Rochel Werner."

"I have seen beautiful women," the emperor muttered to Václav, "the courtesans of Venice, the ladies-in-waiting at the Spanish court, English beauties, but . . . who is she?"

"My wife," Zev said again, fear in his heart. "Frau Rochel Werner."

"Can she speak for herself?" the emperor asked, "or is she, too, without a tongue?"

Rochel moved closer to Yossel, muttered, "Your Majesty," bowing low.

"Where are you from, my dear, and how is it that your marriage went unnoticed, for I, as your monarch, had the right of the first night."

"That is a barbaric practice," Rabbi Loew quickly interrupted.

"I regard it a venerable and highly appropriate tradition." The emperor's codpiece felt too tight, his breeches pinched.

"I believe you want something sewn for you," Václav whispered in his emperor's ear.

"Indeed." The emperor shook his head as if to rid himself of a bothersome fantasy. "I want a dressing gown. A dressing gown like no other before it or after it, of a rich brown, the color of your eyes, my dear, the color of chestnuts, and of a silk so fine it cannot hold still in your hands. Silk as slippery as a fish. Silk worn by seraphim, silk never before seen by human eyes."

"Yet spun by worms, Your Majesty," the rabbi said, in spite of himself.

"Worms?" The emperor was confused.

"He means silkworms," Václav quickly interjected.

Rudolph could envision a fitting session, see the dressing gown drop off him as he slipped wetly into her envelope.

"Embroidered with tulips. Is there any flower more various?"

Rochel could not help but smile a little at the thought of making this dressing gown, she in her room, the soot thick on the hearth, mice skittering where the floorboards met the wall, the stain of rain creating big, damp blotches on the walls.

"A multitude of tulips," the emperor continued. "Yellow tiger stripes on blackest red, white having shades of darkish maroon, white with one line of lavender down each petal and the palest of yellow with magenta blocks, the orange of Portugal. Do you have that, Frau Werner?"

Yossel nodded for her.

"You, the golem, can remember that much?" the emperor said.

Yossel nodded again.

"You cannot speak, but you remember. You cannot speak, but you understand. What is this? I have been fooled," the emperor exclaimed.

"We will see." Kirakos went over to the desk in the corner of the room.

The emperor stood up, stepped down from his dais.

Everybody followed.

Kirakos, with fine affect, dipped the feather quill into a little jar of ink, wrote on a piece of fresh white paper, "What is your name?"

Yossel carefully took the slender implement in his hand, dipped it in the inkpot, tapped it carefully to rid it of any drips, and wrote in a beautiful, ornate hand, "My name is Yossel Ben Loew."

The rabbi gasped.

"Well, well," Kirakos said.

"Yossel, why did you not tell me?" The rabbi found his voice to ask.

"He is mute," the emperor said, "how could he tell you?"

"Did you ever ask?" Kirakos inquired. "But any schooled child can write his name. Can this one reason?"

Yossel wrote, "What walks on four legs in the morning, two legs in the afternoon, and three legs at night?"

"Are you a man?" Kirakos said.

"I am a riddle," Yossel wrote, "made by man."

The emperor looked up at the rabbi.

"He is clever," Kirakos admitted, albeit grudgingly, "but there is clever and there is clever."

He moved closer to the emperor, whispered in his left ear.

"You are right, Kirakos," the emperor whispered back. "I declare, what an invention. And this has happened right under my nose while I spend good Austrian money to bring alchemists from England. Do you know how this creature, this machine, whatever it is, was made?"

"Would you step back?" Kirakos asked the rabbi, the golem, Zev, and Rochel. "We need to confer privately."

"Of course." The rabbi glanced anxiously at Yossel and pulled his little group into a close cluster in a corner of the vast room.

The emperor drew his advisors to him—Kirakos, Kepler, Brahe, and Václav.

"The rabbi used the Kabbalah," Kirakos said softly to the emperor. "No doubt about it."

"Then he must be a magus, for he has made a giant who reasons, no mean feat." The emperor's mind was full of possibilities, yet they needed sorting. "And the woman, my God, she looks like a Tartar, a Gengis Khan, but with gold hair. She is exotic, a queen. I would love to see her wrapped in furs—sable, ermine, mink—riding a fine black stallion naked."

"She is part Russian, her mother was a Jewish whore," Kirakos mentioned.

"Her mother was raped," Václav corrected, "by a barbarian. Now an attack on Judenstadt is planned right here in Prague, Your Majesty. That is why the rabbi made the golem."

"He is not going to cut off our heads, is he?" Rochel whispered to the rabbi.

"He needs our heads." But the rabbi was not at all happy at this turn in events. First of all, he felt the fool for not realizing the full range of Yossel's abilities; furthermore, the emperor seemed smitten with Rochel. No good could come of this.

"This rabbi, he is called a lion," the emperor said to his private group. "Why is that? Where is Maisel, by the way? He told me nothing of this, of the golem, the woman, the attack."

"In Hebrew both his names, Judah and Loew, mean lion," Kepler explained.

"Mr. Lion Lion. You seem to know a lot about Jews, Kepler, why is this?"

"We are friends, excuse me, I mean acquaintances, only in passing."

"Friends to a Jew? And yet you have not told me, your real friend, the friend who pays your wages, about this . . . this golem thing. Your real friend, you keep in the dark."

"The dark is full of light, Your Majesty, all the stars of the heavens. I live in the dark."

"Yes, yes." The emperor waved his hand dismissing Kepler.

"I wonder what the golem's sign is," Brahe mused.

"If you please, pay attention to matters at hand, men, do you not see what we have here?"

Zev whispered to the rabbi, "I have tried to live my life as a good Jew."

"Calm down, Zev."

"I will calm down when we are well on our way out of here, that is when I will calm down." Zev looked at his wife. "Rochel, can you make this marvelous robe he speaks of?"

"Shhh," the rabbi soothed. "Take comfort, Zev."

"In what, I ask you? One minute Rochel drowns, the next minute we are at the castle."

Yossel was trying to catch Rochel's eye.

"Let us hope he does not ask for more than a dressing gown," Zev said.

Yossel was thinking the same.

"So you are afraid that a few apprentices will set fire to your houses, is that it?" the emperor said, calling the Jews back to him. "Why did you not tell me?"

"I tried to, Your Majesty."

"Ah, yes, the yellow roses flying in the air. So, Maisel, why did he not tell me?"

"He made many attempts, Your Majesty."

"I can send some soldiers, Rabbi, many soldiers, my own Slovene guards to stand watch over your little neighborhood, to guard you night and day, if you would like."

"We would like that, Your Majesty. We would be grateful."

"How grateful?"

"Very grateful." The rabbi tried to smile.

"Good, good. You have created life, Judah. You are a powerful man."

"Not really, Your Majesty, and only with the help of the Lord are we able to do anything."

"Yes, yes. If God helped you once, surely He will help you again. This is what I propose: I send the troops to protect Judenstadt, you make me immortal. A simple exchange."

"Pardon me, Your Majesty, I do not understand." The rabbi felt a great weakness in his limbs. It was the afternoon, the time he would be resting in his bed.

"You have not heard of my quest, Loew?"

"I have, Your Majesty."

"That I brought two alchemists to make an elixir of eternal life, that butterflies are at this moment waiting to be born in Vladislav Hall, and once born will be fed with the elixir, that if these butterflies live for more than a day, my faithful servant and others will also drink this drink, just a sip, and that then, all proven safe and well, I will drink of it, thus live forever?"

Just talking of his plans excited the emperor. Petaka had awakened and was yawning. Dear animal, his proud owner reflected, he must live forever, too. He and Petaka, master and pet for eternity.

"You found the spell in your Kabbalah for making life, now find the spell for making me immortal."

"But there is no such spell, Your Majesty. The power of prolonging life and postponing death are . . . out of my hands."

"As could be said of creating life, Rabbi. Do not prevaricate. Did you not make the golem with your hands, with words? Surely it would be a simple matter to extend life."

"Your Majesty, we do not play with the Kabbalah."

"Saving your emperor's life, saving your own and everybody's in Judenstadt, you call play?"

"We do not need the troops to protect Judenstadt," the rabbi decided. After all, they had Yossel. Yossel would be enough.

"No troops? That is well and good, Rabbi, then just the secret."

"But Kelley and Dee, Your Majesty, are to provide eternal life, you have just said so." The rabbi hated himself the instant he said those words, for he knew that he was trying to save himself at the cost of another, which was against the Law and his temperament.

"I want to live forever and a day. If one formula is good, two will be better."

"But Your Majesty—"

"I want to be certain, absolutely certain, Rabbi."

"With all due respect, Your Majesty, we can only be certain—"

"I want what I want, nothing less." The emperor stamped his feet peevishly.

"Please, Sire. Our tradition. It is written—"

"Let me put it this way, Loew." The emperor leaned forward from his throne. "If you do not provide me with the formula, Judenstadt will not survive."

"Your Majesty?" the rabbi gasped.

"If you are worried about a few peasants and their torches, how will it be with pikes and cannons, harquebuses, what if all the instruments of modern warfare are brought to bear on the same crumbling walls, the same thatched roofs, your women, your children? What if the Slovene guards, the imperial army march on your squalid little neighborhood and those who survive are banished from the Empire?"

"But your father, Maximilian, promised the Jews safe haven. In the ancient day, Queen Lubice had a dream about us. This is Bohemia. Such things cannot happen here."

"It is indeed Prague, part of the Holy Roman Empire. It can happen anywhere, Rabbi. Let me remind you that you are a guest in my country, a Christian country."

"We are protected by charter, Your Majesty."

"Parchment is easier to burn than thatch, Rabbi."

"The Ten Commandments, Your Majesty, are written in stone."

"Come, come, Rabbi. Any strong hammer."

There was a collective intake of breath among the many gathered there.

"I am not serious, of course," the emperor said a trifle nervously.

Kirakos was intrigued. The emperor could start on a basically weak or far-fetched assumption, yet build upon it a most logical argument. The monarch was both beyond reason and yet could be quite cunning. Initially, Kirakos's mission had been to pose as refugee from Turkey's harsh rule, present himself as a practitioner of the

healing arts. Thus, he arrived in the emperor's court with recommen-
dations forged and falsified, although in truth he was a qualified
physician and certainly had the touch. When the opportunity to gently nudge the precarious balance of Habsburg power by gently nudg-
ing the balance of the emperor's mind, never too stable at best, had
fallen in his lap, a stroke of luck, how happily had that news been
received by Istanbul, with what great favor was he then regarded by
the sultan himself, Mahomet III, although Kirkakos at moments
remembered Mahomet had ordered the silken cord for each of his
nineteen brothers. But now official acclaim is what awaited him—
garlands of marigolds, plates of macaroons, dancing girls, and laughing boys. Yet he felt strangely empty over his coming victory. No, no,
Kirakos, he warned himself. Do not feel sorry for anyone. Why spend
a moment in regret? Thirty thousand Turks and Serbs had fallen at
the Battle of Kosovo in the Field of Blackbirds.

"What are you saying, Your Majesty?" The rabbi's forehead
matched the color of his beard, a ghostly white, and the tall man
seemed diminished, defeated.

"What I am saying, Rabbi, is if I am not given the secret of immortality, every Jew in Prague will be killed, plain and simple."

The room, quiet before, became so still that Petaka's breathing
was audible.

Yossel stepped forward, motioned with his fingers that he wanted
to write something.

"Very well." The emperor moved over to his desk. Yossel followed.

"Harm a single hair on a Jew's head," Yossel wrote, "and there will
be no secret of immortality."

"He knows the secret?" The emperor asked the rabbi.

"We all do, we all know a part, a piece," Yossel quickly wrote.
"Without all of us alive, the secret of immortality will be lost."

"Touché," Kirakos commended. "Very good, Yossel, you play a
good game."

"But what if it is true?" The emperor sputtered.

"It is not true," Kirakos said. "Anyway, you have the butterflies."

"Yes, yes, I have my baby butterflies. But I do not understand you,
Kirakos."

Zev was in a daze. What secret? What was the answer to what the
golem had posed?

Rochel, who could not read, did not know what Yossel had written, did not know what was happening, except that they, the Jews, as always, were in grave danger.

Kepler looked positively stricken at the turn of events.

Brahe had to relieve himself.

"Rabbi," Kirakos said. "I am sure the emperor wants you to go home and study your books. You and your erstwhile, ersatz son."

"But wait, wait." The emperor was in great panic. "We must arrange a time, a place, a way. No Jew is to leave town, do you understand, no Jew. Now all go, go, just go, my head is hurting. But you." He pointed to Rochel. "You stay here."

"Your Majesty," Zev spoke out.

Yossel stepped up, his arms tensing, his fists clenching.

"She must be home as duty to her husband," the rabbi protested.

"I am the first man in the realm. Duty to me is first, Rabbi."

Rochel cast her eyes frantically about, spotted the window, a pair of doors, the guards, took a step forward.

"Seize her," the emperor commanded.

Two burly Slovenes clasped their meaty arms around her. Others grabbed hold of Zev, and the rabbi's arms were pinned behind his back. Both men were dragged from the room. Yossel, his hands free, about to attack the emperor, was surrounded by fifteen guards, swords drawn. He was going to storm the throne anyway, but Václav deftly moved behind him, requested that the giant bend down, whispered in his ear:

"Make no resistance, dear fellow, I will see that she is not harmed. Go quietly to the hallway. I will follow shortly."

"Take the girl to the green bedchamber," the emperor commanded.

"Please no. Have mercy," Rochel sobbed as she was pulled away.

Zev, the rabbi, Yossel, pressed to the wall in the hallway by a line of guards, could hear Rochel's pitiful protests. The rabbi started praying, Zev began to curse, and Yossel kicked the wall with his heels, his body racked by groans he could not articulate into words. When Václav emerged from the emperor's reception room, the three were at their wits' end.

"I will see to them," the valet said to the Slovenes. Accustomed to Václav's instructions when the emperor was in a low mood, the bur-

ley soldiers let down their guard and quietly marched to their quarters—right, left, right, left—their feet echoing down the passageway.

"What can we do?" Zev wrung his hands.

"Do nothing," Václav answered. "Nothing will happen to her. I will
see to it."

"Do you promise, Václav?"

"Yes, Herr Werner, I promise. I will have Karel bring her back to
you before the night is over."

"Untouched?"

"Untouched, Herr Werner."

"Thank you, Herr Kola." The rabbi glasped Václav's hand warmly,
inclined his head.

"Your loyal servant, Rabbi."

23

A S THE THREE Jews left the castle grounds, the sky became dark with heavy gray clouds, and people, silently pulling their cloaks about them, began to rush home to close their shutters, make fast their doors, herd their animals into their pens. Up at the castle, the fires were banked high with logs. Torches were set ablaze.

"Would you like some nice hot spiced wine, Your Majesty?" Václav suggested sweetly.

"To be certain, what a good idea."

Václav backed out of the room, ran toward the wine cellar, stopping for a moment at Anna Marie's apartments. When he returned, he was followed by several servants bearing a silver bowl of wine and a set of cups.

"This is the life," the emperor cooed.

"It may be, but the Jews do not have the secret." Kirakos had downed his cup in one swallow, quickly reached for another. He felt vaguely irritated.

"If they do not have the secret, they will be killed, Kirakos, and if they have the secret, after they give it to me, they will be killed or have to do away with themselves."

"They will not commit suicide," Kirakos reflected. "These Jews are not Zealots, Prague is not Masada, these are not the Italian Jews during the Crusades."

The emperor was not sure what Masada was. Was it the fortress on a hill in old Israel where the Jews held out against the Romans, killed each other rather than be taken? He was only interested in history which left artifacts he could acquire for his collection of curiosities.

"I propose a toast," Václav said in the midst of this gruesome speculation. "To Your Majesty's health and immortality."

"Rudie, my love." Anna Marie tripped into the reception room all atwitter.

"This is not your night, Anna Marie," the emperor replied, disconcerted by her sudden appearance.

"Do not be grumpy and bumpy, Rudie-boodie." Her hair was done with seeded pearls and her face was painted in the style of the British queen, deathly white with bright red lips. She looked like a doll. The emperor did not like her thus.

"I propose another toast," Kepler took up. "To the Empire."

"I do not wish to tarry too long," the emperor said after the third toast. "The little Jewess awaits me eagerly. She loves me, I could tell."

Anne Marie pursed her red lips into a discontented little pout.

———

YOSSEL, ZEV, AND Rabbi Loew, crowding together against the coming storm, had reached the Stone Bridge. By now the waters of the Vltava were curling in foam-tipped waves and sloshing against the embankments.

"Václav is a man of his word, Zev. Do not worry yourself." The rabbi was distracted.

"But Rabbi, what if . . . that is, how will I be able to live with myself?"

"Life goes on." The rabbi was not paying attention to his words.

"Not if you are dead, Rabbi."

The rabbi stopped in his tracks. "I am so sorry, Zev." A high wave hit the bridge, spilled across. "How could I say so careless a thing?" Perl was right, he reflected, holding up his caftan, wading through the water. There were times when he was indifferent to the fate of his fellow person. Here he was, worried about the whole community in an almost abstract sense, while Zev, the man, was standing right before him in immediate and dire distress. "And you, too, Yossel. Please forgive me for considering you less than what you are. I love you. I love you both."

Yossel was not particularly moved. Yossel Ben Loew who could write his name was the same Yossel who swept the floor and washed the clothes. Was he, in that capacity, any less deserving of his father's love?

The wind, gathering force, was scattering pieces of wood from stalls and other debris in their path. Yossel walked to the front to shield the other two.

"It is one of my great failings, one born of arrogance. I underestimate people," the rabbi rattled on. "I am a man with many faults. I need to cultivate humility. There are many lessons I need to learn. I must be . . ."

Yossel wished the old man would stop talking about himself. Rochel was incarcerated, and when he looked back, the turrets and cupolas, the serrated walkways, the lookout towers, and the zigzagging walls, every detail of the huge edifice overlooking the city seemed to blight the landscape. He wanted to tear the castle down rock by rock.

ROCHEL HAD BEEN placed in a windowless room papered in a print of twisting vines. In the middle was a bed hung with gauzy green curtains. Chests with inlaid wood of hunting scenes were at the foot of the bed. On one wall was a picture of a doe in a forest, her back peppered with arrows. A green-tiled stove, tall as a fir tree, cold, unlit, rose in the corner. There was a small desk on curved legs lacquered in a bright green. Rochel crawled under the bed.

"SHALL I SEND for the orchestra, Your Majesty?" Václav inquired.

"Do, and more wine."

Kirakos, getting more tipsy by the minute, still could not let it go—a mind on a big stalk similar to the complicated mechanism which lay in the tower of the Astronomical Clock, the springs and pulleys, the notched wheels within each other. More perfect than human, was the thing an angel? He thought of the Muslim seraphim—Gabriel, messenger of God, Mika'il, the angel of providence, Azra'il, the angel of death, or Shaytan. Perhaps a combination of man and angel?

"You have not forgotten your love of the butterflies, Your Majesty?" the good doctor asked idly.

"My little prides and joys, I adore my butterflies, and wish to be called from bed, if need be, to attend their birth."

Vladislav Hall was scaffolded with netting, piled high with

mounds of earth planted with brightly colored and fragrant wild-flowers—daisies, red poppies, lupines, asters, cocklespur, bluebon-nets, periwinkles, mustard broom.

"Yes, yes." The emperor rubbed his hands together. "Things are coming along very nicely indeed. Elixir, then the Jews with their secret, all in order and piece by piece in our possession. Life forever, two lives, eternity upon eternity. It is ordained. I am so happy, I do not know what to do next." The emperor, at the thought of his hap-piness, gave himself a little squeeze and began skipping about as if a tarantula spider had bitten him and he was set to dance the taran-tella, like it or not.

"If you will permit me to interrupt your joy, Your Majesty, if the Jews are so clever, why are they not all immortal?" The instant those words slipped out of his mouth, Kirakos wanted them back. He was blundering tonight; in fact, the whole day was pockmarked with mis-takes. Throughout this morning, he felt his throat constrict, as if the silken cord were already bound around it. I cannot fail in my mission, he told himself.

"They have to die," Brahe offered, "for with Adam's fall and no Christ for redemption, they are not permitted eternal life."

Kepler thought it best to remain silent.

"That is not what I mean," Kirakos said.

"When *their* Messiah comes," Václav said, "they will live forever."

"Maybe the golem is their Messiah," the emperor offered. "Is he, himself, immortal?" He had stopped dancing and had thrown him-self, exhausted, back on his throne.

"The golem is the Antichrist." Kirakos immediately knew he had overstepped. And for one wild moment, during the afternoon's events, when it was said that Rochel's mother had been raped, he remembered seeing his own mother's rape. Be quiet and you will live, she had said with her desperate eyes.

"Just throwing a few ideas around." Kirakos laughed. "The pagan figure, Prometheus, crossed my mind. According to legend, he was of heroic proportions, dared the gods."

"You do not think he is the Antichrist, do you, Kirakos?"

"Of course not. If he were the Antichrist, he would have a tongue, a forked one."

Anna Marie let out a little yelp, as if the devil were there right in their midst and had given her a sound pinch on her behind. Kepler looked searchingly at Kirakos. It was obvious that the man was losing his footing.

"Did you say if the golem lives forever, I have to become a golem?" The emperor, whose mind a moment ago had been tinkling clear, a veritable pincushion of ideas, was now muddled. So many things to think about, and the wine, while warming his body, had gone to his head. Then the imperial orchestra arrived, all seventy-seven of them, and they set up their music stands and chairs in one corner of the room, began tuning up.

"I must admit," the emperor confessed, shaking his head, "theology is not my forte." Although he called himself a devout Catholic, he fumbled at what Protestants died over, that is, whether Christ was directly present in body and blood during the Eucharist or if baptism should be at the age of consent. Truth be told, the emperor did not care a fig whether a priest married. Many had concubines, and popes had "nephews." Would he sleep tonight or ever again, that was his concern. He would take a year off eternity if he could sleep one night. Then he remembered the Jewess, but first he must rid himself of Anna Marie.

"If Your Majesty does not need me," Brahe said, for the orchestra was still tuning up.

Brahe, Kepler mused, drank too much beer, and could be a fool when it came to politics. Not that he himself was any better at it, but he, at least, could see that the emperor had to be contained or they all would perish. Stars, planets? The earth would be awash in blood, its own red planet.

Kepler, Brahe thought, was an interfering busybody, altogether too much in affairs of court, state, and Empire. The fool was frittering away his talent in unworthy matters. He, Brahe, ate, drank, made merry, and got a good sleep so that his head was clear for observation. Every night that he did not have to be in attendance at court, he traveled to the observatory, Benátky. On his own, throughout the course of his life, he had mapped the firmament, found the positions of a thousand fixed stars, and discovered that the comet of 1577 moved in an orbit far outside the moon.

"You may be excused, Brahe," the emperor said, "but I will be in great need of your services. My horoscope needs to be cast for thousands of years into the future."

"At your disposal, Your Majesty." Brahe backed out of the room, his legs close together. Free, he ran down the hall to the nearest stair-way, let go a great, golden arch of water.

If two prescriptions for eternity were good, the emperor consid-ered, why not more? The Transylvanian would provide number three, a lucky number, for despite his aversion, what was a little blood if mixed with wine, scented with herbs?

"Kepler," the emperor asked, "do you think it possible to live three eternities?"

Kepler decided the less said, the better, and so he said nothing. Was even the earth forever? Death may very well be the rule of the universe. Stars were suddenly seen which were not there before. In 1572, Brahe and other observers saw a new star. Did that mean they were born and died? For a star, was eternity a minute?

The conductor cleared his throat. The harpsichordist struck a mid-dle A, and the alto recorders adjusted their pitch an octave lower, the serpent players with their S-shaped instruments lower still, along with the long brass of the sackbuts, shawms; soprano recorders fol-lowed suit an octave higher, trumpets, too, the string players. Rochel, who had fallen asleep, was awakened by the sound of the orchestra. A short time later, the door to the room where she was hiding was opened.

24

THE JEWS OF Judenstadt met that very night, no time for delay. And even though rainy and windy, because there were so many crowding into the rabbi's study and the smoke from the stove was backing up, the window had to be opened. The rain whooshed against the building. All the members of the Burial Society were there, Maisel, of course, the sons-in-law, members of the shul, Zev, and other tradesmen, in fact, all male Jews who were bar mitzvahed, and Kepler, the Protestant, who had ducked out of the castle once he was certain Rochel would be rescued by Václav from the emperor's clutches, and Perl because she was the rabbi's wife. The rabbi's daughters with all their children had gone over to Zev's to wait for Rochel to come back from the castle. Yossel had been given chalk, and the one wall without shelves for books was to be his parchment, his paper.

"This is the situation," Rabbi Judah Loew began in the candlelight, his tone solemn. "The emperor believes—erroneously, of course—that because I brought Yossel to life, which, as you know, is something that I have been given the power to do only once and for a specific purpose—"

"Get to the point," Zev piped up. He was very jittery. His Rochel was still at the castle.

The rabbi, sitting at his refectory table, which could have been in a monastery's crude dining hall but was covered with a Persian carpet of beautiful design, raised his eyebrows, continued undaunted. "As we all know, the emperor wants to live forever, and now wants me to help him accomplish that end."

"Live forever," intoned the group. "No end, no end."

"How?" asked a yeshiva student.

"The Kabbalah."

"Kabbalah," echoed the group.

"And in order to have me do it, he is prepared to hold our whole community hostage, initiate a massacre to force my hand."

A contagious shudder passed through the group.

"So," Zev prodded, "If you do not mind, Rabbi . . ."

"This is the point. As you well know, I cannot make anybody live forever, and Yossel, to spare me, spare us all, told the emperor—"

"Told?" Zev asked politely.

"Wrote. You were there, Zev Werner. Yossel wrote—"

"What did he write, what did he write?"

"If everybody would be quiet, I will tell you."

The wind wrapped around the wooden building, which shook like a boat at sea.

"Yossel wrote that we all hold part of the secret of immortality, each one of us in the community, and that if any one of us would be harmed, part of the secret would be dead, hence ensuring that we all live."

Ice-cold rain sliced between the buildings of Judenstadt, pummeled flat the tall grass in the cemetery.

"I do not understand." Zev tried to focus on the matter at hand, but his mind was at the castle.

"What I am thinking, is that we each know a word or a letter."

Yossel's concern for Rochel made his hands sweat, the chalk slip in his fingers.

"My friends," the rabbi conceded. "I want to say this. When I say we each have a word to give to the emperor, it is a lie at worst, at best a prayer. Furthermore, there is a small loophole, or rather a big one," the rabbi continued. "As each of us states a piece of the so-called secret, we will become expendable."

"But if somebody is harmed or killed, you can say the next person who has the secret will kill himself or herself," Zev suggested brightly, "which would keep everybody alive."

"For a while." The rabbi truly did not have the strength necessary for this discussion. "At some point, the point at which the whole secret is given out, he will not need us anymore."

Maisel stepped forward. In his fine doublet, padded short breeches, silken hose, his court attire, he looked out of place in that crowd of paupers, shopkeepers, students. "We will always be of use to him. Taxes, loans—"

"Such considerations have not stopped other monarchs," the rabbi countered.

"Is the emperor's madness the last stage of the French pox?" Zev asked.

"He has shown no other signs of that," Maisel said, thoughtfully stroking his clipped beard. "He is perhaps suffering a Habsburg malady, a disease of their blood. Among his ancestors, there are those who have exhibited these strange behaviors—a great-grandmother who kept company with the corpse of her husband, and, of course, the wretched Don Carlos, not to mention, the emperor's own Don Julius Caesar, who stabbed his mistress in the eye, dismembered her young body, and threw the parts to the bears below at Český Krumlov. In the emperor, the illness manifests itself in vacillations between extreme agitation and paralyzing sadness."

"Perhaps his condition will get so bad he does not remember us," Zev offered. "A secret a day, so that if we draw it out . . . ?"

"To several years?" the rabbi asked. "Then what?"

"Slowly leave town, one by one?"

"The city gates are going to be locked tomorrow morning, and where would we go? And if we go how could we not be noticed until one man was left? Come, come." The rabbi sighed.

"What about Kelley and Dee? I am sure they have been through this whole argument."

"The butterflies have not come out of their cocoons yet," Kepler informed them. "When they do, the emperor needs a week or two for proof of their continued existence."

"Kelley and Dee will be executed however long those butterflies live." Zev believed that God, in the wind and rain, was warning Judenstadt of impending disaster. It was a sign, a bad sign.

"Let us hope Kelley and Dee have their own plans." What those plans were, Kepler was not privy to. He had gone up to their laboratory and found the two in high spirits, the stove going full force, all alembics in use, Kelley poring over ancient tomes, Dee mixing like a cook inspired.

"Those butterflies are going to drop dead, if you ask me. I was once in Vladislav Hall when they had a booksellers' market there, but the reek of horse dung from the jousts, let me tell you, was strong enough to fell a giant. Excuse me, Yossel." Zev smiled at the big man.

"How many butterflies do they have?" the rabbi interjected.

"Must be over a hundred," Karel said.

"A thousand, is my guess," Maisel corrected.

"God knows," Kepler said.

"He does," the rabbi added. "And Kirakos, what is his stake in all this, I wonder?"

"I suspect the more disorder, the better from his perspective." Maisel's long cloak, of the softest, blackest velvet, Rochel's handiwork, gave the impression that he had only to spread it out around his shoulders and he could fly over the houses of Judenstadt and all of Prague.

"Václav, however, is a friendly fellow," Zev mentioned. He said he was going to save his wife. He was going to save his wife most definitely. He had promised.

"Václav is the emperor's son by a confectionary cook."

"My goodness, Mayor Maisel, I did not know that." Kepler was astounded.

"Have you ever looked at his chin?" Maisel continued. "The crinkly red hair?"

"Is there any possibility he will come to the throne?" Zev asked.

"None at all," Maisel answered. "And he does not even know he is the emperor's son."

"And the emperor, does he know?"

"Zev, my friend, the emperor knows, does not know, and does not care."

"Which brings us to Passover, the three malcontent brothers, Father Thaddaeus," the rabbi put in.

"Father Thaddaeus? Does he want to be eternal, too?"

While everybody was aware that Yossel was made to protect them, few knew that he was made in response to a very specific threat. Sparing details, the rabbi told the assembled group the terrible news Karel had brought to him, that a full-scale assault on their community was being planned.

"So we must be prepared on two fronts," the rabbi concluded. "The emperor and the town."

"If Protestants were to take over the Empire, where would the Jews stand?" Zev wondered if he could think straight. Rochel in the castle, Thaddaeus at the gate, the emperor demanding magic words.

"I suspect as usual, Zev, the Jew will be in a bad spot," Maisel answered in his thoughtful manner. "Although it might depend very much on the brand of Protestants. Peasant uprisings are not good for

us, for the peasants, Protestant or Catholic, associate us with the ruling monarch or noble, as indeed is often the case. We receive protection from those who need our money. Yet it is often people like
popes and rulers who set the poorer people against us by edicts and
sermons. Luther, when he saw he could not convert us, hated us.
Sorry, Johannes, it is the truth."

"We have wandered far from our concern," Yossel wrote on the wall.
"Let us look at our problems in proper sequence. We must defend ourselves against not only the townspeople, but perhaps the emperor's
guards as well." After this meeting, he had determined, he was going to
march right up to the castle and wrest Rochel away, for although he
believed Václav was a man of his word, how long could even the most
clever and well-intentioned of men delay the lusty emperor?

The rabbi, weary and saddened, looked about the room, examining each face in turn.

Perl, his wife:

When he had been betrothed to her, he was a mere yeshiva boy,
she a girl in braids by her mother's side. She had a sizable dowry, but
after her father had lost all he had, she became a baker, supported
her parents, and amassed sufficient funds so that she and Judah could
marry, start a household. Passion? It was only when he saw Rochel he
thought of that. Yet, what did it matter? The thought of Perl perish-
ing was beyond his fathoming. He could not endure it.

Maisel, the mayor, court Jew, benefactor:

Circumspect, judicious, strung between two worlds, and wound
very tightly indeed. Maisel and father went from secondhand rags to
cloaks, long and three-quarters, to supplying fur collars, whole furs, and
employing workers, which was allowed of Jews under Maximilian, little by little loaning money, small sums at first, importing lace and fine
glass from Italy, spices from India, larger sums, wool from England,
their shop becoming a warehouse, two warehouses, and a paper mill
and book bindery, their home a kind of private place of negotiation,
until the emperor himself borrowed, or rather took, great sums. Maisel
was financing whole wars, an art collection, immortality in a vial, oh,
yes, it was vile. Maisel, the gentlest of all men alive.

Yossel, the golem:

The rabbi noticed that his golem listened carefully, his face changing from hopeful to mournful, registering the full range of human
expressions. I am the monster who has made a man, the rabbi

berated himself. In his heart, the rabbi wished that Yossel were as intended, a being with no mind, no heart, a schlepper, a schlump, for to know and feel, and yet to be without childhood and old age, was tragedy. His doing.

Kepler, the Protestant astronomer:

The light of a single candle illuminating his small black eyes which could not see very well, in his profession a distinct disadvantage. Johannes—head in the stars, poor as a church mouse, a meek grasshopper of a man, and yet all the while a kind of sublime soul, believing not in a mere correspondence of what is above is below, mirrorlike recipients of governed configurations of the sky, but going so far as to match man, sky, and planets together in harmonic oneness. Was it this connectedness that made Protestant Kepler friend to Jews?

"We must fight back," Yossel wrote, underlining the word *fight*. He held the chalk so tightly that his knuckles bulged like rocks.

"Thou shalt not kill," somebody pointed out. "Is that not our commandment?"

"Perhaps we should reconcile ourselves to our destiny. Perhaps He wishes us to die a good death." This came from the head of the Burial Society, which made the rabbi groan from within. What the man was talking about was kiddush hashem, a very serious matter, martyrdom. Masada, Hannah and her seven sons during the reign of Antiochus Epiphanes, and in the tenth century Jews in southern Italy who killed themselves and their children to escape conversion, and in France and Germany in the eleventh century in the wake of Crusaders "cleansing" European towns on the way to wrest Jerusalem from the Muslims. The rabbi knew that the martyrs who slew themselves and their children did so not in despair, but in anticipation of "the great light" in the World to Come, as example of faith, and only after all was lost.

"I know of that tradition," he admitted. "But if we are to die, God forbid, I choose to die defending our community."

"If I die," Zev said. "I will take one of them with me. At least one."

"Zev," the rabbi warned.

"Just speaking my mind, Rabbi, with all due respect." Zev heard the town crier. Nine o'clock and all is well. Four hours since Rochel had been taken. Four hours. All was not well.

"The golem was created to protect us," somebody reminded.

Yossel wrote, "I can protect you against a few men, but not more than a dozen."

"We have no harquebuses, no cannons, bows or arrows, pikes or spears," Zev pointed out.

"Yes, but we have sticks, stones," Yossel quickly wrote.

"Stones?" the group gasped.

"Well-placed, hurled with catapults," Yossel wrote.

"Stones against cannons?"

"That is the story of David and Goliath," Yossel affirmed.

"You are Goliath," Zev protested.

Yossel felt a pang of guilt like a quill pointed at his heart, for he loved the man's wife, could not help himself, and in doing so had to ask, was there any higher law than love?

"I am not Goliath," he wrote. "Are we not, all together, the House of David?"

"I think we should use verbal tactics to impede the emperor as long as we can and in the meantime build up an arsenal." Maisel suggested this quietly. "We will secretly buy swords and daggers, plan strategy."

"Swords? Daggers?" Kepler was disdainful. "Weapons like that are from olden times, only used for jousts and celebratory demonstration nowadays. It is no longer the age of knights."

Zev gave Kepler a deadly stare. "Maybe where you come from you can afford guns."

Kepler realized his presumption and wished to beg pardon. Before him stood the rabbi's globe—the continents like parched pears, the seas a faded turquoise. He had been bemused at the rabbi's model of the out-of-date Ptolemaic planetary sphere, earth at the celestial center, the brass rings wound around it demonstrating the circular paths of the other planets. Yet he had to ask, where is our place in all of this? He, as Copernicus had, and others, understood the earth was not the center of the universe, that it was part of the family of planets which orbited the sun, but if that were so, were there other rooms, not only on earth, but elsewhere, filled with men and words?

"I can take harquebuses from the castle," Maisel muttered under his breath.

"How can you remove them from under the guards' noses?" the rabbi asked.

"In point of fact, Václav has the key to the room where they are stored," Kepler said.

"Against his own father, he would steal guns?" Zev was incredulous.

"He does not know the man is his father, remember?" Maisel continued. "He lives in a hovel hardly better than the Russian. When his child was sick and dying, he begged for the use of the court physician, was denied."

"Kirakos was the physician?"

"It happened before his time." In point of fact, Maisel sent the Jewish physician, but the child was beyond medicine when he arrived. "Václav is Czech, as far as he knows." Maisel, usually reticent, felt in his element on this strange evening. "A Slav, raised in this city by his mother, a city servant to the Teutonic overlord, if you will, a slave tied to the castle, Václav is, in his heart, one with his country. Believe me, he has little love for the emperor, although the emperor—and this confounds the picture—probably likes Václav better than anything, save his collection and the ridiculous lion."

"What if I do not know how to fight?" Zev confided sheepishly. "What if I am afraid?"

"This is the man who was going to take one with him?" Kepler reminded him.

"Yossel will train us. When the time comes, you will have the courage." Maisel was not sure of this, not even for himself.

"And what will the women do?" Perl, who had been unusually silent until now, took up. "We grew this community in our wombs."

"Perl," the rabbi said, shaking his head sadly, "so blunt?"

"Women will pour boiling water, throw pots, pans from the windows. Children will hold string across the street to trip them. Some will be on the roof to alert us when they come, sound the alarm. They will pile and throw stones, shoot arrows." Soft-spoken Maisel's voice rose in enthusiasm.

"Did you hear something outside?" Zev asked.

"The emperor's guards?" The Rabbi blew out the candles, everybody hunkered down.

"I am back," Rochel called from the street below. She hopped off Karel's cart.

"Rochel, Rochel." Zev quickly ran down the stairs to the front door. Rochel peered up, saw Yossel's shadow at the window.

"Rochel, my wife." Zev put his hands on her shoulders. "Did he touch you?"

"No, the emperor did not touch me." She wondered for a moment what would have been worse to Zev, for her to be touched or to be dead.

"You have soot all over your dress, on your face and hands. What happened?"

"I am Aschenputtel," Rochel answered gaily. "I had to sweep the ashes, tend the hearth."

"Wife?"

"In truth, I have been like Shadrach, Meshach, and Abednego, who walked through fire."

"You know I do not like stories and riddles, Rochel."

"A very curious woman helped me, Zev." She was oddly elated. Just then, Yossel stuck his head out of the window, letting the rain stripe his face.

"Anna Marie, the mistress," Karel added from his seat on the cart, "rescued her."

Rochel, hiding under the bed, thought the footsteps had been the emperor's, but the person who arrived had been a fine lady with pearls in her hair.

"Come out, Jewess," the lady had said, "so I can see your face."

Rochel had crawled out, frightened and in great distress.

"Ach," the woman had said, looking her over, up and down. "You are indeed a pretty one, but why is your hair all cut off?"

"So men will not look at me."

"Did not work, did it? Do you know who I am?"

"A princess?"

Anne Marie threw her head back, laughed heartily.

"Save me," Rochel pleaded.

"Save you? It is myself I am saving. Do you think for the wink of an eye I want to share my Rudie and all that he offers? Be quick about it, woman, go through the stove."

Anne Marie opened the door of the cold green stove, shoved Rochel in. For a moment, Rochel panicked, thought she was trapped, but then she saw light at the other end where the stove reached the hallway, for the great oven was fed logs through that opening so that servants did not have to traipse through the bedchamber. Václav had been there waiting for her, and from there they sped to the courtyard, where Karel was stationed in his cart.

"Go straight home, Wife," Zev ordered. "Clean yourself. I am at an important meeting. I will be along shortly. You run along."

For some reason, those words stung, deflated her exuberant mood. Rochel glanced up at the window. She took off her scarf and, like

Yossel, let the rain flatten her short hair. They stood thus, together although apart, he looking at her, she looking up at him.

"Come to the meeting, Karel." Zev reached up, oblivious of his wife, took Karel in his arms, carried him up the stairs. He set Karel down by the tile stove, wiped his wet head with a cloth. "Warm yourself, my friend. I am grateful to you. We all are. And, of course, to Oswald."

"Very nice to see you, Mr. Vojtech," Maisel said, inclining his head in a little salute. "We were just assigning duties. Tell us, when we are attacked, what can the animals do?"

"The animals will stampede down the street when the bad people come," Karel replied, his fist raised in solidarity. "Led by Oswald, creating havoc and confusion, they will charge through the ranks. I will be throwing bones and rags right and left from my perch."

"Dear Karel." The rabbi could not help but smile at the thought of the faithful but terribly slow mule, Oswald, leading a charge. "You are Catholic. Why should you die with us?"

"I am going to fight with you, Rabbi. Who spoke of dying?"

Yossel felt a sting behind his eyes, turned away, hastily began to write on the wall, "A series of ditches surrounding the wall to be dug during the night, tunneling through our basements."

"Yes, yes." The men chorused.

"Men with the guns in the ditches. Children on the roofs as lookouts. Women with sodden coverlets to quench the fires. Oxen and mules pulling carts with water."

"And the babies?" Perl asked.

"They will cry out, kick."

The rabbi thought of little Fiegel, his favorite grandchild. He could remember when she stood upright, walked for the first time across the kitchen floor into his arms.

"We do not know," the rabbi concluded in a valiant voice, "the outcome of this war which is waged on us here in Prague. We do not know if we will all perish. But, fellow Jews, let us stand together strongly and steadfast. Let us with our very last breath defend our faith, our families, our community, our homes, our streets, and ourselves. However meager they may seem to others, they are ours. This is our God, our life."

There was a great clapping after that, so much that the rabbi had to quiet them, remind them that their meeting was a secret, and they should not all leave altogether, but one at a time, at intervals, so as not to arouse suspicion. Perl went downstairs to start kneading the bread to rise overnight, for in the morning Yossel would take the loaves to the baker's to be baked for the Sabbath. Perl's daily battle with the house and food was her way of attending to the world. If she could keep one corner clean, the food cooked, then she would achieve something.

Zev was the last to go home. The rain had stopped by that time, the wind died down. The sky was changing from black to gray, a border of white light lay on the horizon. The seven hills of Prague would soon be visible and the birds would start chirping, the roosters crowing. Karel would start his rounds. Peasants would be trooping over the Stone Bridge with their produce from the country.

"Do you know . . ." Zev said to Perl in the kitchen, the rabbi keeping her company, sitting on one of the fireplace benches, Yossel outside in the courtyard looking up at the sky.

"What is it you want to tell me?" Perl looked at Zev. He talked too much too often too loudly, true. He was not young, not his fault, nor handsome, just as God made him. But he was a dear, kind man, a good match for Rochel. She must be made to see that.

"Rochel nearly drowned, but she is well. She was almost molested by the emperor, but she escaped unscathed. I am blessed, Perl, for I just think, perhaps maybe, it is possible she may be pregnant."

Quickly Perl looked around, spit out the door; you could never tell if the Evil Eye was lurking. "Do not boast," she hissed at him.

"She looks so well, Frau Perl. She looks . . . radiant."

"Go home, Zev," Perl said. "I believe baby when I see a baby."

Zev looked at Judah, winked, bade him good-bye.

The rabbi turned to his wife. "Why spoil the man's happiness, Perl?"

"Are you so much the rabbi, you cannot see what is happening before your eyes? I want you to talk to Yossel. No good will come of this."

"What are you talking about?"

"You know very well what I am talking about."

"The first free time I have, Perl, I will talk to him."

"Before."

25

EACH MAN, WOMAN, and child in Judenstadt had to be given part of the secret, and for this the rabbi was not going to the Kabbalah. Making Yossel, he had already trespassed into forbidden territory, and to transgress further not merely tempted fate, which was not the way to put it, but would—and this was something altogether different—offend God. Thus, if he did not use the *Zohar, The Book of Splendor*, he would start at the beginning. Sitting in his study, looking out over the Vltava River, the rabbi saw the beginning of spring. The apple orchards across the river were a dusting of white and pink. The hills were a fuzzy green and each morning, at the moment of light, birds took up their wild chirping. The city had withstood its share of snow and cold, rain and mud. Winter was now a memory. Surely, with nature so beautiful, the rabbi thought, nothing could spoil the world. He went back to the Book. If he were to start at the beginning, the words would be nouns, each creature and living thing named by God. Through verbs the creatures came alive, were set in motion. Prepositions and conjunctions connected everything. Adjectives gave color, adverbs quality. Indeed, language created the world.

Rabbi Loew thought of narratives that would convince the emperor—sentences and paragraphs, stories and arguments, lies and gossip, theorems and recipes, speeches and sermons. He thought of fairy tales. There once was an emperor. And they lived happily ever after. The shortest distance between two points is a straight line. One-half cup of oats. He did not want to sound glib or have the combinations of words seem long-winded, too loquacious, nor would it do to be overly succinct, cryptic. He thought of puns and riddles, limericks, poems, treatises, diaries, books, chapbooks, prayers, and the Psalms.

Psalm 18—The Lord *is* my rock; 59—Deliver me from mine enemies; 61—Hear my cry, attend unto my prayer; 70—Make haste, O God, to deliver me; make haste to help me, O Lord; 71—In thee, O Lord, do I put my trust.

The Psalms soothed both heart and mind, were praise and prayer.

The rabbi, looking up from the Torah, could see the silver-blue ribbon of the Vltava River. When he was a young boy growing up in Worms, he had not wanted to be a rabbi. Two of his brothers were rabbis. He did not understand why he could not be a fisherman, ride a horse, have a farm, wear a sword. He was a big fellow, capable of cutting down trees in the forest, walking long distances without tiring. But all too soon, he understood that he could not leave the ringed walls of his neighborhood, and whoever heard of a Jewish fisherman, or a Jew who lived in the woods, or a Jew permitted to carry a sword? His world constricted further when his lessons began. No more running about in the sunshine. After studying all day, he would leave his yeshiva at night, look up at the sky, see the sky lit only by the moon, who seemed, with her gray shadows and craggy face, an old woman. Thus, Judah, returning to his house, his supper, time for prayers, time for rest, another day, became, without knowing how, a rabbi, that is, a teacher, judge, scholar, a leader. He had no great moment of truth, for which he longed night and day, no mystic enlightenment, for although he read unceasingly and spent hours fasting and in contemplation, he never felt closer to God than when he was with his family or friends. He loved being with his congregation, he loved listening to the knocking of the doors by the shammas announcing when work should cease, the Sabbath begin. He loved the summoning blast of the shofar at the beginning of Rosh Hashanah. The gaiety of Purim gladdened his heart. Shavuot, on the sixth and seventh of Sivan, celebrating Moses receiving the commandments, with processions of people carrying flowers and fruit and a meal of barley soup and puddings, strawberry blintzes, that was Eden. And the quiet of the Sabbath was a pool of peace he stepped into, soothing him from the workaday week and preparing him for the coming six days. Rabbi Judah Loew's calling became a habit of a lifetime.

Yes, Psalms it would be. The rabbi did not think the emperor would know a Psalm when he heard a Psalm. Thus, each grown person in turn was given a noun or verb, article, adjective, the whole community covering every part of speech, a grammar of hope, blessings in disguise, double-edged words, powerful words, sorrowful words, words with twists and turns in their letters, upright words, words that rained and words that pained, just a word if you do not mind, and with the words, the rabbi prayed, may there come a miracle for the People of the Book.

At the same time, the small Jewish militia under Yossel's direction practiced throwing stones at crude targets out in a field, parrying and thrusting with small staves in the privacy of their own kitchens. Maisel, with the help of Václav, began to spirit away the emperor's store of guns, pins, and powder. Catapults were constructed in basements and walled courtyards. Yossel amassed a huge pile of rocks. Vessels of water had been hauled up to top floors, string stretched and tested across the streets, brought back inside and wound into tight little balls. Whips were curled into chests like snakes set to strike on the fatal day. The rope maker was kept busy making rope for pulleys to lift and lower kettles, and the few animals were corralled to the end of the street, where they were to be penned until battle. Most importantly, a series of tunnels had been dug going from basements to a ditch circling the outer wall of Judenstadt and concealed by thatches and boards. Lastly, a system of alarms was designed with lookouts posted house to house.

During this intense and clandestine activity, the rabbi had his appointment with the emperor. For this court appearance, Dr. Kirakos, physician and chief advisor of immortality, as well as Brahe, Kepler, Maisel, Rumpf were present. Faithful Václav, of course, was there, as always, in attendance.

"The most propitious time," the rabbi said, "for the giving of the words is after Yom Kippur, Your Majesty.

"So when is this Yawn Kipper?" the emperor asked.

"In September or October, our month of Tishri."

"So long away? It is barely April."

"I have fasted and studied and prayed, Your Majesty, and it seems—"

"Yes," Brahe interrupted. "We will be in Libra in October, the Seventh Sign, an Air Sign, all in balance, ruling planet Venus. The stars will be favorable."

"I have dreams in which a meteor falls on my head when I am out taking a walk to the lion house and I am drowning and dying, cannot get my breath. What if I die before October?"

"No, Your Majesty, you will not die before October," Václav assured him, although he wondered if the emperor's madness would completely overtake him by that time.

"What do you mean, no? You dare say no to me, Václav?"

"Is Your Majesty feeling well?" Kirakos moved forward. "Perhaps if you lie down."

"Lie down? When my head is teeming with ideas? Does the lion lie down with the lamb? Do you think I should lie down on the job? Fie, Dr. Kirakos, fie on you."

Václav ventured a quick glance at Rabbi Loew, as if to say, You see, you see what I have to put up with?

"Perhaps if I visit tomorrow?" the rabbi suggested.

"We have received you today, and today is the day." The emperor tapped his toes. "I am impatient for immortality. October is fall again, when the earth is dying. Where is the beautiful little Jewess, the one who could sew so well?"

"Today is a beautiful day," Václav concurred.

"A beautiful day for what? Do not change the subject." The emperor had not slept the night before, nor the night before that night, and day blended in with the night in a vagueness that distorted even the contours of the room, his throne, the crown.

"What the rabbi is saying," Kirakos said, "is that in order for the words to be effective, Your Majesty, they must age like wine, so to speak, grow like flowers to fruition. To rush is to crush." Kirakos did not understand why he was saying this. Unexpected words, words injurious to his cause these days, just popped out of his mouth in little bubbles, to be followed by the bitter aftertaste of regret.

"If I could sleep, maybe I could live forever, for God knows, I need the strength."

Before the emperor went to bed, Václav read aloud to him from a book by Tasso, *Jerusalem Delivered*, in which there was a talking bird, a wizard, holy war, and a converted witch. Wine, warm milk, hot baths, lovemaking, brisk walks, soft music, valerian root, and opium, nothing seemed to work.

"So this Yawn Cribber? I do not understand, it is a special day? The little Jewess, when is she coming for a visit again?"

"Rosh Hashanah marks the beginning of our ten-day period of

repentance, which ends on Yom Kippur, the Day of Atonement, when we ask forgiveness for our sins." The rabbi stole a glance at Maisel, who, standing straight and tall, attention forward, did not appear to be listening. They both knew that Rochel had been saved by the jealous Anna Marie; however, the emperor's recollection of that incident was confused.

"Where is the golem, by the way, Rabbi?"

"Your Majesty, he is at home washing the dishes."

"Ah, home is best." The emperor sighed. "We look forward to your safe return to your home, Rabbi. You remember, do you not, that not one of you is to leave town and the city gatemen have been instructed not to let a single Jew leave the city? So please do not dream of escape. What do you recommend for sleep, Rabbi?"

Rabbi Loew was going to say a clear conscience, but instead said, "Peace and quiet."

"You are right there. If only I had a little peace and quiet, a little appreciation, plain and simple. You say the Jewess went to Pilsen? Yes, yes, she must be fetched soon as possible. Send a rider posthaste, Václav. We want her in the castle. She loves me, you know. And the robe she is going to sew for me will be unequaled."

Deeply troubled as he was, when he left the court the rabbi tried to put all that was not holy out of his mind, for preparations were under way for Passover, since at the same time that every household in Judenstadt was anticipating an angry mob bent on burning down their homes, each room was being cleaned top to bottom, all traces of flour, wheat, barley, and oats removed. When during the seder Rabbi Loew was reading aloud from the Passover Haggadah and the door was left open for the arrival of the angel Elijah, Perl thought she heard a noise, but it turned out to be nothing—the wind, a mouse, her own fears.

After Passover, the militia continued to practice, but not as much, not as hard. Moreover, the children came down from their daily stations on the roofs, food which had been stored was eaten, the kettles filled with water were drained. Yossel went back to helping Perl in the kitchen, fetching, carrying, cleaning.

Then, on Easter Day, up at the castle, a butterfly wiggled its way out of a cocoon, and then another and another, until the whole of Vladislav Hall was aflutter with yellow wings tipped with orange. "Live, you little buggers, live," Kelley sang to them under his breath, ready at the falter of a wing to make a mad rush under the nets, pluck away a fallen soldier despite the squad of guards and spies watching his every move. Every night, the two alchemists, in solemn ritual, drizzled the blossoms with the elixir from beakers. The butterflies liked it, loved it, lapped it up, wanted more. To this end, a locked, guarded shed containing gallons of the elixir in hermetically sealed jars was set up next to their abode. Undeniably, the recipe, a state secret, had been successfully subjected to all the alchemical stages—the Praeparatio, the Fixatio, the Calcinato, the Sublimato, the Separatio, the Albificatio and Conivinction Sive. The process in its final stages became so elaborate, in fact, and the feeding and tending of the butterflies so much an occupation, that both Kelley and Dee began believing that their concoction was a bona fide elixir that would not only grant immortality to the emperor, but postpone indefinitely their own demise. They talked of how rich they would become, how Prague was not such a bad place after all. At the Golden Ox, when men would ask how the butterflies were, the two would answer, Could not be better, getting fat. They became lazy in their own behalf, letting their minds ignore anything too unpleasant to contemplate, and as the stealthily garnered opium lay neglected in a corner, dreams of escape, if not forgotten entirely, were not of current interest.

Anyway, summer was coming on, each day opening a little earlier, a little brighter, warmer, more fragrant. Crocuses had given way to daffodils and the tulips were blooming. Puppeteers, musicians, jugglers appeared on the streets. In addition to the market people selling spring onions and early carrots, radishes and peas from farms fanning the outskirts of Prague, there were now vendors hawking foreign fruits and vegetables to those who could afford them—tomatoes, their red so brilliant that instantly the dye makers tried to use them to set new colors, pimientos, too, artichokes, cantaloupes, a strange tuber called a potato from the New World, which if set in coals to bake became soft enough for old people and babies to chew. Václav's new baby girl had a potato stolen from the castle, and now regularly ate gruel, in addition to her mother's milk.

With the thaw and the spring sky lucid as glass, Kepler and Brahe, despite the emperor's constant horoscopic requirements, were able to keep their nightly appointments with the stars. Mars was as much an enigma as ever, yet Brahe had faith in methodical plotting, point

by point, degree by degree, and for the time, Kepler was satisfied simply to observe and record, not speculate or bother himself with what
to him was an orbit in obvious deviation from the perfect circle, the
sun as focus.

And one lovely day, in this most lovely of seasons, the river
sparkling like finely spun silk, the air redolent of honeysuckle, Yossel
was sent across the Stone Bridge to Petřín Woods to gather mushrooms, some to be used immediately and others to be strung up to
dry in the cellar for winter. The best of the slick, soft delicious buttons grew in that black, moist soil.

Since the day he had first seen Rochel, Yossel imagined her everywhere. In the graveyard. At the butcher's. On the way to the bathhouse, although he no longer spied on her there, for he had filled the
holes made by Kirakos. He saw her with the small birds packed in
trees tweeting their heads off before the fall of light each day or as a
lone daisy reaching for the sun on the riverbank. He saw her on
rooftops, resting against chimneys, floating in the sky over the castle,
even swimming like a fish in the river. He envisioned her in the
courtyard of the rabbi's house or in the kitchen sitting by the fire. Yet
he despaired of ever touching her again. It was not right. She was
married. He had reconciled himself to the truth.

She, too, always had his image before her. She was able to hold
him in the objects of her rooms and the air outside. He was the warm
wind of spring, the spoon on the table, the table on the floor, and the
floor beneath her feet, the very earth which was home to all living
creatures. She fell asleep at night concocting little stories about him
in her mind, for he was, in his silence, malleable and gave free rein to
her fancy, was hers alone to make up. Once upon a time she met him
crossing the Stone Bridge, once upon a day they had a meal in a
meadow, once they bathed each other with soft, large sea sponges.
The knowledge of him she nursed, cherished. To match the many sad
things, she used him as memory of joy. I have known love, she was
able to say to herself. He listened to me.

And there was something else.

The night Zev, the cobbler, told Perl that Rochel looked pregnant,
he made it true. Rochel taking her husband in the early hours of that
morning as the sun was rising between the seven hills, for once as if
he were a lover, had made the difference. Strangely, in a roundabout
way, although Yossel had never entered her, she thought of it as his

seed, for it was their love, she reasoned, that had inspired her generosity, opened her heart, softened her nest. Like the philosophers'
stone, the catalyst in the process of alchemy, which makes all things
possible, Yossel had transformed her, she believed, into the gold of all
gold. She was to be the most honored and loved being of all the
world—a mother.

Nevertheless, she had not told Zev, not yet. She wanted to savor
the knowledge by herself, keep her baby all her own just a while
longer. She was not ill at all, on the contrary, only a little sleepy, a little slow. The heat of the season suited her, and whereas before she
had found their one room confining, she now liked to sit all day, posi-
tioning her chair so that the sun streaming from their opened window would fall on her face and hands. Drowsily, she let her thoughts
meander while she sewed the emperor's fine new robe, the cloth lus-
trous as light, threads shiny as the eyes of flies.

One of the things she liked to ponder was the mystery of her daring rescue from the castle. Tiptoeing into the bedchamber, the lady, in
skirts held up like wings by a farthingale and a roll of fabric about her
waist, had known immediately that Rochel was hiding under the bed.
Rochel considered her a woman of valor. How generous the woman
had been, for in another minute the emperor was sure to come, and
then Rochel's honor and life would have been lost.

"You deserve a rest from your sewing, Wife. You should not overdo."

It was a particularly fine day. The rabbi's daughters were going
mushroom picking. Karel was going to take them in his cart, come
back in the afternoon to pick them up.

"I am quite fine, Husband." She did not fancy going anywhere
with the rabbi's daughters. She knew they would use the occasion to
belittle her in some way, make her feel wretched.

"We could use the mushrooms, Wife. Dried, they will serve us on
into the winter. Mushroom stew and mushroom pie, is there anything more delicious? Mushrooms with kasha or made in a gravy
over dumplings, mushrooms sprinkled over onions and cabbage, or
large ones on bread."

"Husband."

"Say no more."

Zev did know what Rochel did not know he knew, and he secretly
worried over her. Did she eat sufficiently, get enough fresh air? He
bought milk from the farmer, which she liked heated and mixed with

honey and spices. A day without work would be good for her. When he looked at the blue veins of her throat branching like tree boughs from the wings of her chest, he feared for her, because she seemed so young, altogether too delicate to be a mother. "Go, dear Wife," he finally urged.

When Yossel first saw Rochel in the forest, he thought it was the way he saw her everywhere and in all things; then he realized his vision was real. She had her basket, was in her everyday dark brown skirt, brown bodice, brown scarf. She looked like a mushroom herself, standing on the edge of the forest. He moved closer, hid behind tall bushes. She moved away from the other women. He followed her, keeping well concealed. When she bent down to pick, the shape of her hips outlining her skirt took the form of a tulip; she was getting a little plump, he thought, more womanly, growing up. He caught a glimpse of her leg, ivory against the brown of her skirt. Then she turned. He had not remembered her breasts so full. She lifted her face to the sky, sunning herself with her eyes closed, like a cat. He was only a few feet away. Oh, talk to me, he hummed within himself. Sing to me, sweet bird.

As if she had heard his mind, she turned around nervously. No, no one in sight. She lay down in the grass, one hand over her forehead shielding her eyes from the sun, the other across her stomach. Around her, under her were little insects of the field, shiny red ladybugs and small spiders, ants hardly hatched, slender grasshoppers, all busy. A whole world, she realized, lived on a square patch of grass, tansy and cocklebur. Then a large shadow clouded the sun.

"Yossel," she said. "You scared me."

She did not seem frightened.

"What are you doing here?"

He showed her his basket.

"Ah, you are mushroom picking, too. It is the season, no?"

He sat down beside her.

She did not move away, but she did not look at him, either. She spoke as if addressing the sky.

"Yossel, I wanted to tell you that I do not know what came over me." She shook her head. "No, I do know. I understand it from certain stories—Jacob and Rachel, David and Beersheba. I suppose the passion of God for the world, and man for God, man for woman. I tremble to say these things, to say anything; Yossel, I am so unused to hearing my own voice. You are the only one who lets me talk. You do understand?"

He nodded.

"I feel less alone with you." He touched her most secret self.

He nodded.

"For all your lack of words, you seem more alive than anybody." She had to search. "I should not be saying all these things. I do not know what to say. Is not today a day of days, the blue so perfect, blue as the sea, which I, for one, have never seen and would like to before I die. You have changed my life, Yossel, which I cannot think a sin, and I dare to say this, I care for you so much, but you are not my husband, and there is something else, too, you should know."

Really, what she wanted to do was touch Yossel. She felt helpless in face of that fact. On the other hand, she was so fortunate to have Zev, such a good husband. Before she saw Yossel walking down the road that first day, marriage was her liberty. Zev, by marrying her, gave her the chance for children and honor. Without him, when she died she would have been forgotten. He put food in her belly, a roof over her head, saved her from a wretched life, yet Yossel was the one who made her want to live.

He touched her side with his little finger. It was the softest of touches, so that he was not sure she felt it, but despite the heat of the day, she began to shiver.

"Please do not." Now she had another reason to live, a bigger reason than even Yossel.

He let another finger follow.

"I have to tell you something."

Three fingers.

"No, you must not. I am here with the rabbi's daughters."

His hand touched her side. She closed her eyes, groaned.

"They are nearby." Rochel sat up, looked around. The other women were not in sight and the city was far below, small as a toy. She could hear the church bells ringing one after another. She turned to him, took his face in her hands. He gave her a steady look.

"Yossel." She closed her eyes against his sight. "Dear Yossel, I am so weak."

He put his hand on her shoulder, caressed her arm.

"How can I help myself? What can I do?"

He put his other hand on her other shoulder, moved his thumb so that he could feel her collarbone, which was as delicate as a twig.

"Dear God." She was overtaken by desire. "Follow me," she whispered, and she took his hand, drawing him into the woods, moving steadily through the sticky milk grass and goldenrod, the thatches of blue lupine, wild rosebushes, and tangled vines. Briskly and resolutely, holding her skirt high so it would not catch on any thorns, she led him deeper into the trees where it was shady and cool. Shortly, they found themselves where the trees grew so close together and the bushes clumped in such thick bunches that it was almost black. Parting a way between the solid greenery, Rochel plunged on, crashing down the underbrush, snapping little sticks. Finally they came to a place where the tree branches knit over each other so densely that it was like a cave. All was silent save a whippoorwill who called out, *Whippoorwill, whippoorwill.*

"Here," she said, pulling him down and crawling into a hollow under a thicket of brambles.

He scrunched next to her. She pulled off her scarf, lifted her skirts. He was careful to hold his weight high over her, for he feared to crush her, and he was worried that he might hurt her as he began, but her body closed around him tightly, like a little wet glove, drawing together in a perfect purse of velvet.

"Oh, no, do not stop, Yossel, never stop."

When he spilled himself, it seemed that all of his body, his whole self, flowed into her.

They lay side-by-side, holding hands in their hut, in the forest again; it was still the same day, the whippoorwill singing. When she sat up, her skirts over her hips, his essence streamed out from between her legs in a little pool. Beyond their little shelter, the sun, filtering through the lattice of leaves, hit in triangles and jagged pieces, like broken glass strewn on the dark forest floor. Bees, with their perfect stripes, a miniature, fuzzy uniformed army, hovered over tiny blue flowers. The earth smelled fecund. The world of Judenstadt, really just a row of wooden buildings leaning into each other facing dark alleys, one cobblestoned street, a bathhouse at one end, the synagogue at the other, her dank room with its one table, two chairs, a hearth, a straw bed, seemed so distant as not to exist.

"I need to tell you something, Yossel, something very important."

Then they heard the voices of Perl's daughters.

"Rochel, Rochel," they called.

"Oh, no." She crawled out from beneath their shelter, stood up, shook like an animal drying itself of water. "Yossel." She reached down. "Yossel, I must go."

He released her, she turned, grabbed her basket, began to run.

"We were looking for you, Rochel," were the first words out of Leah's mouth.

"Did you get lost?" Zelda asked.

"Our husbands are waiting for us," Miriam said. "Karel will be here soon to fetch us back in his cart."

"You do not have many mushrooms," Leah observed. "What were you doing?"

From a patch of bushes, Yossel watched the little band of women emerge from the forest into a treeless meadow. Shortly, they sat down, davening in the grass with their legs straight out in front of them. Then they brought their supper out from their basket—water and bread, some cheese and figs.

"Look, look, it is the big golem," Leah, the oldest, said.

Yossel nodded politely, nonchalantly, as he walked down the hill.

Miriam snickered, but they all looked down, did not meet his eyes, for it would have been unseemly as married women, and Zelda betrothed.

"His hand is as big as my head," Leah said when he dropped down out of sight.

"No, it as big as your stomach, Leah."

"Your stomach, Zelda."

"His hair is over his forehead, that is where he had the letters printed."

"What letters?" Rochel said.

"Have you forgotten? The rabbi put them there when he made him," Miriam explained.

"It spells *Truth*, and if one letter is removed, it says *Death*." Leah was prideful of her knowledge of letters. Her mother had taught her how to read, and she had taught her sisters.

Rochel felt a chill move up from her spine. "Leah, you are telling tales? It is only a story."

"No, no, it is true. I heard it, too," Miriam insisted. "He is going to die soon."

Rochel's breath froze in her chest. How could she have missed the letters? Zev had told her once, but she had long ago since dismissed such an idea. It simply could not be true. Or maybe it was true once, but not anymore. "How do you know?"

"Because my husband told me, Rochel Werner."

"Do you believe everything your husband says, Leah?"

"Of course I believe my husband, Rochel Werner, and you would do well to believe your husband, as well."

Rochel felt her stomach cramp. She thought she felt the baby move, but it was way too early for that. She began to sweat. Was it possible to have ice in her lungs and a stove in her stomach at the same time? Was the baby too cold, too hot?

"They say that the emperor is going to start sending for us one by one for the secret," Leah said, waving her bread.

"I do not like secrets." Miriam spoke with her mouth full.

"Look, do you see that wisp?" Rochel pointed to a spot down in the city.

"You are always seeing things."

"No, look. It is very faint."

"I see it, too," Miriam agreed, "a slight thickening in the sky."

"Is that the glassworks?" Leah asked.

"No, that is farther downriver."

"The foundry?"

"Cannot be. New Town is hidden from us here."

"The brewery?"

"It is smoke," Leah said evenly, "coming from Judenstadt."

The women started to run down the hill.

"They are burning us down," Leah called back to Rochel, who was trying to keep up with them, but hung behind. "Hurry, Rochel. We have to throw pots of water from the roof. We have to save our families. Hurry. It is happening, the battle has started. We cannot wait for Karel to come for us. We must hasten home, help. Run, Rochel."

Rochel could not run; in fact, she had to sit down a minute.

"What is it, Rochel?"

"Go along, Leah, I will come behind you. You must hurry. I will be behind you shortly."

"There is blood on your skirt, Rochel, look. It is your curse. What a bad time for it."

"Yes, you run ahead. I need to rest here a moment, then I will come along."

"We cannot leave you, Rochel," Zelda said.

"No, you must. Go along. You have your jobs to do. I will be well shortly."

Rochel, crouching in the grass, holding her stomach, watched them disappear down the hill. By the time they had descended into the city, her cramping had become so severe it was all she could do to hobble back to the thicket where she and Yossel had been together. She dropped to her knees, had to pull herself forward with her hands.

26

A S THE RABBI'S daughters approached the city, the smell of smoke grew pronounced. From the castle side of the Stone Bridge, they could see tall flames. The smoke was not a mere thin trail from a chimney, but rather formed thick black clouds. It looked like the end of the world by fire. The women, who had been walking very fast for several hours, were exhausted, but for the last leg, they ran.

"My babies," Leah cried out, crossing the bridge.

When they saw the people who were shouting and throwing stones and waving lit torches outside the front gates of Judenstadt, their hearts beat loud as drums.

"Get the Yids."

"Death to the killers of Christ."

"Kill the moneylenders."

Instead of trying to go through the rampaging crowd, they quickly, quietly made a wide detour, entering a copse of trees in back of the bathhouse, dropping down into the trench which had been dug weeks ago. Entering the system of tunnels under Judenstadt's walls and underlying all the houses, they quickly reached the rabbi's cellar, where among the cabbages and onions, carrots packed in sand, and strings of drying mushrooms and apples, Perl was gathering her grandbabies.

"Oh, thank God they are safe." Leah and Miriam hugged their little ones to them.

"No time, no time," Perl rasped. "One of you stay with the children, and the others come with me. Leah, you stay. Miriam and Zelda, you come with me. Where is Rochel?"

"She is coming," Zelda said.

"Grandmother, I am frightened," Fiegel cried.

"Be brave, little Fiegel, be brave for Grandpapa."

Then, after the four women said a quick prayer, Perl went up the ladder made of twigs, pushed the trapdoor open cautiously, and she and two of her daughters climbed out of the cellar into the kitchen. Swiftly, they closed the trapdoor behind them, flung a small rag rug over it, and moved the kitchen table over the rug.

"Come along," Perl said to her daughters, as if summoning them to temple and there was not a life-and-death battle raging in their town. As they turned the alleyway corner, however, they were caught up in a throng of panicked people. Small stands and stalls were toppled over, chickens were skittering across the alleyways, and larger animals were tripping over the string stretched across the street. From the rooftops on the edges of their street, some of the women were throwing chests and chairs, pots and pans, slops and boiling hot gruel haphazardly out of their windows. One of the thatched roofs was burning fiercely despite the kettles of water being emptied on it. Another roof was smoldering. In the south vestibule of the Altneu Synagogue, beneath the tympanum above the double doors carved with grapes and leaves on entwined branches, instructions were being given, duties assigned.

"All boys and women on the roofs to stop the fire," Maisel ordered in an even voice. "Men to the ditch surrounding our walls. Archers to their positions along the walls."

There was an array of knives and swords, clubs, guns, and pikes on a large finely polished table in the entryway. "Yossel, you and Zev are to man the catapults at the gate."

Both Yossel and Zev believed Rochel was with the children under the rabbi's kitchen or already on a roof; however, they had not the time to confirm this. Instead, they had to hasten down the street, Yossel well ahead, Zev way behind, to the catapults, the rough wooden boards forming a platform with a cross strip, a kind of see-saw with a bucket swing at the end. These machines were kept in the courtyard of Maisel's house. Yossel wheeled them out. Already there was a pyramid of stones piled up on the two sides of the entranceway to Judenstadt. A group of yeshiva boys was standing guard over them, and none of the townspeople had broken through. Zev sent the boys to the roofs, and then he and Yossel put two huge rocks within the swinging bucket on the ends of each of the long boards. The other ends tipped up.

"The big Jew," the crowd outside the walls screamed in frenzied glee.

Yossel watched them, the brothers who owned the barn where Oswald was quartered, a scruffy trio, drunk and disheveled, their breeches stained with urine, their dirty shirts crusted with spilled food, stubble on their cheeks, boots dusty, their hair uncombed. Unkempt, unschooled, undisciplined, unkind. Behind them stood Thaddaeus, the zealous, jealous priest, hoping to distinguish himself on that day as a warrior of righteousness, this his main chance, and behind him a rabble of apprentices, butchers' helpers, blood already on their hands, bored beggars, a motley bunch spilling out from the nearest brothel, a disorganized, ragged army of discontents who had nothing much to do and always relished a fight. Yet as he continued to look, Yossel saw that behind the riffraff, less bold, perhaps, but no more friendly, were glovers, weavers, bakers, members of the Potters' Guild, an apothecary, students, monks. There were maybe fifty of them, hardly an army, yet deadly enough. The truly frightening part to Yossel was the palpable hate rising like steam from a pot, not a free-floating malice, but a direct detestation of the little community in their midst, hatred for a people who meant them no harm and only asked to be treated as fairly as those who followed another religion.

"Come out, you cowardly Jews," one of them shouted. He brandished his torch and the others raised theirs in support. "Your monster cannot not save you."

Yossel picked up a stone in his bare hand, took a step outside the gate.

"Get that Jew monster."

"Yossel," Zev hissed. "Yoss, Yoss, no, no, come back. Wait."

Yossel moved back.

"Yellow-bellied coward," shouted the crowd.

Yossel took a step forward again.

"Wait," Zev whispered from his post at the other catapult. "Wait until they get closer."

"You poison our wells, murder our children, spoil our maidens, bring the Plague."

Yossel could see the brothers' eyes. They looked as hard as marbles. Thaddaeus's eyes were lost in the folds of his eyelids and puffy cheeks; his mouth was contorted as he spewed forth loathsome oaths and imprecations. However, while the crowd was shouting insults, fanning out on both sides of the wall, underneath the thin layer of dirt spread over boards, scurrying like worker ants out of their hive, one group of the men of Judenstadt had taken their places in the encircling trench. Another group climbed up to platforms below the wall and, heads hidden, positioned their crossbows, ready to sail their arrows at the signal from Mayor Maisel. The women had managed to contain the fire on the roof. Other women had their kettles of boiling water ready should any of the townspeople break through, and an ace group of yeshiva boys had slingshots with pebbles as sharp as arrows. Furthermore, the maidens of Judenstadt, commandeered by Zelda, were ready by the windows to throw down bricks. Each man, woman, and child of Judenstadt was equipped with a dagger, in case it came to that, and the bigger boys and men had swords, including the Rabbi Loew.

"Now," Zev signaled to Yossel, for Maisel had given the command.

Immediately the flag of Judenstadt, permitted by Rudolph's grandfather, a six-pointed star, which, it is said, had been used by King David on his shield, *Shield* being another name for God, was rung up high over the gates. Zev and Yossel pulled down their catapult boards, and up went the rocks, up, up, twisting and turning in midair, and down, down they came right on top of two men, knocking them flat to the ground, crushing their skulls. The crowd drew back as they witnessed this, a sound of horror whistling between their lips.

"Now," Maisel commanded again, as if born to warfare, and with a zing, the arrows arched over the walls and found their marks.

"Now," Mayor Maisel shouted the third time. A dozen guns were fired, and while this group reloaded their harquebuses with balls and emptied their combustible power into the igniting chamber, another dozen guns went off, then a dozen more, and the first dozen were reloaded ready to begin again. It was a relay without letup, the cracking of gunfire constant. Zev kept at the catapult. Then the row of Jews in the ditch behind the sharpshooters threw off their protecting boards, and a vanguard led by their general-mayor Maisel, armed with pikes and clubs, jumped forth for combat. Another man took up Yossel's post, and Yossel, with a Herzegovinian war axe in one hand

and a Venetian dagger in another, both garnered from the emperor's collection, made his way through the chaotic ranks of townspeople, lopping off heads, stabbing hearts. It was utter mayhem. The street outside Judenstadt ran with blood. Bodies lay everywhere, the wounded groaning, gasping their last gasps. But the Jews held their ground. They had successfully defended their community. The smoke cleared, there was a pause. Then, just when it seemed the battle was won, a few of the evil townspeople broke through the gates to Judenstadt, slashing people as they marauded, chopping off the head of a boy, setting fire to the stalls and stands, a shed, the bakery. They headed for the mikvah.

"Stop them, stop them," Rabbi Loew, shouted, but feebly. As one of the sharpshooters in the ditch, he had received a blow to his shoulder. The blood oozing from the wound stained his robe. Still, he would not yield his place.

Suddenly Karel, whom nobody had seen earlier, appeared at the back of the hellacious crowd ringing the ghetto. Sitting high on his pedestal, urging Oswald to a gallop, and holding a whip, he lashed right and left, here and there, whipping muskets out of drunken hands, wrapping necks, scoring scars across cheeks, and striking the skirts of bad women. Unfortunately, however, there was no stopping the throng streaming into Judenstadt. Thus Zev, abandoning his catapult, beat a hasty retreat, and with a group of young boys went down through the tunnel to the back entrance of the walls enclosing their neighborhood. Tearing off their yellow circles and kippot, they came up behind the crowd, and with clubs and daggers they pressed the townsmen between two flanks of Jews, those in the ditch surrounding the walls and themselves. Then still more townspeople, coming from houses and the marketplace on the Square under the Astronomical Clock, popped up behind the Jews. It was hopeless. The Jews would all be massacred. Yossel, who had hacked through the crowd, found himself back at the ditch picking up the rabbi. His father in his arms, the battle-worn giant made his way through the tunnel to the basement where the grandbabies were gathered; carefully, without using the frail twig ladder, Perl and her daughters helping, he hauled the wounded rabbi to the upstairs of his house, set him on his bed. Gently he removed the rabbi's shirt, sticky with blood. He could see that the rabbi's wound went from his collarbone down to where his arm met his shoulder.

"Yossel," the rabbi gasped.

The golem ran downstairs to the kitchen cupboard, grabbed a decanter of brandy and a bunch of clean cloths, ran back upstairs, and, pouring the brandy over the cut, pressed the rags to the wound where the skin had been parted. He tore off some of the bedcloth, dipped it in the bowl of water on the rabbi's nightstand, dripped it over the rabbi's head. Then he lifted the rabbi's head, tried to get him to take a sip of water.

"We are done for," the rabbi moaned, and he closed his eyes, was about to intone, "May my death be an atonement. . . . Hear O Israel, the Eternal is God, the Eternal is One," when suddenly there was the peal of trumpets, a volley of bright, clarion notes, and beneath that sound came the clatter of many horses' hooves.

"The emperor, the emperor," the call went out.

"Go see," Judah said to Yossel weakly.

True enough, there at the gates of Judenstadt was a phalanx of Slovene guards armed with harquebuses bearing the Habsburg flag of twin eagles facing east and west, and being dragged behind them was a huge cannon mounted on a large cart. This martial procession made way between the two battling factions.

"Apprehend any and all provocateurs," the chief officer of the group announced, stopping abruptly in front of the gates of Judenstadt. He called a halt to the rest of the troops, swung his horse so it was facing the pack of harassers, unrolled a scroll and read:

"Hear ye, hear ye, the emperor declares that any person who harms a hair of a Jew's head will be put in the tower for five days. At the end of the five days, he will be brought before the executioner and beheaded. His head will be placed on the bridge on a pike for all to see. The throne will confiscate all his worldly goods."

The officer, fully armored and helmeted in the Spanish style, rolled the scroll back up, and the guards about-faced, and the whole line turned tail, filed out.

"Barber surgeons, barber surgeons," the wounded townspeople moaned, and, indeed, some in shops nearby, marked by columns painted in bloodred and white stripes who had no quarrel with the Jews and had been hiding under their counters, came out and began to attend to the wounded, Jew and Christian alike. The few Christian apothecaries who dealt fairly with all came forth with herbs and medicines. The instrument maker, who had learned his craft in

Kraków and loved Jewish music, helped the Jews. Priests picked their way through the fallen Catholics, administering last rites, although Thaddaeus, the instigator and coward, and the dissolute and despicable brothers, had apparently beaten a hasty retreat and were nowhere to be seen.

Rabbi Loew's cut was not deep, but as an old man he was fragile and would not knit easily. A stone had pummeled his shoulder, the flesh shredded. The rest of his arm was bruised. At the request of Kepler, who had rushed down to Judenstadt to help and was the one who alerted the emperor of all that was transpiring, Kirakos quickly appeared.

"So we meet again," Kirakos said, entering the rabbi's bedchamber, the Russian in tow. Kepler, with Karel in his arms, crowded behind. After one look, the doctor pronounced, "Your rabbi needs a lot of care."

"You are telling me he needs care?" Perl replied. "For that you come across the bridge?"

"Soup and rest. I will have to do some stitching and then he needs to put on this salve when you change the bandage tomorrow. It is a mixture—spider web to mend the skin, good wife, egg yolk, if you please, turpentine, rose oil."

Perl rolled her eyes. She knew all that, could have done it herself.

"And go to the apothecary. He should have the mixture to kill pain."

Everybody knew what that was, too.

Kirakos looked around the room. It was a simple bedchamber, nothing much, a bed, a chest, a chair, the marriage bed where the rabbi's children had been conceived and born. The old man would die in that bed, Kirakos reflected, and for a moment he envied the Jew for his family, the simple goodness of his life.

Yossel was there by the rabbi's side. Most of the women had returned to their families, but he had not caught sight of Rochel. He would pass by Zev's, perhaps knock on the door, smile, for had they not fought well together, been comrades in arms, he and the husband of his dearly beloved?

"Maisel is dead, I hear," Kirakos said. "I am sorry."

"Maisel is dead?" the rabbi exclaimed. "No, no, he cannot be dead, he cannot!"

"He is dead," Perl confirmed. "Mayor Maisel died. And five others, including two women and one young boy who died saving his mother by standing in front of her."

"Dear God." The rabbi hung his head. *Yitgadal Veyitkadash.* Magnified and sanctified is God's name."

"The head of the Burial Society died."

"No, Perl, stop."

"I am sorry," Kirakos said. He was sorry, and he was not certain why.

"We will mourn our loss." Tears began to flow from the rabbi's eyes. "To think I have lived long enough to see this. Maisel, no better man, and a little boy saving his mother."

"The rabbi is tired. Perhaps you would like to leave the room while I stitch him, Frau."

"I most certainly will not."

"Perl," the rabbi groaned. "*Genug*, enough. Maisel, of all people Maisel. Why Maisel, Perl?"

"Why anybody, Judah, why anybody? Who deserves death among us?"

"Needle, Sergey."

"Is needle."

"Thread needle."

"Needle threaded."

As he had with the emperor's wrist some months before, Kirakos sewed a fine hand, neat little stitches, which when the sliced flesh mended would not leave an ugly red scar.

"Now, then," Kirakos said, sitting back, "the emperor wants to know what happens to the secret if some of the Jews are dead."

"You cannot see the rabbi is tired?" Perl asked. "You just said he should rest."

"The emperor wants to know what happens to the secret now that some of the Jews are dead, " Kirakos repeated. "I cannot help that. I must ask. He asked me to ask."

"Out," Perl said, pointing her finger to the door. "Out with you."

"Both the golem and you, Rabbi, must come to the castle to account for the loss of the words. I speak for the emperor, not for myself."

"Do you? Do you always speak for the emperor and never yourself?" Perl asked.

"The emperor has just saved your little ghetto, Rabbi. Your wife would do well to remember." At that Kirakos bade them good day and left, followed by his taciturn assistant.

"They have rounded the corner," Kepler reported. "They are at the gates, through the gates, on the street outside, off they go."

"The emperor will want all the words now," the rabbi said from his bed.

"The butterflies are doing well," Kepler offered hopefully.

"Yes, the butterflies are doing very well," Karel agreed.

"However well they do," Perl said, "they will not live forever."

"We should let you rest, Rabbi." Kepler lifted Karel up in his arms. Perl led the way down the stairs, Kepler behind her with Karel.

"Bring me some chicken soup, Perl," the rabbi called down, "the next time you come upstairs."

"Yes, yes." Before opening the door, Perl turned to the two friends, whispered, "Find Rochel. She is missing."

27

T HE FUNERALS FOR the fallen were held, as was the Law, as close as possible to the day of death before sundown. The Burial Society—Hevrah Kadishah—was busy the whole night after the battle and the next day and on into the second night. All the dead, including Maisel, the richest man in Judenstadt, if not the whole of Prague, were buried exactly the same regardless of their position in life, rich or poor. Each person was washed with water into which an egg had been mixed as a symbol of life. The bodies were cleaned with nail cleaners, combs, and the hair trimmed into little dishes—all made of silver. Then each person was dressed in a shirt, underwear, a linen shroud with a collar. Everything was white. The coffins, of six boards, were placed on straw on the ground and watched.

Rabbi Loew, bandaged and hunched over, gave the funeral service and led the prayer, "What the Almighty does is right," and the coffins—plain pine wood—were lowered into the graves. Each of the mourners, having already rent their shirts, threw three shovelfuls of soil into the graves. Back in the burial hall, Kaddish was said. For a week the closest relatives kept shiva, sitting on the floor, but the rabbi, as soon as the funerals were over, had to give his attention to the whereabouts of Rochel. Karel, in his cart, and Kepler, by foot, had gone all over looking for her, had found no trace. God forbid that she was hurt right in the streets of the town, a lone Jewish woman, unprotected. Perhaps, it was suggested, albeit delicately and reluctantly, that she lay wounded inside Judenstadt, but the houses, alleyways, and all of the various tunnels of Judenstadt, scoured for survivors, yielded nothing. It was at that point that Petřín Woods was mentioned, that perhaps she had never come back to town, for the rabbi's daughters recalled the blood on Rochel's skirt and how she had lingered behind.

"Blood on her skirt," Zev cried out. "That cannot be. She is pregnant."

Yossel paled, nearly fell over. Only Perl noticed this extreme reaction.

Perhaps, in her weakened condition, somebody conjectured, a wild animal or wild man of the forest had gotten her, or maybe she was lost. So it was that groups of men, accompanied by the rabbi's daughters, trudged back to Petřín Woods, beat the bushes, trampled through the tall grass of the hillside calling, "Rochel, Rochel." Yossel, of greater strength than anybody else, relentless in the quest, took off alone into the deepest, darkest part. When it was evening and the search party had to return to town empty-handed, and they gathered in a huddle to walk back together, it was discovered that Yossel, too, was missing. He had disappeared mysteriously, as if the trees had reached forth, embraced him in their arms, swallowed him whole.

It was only then—Zev having broken with the group, still looking for his wife in the dark—that the rabbi's daughters, with much insinuation in their voices, recalled the time they were sitting on the hill having their meal. Yes, Yossel passed them by. And before that, now that they remembered, Rochel had parted from them, was not seen for some time. In fact, they had to shout to summon her and had to share their mushrooms, for she had picked hardly any. Leah also felt duty-bound to mention that when Rochel almost drowned, Yossel was the one to save her. What could she be doing on the riverbank alone with Yossel? Miriam, not to be outdone, wanted to know. Looking back, Leah could see it, believe it, and who said it first, nobody knew, but an unworthy remark was made, and somebody else agreed, nodding intently, that yes, he, too, she, too, had seen signs, for what was the world coming to when a married woman would carry on in such manner? Indeed, Leah, confirmed, Rochel had been a strange one from the beginning, an orphan not of their community, and truly only half Jewish, which could account for her wayward behavior. Of course, she was spoiled by her grandmother, and even Leah's father, the rabbi, had a soft spot for her. When Zev returned to the group, everybody silenced their suspicions, went back down the hill to Judenstadt without Yossel, yet the husbands told their wives, who told their friends, who told their husbands, who told their friends—at the bathhouse, in the entranceway to shul, the butcher's, the baker's—and even the Christians were soon aware, the news traveling like a pack of busy monkeys going from tree to tree. Shortly, all of Prague was chattering that Yossel and Rochel had run off together. Only Perl and Judah would not speak of it. Zev, the loyal husband, refused to believe the pernicious gossip.

WHILE THE JEWS were burying their dead and looking for Rochel, at the castle the butterflies were not fluttering about as gaily as they had been previously. Just the heat, Kelley told himself, expecting that in a few days they would be back to their former state. It was Dee, however, who found the first dead butterfly, its wings neatly folded over its body as if death were a mere resting from flight. He plucked it up rapidly, hid it in the overlap of his doublet, acting as if he had merely bent to inspect the petals of a flower. He did not wish to appear rushed or flustered in any way, so he dallied, humming an English ayre, ambling out from under the nets, and emerging from Vladislav Hall with the greatest unconcern. Pacing himself, he made his way down through the courtyard to the laboratory, pretending to enjoy the rich sunshine of the day.

The laboratory, as usual, was a bustle of activity, the young boys stoking the fire, other boys pumping the bellows, assistants stirring steaming pots, dogs in wheels, by their constant running moving pulleys, for despite the alchemists' protest that it would only be necessary to imbibe the elixir once, the emperor insisted they make a supply adequate for eternity, as if each morning he would take a sip, a boost, so to speak, like a tonic, to ensure his continuous life. At present, the chief assistant was pouring the elixir into jars through a funnel with cheesecloth stretched across its narrow end. Kelley, quite the figure of the magus in his somber colors and calm demeanor, was bent over a large tome, a work of the fifteenth-century mystic Pico della Mirandola, who predicted the future through dreams, believed in sibyls.

"Edward," Dee said, trying to keep his voice even, not betraying a hint of anxiety, "would you come with me to the apothecary's?"

"Why not send one of the boys, John?"

"I need your sagacious advice on acquiring a specific compound."

"Oh, very well," Kelley said. "To the apothecary's."

Dee led the way down the stone stairs in measured steps.

"Fascinating stuff," Kelley said. "Mirandola. He died at thirty-one. A pity he did not have the elixir."

"He may not be the only one to die young." Dee, looking back at the guards whose job was to follow them everywhere, said a little louder than necessary, "We are making good progress with our batches of elixir, are we not, Master Kelley?"

"Many funerals in Judenstadt," one of the guards mumbled. "Maisel is dead."

"Maisel is dead?" Kelley gripped Dee's arm.

"The big man, he ran away with the shoemaker's wife," the other guard added.

Kelley looked closely at his friend. Dee put his finger to his lip.

The apothecary's was composed of two rooms, one completely walled, floor to ceiling, with little drawers faced with porcelain on which the names of substances were labeled in gold letters. Spanning the front of the room was a long oak counter. The next room was the apothecary's laboratory, where he kept his various mortars and pestles, his small furnace and many little pots suspended over braziers. Herbs were tied in bundles on the beams of the ceiling.

"We will be waiting outside," one of the guards let Dee know.

Dee spoke to the apothecary briefly and the man said he must step into the other room to grind the substance to a fine powder and would be right back.

"It is a beautiful day, is it not?" the apothecary remarked.

"Lovely, to be sure."

"I will return shortly."

"Take your time," Dee replied amicably.

As soon as the man turned his back and left the room, Kelley whispered, "Yossel has run away, Maisel dead, what is happening?"

"More than that, my dear Edward. The first butterfly expired today."

"Good God. That means soon we will be on the chopping block."

"Edward, be calm."

"Calm? Calm?" Kelley started to seethe between his teeth; his head felt as if it were spinning off his neck. He looked up at the spiked puffer fish the apothecary had hanging above the counter, tried to gain a fixed point to still his dizziness, settled on the guards in the doorway, then looked hastily away.

"I need a drink," he said to Dee, feeling time, like two shutters, close around him.

"It will cloud your head, Edward."

"It will soothe my heart, John." Kelley remembered vividly when his ears were cut off, the excruciating pain. He had been placed in the center of the town square. His father watched, stated later that it served him right. Kelley never saw the man again.

"Here we are, gentlemen." The apothecary returned to the counter. He handed them a little cloth bag closed by a drawstring. "This should cure your rat problem."

"The emperor's account," Dee said. The two stepped out of the shop.

"Our throats are parched." Kelley looked back at the guards. "Are not yours? Hot day."

" 'Tis," answered one of the guards.

" 'Tis indeed."

"And you must be sweltering in your livery." Kelley despised uniforms of any kind.

"Am."

"Am indeed."

Kelley shot Dee a glance, and the four of them made their way down to the Golden Ox. Already at nine in the morning it was filled with the regulars—tinkers, itinerant musicians, puppeteers, Karel, Kepler, Brahe, Jepp, of course, and the peddlers who carried a box hung from their neck on a strap, which they could open up to show their wares—rows of needles and threads, silk ribbons for the ladies nested in red velvet.

"Join us," Karel invited.

"How now?" Kepler greeted the alchemists using one of their own British expressions.

"Bad is how now," Kelley answered. "Could not be worse."

"Edward."

"Oh . . . wonderful," Kelley amended. "The world is a wonderful place, I love it so. I love it to death."

"Yes, Maisel is dead, and Yossel is gone." Kepler hung his head over his tankard of beer. Brahe was having a little snack—sausages fried with onions, and a leg of veal roasted with strawberry leaves, sorrel, and endive sprinkled over it, and pottage boiled with violet leaves and marigold flowers, not to mention several jugs of beer.

"That is not all—" Kelley began before he was knifed with Dee's elbow.

"Terrible about Judenstadt," Dee interrupted.

"Our guards," Kelley introduced. How to get rid of them was the question.

"Pleased," said Brahe.

"The emperor's beer," Kelley ordered from the barman, as if he had any choice.

A group of revelers had taken up an old Czech song, "A Nest for Every Bird."

"After the Feast of Corpus Christi, true enough, the emperor will be asking the Jews for their words," Brahe said, trying again to be chatty. "He has moved the day up a bit."

"And the elixir, too," Jepp interrupted. "Since the butterflies are doing so well. Václav, a few courtiers, then the emperor himself are going to take it, for he has overcome his inhibitions."

"Yes, the emperor has not slept a wink in four days," Brahe informed them. "He can no longer sit still. He talks constantly, and much of what he says makes no sense, he is so anxious."

"They say," Jepp said, "that he sees things."

"What things?" Kelley sat forward, very interested.

"Ships in the sky. He thinks he is losing his teeth."

"He has no teeth," Kelley replied.

"Five, the five that he has." Jepp smiled, revealing his mouthful of small but perfect pearls.

"It is the new moon." Kelley shrugged. "Or the old moon. Some moon."

"Come, come, we are on the cusp of Cancer and Gemini," Brahe said, "and the emperor's birthday is soon, July eighteenth, a celebration to be sure. Have you not noticed the many guests already arriving at the castle, many people of the town taking on additional servants?"

"We have been so busy in the laboratory, Brahe," Kelley said, looking straight at Dee.

"Entertainments and foods of all kind, a great birthday party."

"Melons are shortly to arrive," Jepp explained. "A turtle all the way from London."

London, Kelley thought. London.

"Hazel grouse and ortolans."

"What are ortolans, Jepp?" Brahe asked.

"I do not know, but expensive, that is the main thing. And oysters from Paris, pineapples from Afric, or did Cortés bring some back from New Spain, herring from the North Sea, partridge and quail, cauliflower, green beans, crystallized sweets from Italy, toasted grouse from hell—"

"Jepp," Brahe said. "Do you not think you should watch your language? You are in the company of courtiers, gentlemen."

"Yes, Jepp, in the company of pretenders and hypocrites," Kelley amended.

"Come, come, Edward," Dee said gently. "Do not be so hard on yourself."

"But this party," Kelley took up. "Much wine?" He tried to make it a delicate inquiry.

"The Vintners' Guild," Jepp said, "has never had so much work in their whole lives."

"Yes, and we, Kepler and I, are to be seated near the emperor's table," Brahe added.

"How nice for you," Kelley mused, remembering the stash of opium in the corner of their tower laboratory. Golden Prague was the watchword. Sleepy Prague. Sleepy, sleepy Prague.

"How are the butterflies?" Kepler asked.

"Could not be better." Kelley finished his beer in one tip.

"Yes, they will have a procession first to St. Vitus Cathedral, a service, of course," Jepp said. "There will be singers and musicians, players, jugglers, dancing bears. A bacchanal."

"Must be getting back," Kelley said abruptly. "It would not do for us to sit the day away."

"Good-bye, Karel, Johannes; good-bye, Tycho."

"Why all this good-bye?" Brahe asked. "We will be seeing you tomorrow."

"One thing more. Do you think Dee and I will be invited to the feast?"

"To be sure," Brahe answered Kelley. "Everybody is going to be invited."

"The emperor's account," Kelley told the tavernkeeper.

The two alchemists strolled up the hill to the laboratory, hands behind their backs.

"That silver nose of Brahe's," Kelley said. "I always worry that it will slip off and we will have to see the hole in his face where his nose used to sit."

"Should talk, Mr. No Ears."

"At least I hide my shame with my hair."

"What do you suggest Brahe do?"

"Wear a veil like a Turkish woman."

"You know, this party . . ." Dee mentioned, his words measured and soft. "The birthday party might be a good occasion."

"I have been thinking the exact same thing, John. It would be fitting, would it not, on his birthday? He will be drinking and merely fall asleep. He has been having trouble sleeping, has he not? He will just keep sleeping forever. It is sweltering today, have you not noticed, and the road so dusty. Sometimes I long for the dampness of England."

28

T HE TALKING IN the curtains went on all day long, his dead cousin, Don Carlos, chief among the babblers. There were times when he felt he was not walking on the ground, rather floating above it, skimming the surface, as if wearing ice skates. He could not get enough of Anna Marie, yet she sickened him. The Jewish seamstress had vanished. How would he ever get that dressing gown made? He must have it. He must have her. He wanted Tintoretto's *Susanna Bathing.* His many beds were bumpy, scratchy, made his back sore; no wonder he could not sleep. Sometimes he wished Václav would just take a club and hit him to sleep. Ambassadors, nuncios, peasants with petitions, council meetings, Petaka was sulking, the spoiled beast, and the damn stag with the golden horns in the Stag Moat was seen with tears of glass. On top of it all, guests were arriving for his birthday, as if forty-nine years on this wretched earth were cause for celebration. Vilem Rosenberg, supposedly his advisor, was at Český Krumlov for the summer, a palace near the border of Bohemia and Austria, the same castle where his son had killed his mistress. Could Rosenberg not choose a better place to conceive an heir? Who had sent the birthday invitations, anyway? It was a vast conspiracy to disgrace and discredit him, humiliate and mock. The next thing, they would pull the throne out from under him.

"Where is the golem?" the emperor demanded of the rabbi, who had responded to the summons to court.

"Yossel is not to be found, Your Majesty," the rabbi answered, bowed, bruised, and bandaged.

"And Maisel?" The other members of the court were there. The emperor was pacing in front of them, his doublet soiled and rumpled.

"Maisel is dead, Your Majesty." They would not place his tombstone until the yahrtzeit, but the rabbi visited his grave once a day,
talked to him. Maisel, how I miss you, my dear friend.

"Mayor Maisel dead? My court Jew dead? In that case, somebody
must be sent over to his home to confiscate his belongings for the
crown, empty his coffers."

"His widow, Your Majesty, his family," the rabbi said.

"Fie on them. Václav, dispatch some guards immediately to the
Maisel house. Have them strip the place. And come right back
afterward."

"Your Majesty, if you do not mind, would you excuse me for a
while?" Václav appealed.

"No, no, come back, come right back." The emperor sat back down.

"Your Majesty." Václav shuffled his feet, cleared his throat. "I am
needed at home."

"Nonsense, your presence is required at court." He crossed,
uncrossed his legs.

"His son is ill," Kirakos said. Why did I have to say that? he asked
himself.

"Whose son is ill? Maisel's son? Not my son. I have no son worth
mentioning."

"I do think, with all due respect," the rabbi said, "that Maisel left
his wealth to his family."

"Loew, whenever a Jew dies, all his goods revert to the state, to me."

"I have not heard that, Your Majesty."

"Now you have." The emperor was up and pacing again.

"He has a high fever and a cough," Václav said.

"Who has?" He stopped in his tracks.

"My son, Jiří, Your Majesty."

"So with the golem gone and the little seamstress, where is she, the
love of my life, and Jews dead, what happens to the secret?"

"I have the secret." The rabbi and Perl had worked out the new
plan the night before, when the summons to court had arrived.

Kirakos looked around. They were all there, just about. Václav,
Rumpf, Pistorius, Crato, Kepler, Brahe, Petaka, Kelley and Dee, several pages, the usual guards, Jepp, who did not count, no Maisel.
Kirakos had never engaged Maisel in a conversation, had not liked
him, not because he was a Jew—for had not the Muslims and Jews a
common father, Abraham?—but because Maisel was a man without

apparent weakness. Now he missed him. The emperor had borrowed, never repaid, untold sums from him. Now he was going to
rob him again.

"How can you, alone, have the secret? If you had died, what then?"
If only his mind were not in such a disordered state, and for this the
emperor blamed them all. His court was a hodgepodge of ineptitude.
Brahe, all his notations, what did they add up to? The dwarf following
like a tail behind him. Kepler was in love with Mars. Did he, the
emperor, want to live on Mars? Would it help him in his quest for
eternity? Did Mars care a fig? Looking at Kelley and Dee, the emperor
knew they were as good as gone. The minute he drank the elixir, to the
tower they would march, and from there straight to the block. Pistorius,
his sanctimonious confessor, inspired falsehood. Crato, the second-in-
standing physician, was, to his mind, incompetent. Hoefnagel, Spranger,
all the artists, goldsmiths, Pucci was a pain, the orchestra a huge
expense, the master of the horse, for God's sake, he hardly rode anymore. Kirakos speaking up on Václav's behalf?

"Majesty?"

"Hush, I am thinking, Václav."

The rabbi, in his robe, pointed hat, looked like a medieval wizard.
"I can make you immortal," he was saying, his words reverberating in
the emperor's head like an echo. *Im-mortal, mort-al.*

"Your Majesty, if you will . . ." Václav beseeched frantically.

"Everybody quiet." The emperor popped up, plopped down. "So
you, alone, will be telling me the secret, Rabbi?" He was dizzy, disori-
ented, here in his own castle.

"Not exactly." Truth be told, the rabbi was flailing, making up a
solution as he went along. Perl suggested that he be sparing of words,
then she had contradicted that ploy. "Talk, talk a lot, the more talk,
the more difficult it will be for him. Confound him. Who likes to
admit, particularly an emperor, and in public, that he does not understand? Vanity, Judah."

"Your Majesty, it is the sum of words. I quote: 'Words do not fall in
the void,' and numbers come into play, too, for certain combinations
of letters correspond to numbers."

"What sophistry is this? Do not speak in a circle, man, come
straight out."

"There is the story that it takes thirty-six just men to hold up the
world, and for instance, we say that the names of the angels and

those of God total 301,655,172. In the *Zohar, The Book of Splendor,* we read that he who gets up early can see something 'like letters marching in the sky, some rising, some descending. These brilliant characters are the letters with which God has formed heaven and earth.' Of course, God is infinite and the universe is a concept that the ordinary man has trouble grasping, but you, the emperor . . . I am sure you comprehend."

"Robert Fludd, in *On Music of the Soul,* explains that musical intervals are the organization of the heavens. His thoughts on the harmony of the universe are like Pythagoras's views," Kepler added, inspired by the mention of numbers.

"Your Majesty, I hate to interrupt."

"Then do not, Václav. And you, Kepler, we care nothing of Pythagoras or floods, either."

"My son . . ." Václav was wringing his hands, standing on one foot, then the other.

"We are dealing with something of far greater consequence, Václav, than your son."

"So the words equal numbers, and the number is 301,655,172?"

"It is complicated." The rabbi noted that the emperor was not completely addled.

"It would seem so," the emperor returned tartly.

"Each letter in the Hebrew alphabet corresponds to a number, and in a sense, only in a sense, would you be golemlike." The rabbi had to be careful here.

"My son is sick," Václav said. "He needs me. I would like to tend to him."

"Hold your horses, Václav."

"I have no horses to hold and respectfully request that Dr. Kirakos look at him."

"I would like to know," Kirakos asked, "why Jews get these magic words, not others."

"We are God's firstborn, Doctor, in the sense that we accepted the Torah."

"But I have heard that other people, Christians, can become Jews."

"It is rare, and we in our community do not seek to convert, for the penalty is severe," the rabbi replied.

"But if?"

"It is an ongoing discussion, Doctor, but in my humble opinion, if a Christian becomes a Jew, he has always been a Jew." The rabbi stroked his beard thoughtfully.

"Not by blood, certainly?"

"By temperament."

"Is that stronger than blood?"

"It depends on the person."

"But if a Jew becomes a baptized Christian, a *converso*?"

"Once a Jew, always a Jew."

"But you are now talking of blood, Rabbi."

"No, temperament." The rabbi shrugged. "I do not split hairs, Dr. Kirakos. Hillel said, 'Treat each other well, all the rest is commentary.' Rashi—"

"I do not care about all that." The emperor brushed aside the debate with a flapping of his hands. "My goal is nothing less than eternity. To be brief, I am testing the elixir on my birthday, will partake of it on the day following, and on the same day I will receive the secret words, not your holiday, Rabbi, but my birthday, my entry into eternity. The golem will be there? How does the golem fit in to the festivities? I would become the golem?"

"No, no, I am not saying quite that."

Václav gave Kirakos a steady look, then he left the room, bowing low and backing out.

"I have a headache," Rudolph shouted after him. "Do you hear me, Václav?"

"If I can be of assistance, Your Majesty." Kirakos stepped forward.

"The good must suffer, Kirakos, so I suffer. I hear tell that you have power of life and death over the golem, Rabbi. That is the part I do not like."

"He was made to serve for forty days, then return to the earth. Already he has lived beyond that time." The rabbi dared not think of what was ahead. "Your proposed term is eternity, is it not?"

"Excellent, but I have to know exactly what will happen. Will I repeat the words? Must I be standing up or lying down? Is there a special ceremony? Should I fast, heaven forbid? It will not hurt, will it? It cannot. And I must remain my handsome self forever, too." The emperor put his head in his hands, then he lifted his head. "Now go, all of you, just go."

Kirakos, in the hallway, looked both ways, and then, quick as a wink, he darted out, sped across the courtyard to his room. "Hurry."

He gave the Russian a swift kick. "Get my bag, my wax coat and mask, my needles. We must speed to the imperial stables."

Václav was a little below the Golden Ox when he heard a horse behind him. Two horses. It was Kirakos and the Russian, apparently out for a ride. He turned his head, ran on.

"Here," Kirakos said, reaching his hand out to pull Václav on behind him. "Make haste."

"I am going to my son."

"Yes, we, too." Kirkos hauled Václav on behind him, and with Václav's arms around his waist, Kirakos took off at a fast gallop, the hooves of his stallion clattering against the cobblestones, the Russian's horse behind. Down the hill, along the river, they had to slow up and wend their way across the Stone Bridge, which was full of peasants bringing vegetables and wares to market. Then, picking up again, they raced, bypassing Old Town, and approaching New Town, the horses climbed up the small hill toward the Slavonic Monastery. At the rickety wooden house behind the cattle market, Václav slid off the horse. Kirakos put the long cloak stiffened with wax over his clothes, the strange mask on his face.

"Tell your son not to be frightened," he said to Václav. "I dress so fleas do not penetrate."

"What fleas?"

"Plague fleas."

"The Plague?" Václav gasped. "He does not have the Plague. No, not the Plague."

Václav's son was in bed and his mother was sitting in the corner, holding the new baby. The floor was dirt, and there was only one table of rough, splintered wood, a chair made from half a barrel, a crude, three-legged stool. A tattered coverlet, patched in fur and velvet, silk and linen, and other discordant fabric probably filched from the rag bag in the castle, was thrown on a line dividing the room. Kirakos could smell stale food, standing water, and sickness. He approached the bed, then quickly moved away. "Back," Kirakos warned. Then he moved to the bed again. "Tell me, child, backache and vomiting?" The boy's eyes were glittering with fever and his face was dotted with red spots. When Kirakos lifted the child's gown with gloved hands, he could see the whole body covered with the same red spots.

"Be strong, father," Kirakos said, turning to Václav. "Be strong for your son, your wife, the baby. It does not look good, not good at all; he has the pox."

Václav's wife, hearing the word *pox*, broke into a high, keening wail sharp enough to pierce the heart of a stone. Kirakos crouched down, shook her shoulders.

"Stop that. You will scare the child."

Václav, close behind Kirakos, pleaded, "He will live, will he not? Tell me, tell me he will live, Kirakos. You can save him. He will live? Kirakos, save him, please, I beg of you."

"If it is the black smallpox, the spots will become black. He will certainly die."

"The other pox?" Václav faltered. "If it is the other?"

"The sores will fill with pus, he will resemble a cobblestone street, the pustules will turn into scabs, fall off. He may lose the ability to speak. He might live."

"Dear God, have mercy." Václav fell to his knees, put his head to the ground, pounded it.

"Let me look at you," Kirakos said. "Sergey,"—Kirakos poked his head out of the door—"come in here, put something over your face, and take Václav's clothes off."

The Russian, with a cloth tied around his mouth, undid Václav's livery, its festive colors of scarlet red and gold absurd at this moment. Kirakos gazed at his chest, back.

"Undo the breeches." Kirakos did not know what it was that caused the disease, but he imagined it tenacious tiny beetles with many hairlike feet, viciously invisible scorpions somersaulting through the air, legions of them adhering to the skin, tunneling into the roof of the mouth, entering the ears. He peered at Václav's skinny shanks, his groin.

"No signs yet," Kirakos said. "Have you had a cough, fever?"

"No," Václav said.

"May I take a look at your wife and baby?"

Václav's wife was still sitting on the floor, her baby clutched to her. She had stopped screaming, now was sobbing and hiccupping, her eyes glazed with tears.

"I do not see any pox on the rest of you," Kirakos said, "but heed me well: The mother and baby must be sent away. Do not touch her. You may make her sick or she may make you sick. The boy can be kept clean, cool, fed; he needs lots of water. I will send the Russian back with some food from the emperor's kitchen. Oranges from

Valencia, and something called coffee. Chipped ice from the slabs stored in the castle cave."

"Opium?"

"For certain, but one of the worst things about the pox, Václav, is that opium does not entirely dull the pain. It is uncanny, but the patient is aware of what is happening to him. He is not in pain now. Remember, too, you do him no service to cry. Some fresh eggs which he can have mixed with cheese, a little pepper, soft white bread soaked in milk sprinkled with sugar. You will have to wear a mask of cloth over your face, which, along with your clothes, must be discarded every time you leave him. The pox seed is most pernicious, dear fellow. It flies through the air silently, stealthily, landing on everything. Bathe yourself well with hot water after you tend to him. Do not let him breathe upon your face, do not let your bare skin touch his skin."

"You touched him."

"With gloves. I shall lend you them and my wax coat. I will tell the emperor you do not wish to pass on to him the pox. He is not immortal yet."

Václav nodded. He could not see Kirakos's face under his Plague mask.

"God will reward you, Kirakos, for your kindness."

"That remains to be seen, does it not? Do as I say, it is the only way. Do not give in to despair. The boy must see hope, faith."

"Kirakos?"

"Yes?" He himself had little hope in the child's recovery. He had heard stories of skin turning into charred sheets, blood oozing from the eyes, ears, nose, and mouth.

"I thank you." Václav began to weep piteously.

When Kirakos and Sergey got back to the castle, they threw their clothes and shoes in the bonfire outside the kitchen, then they rushed naked to the basement, submerged themselves in a half barrel each of very hot water, scrubbed their skins vigorously with pig-bristle brushes and hard soap made of lard, potash, and marjoram. They washed out their mouths with a hot mixture of peppermint leaf and rosewater, and with a fine comb dipped in hot oil combed through their hair. Then they had the horses washed down, brushed briskly clean, and sent out to a breezy pasture. That night, the Armenian physician prayed for the first time in many days. "Allah, do not let me catch the pox."

29

Y OSSEL AND ROCHEL were in the same little hollow where they had made love. When all of Judenstadt had gone out look- ing for Rochel, Yossel knew where to find her, and there she was, curled up in a little ball, incoherent with grief. To his mind, she needed the care of a woman, but when he turned to fetch one, she held on to him, and at the sound of the voices of the other searchers, she buried her head in his chest. Yet after a few hours, she let him carry her to the stream, and despite her expressed desire to die, she lowered her head, drank, permitted him to stanch her flow of blood with fistfuls of moss. Bundling the remains of her miscarriage in her bloody underskirts, he buried them by the stream, and tearing off the sleeves of the silk shirt she had made him, he bathed Rochel like a baby, making sure no rem- nant of blood on her legs remained. Then he picked strawberries for her to eat; pungent watercress he plucked from the stream, and he ripped strips of dandelion greens from the ground; he gathered soft honeysuckle to be sucked at the stems. He wished for peaches, apples, and plums, but they were not yet ripe. To make their shelter more sub- stantial, he broke thin branches into strips, and taking stiff strands of long grass, wove them together like a thick piece of cloth. That was their roof. He bunched thick brambles on three sides, tying them with roots. That was the sides of their house. Padded-down moss provided floor and bed.

When the baby started to leave her, she had slithered in under the branches into the thicket and, holding her thighs together, prayed hard. Sucking in her breath, she tried to keep it in her body, com- manding it back, but the cramps turned into spasms racking and twisting her whole body, and the unformed being slipped out between her locked legs. Rochel did not want to look, but holding the moment to her heart, she knew: This is all I will have of my baby.

"I never want to go back," she said that first night, resting in Yossel's arms.

The second night, strong enough to sit up, she said, "I have to go back."

He shook his head no.

She asked if anybody in Judenstadt had been killed in the fire.

He nodded yes, held up his fingers to six.

"Zev?"

He shook his head no.

Zev was alive. After a day of pretending the world did not exist, it had become increasingly clear to her, as she lay in their tiny hut, that she could no longer evade her responsibilities. She had to face the world. She pushed up Yossel's unruly hair, saw for herself the letters the rabbi had written spelling Truth, EMETH, which with the erasure of one letter would be death, METH.

"I cannot read, Yossel," she began, "but I know the rabbi must . . ." She could not say the words *kill you*. "Yossel," she started again. "You know everything, but you do not know this. Think of me as your looking glass. I say that on your forehead is a word. The word spells Truth, life, God, all that is, and if one letter is taken away, the word spells Death, nothingness, that which is not. When the rabbi made you, he put it there. It was part of the . . ." She fumbled for the right word. "It was part of the promise. We all live to die, but you sooner than most. The rabbi will erase the letter, and when he does, you will go back to earth. He has no choice, Yossel."

Yossel recalled how looking glasses reversed words, flattened and distorted, did not tell the truth. The Hebrew letters on his forehead were, he had deduced, a kind of signature and reverent acknowledgment that the rabbi, not God, had made him. The Truth was he was a golem, extraordinary and individual, more of a man than man.

"Do not think you can go to the stream and take the whole word off, Yossel."

He looked at her with longing. How sad everything had become. He could remember her laughing. But he knew her lost spirit was grief for her lost child.

"You will die instantly if you erase it." She told him he was made only for a time and a purpose and that the time and purpose were over. "I cannot bear you dying, Yossel. We must not permit it." She started to cry. Yet she jerked her shoulders away when he reached for her. "I have hurt, nay, more than hurt, damaged so many others. Listen to me, Yossel."

Yossel pointed to the castle, and then back down in the direction of Judenstadt.

"No, no, you can do nothing about that." She did not believe that some incantation, spell, or combination of words would deliver the community from the emperor. "You must look to yourself, Yossel. Do you understand? I must go back, and you must save yourself."

He took her face in his hands and kissed her.

"It is no good, Yossel. I have broken all the laws." She remembered a story her grandmother had told her, that when Moses broke the tablets of the mitzvot the first time he came down from Sinai and saw the people worshiping the golden bull, all the letters flew back to God, but that the broken tablets were gathered up and later taken with the new mitzvot in the ark. The story was a midrash, her grand-mother explained, a lesson about how you must carry your faults and your failures on your journey.

"You understand why I have to go back?"

He truly did not.

However, she gained confidence as she spoke. She knew she was right. Already each plant portended the coming of winter—the desper-ately taut leaves of the trees, the stick-straight blades of grass, the fruits boasting and bursting in the sun. The grass would become a tough, cut-ting stubble, the day lilies would die, the butterflies rest forever from their flight, and the golem . . . The languor of the days already held a hint of ice-cold winter.

"It is my city. My life."

Yossel pointed north, over the seven hills.

"Pretend to be Christians?"

He did not mean that.

"Unthinkable."

He shook his head. He did not want to be a not-a-Jew, as if he had any choice.

"The whole world is declared. We are Jews." She knew that there were some in Judenstadt who did not consider her a real Jew, and also regarded Yossel as a goyish servant and not a Jew; yet, to her mind, was there anybody more Jewish than the two of them?

He, on his part, just wanted to live with her someplace safe. They could go north to Melnik, Litomerice, Usti nad Labem, and on into Germany, or they could go south along the Vltava River, passing Český Krumlov, on through Austria, and into Italy, to Venice. The world was a large place. He was a big man. He could work, make their living.

"Yossel, we cannot be anywhere else together. That is a dream. You must not return to Prague."

She was wrong in this, he told himself, for he would never let her go.

"I cannot leave and you cannot go back. You will die. The rabbi will be bound to the promise. I could not stand it."

Yossel shook his head, almost smiled. He had carried the rabbi, his father, in his own arms to his bed when he was wounded. How dissonant her words sounded, like the noise of a hundred seagulls screeching, how against God and nature it went, the nature created by God. His father erase him from the face of the earth? His father had made him. He, Yossel, was an act of conception greater than any union between man and woman. He was fruit of his father's mind and most deliberately formed in his every part, although, to be strictly honest, he wished for a voice. However, he acknowledged, perfection did not yet exist in the world.

"Listen to me, I will go back. I will tell them I was lost in the forest."

Yossel shook his head no. If she insisted on going back, he would act as if he had just found her, that he had been looking all this time.

"I will tell Zev I wandered away and could not find my path. He does not know about the baby. He does not know we . . . He knows nothing."

Yossel shook his head no, no, no.

"They will be mourning the dead still, and I will slip back, mourn with them, repent. Zev is a good man. He is generous of heart. I will spend the rest of my days with him."

Tears collected in Yossel's eyes.

"Yossel, do not cry. Please. It is the only way. My duty is to follow the teachings of the Torah, do good deeds. I have never done a good deed in my whole life, and do you see how I have been punished?" She broke down. "An innocent child . . ." She could not continue.

How could she be so obstinate and so wrong? He could not follow her logic. She was using words she had never used before. Were not the two of them married in the most essential way?

"I have to go back because of what I was taught." And she began to prate like a child at lessons. "I salt the matzos, I bless the bread, on the first day of Rosh Hashanah, I go to the banks of the river and cast my sins into the water. This is the blessing for the washing of hands. Put your extra coins in the pushke, the charity box. It is a mitzvah to not engage in gainful work on Shabbat." Then she stopped. "Daily life adds up to something, Yossel. Perhaps it is all we have."

That is what she had. It is a lot, she told herself, everything.

"You think I can be a righteous woman with you, live somewhere else?"

Yossel nodded yes, yes, that was what he wanted her to understand.

"Yossel, listen to me. To be a Jew is to live honestly." So saying, she was lying, for was she not deceiving him with this train of thought? She understood far too well that when she went back she would not be welcomed as a prodigal daughter, but rather regarded as a pariah. Ostracism and punishment awaited her. But she could not have him believe that, not for a moment. She had to lie in order to save him. He would be her one good deed.

Live honestly, he mused, is that what she calls it? The first day of his life, he considered Prague beautiful. Now he understood that Prague was a squalid city full of hate and spite, and he realized within the walls of the ghetto, Rochel, confined to a room little bigger than a cell, was a prisoner. That was the truth. What could she know of other places, the world at large? Except once she had looked into his eyes.

Realizing, however, that he could not convince her otherwise, he acquiesced, letting her think that her argument prevailed, nodding as if accepting her proposal, permitting her to believe the unbelievable, that is, that he would allow her to go back and never see her again. She could go back, return to her former duties, her husband, her room, and he would go far over the hills, defying, evading the fate she described, which was nothing more than her fear manifested, a fanciful rendition of ghetto gossip. The rabbi harm him? Pure folly. "Abraham, Abraham, do not hurt your son." God was merciful and just. He did not require blood sacrifice. His own father loved him, Yossel Ben Loew, with all his heart and mind. It would take only a few days in her former existence, confined within the damp walls, sewing without adequate candlelight, Yossel reasoned, for her to come around to his view, and just as she was regretting her decision, sensing herself trapped and doomed to her narrow life, he would return from over the mountains. By then he would have found a town, work, a room, and be able to take her away. She would see.

They silently walked together out of the woods and down the grassy slope, as far as they could without being detected. Tears spilled out of her eyes.

"Yossel, Yossel."

He groaned in reply. For a moment, she almost changed her mind. But then she heard the bells, all the different bells of the city noting their individual hours. It was time.

Assured that she had saved him from certain death, bracing her resolve to accept sneers, divorce, all that lay in store for her, she headed on into town slowly and haltingly because the blood had not stopped coming. Before crossing the Stone Bridge, she stopped to rest in Master Galliano's shop by At the House of the Three Ostriches. Master Galliano's wife took the weary traveler to the back of the shop, had her stretch out on a cot, and brought her water to drink and some bread and cheese. The kind woman took off Rochel's dirty clothes, wiped her clean with a rag, dressed her in a fresh skirt and bodice, and from a scrap of fine blue linen made her a new scarf, careful, as was prescribed by Jewish Law, not to mix animal- and vegetable-based garments.

Rochel was touched by this woman's concern. The cloth piled high in the shop reminded her of her dear, dead grandmother and the nights Master Galliano brought fabric and thread across the Stone Bridge in a wheelbarrow. That had been a good life and she had not known it.

Master Galliano, too, was emphatic, almost stern. "Rochel, your people are doomed. If not the emperor, the townspeople will destroy your neighborhood, for Thaddaeus preaches to their restlessness, makes them fear the future. He has singled you out not only as a Jew, but a sinner. It will not go well with you. People know about you and the golem. You must let them think you are dead or gone."

"You do not understand, Master Galliano," Rochel protested. "I let my passions cloud my mind and overrule my duty. I lost my child, ruined my husband, brought dishonor on my people. I deserve chastisement, retribution, must pay the penalty for all the pain I have caused."

"Child, you are so mistaken. Youth is not a crime. Stay, hide here with us."

She would not hear of it. Like Yossel, they did not understand. Bidding Master Galliano and his wife good-bye, Rochel left their care and headed toward Judenstadt. Out in the river, she saw Václav rowing. He was weeping. Fisherman were on the bank mending their nets. The Stone Bridge was getting crowded. And shortly, as she anticipated, people recognizing her began to spit: "Whore, whore." Steadily, she kept walking. Holding her head high, she passed through the gates of Judenstadt. Her own people turned their faces away: "For shame, for shame." The rabbi's door was open. Perl was at the fireplace, stirring some porridge, grandchildren arrayed around her. As soon as little Fiegel saw her friend, she started up:

"Rochel, Rochel, we were looking all over the place for you."

Perl turned slowly from her kettle, gave Rochel a hard look, and then, not able to restrain herself, she lurched to embrace the young woman.

"My poor child." The two women held each other, cried.

"Who is it, who is it, what is all this ruckus?" The rabbi hobbled down the stairs with difficulty, his shoulder still sore.

"She has come back," Perl said.

"I see that," the rabbi replied slowly, standing on the step. "Yossel? Where is he?"

"I sent him away," Rochel said. She could see relief wash over his face. Then she hung her head, would not meet her rabbi's eyes.

"Come, now," the rabbi said. "Stand straight, Rochel, be brave. Be a woman."

30

K ELLEY DRESSED LIKE a servant, presented himself to the castle kitchen as a servant, and in the clamor and confusion was believed to be a servant and hired to work in the kitchen for the emperor's birthday. The emperor's kitchen included storehouses, larders, a boiling house with a cauldron kept going night and day, a pastry house for savory and sweet, a confectionery, a spicer and chandlery, an ice house, and the great kitchen. The master cook had twenty-five assistants in addition to children turnings the spits. There was a scullery where silverware was boiled and pewter scoured with sand. Water was piped in from the river. Over all was a chief clerk who had his own office and kept the kitchen accounts. The great kitchen had several massive fireplaces, some with windup jacks, a mechanism for turning a spit more advanced than dogs running in a wheel, although there were spits with dogs in wheels as well. Along one wall were charcoal stoves with small pots and ovens. The bread ovens, however, were in a separate house by the river because of the constant threat of fire.

The feast was not until the evening, but already at early morn there was much to be done and Kelley was set to work at once in the confectionery shaving sugar for marzipan, breaking up nutmeats, picking pits from cherries, and cutting shapes of clubs and hearts in the soft dough to be baked straightaway. There were to be, he soon discovered, several tasters for the emperor that night—the emperor's professional taster, Master Shrack, a walking waste of bones, who from years of tasting had developed an aversion to most food and never finished a meal, and two other new tasters brought in especially for the occasion. Václav, who often tasted, had not been to the castle in some days because his son was sick. Nobody knew if the son was still living or if Václav himself had taken ill. Kirakos also was ill with something or other, no doubt too much drink. Everybody was too busy to check in on him. He was a doctor, after all, and could cure himself. The elixir was to be tested after dinner in a special ceremony held in private.

Heavy damask napkins, candles, silver plates, golden spoons were taken out of the locked supply room. There were to be knives for all, as well as forks, although most would prefer to eat with their fingers as God intended. Guards were already stationed at each setting, lest anybody be tempted to make off with any of the golden plates. Great bouquets of roses and lilies from the gardens, and the more fragile flowers, were brought at the last minute from the royal greenhouses, and ferns were already picked from stream beds and stored in the icehouse and cool safes where butter and other perishables were kept. Violets were put to float in bowls of ice. The emperor's table was decorated with tulips, which, while not in season, were kept growing in special greenhouses year-round. Pears, oranges, plums, apricots, peaches from southern climes, and berries of every sort were piled in artful pyramids. In all the commotion of servers changing into livery, the musicians and other entertainers arriving, meat being basted, pies being checked, vegetables warmed, and gravies mixed, the others did not notice Kelley as he made his way down to the lowest level, the wine cellar, where the castle's wine was kept in big wooden iron-hooped barrels and the floor was strewn with sawdust to keep it from getting slippery. All afternoon the carriages had been arriving in the courtyards. From the kitchens they could hear the clip-clop of horses on cobblestones, the roll of heavy wheels, the swish of taffeta skirts.

"I am here to serve at the emperor's table, his wine," Kelley announced.

"Ah, good, good." The master wine server showed him where the earthen wine jugs were shelved, how to twist the knob on the casks. Each guest would have his own jug kept full by the server who stood behind him. By the door was a vat of honey mixed with clove and ginger. For every jug there was to be one scoop of sweet.

When the volley of trumpets for the summoning to the table sounded, Kelley pulled his serving cap tight around his face. He only needed a moment when he could drop the opium in the wine, stir it

well with the honey mixture. True, he was frightened at what he was
about to do, but he knew he could not let any scruples stand in his
way. More butterflies had died. Soon people would notice. The volley of trumpets sounded again. That was their signal in the wine cellar. He stepped forth with alacrity, drew the wine, made his way
down the long row of barrels, dug into the honey vat, and, spooning
in the dripping goo and spices, made his way out. Quick as a rabbit,
he ran up the first flight of stairs, and for one moment was alone. This
was his chance. Inside the purse which hung on his belt, the pods
were already crushed and mixed with nutmeg, cardamom, and mace.
"Drats, double drats," he muttered to himself, although in one small
sense, only in a tiny way, he was relieved, for now all the servers were
at the door. Before them the room was a blaze of light. Chandeliers
of the finest crystal hung from the ceiling, glittering with candles.
The emperor sat on a new throne of gold, with a velvet canopy
topped with a small replica of the crown and bordered with tassels
and gems. Close at hand were his scepter and orb. Next to him were
various nobles and officials. He was wearing, despite the heat of the
day, an ermine robe and, of course, his heavy crown. Below the dais
where the throne was placed, Kelley made out the many more long
tables. Dee was in his usual black, watching the emperor assiduously,
as if by stare alone he could strike him dead. Head low, Kelley
marched in, leading the line of servers, and with adroit skill poured
the emperor's wine and then stood at attention behind him. To his
right and left, on low stools, were stationed the tasters. The emperor,
who never looked at servants anyway, did not recognize Kelley in his
serving apparel.

"To the Empire," the emperor said, lifting his golden goblet high
aloft for the grand toast, after the tasters had sipped. That was the
cue for the chamber singers and seventy-seven musicians—some
with recorders, large and small, others with the twisted pipe of the
serpent, the viola d'gamba, and lutes of various kinds—to troop in,
Pucci first. A group of servers began presenting the food. The first
dishes were seafood—oysters, packed in ice and nettles, brought in
fresh from the Atlantic coast, and pâté from the Netherlands, pike,
jellied eel, porpoises, and seals. Throughout, wine was drunk. The
second course was announced by a silvery peal from the trumpeters.
This was game—venison, boar, pheasant, quail, bittern, woodcock,
partridge, heron, egret, wild duck, crane. Wine, more wine was served

up. Domesticated meats came next. One hundred oxen were served, two hundred sheep, fifty swans, and over a thousand geese, two hundred capons and kids. Wine, more wine. In addition there were cold pies and creamed dishes. Of course, ham and squab straight from the spit, radishes and cherries, asparagus grown in the palace garden, artichokes aplenty. Butter instead of lard was used as a flavoring, and condiments such as lemons, capers, and anchovies were the seasonings. The meat, relatively fresh, unlike peasant food, was cooked quickly, did not need great quantities of salt, pepper, vinegar, and garlic to disguise the rot. No ears and feet, snout, belly, or back, first cuts all.

"Wine, more wine," the emperor called.

Kelley rushed downstairs, drew more wine. From the floor above, he could hear the musicians playing music by Alessandro Orologio. Despite the thick layer of sawdust, the floor was getting slippery. At the vat, he opened his purse. He must do it, do it now. He had assured Dee he would not be a coward. Quick, Jack be nimble, but he found the purse slipping out of his hand. Jesus, he was sweating like a bloody pig.

"Hurry, hurry." A server rushed in. A horde of maids and manservants followed, pushing their way. By the time Kelley was upstairs again, the theatricals had started. He poured the wine, positioned himself behind the emperor. Kepler, nearby, not looking up, was picking at his food, and Brahe, ravenously consuming all in sight, also did not notice Kelley. Dee stared down into his plate, appearing sick.

Pride came first in the little drama, a handsome youth done in tones of purple, aristocratic in the fashion of the Venetians, each leg of hose a different color, and a velvet hat, large and floppy, worn over one ear, with an ostentatious, gleaming brooch fastened to one side. He strutted across the parquet floor like a peacock, advanced on the ladies, hands on hips, looked on the gentlemen with an impudent stare. I am Pride, your very own, do not cry, do not moan. Feed me praise every day, I will never go away. Avarice, a fat, florid man, trod close behind with a big pouch of coins hung on his belt. He clinked and he counted, he fondled bolts of fine cloth brought out for his inspection, and disdained the music of the lute, he was so intent to be seated with his book of accounts. Gluttony was a very fat fellow indeed, several pillows stuffed into his doublet, with grease on his chin, a big bib spotted with food stains. He carried a drumstick in one fist, a pie in another. Gluttony is at your table, confine me not to the stable. Lust pursued a young boy dressed as a comely lass who had apples for breasts and bolstered hips. Sloth snored, walked in his sleep adorned in a nightshirt and cap. Anger arrived punching the air, snarling like a dog. Envy followed, coveting all—Pride's purple coat, Avarice's coins, and Glutton's food, even Sloth his sleep. Then Anger hit Pride with a club in his face, stabbed Avarice in the back, ran Gluttony through with a pike, exploding his belly into a string of sausages, strangled Lust about the balls, smothered Sloth with a pillow, and throttled Envy with his bare hands.

Those old morality plays, Kelley thought, how tired they seem when you have Shakespeare. The orchestra took up an old Czech folk tune. "He who only looks up to heaven," the singers chorused, "may break his nose on earth."

"Wine, more wine."

Up and down, down and up. He feared the whole evening would slip through his hands without a chance. Cannot, cannot fail, he recited to himself. To fail would be to accept death, his death, Dee's. Yet he had never killed a man, and in truth, despite his brave words, the thought troubled him. Dee, perhaps should have been the one. After all, he was used to war, had participated, in various ways, in the destruction of the Spanish Armada. However, Kelley reassured himself, he had forged and foraged, robbed, tricked people of their purses, been a cutpurse. But never a cutthroat. Never a cutthroat. Do not think upon it, Kelley, you rogue, he told himself. Cannot, cannot fail. And finally he had a chance on the stairway to stop and, unseen, pour in the crushed poppy heads, mix them well. In point of fact, it was an altogether good time for the dirty deed. The emperor was already drunken and sleepy-looking. Guests were lolling about, throwing bones to the floor to be gobbled up by the court dogs. Petaka was well satisfied in the corner with what appeared to be half a cow. A few musicians remained playing tunes in a most desultory fashion.

"Wine, more wine."

The emperor put his goblet down, sat back, took it up, looked about, gesticulated with his fork, paused, slowly brought the wine to his lips, put it down. And then he raised his glass, threw back his head, was just about to commence to drink.

Dee raised his head to reveal an agonized look on his face. He put his hand to his chest as if wounded, opened his mouth.

But it was Kelley who began screaming first, "No, no, do not, cannot."

"No, no, do not drink." It was Dee, then Kelley, then the two of them in chorus shouting above the roar of the crowd. "Do not drink, Emperor Rudolph. Do not."

"What? What are you saying?" The emperor was flustered.

Kelley, following his second thoughts, moving his feet, rushed forth, grabbed the goblet, and in one splash dashed the liquid on the floor.

"What in God's name are you doing?" the emperor exclaimed.

"Do not drink, you will die."

The emperor stood up. "Kelley, Dr. Dee, you talk thus?"

"No, do not drink," John Dee concurred, rushing up to stand beside his partner.

"The wine is tainted," Kelley said.

"The wine is tainted." The cry went out. "The wine is tainted."

Kelley now had third thoughts. Dear God, why had he not let it happen? Why such cowardice? Why could he not, as many did, kill a man? Kill his enemy? Kill his killer?

Dee, who a moment before had been seated, praying for God to forgive him, was now in great confusion; he did not know where he was, he was so dizzy. In another second, he would have been a murderer. They had not presented murder in their list of sins.

"It is poison, Your Majesty," Dee affirmed quietly.

"Poison?" The emperor stood up, wavered.

"Poison?" everybody chorused.

"We could not do it," Dee said, wringing his hands. "We could not do it. We cannot."

"Death is afoot," somebody screamed.

Anna Marie, who had been seated at a lesser table, bounded forth, tripped up the little box of stairs to the emperor's table, threw her substantial body over the emperor.

"Murder in the castle," somebody shouted.

"Get them," commanded the emperor, restored in a moment to his full wits. He extricated himself from Anna Marie with some difficulty. "Get the murderers."

Kelley and Dee walked swiftly to the edges of the room, picked up their pace, and, turning a corner to the hallway, began to take large granddaddy steps, giant strides, a big hop and a skip, and finally broke into a crisp run.

"Stop them, stop them," the emperor cried. "Somebody check the butterflies."

Guards rushed forth, their sabers unsheathed.

"Run," Kelley hissed. "Run. Run as fast as you can."

"Arrest the traitors," bellowed the emperor, "drag them to the Dalibor Tower for immediate execution."

In the corridor above the kitchen, Kelley sped to the right toward the bedchambers, pushing John Dee to the left. Kelley hopped up several flights, stumbled, fell down, righted himself, opened a door, and slipped inside, quietly closing it behind him. Crawling under a bed, he tried to control his breathing. John Dee sped down to the wine cellar, then up the outside stairs to the kitchen courtyard, and then, without turning back once, he headed straight for the Golden Ox.

It took the guards about an hour to find Kelley under the bed. He was pulled, weeping and wailing, to the jug, a hole, standing room only, in the Dalibor Tower.

Part V

31

TYCHO BRAHE THOUGHT he was going to die from an overfilled bladder during the emperor's birthday party, and when he was finally able to run out of the room to relieve himself, his belly about to burst, he feared he might wet his breeches, disgrace himself. It had been that way for hours. Yet to absent the dinner before the emperor would have been impolite, a breach of decorum, and so he held his waters like a man, like a true gentleman. When the mad melee started and he gratefully rushed to the stairway, fumbling hurriedly at his codpiece, anticipating the ease of release, a great golden arc returning comfort and peace to body and soul, he sighed happily. Yet, after the first few drops, nothing more came out, and an excruciating pain seared his stomach, arched up his legs, gripped his groin. His feet buckled and he had to grasp the wall.

The air around him thinned, darkened. "Jepp, Jepp," he bleated from the stairwell. Barely able to hold up his bulk, sweat trickling down his back, his face, and coating his hands, slipping and hobbling, Brahe made his way back to the dining hall.

There he found fights between courtiers had broken out. Servants, dodging the flying clots of food, scurried for plates, goblets, and silverware to claim for their own. And a group of roving marauders happening to pass by, hearing the commotion, swarmed in to grab what they could. The emperor had disappeared. Brahe spotted Jepp under a table.

"Get Kirakos," Brahe groaned to Jepp. "I cannot make my water. Be hasty about it."

Jepp, low to the ground, skittering along the edge of the room, raced down the hallway, scooted across the courtyard, and with as big a stride as his short legs could afford him, bounded up the stairs above the emperor's galleries to Kirakos's door.

"Do not come too close, Jepp." The dark room smelled of pus and urine, stale rags.

"You speak German, Russian."

"Yes, I speak the German, Jepp, now go."

"Brahe has a stomachache, Russian."

"Better a stomachache than the pox."

Jepp could not quite make out his words. "A stomachache is better than to be a sot?"

A wet cloth covered Kirakos's face; another one was thrown across his stringy neck. The Russian, like a blackamoor slave, waved a clutch of plumes from At the House of the Three Ostriches above his ailing master. The room was cool as a cave.

"He is sick, you cannot see? Begone," the Russian hissed.

"But what happens when the doctor is sick?" Jepp was at a loss.

"You pray," the Russian said, and indeed the little wooden crucifix he wore on a string around his neck was in his hand. "Get another doctor, the Crato, somebody else."

"The rest of them are quacks. You come," he said, turning to the Russian. "If you can speak, you can heal."

"Nyet," Sergey said. "I cannot leave."

The Russian lifted the rag, pointed. "What do you think those things are on his face?"

Kirakos lay inert, his eyes glittering like chips of flint in a field of red pustules.

"The pox," Jepp screeched, backing out of the room.

MEANWHILE, OUTSIDE THE walls of Judenstadt, a crowd of drunks had gathered.

"The witch is back," they chanted.

"The adulteress has returned."

"Death to the Jewess."

Hastily, the table over the rabbi's trapdoor was moved away, the rug taken up, and Rochel descended the twig ladder, was told not to make a sound.

AS KELLEY WAS being dragged away, Dr. John Dee got into the back of Karel's cart, pulling old clothes, bones, refuse, and rough sacking over his head and body. Oswald, in bliss a few moments before, eating and defecating at the same time, was annoyed at this turn in events.

THE EMPEROR, WHO had sequestered himself in his Kunstkammer with Petaka, admitted only one person, Rumpf, his haughty advisor. "Find Václav," he barked, staring at his prize Dürer, *Garland of the Roses*, seeing his own face in the painting—in place of Maximilian, his relative—kneeling by the Virgin, or he could be St. Dominic giving out the garlands of roses, or a cherub, or Dürer himself, leaning against the tree, taking it all in. Those were different times. At the moment, the emperor would have liked to be anybody but himself.

"Václav is in Karlsbad with his recovering son, Majesty, taking the medicinal waters."

Rudolph turned from the Dürer and fixed his gaze on his favorite portrait, Arcimboldo's depiction of him as Vertumnus, the ancient Roman god of vegetation and transformation, in which his nose was a pear, apples his cheeks, cherries his lips, blackberries his eyes, with a great head of grapes. When had he been able to pose for pictures, give his heart to art, delight in his collection, find pleasure? How had it all gotten away from him? Boyhood in Spain, beloved brother Ernst by his side, hunting in Viennese forests as a young man. The first time he saw Anna Marie. He had asked Strada, his antiquarian: Who is this pretty lady? My daughter, Your Highness. Anna Marie had been shy and slim as a girl then.

"Václav's son is recovering from what?" Rudolph wondered if he could recover from this chaos.

"The pox, Your Majesty."

"Why did not somebody tell me of this? If the boy has the pox, then Václav could give me the pox." The emperor pushed his sleeve back, checked first one arm, then another. "And how could Václav afford to take his son to Karlsbad? Václav must be fetched. It is an imperial crisis. Every able-bodied man must be at my disposal. Get a messenger to ride for Karlsbad instantly, immediately, right away, do you hear? Have the guards locate Dee and Kelley; the scurvy miscreants will be so racked and ruined, they will pray for death."

"Kelley, yes: Dee, no."

"No? No? Do not say no to me. Dee has vanished in thin air? Now you see him, now you do not? He is not a real magi, he is an imposter, and Kelley must be executed as soon as possible. Have the city gates been closed to all? Have a platform built on the Square for the execution. Where is that damnable Rosenberg?"

"At Český Krumlov, Your Majesty."

"That haunted castle? Do they expect to conceive a child there? More like a monster."

The emperor put his head in his hands. The heavy thump of Don Carlos's dragging foot was like the beat of a drum, louder every day. He got back in his chair, drew his cloak about him, feeling the chill of close-by death, although it was a sweltering summer day.

"The captain of the guards will take care of everything, Your Majesty, do not worry."

"Do not worry? The captain of the guards may very well take care of a palace coup. Woe is me. I must start drinking the elixir. Did you notice they wanted to kill me before I was immortal, while I was a mere vulnerable mortal? Where in God's sake is Kirakos?"

"He is abed, I have heard, Your Majesty."

"People at Karlsbad bathing in medicinal waters, people taking the country air at their castles, people abed—what is this spreading through my realm like the Plague?"

"Perhaps it is the Plague, Your Majesty."

"We have not had Plague for three years." The emperor stood up, put his hands behind his back, paced. He was only wearing one shoe. Where had the other one gone? "Are you trying to befuddle me? Is it Plague or pox? Kirakos is sleeping? Wake him."

"Kirakos attended the boy, Your Majesty."

"Ah, yes, I remember the fool must run after Václav. So he has the pox, has he? What was in his mind? I wonder. Now he will pay dearly for his good deed. Everybody will pay for everything. What are the butterflies doing? How are they doing? We have vats of that elixir ready, thank God."

"Beg pardon, Your Majesty, but the butterflies are all dead."

"Dead? Dead?" The emperor jumped up again. "How can the butterflies be dead?"

The butterflies, having given up their day, lay in a thick velvet carpet on the floor of their netted city, wings folded in an attitude of prayer.

"I am sorry, Your Majesty."

"I told you they were mountebanks, saboteurs, treasonous, ungrateful murderers. And where in the hell are Brahe and Kepler?"

"Brahe is sick, Your Majesty."

"Of the pox, too?"

"They do not know. He cannot make his water."

"I am not surprised. I told Brahe he should stop stuffing and drowning himself. Kepler, is he abed, too, or taking medicinal waters, or is he mooning at the moon? Brahe should have known."

BRAHE WAS IN too much pain to know anything but pain. A rosary had been placed in his hands and a tablecloth wrapped around him as a dozen Slovene guards bore him aloft, with an entourage of priests and birthday revelers following him to his home below the Strahov Monastery. Jepp led the small procession.

"Make way, make way," the dwarf called out. "Make way, make way."

"Kepler," Brahe moaned.

"Somebody get Kepler." Jepp hated the scrawny scarecrow, but he knew that his master considered Kepler his heavenly heir.

"I am here." Kepler had seen Brahe stagger back into the dining room, lost sight of him. Now he stepped forward.

"My dear colleague," Brahe groaned, his arms akimbo while his stomach rose like a whale from the surface of the seas. "I am going to die."

"You are not going to die," Kepler said, taking Brahe's hand.

"I want Monteverdi played at my funeral, *Zefiro torna.*"

"Hush. You will be fine."

"I am dying, Johannes, give me some credence, give me this due."

"You are not dying. You ate too much."

"I know all too well how that feels and it is not gluttony alone which tortures me. I tell you, the very devil has entered my tired carcass, is squeezing my bladder with his treacherous talons. . . . I want you to be with me until my end. Jepp, Jepp, where are you, Jepp?"

"I am right here." Jepp was holding the other of Brahe's hands, the rosary dripping between them.

Frau Brahe did not seem to be home, the servants had vacated the premises, and the children were nowhere about, for their toys were abandoned on the floor, dishes were left on the table, and the whole house was as empty as if a wild wind had blown through, and all the people, fearful of storm, had sought shelter elsewhere. The guards settled poor Brahe in his bed. Crato, the next-to-best palace doctor, was sent for.

"You are not going to die," Kepler repeated.

"I wish, Johannes, you would believe me. You are denying a dying man his last say. I held my water too long. Now it is poisoning my body. I will die of politeness."

"You are not going to die of anything, Tycho."

"So you are saying I am immortal like the emperor hopes to be?"

"You are too young to die." Kepler was trying to convince not only Brahe, but himself as well. How could Brahe die? He was the very spirit of life, a man who enjoyed everything.

"I am not young, Johannes. I am old. It is the way of the world. My time is upon me."

"But you are at the height—"

"Of my powers? Come now, Johannes, my powers were never very high. I have a methodical mind, yes, but . . . Jepp, Jepp, where are you, Jepp?"

"I am right here." Jepp had, in fact, crawled into bed with Brahe.

"Jepp, you have served me well, but I am done for."

ROCHEL CROUCHED UNDER the strings of dried apples and amid the turnips, cabbages, and jars of pickled onions in the rabbi's cellar. She was not sure how much time had gone by, but it seemed that she had always been there, knew nothing else. Finally she heard a voice. It was the rabbi. The door opened.

"We need to move you to the Altneu Synagogue. Come, it is night. Nobody will see." The rabbi knew Rochel would not be safe anywhere in Prague. Even within Judenstadt, there were whispers and murmers against her. Everywhere and to all people she was a ready target for approbation and hate. She was not a modest woman. Was there anything worse?

"I am resigned," Rochel said, yet she offered no protest, finding herself readily following him up the street in the thick darkness, climbing the stairs in quick step, ascending breathlessly to the attic of the synagogue.

"Eventually—nay, soon—we need to get you out of Prague," the rabbi whispered. "The city gates are closed, but Karel can hide you in his cart. They let him go to the dump by the Pest Cemetery twice a day. We just need to fix a time."

"Why are you doing all this for me, Rabbi? I have sinned."

"Sin is between you and God, Rochel. You are a Jew and owe it to yourself, to all of us, to survive." He gave her a weary smile.

She sat down on the dusty floor by the one window, careful not to let her shadow show. All about her were discarded and tattered prayer books that, according to Law and practice, could not be thrown away. If she knew how to read, she would have read, been consoled, for despite her determination to meet her fate, as soon as she arrived back in Judenstadt, she had lost her courage and resolution. It had completely vanished. Indeed, she was so frightened, she regretted her decision to return. Why had she not gone away with Yossel? Or hidden at Master Galliano's? Now she just wanted to be forgiven. She had returned for her own just punishment like a child holding out her hand for rapping. Had she somehow believed that if she demonstrated regret, humility, and a willingness to be good ever after, she would escape persecution?

Dear God, she prayed, have mercy on me. From under the slanted roof, she caught a glimpse of the ribbon of the river, the lights of the castle twinkling like stars fallen to the earth. The world was so lovely. Thus, her fears, for a little time, were lifted by hope, even as the soft swipe of the dark wings of the Angel of Death brushed against the beveled window.

ALL ABOUT THE city there was a restlessness afoot, an ill wind stirring. Under the Astronomical Clock, a herd of sheep had gotten loose and were milling about. Horses began to veer off the path along the bank of the river, dead fish washed up on the shores, cows, previously docile, began to kick at the wooden sides of their barns, pigs, not yet led to slaughter, squealed heartrending cries, and dogs ran yelping. People, too, began to act strangely. Some shrieked confession on the street. In other parts of Prague, church doors flew open, and although deserted by their priests, they became packed with penitents scraping toward the altars on their knees. Footpads and cutpurses in their heyday began stealing goods from toppled booths and shops.

"The emperor is dying of poison, the Turks are coming, devils have been released from deep with the earth, a meteor is going to fall from the sky," the cry went up. Accordingly, there was nothing to be done but grab the children, put whatever worldly goods could be borne on backs and in carts, and get out of town. In the middle of the night, the townspeople started to troop in ragged parade toward the city gates.

"Let us out, let us out," they droned in ominous unison.

AT BRAHE'S HOUSE, everything was in great disarray, too.

"I am drowning in my own piss. Where is that damn doctor?" Brahe seethed.

"Ticki, Ticki, Ticki, my love." Frau Brahe jiggled in.

"Careful, my pet," Brahe warned. "Tummy is hurting."

Frau Brahe's face was red, and like her husband, she was not small.

"The doctor is on his way, Tickie-Boo. We heard that the Plague was coming, so the children and I hid in the cellar, then we heard tromping overhead. At first we thought we were being robbed. . . . Cure him, Johannes, do not stand there like an idiot. Make him well, by God." The strings which Brahe used to keep the silver piece attached to his nose had been undone and his face, with a valley where there should have been a ridge, looked like ruins, but every night he made himself naked for his wife, and to her his ravaged face was dear and familiar.

"Let me have a good passing. Just grant me that," the big man moaned.

"NOW IT IS up to the Jews," the emperor said to Rumpf, handling various of his treasures—his mandrake root in the shape of a man, his agate bowl, which supposedly was the Holy Grail, his powder horn made of narwhale horn. "I cannot be denied eternity because of those false Brits; they will not get away with it. Nobody will get away with anything. Where is the golem, where is the rabbi, where is the Jewess?"

"WHERE IS THAT crapacious Crato?" Frau Brahe asked Jepp.

"Father, Father." A troop of merry children crowded into the bedchamber.

"Guess what?" a bright-eyed little girl, plump like her father, said.
"The army has been called up. Pigs have broken their pens. Can I
have a pony, ple-ase?"

Brahe groaned.

Crato arrived at the sickroom, bag in hand. The man was so old, he
could barely walk and hardly see. He had to feel his way to the
patient with the aid of a stick. Hair stuck out of his nostrils in twin
flames. His ears sprouted angry tufts and his eyebrows were so bushy
his eyes were buried in a lair of hair. As soon as Kepler saw the physician, he realized all was lost.

"What seems to be the matter?" Crato asked in his distracted fashion.

"I seem to be dying," Brahe sneered.

The grizzled gray dragon, sorry excuse of a physician, nodded as if
agreeing.

"Truth be told, I cannot pass my water, Crato. I am bursting. Have
mercy, puncture me."

"Oh, my, it seems that a bleeding is called for. Somebody fetch an
astrologer to see if the stars are propitious. When were you born,
Brahe, on what day?"

"For God's sake, I am an astrologer, astronomer, myself, Crato, and
know well I do not need to be bled. I need to be pierced. Somebody
get me a pick, a needle, an awl, a dagger."

A man if possible more elderly than the physician shuffled into
Brahe's bedchamber carrying a roll of charts and a large tome. Crato
had already taken out his blades, a bag of sawdust to catch the blood,
his blood cup.

"Is this happening to me?" Brahe groaned.

"And also the leeching?" Crato asked the newly arrived astrologer.
"See if it is a good time." A jar full of the slimy, white worms was
brought out, placed in good view of the suffering Brahe.

"I think, too, while we are at it, we should send for Pistorius, the
confessor," Crato suggested.

Brahe closed his eyes, wished to die that moment.

"God be praised we are not in the dog days of August, otherwise we could not bleed," the astrologer announced. "No bloodletting, no copulation in the time of flying snakes." He fixed Brahe with a steely glance. "If phlegmatic, bleed in Aries. In Libra for melancholic, in Cancer for choleric. Not advisable to bleed for spleen disorders when the moon is in Cancer."

"The moon is in Cancer, you fool," Brahe said, remembering, when forecasting for himself earlier that day, the stars telling him that this month would be fraught with difficulties.

"Ah, so it is in Cancer, but is it your spleen, my good fellow? How are your humors?"

Brahe looked at Kepler. A melancholy recognition passed between them. Brahe regretted he had wasted so much time hating his friend and colleague, slighting him in conversation, withholding valuable information, and depriving him of many small courtesies. To think he had prided himself on the observatory he once had on an island in Denmark. The edifice itself was now vague in memory, but what he remembered clearly was the view of the lake, the thick forest, the quick calls of birds in the morning, the sudden splash of a fish jumping out of the water. How stupid he had been. A delicious breeze was coming through the open window now, and although he was still in pain, by breathing deeply, some of it was eased. It was late and the noise from the street had calmed down. Night cupped the earth, a black sieve with holes of bright light. How he wanted to live, if just for one more day.

"Perhaps a sip of water," Kepler said.

"I never want to drink water in my life again." Laughing hurt. "It is important, Kepler, that you propagate my ideas. I know that we may be at odds in some matters, that you believe the sun is the center of the planetary system, but do not ignore what I have done."

THE EMPEROR, TIRED of pacing and weary of waiting for the capture of Dee and the summoning of the rabbi, and no longer interested in his curiosities, decided to entertain himself with a book from his vast library, a volume he had acquired as a gift from his uncle, Philip II of Spain, on the instruments of torture used by the Inquisition. Each instrument was illustrated. For instance, the garrote was a frame attached to the ceiling and hung with cords to wrap around limbs, tightening until they cut through to bone.

"ARIES IS A fire sign creating hot, choleric diseases," the astrologer was droning on. "Do not shave when the moon occupies this sign. Noxious vapors gain access through the pores. Diseases are attuned to seasons of the year. For instance, ulcerations and blotches come in winter, migraines and leprosies at the turn of the year. In spring the lunatic diseases are most prominent and rheumatisms, gouts, and colics. Ague is definitely a winter disease."

DEE, SUCCESSFULLY GETTING through the city gates in Karel's cart, concealed in a pile of clothes in a puppeteer's wagon heading toward the German states, prayed that he would see his friend again, that they would meet in London and, over several stout mugs of good British ale, laugh about their time in Prague. Above him, swinging with the rhythm of the wagon, hung the many puppets—Kasparek, the Czech hero, the Night Hag on her broom, the Jew, the wild man of the woods, the devil, the winsome maid, the evil emperor.

THE STRAPPADO WAS a pulley which pulled prisoners up by the wrists with weights attached to the ankles. This pulled the shoulders out of the sockets. Ingenious, the emperor mused. This was the torture Machiavelli had endured when he fell out of favor with his prince and patron.

KEPLER HAD FALLEN asleep sitting in the corner of Brahe's room, Jepp had fallen asleep on one side of the pillow, Frau Brahe on the other, and the Brahe children had arrayed themselves around the bed as if their father were a fire to keep them warm. Brahe was listening to the sound of his own heart beating its solitary rhythm. During the night he passed some water, which offered some relief, although the urine was bloody and, when held to the candles in the sconces in a clear glass receptacle by the physician, revealed little gobblets of pus. Not a good sign.

WATER TORTURE—NOW, that was a favorite, the emperor reflected. The prisoner was bound upside down to an inclined ladder and forced to swallow a strip of linen. Water was poured down the throat and must be swallowed to avoid choking on the cloth. The belly became distended and water poured through all the orifices.

WHEN THE FIRST small skim of gray cut across the horizon, Rochel straightened her tight legs and imagined Yossel far away in a tall and clean city of the north, or perhaps he had changed his mind, traveled toward the Italian states. The word *Italy* was itself warm, full of joy. *Venice* sounded like victory. She had never been in a boat, not even on the Vltava, and to think of a whole city afloat was beyond her comprehension. Then she chided herself. What caprice it was to dabble in such fancies, for it was just that kind of dreamy desire for adventure that had led her astray. Boating and sunshine, the utter presumption. Indeed, her vanity had not led to victory, but rather endangered her whole community, just as the rabbi's daughters had predicted that day long ago when she resisted having her hair cut. She heard a sound. Quickly, she bunched herself up, made herself into a bundle of rags.

"Rochel, hurry," the rabbi hissed. "They have guessed you are here. We have to move you again. Zev will have you back."

"Zev?"

She dared not contemplate what she had done to him. "I cannot go back there."

"You must. Nobody will suspect that you are with him in your own room."

FOR WOMEN, THE Spider was best, the emperor read. Hooks used to shred the breasts, pokers, pincers in the vagina, gunpowder piled on the pubis, long hair soaked in oil, burned, stones heated to white-hot, inserted in armpits, hands dipped in hot tallow, fingers lit like candles.

32

KIRAKOS KNEW HE was going to live when he was aware of the smell of flowers.

"Sergey," he croaked.

The Russian, ever at his side, lifted Kirakos's head, helped him balance on his elbows.

Propped up, Kirakos could see bunches of color—blue and white, bright orange geraniums, brilliantly yellow daisies, opened tiger lilies, and flowers he could not even name—newly picked, in vases, containers, big buckets by his bed. He was in a garden.

"I am alive," Kirakos said, as much for himself as for the Russian. All his objects, his books and large pillow, the rug on the floor resembling a pool of dark roses, existing in their separate, self-contained grace, were meaningful in this, the most precious of worlds. He looked at the Russian—impassive, with his long, dark hair, harshly chiseled features, his peasant garb—a shapeless shirt belted at the waist with a dirty piece of cloth, and rough breeches that were long and tucked into his worn boots.

"Who brought the flowers?"

"I did, master."

"Who has bathed me?"

"I did, master."

"Who has fed me?"

"I have, master."

"And tended me night and day. How many days?"

"More than seven, master."

Kirkos held up his arm, examined it. The skin had not turned black and scaled off him in big sheets. He had not excreted his intestines. Blood had not flowed out of his ears. He could talk. He did not have the many pink bumps he had observed on himself when he was still able to open his eyes. Now he could not only open his eyes, but he thought his vision was never better.

"Sergey, you have seen me through the pox."

Sergey hung his head as if he had done something to be ashamed of.

"Why did you do this for one who is both harsh and mean-tempered. I, a slave, kept you a slave. Why did you save me?"

The Russian shrugged his shoulders

"You could have gotten the pox, do you know that? You value your life so little?"

"I value the life much."

"Sergey." Kirakos sighed. "My friend, I have been bad to you and to others."

"You save the boy, he lives the life." Sergey smiled a little.

Still weak, the Armenian physician had to lower himself carefully back down on his pillow, but in truth, he had never felt more alive. Everything was washed in soft new colors, and his awareness of the world was exquisitely lucid. Suffused with joy, Kirkaos felt his fingertips, his toes, each limb and part of him glow.

"Mankind is curious and the more I think I know, even about myself, the less I can apprehend. Before I say my prayers, Sergey, 'In the name of God, the merciful, the Giver of Mercy,' how is it at the castle?"

Sergey took a big breath. "They tried to kill the emperor, and then they change the minds."

"What?" Kirakos sat up straight again.

"The Kelley, the Dee."

"What are you telling me? What has transpired? How are the butterflies?"

"Dead, all dead, and before they die, the Kelley and Dee put poison in the emperor's cup, too much opium it was, and when he went to drink at his birthday party, they say: 'Stop, do not drink.'"

"Kelley and Dee tried to poison the emperor?"

"*Da, da.*"

"I see. So they could not kill him. Interesting."

"The emperor, he is not grateful."

"So in order to save him, they revealed themselves as murderers and were arrested."

"Kelley arrest. Dee escape. The guards are hunting."

"Clever, those two. Opium in wine would seem like too much wine. And a taster would not be affected. Only the person who drank the full draught would fall into a deep sleep, a deep, deep sleep. They would not be quick to rouse the emperor after a grand party. Ingenious idea. However, they had not the heart nor the stomach." Kirakos looked up at the beams of the ceiling. The world, which was so beautiful a minute earlier, stretching before him like a shimmering, clear lake, was muddied with his misdeeds.

"But wait, I vaguely remember Jepp was here. Why was Jepp here?"

"The Brahe, my lord, is dead."

"Dead? Of what? How could he be dead? He is my chess opponent."

"At the feast he could not pass the urine. They say the bladder, it exploded."

"Bladders do not explode." Kirakos tried to jump out of bed, found that his legs were wobbly. "Help me to the window, Sergey."

The Russian held Kirakos up, and carefully he helped the physician hobble to the window. Kirakos stood there, basked in the warmth of sunlight, knowing that he could only allow himself this short reprieve. He could see the valley of Prague, the snaky line of the Vltava River, the tops of trees, the spires of Týn Church, the occasional red-tile roof. Yes, he would have to get strong, get up, navigate through these troubles. Brahe dead? Kirakos imagined them crisscrossing paths, Brahe on the way to death, he back to life. If anybody, he should have died, not Brahe.

"So did they put warm compresses on his belly and groin, give him valerian and opium for the pain, and make him drink lots of boiled mint water, some drops of honey, steady massage of the stomach, baths, a gentle purge."

"I do not know. Crato went."

Kirakos shook his head, turned away to gaze out of his window. He had an itch in his eye, had to dab it with his sleeve. Below, in blur, he could see the changing of the guard, and servants, in the courtyard, were sweeping away the debris of the debacle, the broken glass and crockery, spoiled food, destroyed furniture.

"The last thing he told the Kepler was, 'Let me not seem to have lived in vain.'"

Kirakos closed his eyes, had to rest his head against the Russian's arm.

"Not lived in vain," Kirakos repeated.

"Are you feeling sick again?" Sergey asked.

"Oh, my eyes, my eyes hurt. Help me, please, Sergey."

They walked slowly back to the bed, and Sergey got Kirakos settled.

"The Kepler is now the imperial mathematicus."

"Nice title. I hope it will help him collect some salary. Brahe dies, I live. And the boy lives and they have not found Dee?"

"No, master."

"Not master. Kirakos. Do you think we could have some wine now that I am better?"

"Maybe in a day, Kira-kos. Maybe a day, two day."

"Yes. You are absolutely right. Soft bread, figs, a bowl of almonds, and you know what I really would like, you have never tasted this, Sergey, but it is something that can wake the dead and make life worth living. Coffee. Coffee. In my country we drink it daily, often, in big bowls, and you can go to a coffeehouse, much like a tavern here, and you can sit down on low stools and lounge on pillows, and you can have conversations, play chess, and drink coffee, be served sweets. Is there nothing more pleasurable? Truly that is a kind of paradise." Kirakos pulled the bell by his bed. "And we must go there, to Istanbul, of course."

"Is far?"

"If one is healthy, nowhere is too far, Sergey; if one is healthy, nothing is impossible. But you must tell me. They are all seated at the dinner. I can imagine that buffoon, the emperor, one arm around the plate as if the plate would take legs, run away if he did not eat fast enough."

A servant appeared. "You called."

"Two bowls of coffee, a plate of grapes, some bread and butter, figs and dates, almonds."

The servant left. Sergey continued.

"At the feast, the players, they put on the play, the musicians make the music la-la-la, the food and the wine is coming up from the cellar and kitchen, up, down, up, down, and the emperor's table, he is served on gold plates, the others silver plates."

"Yes, yes. Gems on every finger, fur on every coat, the ladies like lilies in their widespread skirts. The vision sickens me."

"And they bring in the big bird with all the skin and the feathers still on."

"Some hapless peacock. Where are you, Sergey, in all of this?"

"I am at first in the kitchen to see if there is the food which you could eat, some porridge, the groats boiled in the milk, something to go down your throat easy as water without the chewing, when I hear above me the sound, it is like the wild horses running across the steppes, the Tartars, the Mongols, the Cossacks, and the earth shaking from the hooves. I jump up the stairs, step by step up I go, and what do I see? Women scream. Men take out the swords."

"Good, good, I like that. So Dee and Kelley could not kill even to save their own hides."

The Russian was standing now, excited and flushed in telling the tale, and for the first time, Kirakos noticed that he was a rather handsome fellow. "We must get you some new clothes, Sergey, get your hair trimmed by the barber, and good boots," he said. "The shoemaker in Judenstadt and his wife, I understand, can make good clothes and strong shoes—"

"The shoemaker and the wife, master, she has—"

"Kirakos, Sergey. How nice the air is, do you not love the summer? Has anybody been to see me besides Jepp?"

"The man who carries your messages."

"You know about the man who carries my messages?"

"I do."

"What else do you know, Sergey?"

"I know about the silken cord."

"Ah, yes." Kirakos felt his neck. "I am thinking maybe not Istanbul after all. Let us get off that subject. You were telling me, the shoemaker and his wife . . ."

"The shoemaker and the wife, the people want to kill her."

"Why?"

"Because she lay with the golem."

"My, my, so that is what happened." Kirakos tried to sit up again. Sergey arranged the pillows for him.

"Thank you, Sergey. The golem is a complete man, after all."

"They will stone her," Sergey said. "The people in the town will stone her, and they say the people in Judenstadt do not wish to keep her, so they will put her out. She is hiding."

Kirakos sighed. "One of those old customs, stoning. Adultery is a serious crime, for a woman. As a Jewish woman, they cannot put her in a nunnery, obviously, but she could go to a brothel."

"The emperor says she loves him, wants to be a royal mistress."

"Another of his delusions. But that would be a solution. Better a royal mistress than stoned. But somehow I do not think she would accede to such an arrangement." Kirakos got out of bed again, this time with more strength. He went to the window, looked up at the sky. He preferred sundials to clocks and could actually tell time rather accurately by eye alone. It was nearly twelve in the morning, and he wondered where the servant had gone. He was starving. "And Yossel, the golem?"

"He is gone."

"So very manly of him, yet who wants to die? Nobody in Prague, it seems. I can understand that. The emperor and his quest, how ironic that in fact his life was, in a sense, extended by the very people hired to do the job, although they wanted to end the job."

"It is said the emperor sees the spirit of the dead brother, he thinks he is in the Spain, he calls the Rumpf Don Carlos. He sleeps on the floor in the Kunstskammer, will not leave that room. He thinks the Petaka is sick with the pox and prayers are being said for the lion at St. Vitus Cathedral; the Crato is called in to cure the lion."

"Let us hope he does not try to bleed the beast. Unlike the emperor, Petaka has a few teeth left. Maybe the emperor and Petaka can be put away somewhere."

"Where?"

"In a spare room. Surely the castle has many. It has been done before. Don Carlos. Don Julius Caesar. Juana the Loca. A familiar thing, no doubt, for there has been a good deal of inbreeding. Habsburgs marry each other, keep it in the family, you know, royal blood, weak brains, jutting chin, bad teeth. Charles V could not close his mouth, drooled in five languages. They dug up graves to trace the jaw. It turns out the source was a Hungarian princess, not a true Habsburg after all. Rudolph was both nephew and brother-in-law to Philip of Spain, who was the son of Charles V, who was the son of the father of both his mother and father, something like that, confusing."

The servant came in with a tray which held the steaming bowls of black coffee, grapes and bread, some slices of cheese, dates and almonds, figs and sausage. Kirakos helped himself, avoiding the sausage.

"This is coffee, Sergey. Sip it, savor it, love it. Good for headaches. And this is a fork. They use them at court. With the prongs you can hold your meat fast while you cut it and poke it right in your mouth. It serves for all but soup and gravy. They are very proud of it here."

The Russian tried to manage the fork.

"That is right, a firm grip. Now, tell me, I cannot believe that a man is sick a few days, turns his back for a moment, and the whole world is in shambles."

"The people say there is going to be the civil war. The caravans, the people of the city, they are trying to leave Prague, but nothing can go out. All the houses, they are being searched for Dee. The town people want to burn the witch, they say she has brought misfortune on the Prague."

"What witch? There is a witch in all this, too?"

"The adulteress."

"I thought you said they want to stone her."

"Both."

"Fortunately, the poor woman can only die once."

The physician rubbed his eyes again.

"This is troubling news, Sergey. It is time to leave the city, yes, I think so, and if not Istanbul, where?"

"I was a child in Novgorod. It was the city with the beautiful cathedral of St. Sophia like the one in Kiev. We had guilds for the trades, schools for the children, monasteries. The city people choose the mayor. One day, Czar Ivan the Terrible came to our town. He torture the people. If they live through the torture, they were put on the sleighs, sent down the hill into the ice water, where the army waiting in the boats hacked them to pieces with the pikes and the axes. Twenty-seven thousand of the people killed, every day a thousand. One-third of us die. When I grow up, I do not want to be in the czar's army. I run to the West."

"West, you are right. West is good. Ivan the Terrible, Suleiman the Magnificent, Rudolph the Mad. Yes, yes, I agree, but the gates to the city are closed. Did you not tell me that?"

"Karel takes junk to the dumps near the Pest Cemetery every day."

"Is that so?"

"It is."

"I have heard, Sergey, there are parts of the New World where trees bear huge stalks of yellow fruit, and nuts are the size of bladder balls with sweet white meat inside, and that coffee grows like weeds."

33

R OCHEL HAD ALWAYS regarded her fingers as the one part of her body she had control of, yet at the same time they were independent, as if HaShem, or at least something grand and external to her meager self, worked through her hands, guided her needle. Throughout her life she had always been in the middle of a garment or starting or finishing a new piece, and when she was doing other things—cooking or cleaning, in bed with Zev, before Yossel, even when dreaming—the sewing she did with her fingers was there in her mind. It was as if she had lived in two worlds at once, so that if she was sad, she had something to be glad about, and if her surroundings were drab, what she could do with her hands was glorious. Consequently, although patterns and garments were prescribed— doublets, cloaks, breeches and gowns, flowers and vines—each garment took on a life of its own, configured itself in the end through the mystery of her fingers, even though it was also struggle and labor. She appreciated other people's needlework, too. She had heard from Master Galliano that in a land far off to the east, silk clothes were decorated with dragons in stitches so fine they seemed woven into the fabric itself, and she longed to see the coronation robe used by the Habsburgs. Red, Master Galliano had described it, with gold thread, done by Muslims, a palm tree in the middle, camels as well as tigers and Arabic lettering all along the border. If she could make a robe of her own designing and desiring, it would have people standing on a chessboard, for she had seen the one in the rabbi's house many times, the small battalions of brown and blond wood fashioned as delicately as toys for a prince, each standing in its prescribed square. A chessboard and the sky raining stars of all different colors.

Or she would do one of a big blue fish swimming in pink water. Or a wide full-length cloak with tassels and buttons, ruffles and bells, embroidered faces. Or birds of bright plumage taking wing over a city, like fireworks shooting high into the sky.

Yes, she would like to do doublets and gowns adorned with exotic animals, a Noah's ark of wonderful new creatures being discovered in faraway Afric. Animals long as snakes, fat as pigs, with thick, scaly hides and long snouts who lived under the water, and some who had a single tusk on the top of their mouths and skins like a suit of armor. She had never seen an elephant, but she knew they were bigger than anything. The first lion she ever saw was the emperor's. She would like to see a tiger and a monkey and what was called a giraffe mottled in blocks of brown and white. Some of these animals were brought to fairs, taken for show all over Europe.

Now she knew she would never see these animals, never make anything again, never be with people at a fair. Indeed, since Rochel had been back at Zev's, she dared not look her husband in the face, and, huddling in the space between the bed and the wall, she had nothing to do but dread her death and regret her life. She was defenseless in the world and all alone. Even her faith in HaShem was not sufficient. She had nothing to put between herself and her fear. Nothing. Rochel could hardly remember her lover's face. It was as if Yossel were less than a memory or a dream; it was as if he had never been except to cause her grief, bring her to this final downfall. She was too frightened to remember his touch. That she loved him did not matter anymore. In her room, Zev's room, in her corner, her head was riddled with contrariness. That she had once considered re-creating her life seemed now the height of folly. Yet she was greedy. She wanted to live.

"Wife, come out." Zev knelt on the bed, pleading with her, rubbing her shoulders as she hunkered in the closed space between the bed and wall.

"Please, Zev, leave me, leave me alone."

"You are my wife, how can I?"

Rochel shuddered. Had he shunned her, denounced her, ranted and raved, asked for a divorce, that she could have understood. She had lost his baby, Zev's baby, their child. She had dishonored him, brought shame to her community. There was no end to her evil, and yet he was begging her as if he were the one to forgive. The one day she had been back in the room, she had moved from her spot behind the bed only to empty the slops in the ditch. She had not eaten, but her body still went on, waste moving through her with unrelenting indifference.

"Rochel, my love."

How could he love her? Had he not agreed to marry her out of charity? Was he not pleased merely with her deftness with the needle, finding pleasure in her youth and his rights of possession? That was what he meant by love. What she meant by love she no longer knew. The word crumbled in her hand.

"How can you stand me, Zev, when I cannot stand myself?"

He had only her bowed back to look at as she hid herself between the bed and the wall; nonetheless, it was a dear back, and the tendons of her neck threading up to her dear head broke his heart. Her heels, held under her hips, visible in patches through her torn hose, small moons of reddened flesh, created a tenderness he could barely endure. If he could see her eyes, the way she widened them like twin babkas risen to perfection, and her mouth, made for wedding food— white flour loaves, golden chicken soup—he would consider himself a lucky man. But it was not the flesh alone, the lift of her stride, the expectancy of youth. It was the way she said *husband*, how she grew still as it darkened at night, like a little animal retreating into its hole, and how she loved the morning sun, how she had transformed their room to a home and made food into meals, and—could he say it?— how she sang, a little bird, she was, the wave of her hard worn hands over the Sabbath candles, her ironic half smile as if she perceived the truth behind the world of falsehood, and her daily, close proximity, as a woman, to the presence of God. And it was not that he did not grieve over what had happened. He could not think, did not let himself think of another touching her. And it was not that he did not know that their baby was gone, and that he, a man getting on in years, did not need a son, for a Jewish man without children is only half alive. No, it was not that he did not care. He cared. His sadness pressed him flat to the ground so that his heart was like a piece of worn leather. Yet he loved her. He loved her. What could he do?

"I am partly to blame," he said.

"That cannot be."

"You were young."

"Most women are betrothed by thirteen, marry at fourteen. Eighteen is not young."

"And I, I am old, obstinate, troublesome, blind to the needs of a woman. I did not give you a chance. I am not handsome."

"Zev, what is handsome, what is beautiful, what does all that matter? You are a good man, a good husband, more than a good husband. You are a saint."

"I talk too much. I am a glutton. Sometimes I am so quick to eat, I hurry my prayers. I did not attend to your every need, treat you as a wife should be treated in our faith."

"Zev, please."

"I admit I was overwhelmed by your youth and beauty, coveted it, hoarded it. That first night, our wedding night, I gazed upon you like a man out of his wits. I had impure thoughts."

"But I am your wife."

"All the more reason to respect and honor you." He reached for her hand; she did not pull back.

"Please, do not blame yourself. Blame me. I am so sorry, Zev, about everything."

"I, too."

"My heart is breaking, Zev."

"Mine, too, Rochel."

They pressed their faces to each other, so that it could not be told whose tears were on whose face.

"What is to happen to me?" she whispered. "Are the townspeople going to kill me?"

"No, Rochel."

"How do you know?"

"Because I will not let them."

34

"WE WANT THE adulteress, the sinner." These were the people who had left their homes in a panic and were camped out on the Square below the Astronomical Clock waiting for the city gates to open. War was imminent, they believed, the end of Prague, if not the world, at hand.

"Yield up the golem girl." Some of the women beat pot lids with wooden spoons to the rhythm of their demands.

"The Jewess has sinned." Thaddaeus was at the forefront of the crowd. He believed that *Jew* and *Satan* were synonymous words, but if any word could be worse than *Jew* it was *Jewess*, for certainly before Christ's death came Adam's fall through the temptation of that nefarious woman, Eve.

"Jewess adulteress," the crowd responded.

"Give her up." This was a voice, either that of a woman or a young man, from within the walls of Judenstadt.

"Who says such a thing?" Rabbi Loew was aghast. He had come out of his house to assess the commotion without the walls, only to find that many of his flock and congregation were out of their homes and had gathered on the one street of their community.

"We should all die for a mamzer, one who is not even a Jew?" Leah, his oldest daughter, questioned loudly so that all could hear.

"Hush," the rabbi hissed angrily. "She is a person, and a Jew."

"Enough of a Jew that we must all die for her?" Leah pressed.

"Am I hearing a daughter of mine?"

"Is she more your daughter than I am?" Leah pressed. "Do you value her above us all?"

"I am frightened, Papa," Zelda cried.

"Do not be." The rabbi hugged his youngest and turned to his eld-
est. "Come inside, Leah, we must talk."

"Her husband is hiding her," another person in Judenstadt said
altogether too loudly.

"He took her back? How can that be?" Miriam cried.

"Miriam, Leah, Zelda, inside immediately." The rabbi was furious.

"He took her back, he took her back." The news traveled from person to person.

"ZEV, DO YOU hear that?" Rochel got down off the bed, moved to
the small space between the bed and the wall again.

"It will blow over, it is just talk; soon it will be night, Rochel, just stay
still." They stayed still, she in the corner, he hovering over her on the bed
until the shammas knocked on the door to signal the beginning of the
Sabbath. Then the sun went down, darkness descended, and the noise
without silenced, for despite the horrendous events in the city, in
Judenstadt it was the beginning of the Sabbath. Women had spread the
table with a clean white cloth and laid out bowls of onions and carrots,
parsnips, and platters of gefilte fish, the boned fish meat ground with
matzah meal. Earlier in the day chickens had been roasted, kreplach
filled with meat, honey cakes and challah brought back from the bakers.
Now the candles were lit, the families gathered.

"It is the Sabbath," Zev said to Rochel, and the two of them, she
still on the floor, he above her on the bed, thanked God for allowing
them to live until that moment. Zev divided up some nutmeats, and
they shared the sweet, Sabbath wine from one cup. "L'chaim," Zev
toasted softly. To life.

A few hours later, as the town crier announced from the bridge,
Ten o'clock and all is well, there was a light triple knock.

"It is I, Rabbi Loew," a voice followed.

Zev ran to the door, opened it a crack, peeked out.

"Get Rochel ready," the rabbi whispered. "Karel is coming to the
back gate. Here are some clothes for her to wear." He passed a bundle
to Zev. "Let her take nothing that shows she is a Jew or a woman. She
is to ride with Karel out the city gates to the dumps and cemetery,
where she will join a merchant caravan traveling to Frankfort, from
there to Amsterdam."

Amsterdam. Rochel remembered the blue tiles on the emperor's stove, the pictures of the wooden shoes, the windmills, ships. Was the Dutch country bathed in blue like the tiles? The blue of a glass vial she had seen once from Venice? She imagined the sun on her skin— pale winter sun filtered through frost, and summer sun as bright as the gold embroidery on the emperor's Muslim coronation robe. Her spirits rose, and the qualms concentrated in a hard knot at the bottom of her stomach dissolved like fingers of water stretching up on the shore, bubbly and full of sparkles. She wanted to live. She had her hands. She could work. In her mind's eye, the trees of the Black Forest parted before her like the Red Sea, showing a path. Similar to the pattern of her grandmother's old stories, she would come to a clearing, and in the clearing was a house, and in the house, warming her wings by the fire, was the angel of mercy.

"Rochel," the rabbi chided. "Be quick about it."

Rochel rushed about the little room, putting things in the middle of a large brown cloth spread on the table—some onions, a cabbage, a stale loaf of bread, the stoppered jug of water. Then she swiftly unwrapped the bundle the rabbi had given her, found a cap, breeches, hose and boots, a strip of wool to flattened down her breasts, a plain peasant overshirt, and a long cloak. Hands trembling, she shed the skirt and bodice Master Galliano's wife had given her, stepped out of the underskirt, untied her scarf. Looking in the mirror at herself in the boy's clothes, she saw that with her short yellow hair, slight body, the cape hiding her hips, she could easily pass for a Czech boy. Turning, she took a last look at her home, the strips of leather still hanging from the wall, the garland of wooden shoes, the long table laid out with patterns of cloaks and gowns. Could she shut the door and leave all this behind? Could she leave a roof over her head, food in her belly? In a heartbeat. Without another moment's look back. Moving toward Zev, she said:

"Husband, it is fortunate for you I am leaving, for you will be able to divorce me without any trouble."

"I am coming with you," he said.

"You cannot, I am a disgrace to you."

"I am coming."

"It is dangerous."

"Quickly, Wife," he insisted.

There was another knock.

"Rochel." It was Perl. "Karel is waiting."

Zev took off his cloak with the yellow star, the fringed tallit katan with the two bands of blue his mother had woven for him, his kippah. He kissed his tefillin, the little leather boxes mounted on leather straps he used for weekday prayer, and, with his prayer shawl, put them into the cupboard. Using Rochel's scissors, in two snip-snaps he cut his two pe'ot off, trimmed his beard. He looked diminished, perplexed, not himself.

"Oh, Zev," Rochel cried.

"I am coming." Grabbing a coverlet from the bed as his cloak, he threw his cobbler's tools into a leather bag.

Following the rabbi and Perl, they crept through the graveyard, where Rochel's grandmother, Dvoira bat Avrom, Deborah daughter of Abraham; and Zev's first wife, Etta bat Dovid, Ester daughter of David; the Yakovs, Moshes, and modest Minnas, all the generations, were bedded together, one atop another. Pressing against the walls of the houses, keeping to the shadows, they shuffled along the alleyway toward the back gate, passing the bathhouse where Václav, as a boy, had left Rochel presents, and later the baby had been abandoned, and still later, Kirakos and Yossel had spied on her. Under the old oak, which had shaded the play of children and where the old people sat out their days, the patient Oswald was waiting, pawing the ground.

"Remember us here in Prague." Perl put her finger under Rochel's chin. The old woman was no longer the proud peacock of her household, the august rabbi's wife, dispenser of wisdom and comfort. Perl was tired.

Rochel climbed into the cart. Zev climbed in after her.

"I was told only Rochel," Karel said.

"I am coming, too," Zev insisted.

"Zev," Perl began, "do you think it wise?"

"I am going with my wife."

As Rochel lifted the dirty piece of cloth and piles of old clothes, she saw two people.

"Greetings," Kirakos said.

Sergey did not say anything.

Zev scooted down under the clothes by Rochel.

"It seems we run a ferry service," Karel said to Oswald. "Go slow, old fellow."

So off they went, Oswald straining to pull his heavy load, through the Square and toward the city gates. Although the hour was late,

Celentná Street was blocked by a rowdy horde under tents sheltering all the accoutrements of home—pots, pans, mangy goats. Puppet shows were being put on and musicians were playing their instruments loudly. Squealing children ran about between the dozens of little cooking fires snapping and crackling under kettles of gruel, malodorous fish stew. Despite the air of frivolity, the talk was that infidel Turks were arriving momentarily, the bald-headed warriors who ate babies alive, and on their heels, foreign Protestants, who would join with the Czech brethren in desecrating churches, shattering icons. Others had heard that in certain quarters crypto-Hussites, nested in the city all along, remembering their torched hero of the century past, were sounding the clarion call for loyal followers. Anabaptists of every stripe were popping up like mushrooms, like the sect in a small town in the German states who went naked and believed in sharing all, including wives, for which they were rooted out and soundly burned. However, the Czech Protestants, eager to leave town because they had heard that the Catholics were going to make a big bonfire and burn all heretics, had their own separate encampment. The rival religionists glared at each other across the Square.

"We will have to wait until the crowd thins to pass through," Karel said, as if talking to Oswald, "on the other side of the bridge."

The junkman guided his patient mule to Bridge Strasse, where many nooks and crannies and stone mansions surrounded by gorgeous gardens provided quiet shelter for the night. The relief, in the doorway of the Customs House in front of Judith Tower, of a king and kneeling man, belied the chaos in the realm. At the House of the Three Golden Bells, Karel pulled Oswald into a peaceful courtyard full of sleeping pigeons, their heads tucked under their wings.

"Be tranquil, old fellow," he said to Oswald in a voice the four in the cart would hear.

Rochel, who had been so exhilarated over the prospect of escape, was now subdued. What had initially been conceived as uncomplicated now revealed itself to be fraught with danger. How would they get through the thick clot of people on Celentná Steet? She had not seen them, of course, but the noise was sufficient to alarm her. Would the guards at the gate look inside Karel's cart before they let it go through? Would more soldiers be stationed at the dumps and around the Pest Cemetery? Would the townspeople look for her in Judenstadt at the cost of its inhabitants? Furthermore, she had no claim, she realized again, to strive for advantage, to leave her people as hostage to her crime. If Karel was discovered with his illegal load, would they all pay the cost of her indiscretion? Yet Kirakos and the Russian, in a tight embrace, seemed oblivious of peril, Zev was slumbering, and the tower watchman was announcing the hour as usual.

Twelve o'clock and all is well.

Karel was asleep at his perch when he heard a loud voice: "What are you doing here?"

"The Golden Ox is too noisy tonight. I cannot get through the streets to Oswald's barn."

"You must move on, Karel. We guard these houses, must not let anybody near."

Rochel felt the cart lurch, move forward for a bit, turn, then stop abruptly.

"We cannot go any farther tonight," Karel said to his poor mule.

Rochel peeked out. Ahead of them was a solid wall topped with red tile.

"But we cannot stay here," Kirakos exclaimed, throwing off the coverlet concealing them all. "We are too close to the emperor."

"They will never think of us here," Karel assured him. "Up ahead is a secret spot." When they arrived, the Russian lifted Karel off his perch and carried him along the wall surrounding the castle gardens, the rest following, and shortly they found a small green door, which with a gentle push gave entry to the emperor's rose patch.

"Oh, my," Rochel said. The scent was overpoweringly sweet and the flowers, black in the night, clustered in the bushes like small baby heads. Sadness and longing for her child who would never know this, never see this, pierced her.

"Shhh," Karel hissed. There was a sound of hooves on the road to the castle, and then they saw above them a group of guards in military formation, and in their midst, pulled by a pair of black horses, stood a cart mounted with a cage.

"It is an animal for the royal menagerie," Karel said quickly and quietly. "Hurry, hurry, our refuge is just ahead." Weaving furtively among the roses, they approached a pile of twigs, and suddenly a voice came forth.

"Who is it in the dark of night has come to share my sorry plight?" It was indeed the same person who had helped Kelley find the right butterflies to fool the emperor, the assistant-assistant gardener.

"Karel, the rag and bone man, and friends, butterfly man."

From inside the frail structure, some dogs began to bark. "Hush, Teta, Anjelica, Žižka." The butterfly man poked his head out of a flap. "Last time I had a guest, he promised me shoes, a cloak, elixir, the very best."

"Yes, yes, we will get you that and more. Just for the night is all we ask," Karel begged.

"That is how it always starts, just for the night, do your part. Oh, well."

The place was musty and cramped, and by the light of the one lit candle, Rochel saw the three dogs, one with only three legs, a large tabby cat, bald in spots, rolled in a ball, a bird with a mended wing. The butterfly man slept in a cocoon of quilts, the bird, like king of the hill, perched on his rump. The rest of them curled around the embers of the fire in the middle of the hut. Rochel had only been in such close proximity to her grandmother, her husband, Zev, and for a short time Yossel, and now here she was packed in, cheek by jowl with a whole menagerie.

PERL WAS CLEARING up after breakfast, happy that Rochel was, by now, well beyond the city gates. She believed that part of the trouble was that people had not been able to forgive Rochel her difference—not just that she was foreign, for there were Jews in Prague who were refugees from Spain and other countries, but that Rochel had Christian blood and was in body friend and foe to both groups. No wonder the child had grown up lonely, believing that something was wrong with her. And those slanted eyes, high cheekbones, and full lips were startling, a constant reminder. Perl could understand, also, how it had happened with Yossel. One look, the language of eyes. It had never been that way with Judah, for from the first day, indeed, since children betrothed to each other, they were an old married couple with a long habit of each other. Passion, look what it led to. Yet her heart was not at ease, even with Rochel safely outside the city walls, and that was because of Yossel. She missed him as if he were her real son. Truth be known, not a minute went by throughout the day without thought of his well-being. And although she was a woman who did not believe in wasting time on what she could not remedy, she felt immense remorse that she had not given him a mother's true love when he was there, or perhaps, she reasoned, she had not known how to show it, having never experienced passion.

KAREL REALIZED, ON waking up in the hut, a dog on his face, they would have to wait until the afternoon to go through the city gates because he would have to account for a most speedy collection of junk if he tried to approach the dump in the morning and consequently might be searched. Thus, after crossing the Stone Bridge with his load of passengers, he angled his cart through a small alleyway behind Týn Church off the crowded Square, and at a designated spot had Sergey hop out, pull the knocker with the female hand holding a globe.

"Who is it?" came a faint voice from within.

"Golden Prague," Karel called out the password from his wagon

The barely opened door revealed the young man who sold Kelley the opium to poison the emperor.

"May we stay for just a little while?" Karel asked. "My friends need to hide."

"Do you think I do not have to hide myself?" the student said.

"For the love of God, Gregor."

The student sighed and opened the door wider. Sergey, carrying Karel, and Kirakos, Rochel, and Zev were admitted into the windowless room. Rochel looked about. Bed, chair, table, lantern, and many, many books.

"We thank you," she said to the student.

"I am going to Týn Church to pray," Karel announced, to the surprise of them all. "If the Russian will take me."

"Everybody thinks Sergey is still at the castle. Why do you need to pray?" Kirakos asked. "We will soon be through the gates."

"Just for good measure." Karel feigned cheer. What he felt, at the moment, was great trepidation, for he had not liked the milling bunch camped out on the Square like soldiers ready for war. He had not liked it all. They were a rowdy, angry lot, many of them too besotted to control their manners or possess their wits. He must have a second look at them, and while he was at it, a prayer or two would not hurt.

"People from the castle often ride with me. Sergey will be no curiosity."

As soon as the two left, Rochel looked about the bare room. "You can read?" she asked the student. The two women, despite their shorn hair, caps and breeches, banded breasts, had immediately recognized each other as women. What kind of city is Prague, Rochel had to wonder, where the women must be men, Jews Christians, and Christians at each other's throats? How many others, each in his or her own way, were living a life of not-what-it-seems, players in a drama, going home to take off a mask, step out of costume?

"I can read," Gregoria replied.

Rochel picked a book off the floor. "May I?" She opened it, put her hand on a page, as if yearning and meaning would meet. She was actually touching words with her fingers, for the paper was rag—not parchment—print, which would not fade from sweat rubbed off from a finger.

"What does it say?"

Gregoria took the book. "It is a British story about a group of pilgrims on the way to a holy shrine."

"They are holy?"

"Ordinary people with all the human foibles; that is what makes them interesting."

"Ordinary people like us, like me?" She was incredulous. "Not princesses and princes, not the ancestors, prophets?"

The student smiled.

"They are very good people, then, like Aschenputtel, who swept the ashes in the hearth?" Rochel could not fathom that there would be a whole long story about ordinary people.

"Not particularly good, some bad. In the story of Aschenputtel, she married the prince through extraordinary virtue. Most people are not like that."

Rochel observed that the words on the page did not go every which way. In their lines of German, they seemed to have the precision of stitches marching across the page. Within a glance, she could detect repetitions. The paper was thin, the cover cloth, yet the book was a solid object, an imposing presence, not whimsical or flimsy. Of course, she had seen Hebrew letters. Zev had a siddur, a prayer book, and a Torah, the five books of Moses, and the book of prophets, and she had seen the explication of the Torah, which was the Talmud, while she had hidden in the Altneu attic, but those books, that language, seemed inaccessible to her, too holy, beyond her reach.

"I am going to learn to read someday," Rochel announced.

KAREL, NOT PARTICULARLY religious, the Russian at his side, found himself praying with great fervor to the cold alabaster stature of Mary and elegantly tinted Christ on the windows. In his village, the church was a hut marked by the bare wooden cross fixed to the chimney with twine, and he had always thought of Christ as a man of the people—somebody who liked to talk, eat a good meal, a person who got angry, had doubts—and as for Mary, what mother was not long-suffering? He prayed that they would get through the gates. He prayed for Václav's son and Kepler and his family, the well-being of Judenstadt. He prayed for Kelley and Dee. And lastly, he prayed for Oswald, that he would always have enough oats and a warm place to sleep. On his way back to Gregor's room, carried by Karel, he happened to look up at the Astronomical Clock, for he had always loved it. The topmost part of the tower was home to the carved figures of the apostles, who appeared after their hour-long domicile with a tug of the rope by Death. Below this panoply was the clock itself with Arabic numerals in a rim of black edged in gold, and on the inside circumference were the Roman numerals with the inset circle of an astronomical clock. This showed the movements of the sun and moon through the twelve signs of the zodiac. The bottom third of the clock was the seasonal calendar adorned in gold leaf depicting harvest and planting. There were figures, too—bony Death with an hourglass, the turbaned Turk, Vanity, who looked into a mirror, and as if for the first time, he realized that Greed was represented by a deformed figure of a Jew. No, he wanted to say, they are not like that.

Sergey and Karel were back in the room only a few minutes when a strange silence fell across the Square. Those of them in the student's little cell could feel it, and had there been a window, they would have seen a mass of black clouds stream across the heavy sky in an angry race. Then, there was a slight tensing in the air, a hint, a small disturbance. Leaves rustled nervously and animals moved about anxiously; little babies started crying, and soon whole branches of the trees near the Square were swaying and the tall grass in the fields surrounding the city lay flat as if a giant broom had swept across the land. Then the heavens broke open in a huge crack, lightning struck, thunder rolled, and buckets of rain fell down. The people in the Square snatched what they could of their belongings and ran for cover in doorways and taverns, churches and empty rooms.

UP AT THE castle, the emperor, hardly aware of the strong winds and heavy rains, picked at his food—carp stuffed with onions, salmon in the Polish style, a spiced custard with dates and raisins from the Orient, cream of almonds. He had not changed his clothes since his birthday; his skin was crusty. Petaka, under a large trestle table, would not come out. A whole slab of beef lay on the floor beside him, dotted with flies. The animal was shedding.

"Your Majesty, it seems that Petaka is going to die." Rumpf, who was taking Václav's place these days, hated the decrepit beast, but he did not want to be blamed for its death.

"What? What say?" Deep within the murky chambers of his mind, the emperor listened. "Petaka, Petaka, what is wrong with him?" The emperor remembered, like a sharp pain in his side, that Brahe had foretold that when the lion died, so would he.

"Pistorius suggests he confess."

"Confess? A lion, you idiot? He is without sin." And the emperor recalled with a jolt and a flutter of frustration that the city was filled with roving bands of looters, that the rumor of war caused great numbers of people to amass at the city gates with all their belongings on their backs. And the Empire, who knew the state of the Empire? Were taxes being collected, the Turks held back, was commerce conducted according to the interest of the emperor?

But first things first. Petaka was to be nursed back to health with calf meat finely minced, soft bread soaked in lamb blood, and pigeon breast sprinkled with shaved sugar. A hundred archers were assigned to go out in the rain that very instant and with the finest arrows shoot down the day's supply of pigeons. The prettiest calves were to be sought out near and far.

The number two concern was: "The rabbi, the rabbi, his words for eternal life."

"Not to be found, and Judenstadt is in turmoil," Rumpf informed the emperor. "The townspeople are clamoring for the life of the adulteress. They say she has brought a curse down on Prague, and if she is burned, the misfortune will be lifted."

"Lies, prattle, hearsay, and bosh. Kill a beautiful woman? What absolute nonsense. Old, unsightly witches, that I can understand. But to waste such a woman?"

"A Jewess, Your Highness?"

"She has Christian blood in her, Rumpf, is half Christian, that is the gossip, and she will quickly convert when she is a royal mistress. Send a troop of guards to protect Judenstadt."

"She is not there."

"Then she must be found, brought straightaway to the castle, bathed, powdered, oiled, dressed, prepared, and as soon as the rain stops, Kelley is to be executed. We have tarried too long."

"Night will be falling soon, Your Majesty."

"And so will your head unless you do your duty. Tell me, where are Kepler and Brahe?"

"Brahe is dead, Your Majesty."

"What?"

"They say he swallowed some of the poisoned wine. You yourself appointed Kepler imperial mathematicus. And Kirakos is ill with the pox."

"Do not tell me he died."

"He cannot be found."

"Has anybody looked in his bed?"

"The bed is empty."

"Under the bed? In the closet? Everybody is buried or on vacation. Do you notice me going anywhere for the summer? No, I am right here, in this hot castle, and now, of all things, it is raining. Surely a horse has gotten through to Karlsbad by now."

"The road leading to the bridge is blocked with processions of monks and priests chanting and flagellating themselves. Nuns, fearing the wrath of Protestants, and pretending that their wedding rings signify earthly marriage, are leaving their nunneries."

"It is time somebody did something about those nuns. Tell the captain of the guards to cut a wide swath, indeed, cut down whoever and whatever is in the way. Dee is the one I want. The trail is growing cold, Rumpf."

"Dee? They say—"

"Who are these gossipers, the kibitzers, the yammerers, the eavesdroppers, the yappers, the loose of tongue, ready red lips, words so cheap all must be spent in a spurt, dear God, save me from the talk of Prague. As soon as the storm clears, the execution platform must be built for Kelley, Dee found. Go down to the Golden Ox, bring me the junkman."

WHEN THE SKY cleared that evening, Kepler went out to the serene white marble terrace of the summer palace, the Belvedere, below the castle and next to the singing fountain. This is where he liked to spend his nights since the observatory at Benátky was closed, he alone with Brahe's sextant, the large record book, finely sharpened quills, and bottles of fresh ink, the few tools of his trade. He had inherited all of Brahe's record books, meticulous records of positions of the planets and the constellations. The coming September was going to be a wonderful month for his observations, for Mars, on most nights small and dim, would be visible north of Regulus in Leo the Lion, progressing slowly away from the sun. Usually he felt very close to the planets and the stars, earth but an island in a sea of sky, and each point of light a stepping-stone, but recently, and on this night, the heavens, despite the clarity of the sky, appeared inaccessible, as if they were shunning him, as if he were unworthy of his task. Worse, he supposed, was not the indifference of the heavens above, but that he, puny human that he was, had meddled and caused grief on earth. Johannes Kepler, mind your stars, he told himself, for he had offered false cheer to Kelley and Dee that day in the Golden Ox and, not stopping there, had involved Rabbi Loew, which led to the deception that eventually ended in disaster, as in the Greek—dis + astro. This he had done, knowing the world spins on its course, turning into night without mankind's interference. How much, he wondered, can we plot our own course, how little intervene? What did the stars determine? Given the great mysteries of the heavens, was there really any correspondence between God's mind and our own? Could we ever understand what kept the planets to their appointed paths, and what those paths might be, and how the earth played partner to the sun? Or was it best to leave the mysteries unsolved, the paradoxes unrecognized, simply plod on, reap the harvest, make the bread? How different was the magnificence of a planet compared to our daily lives? And yet we lived on a planet.

He heard a wagon come down the road. So late, what could it be? The owl, Athena's bird, princess of the night, hooted. He held the sextant before him, peered into the sky. Mars was in the Lion. His poor, dead colleague, Brahe, had done four sightings of Mars. Tonight the North Star, the tip of Ursa Major, twinkled, as if just for him. Then he heard the cart again. He turned and saw several wagons filled with cut wood head down toward the Stone Bridge toward Old Town, and behind them were two cartloads of men holding burning torches in their hands. It was an eerie sight.

Within the infinite universes of Bruno's conjectures, planets and stars were dying daily and being born. Tycho himself had identified a star in 1572 not seen before, a new star, Nova Stella, and a comet which was much farther than the orbit of the moon, indicating that it was all bigger and more complex than had been thought before. Perhaps too big, too complex. Mars' orbit was costing his life, not the seven days he had initially boasted to Brahe, or the seven weeks, seven months, for it did not seem to fit into circles, epicycles, yet it had to be a circle, for was that not nature's perfect form? A stone thrown on the pond rippled out in concentric circles, the petals of flowers bordered its circular heart, the great sun was a circle and so too was sister moon. If the orbit of Mars was not a circle, what then? If the speed of orbit, was not constant throughout its orbit, what made Mars slow, pick up speed? If the center of the planetary system was not a point in the earth's orbit around the sun as Copernicus had speculated, what then?

Dogs began to bark as the wagons made their way down the hill. In the sky, the Big Dog, marked with the bright star, Sirius, was easy to locate, as was the Hare, Unicorn, Giraffe, Crab, the emperor's sign. Venus was always covered by her own clouds, Jupiter with his moons, Venus bright and beautiful, but Mars, the red planet, although elusive, he thought had the most to tell him, and even before Brahe had assigned him the task of charting its course, it was the planet he had the most affinity for. Although his eyesight was not that good, Kepler believed that, when studying the heavens, he saw with a kind of third eye, an inner eye, as if instead of merely looking outward, he was apprehending something that lay within, an essential self, not the self that sweated and labored in the world, but the self who was kin to stars. He wondered if Columbus and Magellan on their voyages heard the presence of continents as if listening in on their own heartbeats, felt the sway of palms on shore in the rhythms of their blood.

Then Kepler realized. How had he been so dense? The wagons filled with wood, the carts of men—they were all to finish building the execution platform in the night, so Kelley could be executed as the sun rose. Kepler berated himself for being concerned with the heavens when the imprisoned man had only death to contemplate.

WHEN KELLEY WAS in the jug, he could not contemplate, only stand, not move at all, and all was dark and dank. For a bit, he thought he may already be in the grave. When they brought him up to the larger cell of the tower and washed his body down, he was in bliss. And in the caged cart, Kelley greeted the bright sunshine of the day with something like happiness. He could not account for it, but even when he saw the platform and the ugly crowd of people and knew his death was nigh, something like peace descended on him. So it was to end, he thought, most fittingly, for he started with pies and muffins snatched from the baker's rack, clothes from lines, coin from pocket and purse. When his ears were cut off for forgery, the schoolmaster, who was the one who taught him to mimic any hand, prepared a poultice and bandaged his sore head with rags. After that it was on to London, shows in theatricals, now you see it, now you do not, fortune-telling as a sideline, cards, plain or tarot, hands. He could peer into a face, tell a life, if not a lie. The first time he saw Dee in his scholar's robe and skullcap, long beard and spectacles, he thought he could fool him. But Dee was nobody's fool, and where was his dear friend now? On the way to London, Kelley hoped.

In his last second, Kelley prayed to Madami, his guardian angel, asking that it, whatever it was, be swift and painless. And amazingly, for all his bad ways, he did not he feel the pull and heat of hell. First arrived was Madami, radiant and happy. She was really not a young girl. She was not old, either. She was, of course, an angel. Then he heard music, nine tones in harmony. The Enochian angels, who had been hovering overhead all along, descended one by one without the need of any ladder, more in the way angels descend when little children are lost in the woods or innocent maidens call for help. They lifted Edward Kelley high over the city on a great wave of rosy air. The Vltava River shone like a glistening serpent gliding between the hills, the Stone Bridge a tiny band of black on its sinuous back, the walled Judenstadt a huddle of blocks, the ruins of the Vyšehrad rubble, the Old Town Square nothing but a patch of gray.

At the very same moment Kelley ascended over Prague, Rabbi Loew, in the attic of the Altneu Synagogue, after a night of prayer and fasting, had given up hope for a satisfactory solution to the problem with the emperor. Barely able to walk, he was so distraught, he had to drag himself to the tiny window overlooking the Vltava River, for the frame of the window seemed on fire, yet when he drew closer, he saw it was not flames, but a brilliant white light. How curious, the rabbi thought, for the dazzle did not blind the eye. On the contrary, the rabbi could look right through the window, and, comfortably as strolling through a grassy meadow, he was able to step through, enter an illuminated passageway. A hand, Elijah's hand, enfolded his, drew him forth. Before them pillows of mist parted, brushing against the rabbi's feet. The first vision was of roses. Each petal was precious and every bud was a whole paradise unto itself. Awe, in raiment of a transparent gold, guarded the gate. Transfixed, the rabbi could not stir, yet the gates opened before him as if they had been waiting an eternity for his arrival. In a ripple, with the sound of bells like the little bells topping Torah scrolls, a succession of gardens opened out into each other. Judah Loew, who in his long, pious life had never been granted vision or direct experience of God, passed through each portal like one who had been endowed special vision. One garden had trees taller than any ever seen, with birds in their canopied tops singing melodies sweeter than the sweetest honey. Humility came in the guise of kitten-faced pansies. Trust was marigolds. There were myriads of tulips in a rainbow of colors. Exquisite fragrance wafted in the soft and gentle breeze. Four rivers ran beneath his feet as if represented on a map, yet were as immediate as the fingers on his hand. Was he was in Safed, the holy city overlooking the Hula Valley in Israel, where all was blue and light and Ari, the Lion, had lived and taught? Judah felt like a cub again. He felt rending passion and enormous calm at the same time. He felt he had given birth to himself and, touched by Light and Love, was perfect. Passing through all ten gates, the Rabbi Judah Loew, swooned in the feminine presence of God, the Shekhinah, and he entered Her in ecstatic embrace. Finally, he had been given enlightenment, and throughout the rest of his long life, he would be grateful and satisfied.

35

WITH THE ADVENT of the afternoon, the little group of travelers, who had wondered in their hiding place at the great roar in the Square that morning, bade Gregor, the student, good-bye, and Karel's cart was again able to head toward the town gates despite the encampment on the Square. Those who had run for cover during the storm had returned full force, to be treated by the unexpected spectacle of Kelley's execution. By the time Karel was on his way, the blood was still drying on the boards, Kelley's body removed to the Pest Cemetery, and the head taken on a pike to the Stone Bridge, where all could witness the penalty for treason in the Empire. Vegetable vendors were again spreading out their cloths, pyramiding their squash, arraying their cucumbers and radishes. The scrivener, who wrote letters for people, put up his box under the Astronomical Clock. Rochel, under the damp, dirty cloth, could hear the voices of children at play. It was going to be fine, she reasoned, only a few minutes' ride, no need for the fear she had experienced the night before. It was not a chasm she was leaping over, no precipice she had to cling to, not a mountain she was scaling. She was merely leaving Prague. Good-bye, Prague, good-bye, Perl and the rabbi, and most of all good-bye to her child left behind up on Petřín Hill. If she could, she would turn time back, but she could not. She was convinced, however, that Yossel was safe somewhere, and she was hopeful that in a new town where nobody knew them, she and Zev would not have to face acrimony and blame and could start anew. For all this she thanked and praised HaShem. The cart bounced along for a while, and then one of the wheels caught on a loose cobblestone and the cart wavered a little, righted itself, swayed to the other side.

"Oswald, Oswald," Karel called out.

They slowed, then picked up their pace. Again a wheel snagged on an object. Limbs broken off from trees in the storm littered the Square. Oswald, however, threaded his way carefully, surefooted and calm as a mountain goat used to his rocky terrain. Yet, once more the wagon wheels overran something, and then, wobbling, the cart, like a boat on rough water, heaved, toppled, and in a clumsy spill, the coverlet, all the rags, Rochel, Zev, Kirakos, Sergey, and Karel fell in a heap to the ground in the middle of a group of children.

"Oh, no," Karel moaned.

Boys and girls played chase, leapfrog, and blindman's buff, mothers balanced babies on their aproned hips. Rochel began to right herself, smiled hopefully. They could help get the cart up, and the four would be able to continue their trip.

"The junkman's cart has hit a rut and overturned," a boy called..

"Five cabbage heads rolled out," another child returned.

"The adulteress," a woman pointed out. "Look, it is the adulteress in a man's clothes."

Cries of "the adulteress" echoed through the Square, and immediately a ring of girls and boys surrounded Rochel, clapping and chanting, "Witch, witch, burn the witch."

Rochel saw Kirakos and Sergey scramble under the execution platform. Zev was lying beside her. Karel, where was Karel?

"Zev, Zev, hide under the platform," she called to her husband.

More boys and girls had fanned out in a dance. "Witch, witch, burn the witch."

Rochel started to tremble.

"Witch, witch, burn the witch." The song grew louder as more children joined in.

She could see that Kirakos and Sergey, caught by the crowd, were being cuffed. And Karel, she saw that Karel, holding his torso tightly in his arms, was being kicked. Zev was knocked to the ground. The group of women and children about Rochel thickened, drew closer.

"My wife, my wife," Zev screamed, getting up on all fours, pushing his way between the legs of the boys and men and skirts of the girls and women.

"He is going to his whore," a woman screamed.

"Whore, whore, do you want more?"

Some big boys began to pry loose some of the larger cobblestones.

The first stone fell short, but the second hit Rochel's stomach. Zev stumbled forward.

"Get the cuckold, too," A woman shouted.

"Double back, Sergey," Kirakos, still weak from the pox, gasped. "Try to get to them, pull them away from the crowd."

Sergey, his head lowered, his arms in front of him, pushed through the roaring throng like a wild boar. Barrels of beer from the taverns At the Red Ax and the Unicorn had been rolled out to the street and tankards of sloshing suds were being distributed free of charge. It was a jovial occasion, a holiday, outrageous festivities, a bacchanal, a carnival. Sergey, however, with blind determination, began to make considerable headway through the uproarious crowd, but just when he thought he could reach Rochel and Zev, he saw that the innermost ring around them was a band of people three bodies thick, arms linked, leg to leg. Zev, crawling bit by bit, had reached his wife, and wrapped himself around her, so that his body shielded hers.

"Zev, Zev, go back," Rochel moaned through her broken lips. "It is only me they want."

Karel, on the other side of the ring, moving arm by arm, dragged himself forward. "Not a hair on a Jew's head must be harmed, the emperor's orders," he shouted.

For a moment the stoning ceased.

"What emperor?" Somebody said. "The emperor is dead."

"The emperor is dead." They took up the shout. "The emperor is dead."

"The emperor lives. The emperor is alive and well," Karel assured them.

"The emperor is alive and unwell," came the reply.

"The emperor is mad," echoed the chant. "The emperor is mad."

A rock hit Zev, mashing his ear.

"Guards," Karel shouted. "Where are the guards?"

The guards were on the bridge, on Petřín Hill, among the ruins of Vyšehrad, at the Golden Ox, in the Slavonic Monastery, on the emperor's orders, looking for him, Karel.

"Help," Karel screamed. "Somebody please help us."

Sergey, powerless, distraught beyond measure, now stood by the overturned cart. He wept into Oswald's neck, holding his wooden cross to his lips.

Kirakos, lying in the street on the edge of the crowd, squeezed his eyes shut, put his fingers in his ears. This is not happening, he repeated to himself, knowing in his heart of hearts that he was as guilty as anyone, as everyone.

Another cobblestone hit Zev's back. He started to mumble, "Blessed art Thou, O Lord our God, King of the universe, the True Judge."

Karel steathily dragged himself along by the use of his upper extremities alone. But just as he was ready to barrel himself forward like a human cannonball, stop those hurtling stones, his long, strong arms were grabbed, pinned behind his back.

"Have mercy," he screamed. "Have mercy on them."

But it was not to be. Held high aloft, made to bear witness, he could see Zev cleaving to Rochel and Rochel clinging to Zev. Karel prayed that they die quickly, knowing that the faster they died, the sooner they would find themselves in God's tender embrace. Shortly, as if in answer to his prayer, Rochel and Zev stopped struggling. They lay motionless. The townspeople looked away, not meeting each other's eyes. Silence spread across the Square. The sun was still in the sky. Clouds, fluffy as pillows, scudded overhead in oblivious parade. Somewhere birds were chirping, children playing with toys, people sitting down to their afternoon meals.

Karel, released from his restraints, looked across at the two broken bodies, husband and wife. They had not deserved this. Who deserved such a thing? How could God permit such cruelty? He tried to recall the words of his catechism: Who made thee? God made thee. What did God make? God made all things. Why did God make all things? For his own glory. How can you glorify God? By loving Him and doing what He commands. Then he noticed a slight movement. Rochel's back was rising and falling very slightly. Yes, yes, she was breathing. She was alive, barely alive, but alive. If he could inch his way to her, drag her to Týn Church unnoticed, maybe, just maybe . . . Or if he could put her in the cart as if she were dead and take her to Judenstadt, or if finally the crowd dispersed in shame . . . But before he could accomplish anything, move forward, somebody else noticed her breathing.

"She is alive," a woman shouted. "The Jewess lives."

"Finish her off, finish her off, and then to Judenstadt," came the chant. The women put down their babies, dug up the biggest stones they could heave, made ready. The children filled pockets and pouches with pebbles. The fathers and grandfathers behind them tried to get a good view.

But abruptly, like a sudden change in weather, the earth started to shake.

"What is that?"

Then, from the outskirts of the circle, came a bellow.

People looked at one another.

"The golem," somebody shouted. "Look. He has come back."

Yossel, with huge strides, parting all in his path, made his way to the center of the unholy circle.

"Yossel, Yossel," Karel cried out. "She is alive. Save her."

Rochel's arms were clasped in Zev's so tightly that the golem, with the strength of twelve men, had to lift them both from the street, fling them over his shoulders. He carried them thus, one on each shoulder, inside Týn Church, spread them on the altar. The crowd filed in behind to see.

"She is not alive after all," somebody said in hushed tones.

"She is dead." The three words echoed around the nave. She is dead, she is dead.

Yossel bent down over Rochel. Her bruised eyelids lay like dark blue butterfly wings atop her cheeks. Blood, crimson as a cardinal, feathered from one leg and arm, pooled beneath. No breath came from her mouth or nose. The giant put his ear to her chest.

"Now the monster can bury her with the cuckold."

"At least she got what she deserved before he got here."

Yossel bolted up, stretched out his arms, threw back his head, and from deep within his being, unobstructed by tongue or the ability to form words, came a groan unlike any had heard before. Indeed, each heard it differently. To one it was the cry of a hawk whose nest had been invaded, to another it was like a ghost in the cave of a dream, to another it was the wail of a bear who has lost his mate, to the rabbi and his followers who had now flooded out of Judenstadt, it was a cry of great pain from a human being suffering at the hands of the world. Yossel turned around in the aisle of the church, his eyes blazing.

"Run," the shout went up. "The golem is amok."

The fathers and grandmothers, children and women, tumbled out of Týn Church, stumbled onto the street and began to run as fast as they could.

"Get the rabbi, get the rabbi," the call went up. "The monster is on the rampage."

"The rabbi is here," somebody answered. "He is here."

Yossel, with his great feet, strode up the aisle, and with a mighty pull tore a heavy crucifix off the church wall, and holding it high overhead, he lumbered forth.

"He is defiling our church, desecrating the cross."

Without hesitation, the golem threw it across the church, where it hit the wall, shattered. And then, in mad succession, he pounded out unto the Square, kicked kettles off their tripods, smashed stalls and lean-tos, pulled the cloths from under the arrayed piles of merchants' goods, toppled the scrivener's box, and as people ran to get away, he grabbed the stones they had dropped, flinging them right and left. His fists were hammers, his feet slings that went back and forth, and his chest a great wall. With one massive hand, he grabbed a branch left over from the storm, bit the leaves off, chewed them up, spit them out, and advanced, brandishing his weapon, brushing the ground with it, twirling it over his head, thrashing it side to side like an angry animal beating its tail. He arched his back like a snake uncoiling from a winter's sleep. He charged like a horned bull. He was unstoppable, a force of nature, a machine without master.

Back in Týn Church, as the murderous crowd fled from Yossel's wrath, Kirakos and Sergey entered, Karel pulling himself behind them. Kirakos knelt beside Rochel, put his mouth over hers.

"She is not alive, is she?" Karel asked the doctor.

Kirakos began to blow puffs of air into her mouth. He had seen, when a child, his mother breathe into the mouths of baby lambs when they were born still and blue.

"Sergey," Kirakos commanded, pausing for a moment, pulling off his turban and ripping it in two. "Tie it around her arm, and the leg, too. Stop the blood flow."

And he resumed, saying in his mind, Breathe, breathe. Make her breathe. Please breathe.

And then shortly, as if waking from a nap, Rochel blinked, opened her eyes. "Zev?"

"Your husband is dead," Karel said.

"He cannot be."

"He is."

"No." She began to recite the Shema: "Hear O Israel, the Eternal One is our God, the Eternal God is One."

Karel dragged himself to where Zev lay on his back. His eyes were closed, but lo and behold, his chest was moving up and down. "Wait, the husband lives. He lives. Water, Sergey, bring some of the holy water from the font." Karel uttered, "Thank God."

"Not yet," Kirakos said. "We have to get out of town."

Yossel, now by the banks of the river, was seeing everything through a wash of blood, yet he could make out the rabbi running toward him, Perl behind him.

"Yossel," the rabbi said. "Come home."

Home? Did the man say home? What Yossel wanted to do was rush up the stairs of the rabbi's study, push everything off the rabbi's tables, spill the mixed ink, snap quills, destroy all his father's fine things. Without further ado, he ran straight to Judenstadt, barged into the rabbi's house, bounded up the stairs, and with one sweep he did break the globe of the world like an egg. That was what he thought of it—the world was a diseased onion, soft with black rot. He dented the armillary. The heavens, too, had failed, for had God interfered? He tore pages out of books, made into shreds what was called learning. Was knowledge of any use? What was civilization? For one's civilization was another's slavery. He ripped up maps, smashed glass, threw books out of the window, shelves were emptied of all their contents, chairs overturned, the legs pulled out from under the table.

Those who had been disdainful of Rochel, the ones who had snickered at her behind her back, those who had ostracized her, who had not a kind word for her, those who had forced her into exile and death, he sought. He would get them, show them. The three sisters—Leah, who had instigated; Miriam, who had copied; and Zelda, who had remained silent—crouched in the cellar, the trapdoor locked from the inside by three heavy bolts.

"Yossel, stop, stop," Perl called out after him.

But there was no stopping the giant. Looking for the rabbi's daughters, he charged through Judenstadt, tearing apart whatever he could get his hands on; fathers of children ran forth trying to bind him, hold him fast, knock him down, hoping that the golem would not hurt a Jew, for he was one of them. But was he? Had he ever been truly a member of the community? Yossel did not care anymore. And the emperor was to be next.

As he crossed the Stone Bridge, a line of men and big boys from Judenstadt ran after the enraged golem, several with axes and hammers. Somebody would have to shoot him with a harquebus, pierce him with an arrow, they decided. But he was too swift, his stride too big; he was faster than any living person, and the Jews had no horses, and the few guards who saw him believed that he was the devil predicted and finally arrived. They fled to the shelter of the castle, spreading the word, sounding the alarm. The emperor and Rumpf cowered in the secret compartment of the Kunstkammer, Petaka at their side.

"Yossel, Yossel, stop, for the love of God, stop," the rabbi begged, trailing behind him.

But the golem did not love God. He did not love anybody. He had come back to claim his love, take her away, rescue her from her life, for he had found work in the mines, a room in Kutná Hora, and now she was dead. Now they were all at his mercy. How pitiful they were, with their things and puny lives, their rooms and shelves, tables and chairs, their ailments and complaints, their rank smells, the way they put food in their mouths, their stares and spiteful mouths, their spit and phlegm, crabby genitals, raw bottoms, the grimy creases ringing their scrawny necks, and Grandfather sits there, we say our prayers, if we die tonight our soul to keep. What right had they to touch Rochel, to touch her? He remembered her lovely skin, the soft hollows behind her knees, and her pretty feet. She, who had been open to the world, was crushed like a baby bird fallen from its nest. He could not stand the thought that soon worms would take up residence in her sweet mouth and the curl of her ears, devour her wet brown eyes, and in a year's time by her yahrtzeit, her body would achieve the color of chalk, the feel of shell, the purity of bone, and in ten years, all of her would be dust. He could not stand it.

EARLIER THAT MORNING, a group of Brahe's friends had decided to meet at the Golden Ox. The funeral cortege several days before had been led by a team of black horses, Brahe's horse foremost, empty-saddled, carrying Brahe's favorite spurs and cloak. There were many speeches from august personages, although, of course, the emperor did not leave the castle to attend. Now a contingent of mourners were meeting to toast their fallen fellow once again in the cozy confines of the well-known Golden Ox, the site of many a happy occasion. The good men reminisced sadly and fondly about Brahe's silver nose; the elk he had in Denmark, which, drunk, fell down the stairs; Brahe's great generosity; his appetite for drink, life, and food; his fine chess game, speaking of which, what had happened to his worthy opponent, Kirakos? Jepp wept copiously. Kepler, who had inherited all of Brahe's records, including plot points of the orbit of Mars, with the promise that he would make the dead astronomer immortal, looked lost. Frau Brahe was inconsolable. And then, in their midst, Václav appeared.

Václav Kola, the emperor's valet, had returned with his small family from Karlsbad. Some people had believed Václav would never be seen in Prague again, for it was well known that the emperor had not been sympathetic to his son's illness. Talk of his departure included various conjectures, such as Václav traveling to Vienna to become a confectioner for a fine noble family. Others speculated that he had stolen so much from the emperor's Kunstkammer that he had enough gold to become a proud landowner with a palace overlooking the Rhine River. A few surmised that Václav had met Yossel on the road out of Prague, and together they were planning to tour Europe as an event for fairs and market days—the Biggest Man in the World. This idea came about through word from some merchants that a Yossel-like man had been sighted in Frankfort with that same group of fools who came to Prague and wandered Europe begging for money. Somebody had heard that in Bruges there was a man so strong, he could uproot trees; even in London town, where the people were taller from long-ago Viking blood and were not startled by one of his kind, came reports of an enormous man in the pit at the Globe Theater. No matter that to reach those distant locations in so short a time, Yossel would have had to fly.

But Václav said no, he had not seen Yossel, and yes, his son was better, and yes, he had heard about Kelley's tragic demise. How very unfortunate it was that poor Brahe had died of politeness. Then, as they were raising one more jug in honor of the noble Dane, the assembled friends of the dearly departed heard screams, and suddenly the door to the Golden Ox was thrown open and something like a bear, an animal on its hind feet, stood there snarling.

Indeed, Yossel had a demented look in his eye, and he moved not with his former grace, but stiffly, like one governed with ill will, nay, with supreme menace and evil intent. His great hands, held out in front of him, were covered with blood.

"Yossel?" Václav asked. "What is wrong?" For the group had been sequestered in their drinking hole all day and were not aware of the disturbance in the Square.

"He has the moon disease."

"He has been bitten by a mad dog."

"He is afflicted with the last stage of the French pox."

The golem moved forward, his eyes not leaving the faces of the crowd. With his foot, he tipped over a table, kicked a bench. The patrons ran to the back of the room, pressed themselves against the wall. Behind Yossel, the rabbi and other Jews who had been following entered. The rabbi grabbed the golem's shirttail, tried to hold him back.

"Yossel," the rabbi said. "Stop. You will not solve anything this way."

The golem turned, looked at the rabbi as if he did not know him.

"Somebody call the guards," one of the frightened drinkers suggested in a small voice.

Meanwhile, the tavernkeeper, standing by the fire behind Yossel, unsheathed the knife he kept strapped to his belt.

"No, no," the rabbi said. "Do not hurt him."

"He will kill us all."

The golem took a step toward them. The crowd could go no closer against the wall. The tavernkeeper circled the room slowly, quietly, so that Yossel would not notice him. All eyes were on him for rescue.

Then Jepp stepped forward.

"Yossel," he said. "Tell us, please, what has angered you?"

"They have killed Rochel," the rabbi answered for him. "She was stoned to death in the Square. She and Zev."

"No." Václav started to cry. "Not sweet Rochel."

Everybody began to cry, Jepp the loudest of them all.

Yossel looked down at the small man.

"Come, let us wash your hands, dear fellow," Jepp said, sobbing.

At that, Yossel's knees buckled and he fell to the floor, his legs spread out, his eyes cast down, looking for all the world not like a monster, but like a harmless half-wit. He was spent, hollow, a mere husk. He did not know what had come over him, except that it was grief, grief and rage. He had succumbed to the lowest of human emotions—anger—and being the colossus that he was, in his fury he had hurt many who were perhaps innocent or powerless, and he had destroyed parts of the city. Furthermore, in retrospect, his whole short life seemed a waste commensurate with his size, a huge, frenzied, fumbled series of bad choices leading to worse choices. He had cast evil far and wide. The tavernkeeper brought a bowl of water, some rags, and Jepp washed Yossel's hands

If he had been able to talk, the big man would have confessed, It is my fault, for it was I who caught her eye. From the first day, I coveted my neighbor's wife, and I tempted her, and I caused her to lose all that was precious to her—her child, her honor, her home, her husband, her life.

"Take him," Václav said to the rabbi. "Take him home before the guards get here."

"Come, Yossel," the rabbi said gently.

The two walked out, father and son, son following his father. The others of Judenstadt hung well behind. As they traveled over the Stone Bridge, Yossel could see all the havoc he had wreaked, the broken carts, toppled goods, spilled milk, broken windows. People hung back, scampered to corners, crawled under tables, hid in closets. Yossel hung his head in shame. Weakened by the sight of all his evil, his strength gone, he stumbled toward the gates of Judenstadt, understanding that he was not a man who had the strength of twelve men, but a golem. He could never have been married to Rochel, have a household, be a real Jew. He knew that he must return to the mute, formless earth of which he was made. He gestured toward the Altneu Synagogue.

The rabbi stopped.

Yossel nodded yes, it was time.

"Let us ask God, Yossel. We will pray." With great sadness, the old man, followed by the golem, walked to the Cervena Street entrance, passing under the portal of the south vestibule decorated with clusters of grapes and vine leaves.

"Yossel, my son," Perl cried, running down the stairs from the women's section.

"Perl," the rabbi cautioned. "Perl, it is out of our hands, let him go. Rochel and Zev are dead. Prague is in shambles. All is lost."

"No, Judah, she lives. Rochel and Zev. They both live."

Yossel halted. What was this?

"Yes, yes, you have saved them, Yossel. They live. Karel has just returned from the dump, and with his own mouth told me that when all the people were fleeing in terror, afraid you would kill them, and the guards in great panic deserting their posts, Oswald was able to pull the cart right through the city gates free as can be, no one to stop them. Yes, yes, Rochel and Zev will recover from their wounds, and with Kirakos and Sergey have joined a merchant caravan and are on their way to Frankfort, and from there to Amsterdam. It is true. You have saved them, Yossel."

"That is good news indeed, Perl."

"Not only that, Judah." Perl clapped her hands like an excited little girl. "The townspeople have all returned to their homes, locked their doors, covered their windows, for they expect reprisals. They have promised to leave us alone. They realize that the golem will not let a hair of a Jew's head be harmed."

"Well and good, Perl."

"Yes, Judah, I know. So for now, for a little while, we are going to be left in peace."

Judah did not say anything more. There was the emperor to worry about. And in his experience, peace was fragile, goodwill a whim, yet his vision, his tiny glimpse of Paradise, if it had not changed everything on earth, it had changed him. He had hope.

Yossel looked up at the sky, saw a flock of geese traveling in the pattern of a V. Soon it would be autumn, the leaves turning yellow and brown. He had never seen autumn, would like to see it, but that was not to be. Rochel would see it through her eyes, and he imagined her, in her blue forget-me-not skirt, peering at the sky. He bent down, lifted his mother, looked at her hard, as if to take the memory of her with him into the earth.

"Go, Perl," the rabbi said gently. "Leave us." Then he turned to Yossel. "I cannot, Yossel."

The golem nodded: Yes, you must. For really, why would he live, how could he live? Who knew when he might get out of hand again? Rochel would never be his. Indeed, he had no future as a man, as anything, really.

"I cannot, Yossel. You are a Jew and a mensch."

The golem smiled at the compliment.

"You can go away." The rabbi said this, unsure of the consequences.

Yossel's eyes beseeched the rabbi's: Do what has to be done.

The rabbi hung his head, sighed deeply, and with the most meager of nods, assented. The two continued into the synagogue. Before them was the bimah, the raised dais from which the Torah was read, the curtained ark where the sacred scrolls of the Torah were kept, and to their right was the rabbi's chair. It was dark in the room without the candles, and the silence made the sense of solemnity complete. They ascended the stairs to the attic, where the books too frayed and old to be used anymore were stored. Rochel had been here, Yossel knew. He could smell her all around him, the scent of mushrooms at the edge of the forest, and the tiny white lilies which hung like bells that she liked better than any flower, lilies of the valley. Yossel, as instructed by the rabbi, obediently lay on the floor. He did not close his eyes and he was smiling, for in his head he was seeing her as he saw her on the first day of his life, singing at her work, letting the sunshine spill over her head and neck like melted butter.

Then the ceremony began. The rabbi walked around the golem seven times in one direction, seven times in another, as he had at Yossel's birth. He bowed to the north, the south, the east and west, and, standing at the golem's feet, he intoned the prayer for the dead. "Magnified and sanctified be His great name in the world that is to be created anew, where He will revive the dead and raise them up into life eternal . . ." Kaddish, Yossel thought with a smile, somebody is saying Kaddish to comfort my survivors.

"Yossel, one thing I want you to know," the rabbi finally whispered, bending low. "Two things. One, love is eternal, and two, death is an illusion."

Yossel hoped it was true, yet wondered that if it were true, why did people mourn the dead at all? But he had no tongue, no time, and so let it be. So many things, in this world, had to just be left, he had learned. And then the rabbi kissed Yossel, licking out the Hebrew letter E of EMETH, Truth, leaving METH, Death. Without a speck of pain, as if falling into a peaceful sleep, Yossel the golem turned to dust, leaving an imprint of his thumb which stayed fixed to the floor, marking, as prisoners do the walls of their cells or as lovers carve their initials within hearts, in the same manner in which we all are inscribed in the Book of Life.

36

I T WAS VERY early in the morning of a cool day in fall, the sky still dark. In the daylight, the leaves in Petřín Woods looked like the pale continents in the rabbi's broken globe. The flowers in the imperial gardens were now strawlike chrysanthemums, asters, dahlias, but in the dark they looked like spikes and heads of hair. The trees and hedges, clipped in the shapes of animals, looked like a shadowy zoo. It was a Friday morning, near the beginning of the Jewish New Year, Rosh Hashanah. At the castle, the emperor was preparing for the rabbi's visit. They had not discussed the details, but Vladislav Hall was readied. A bed had been brought in, for the emperor was certain, as certain as he was about anything these days, that he had to be supine while the rabbi worked his spells over him. His dressers had attired him for this occasion in his crown, of course, and a splendid doublet of green velvet with panels of satin, a small cap of the softest wool in a tint of green lighter than his doublet, a sea green. His sleeves were slashed to show an undergarment of brown silk, and the small buttons of his doublet were emeralds. The edges of his sleeves and fastenings were blue, which matched his bright blue hose, and his shoes, high-heeled, were tied with blue bows. He was also wearing, as he always did, the little amulet he had received as child. It was a gold case bejeweled with pearls, coral, and eastern emeralds. Inside was a little cake made of toads, virginal blood, white arsenic, dittany, and mandrake root to protect him against the Plague. His beard was newly shaped, his hair fashioned and cut. Beside him were his orb and scepter.

"So, Václav, what do you think?"

"You look very well, Your Majesty." Václav hated to be up this early. It was an unnatural hour to leave your warm bed, for more and more over the last month, as the emperor had become increasingly befuddled about who was there and who was not there at his side, Václav had been able to sleep at home with his family. His little daughter could push up on her legs, would soon be walking.

In truth, the emperor had good days and bad days, mostly bad days, when the thread of a discussion proved too thin or frayed or knotted for him to continue. Sometimes he was no longer certain whether he was emperor or not. He called for his brother, Ernst, long dead, and feared that his cousin, the notorious humped-back, limp-footed Don Carlos, was occupying the throne. The curtains held a veritable throng of assassins of every religious persuasion. August skies were filled with snakes in the air. September boded no better. Rudolph looked out on the green hills of Prague, saw the dusty brown of Madrid. His collections offered little solace, hardly suc-ceeded in keeping him tied to the world. There were moments he believed that on the very first day of the Christian New Year, 1601, he succeeded in killing himself, and that he had descended into a hell walled in blood and floored with sharp rocks.

Yet, on this day, the day he was to become immortal, he was quite coherent. Indeed, it could be said, and most certainly was said, that the emperor's desire for immortality was his one link to sanity. On the other hand, it could be argued, which it frequently was at the Golden Ox, that his obsession was what finally had made him thor-oughly and irrevocably mad.

Initially, a select audience was chosen to witness his entry into eternity—Anna Maria, Rumpf, the dubious advisor, Crato, who in his dotage was the new number one physician, Pistorius, the Confessor, the Burgrave Rosenberg, Kepler, and Václav, of course. But the rabbi cautioned against an audience, for Rudolph had forgotten, as he had so many other things, how these kinds of things must be exclusively exercised. The day, however, had been designated as auspicious by Kepler. The constellations were in Libra, and one could, facing north, see Hercules and the Dragon, the Giraffe and Charioteer. It was also the eighteenth day of the month. In the Hebrew alphabet, the num-ber 18 was a combination of letters which spelled *chai*, life..

The Rabbi slowly climbed the hill up to the Hradcany, stopping at the Summer Palace, the Belvedere, where Kepler was waiting for him on the white, marble terrace. He and Kepler were taken over the stag moat bridge. To their left was the Powder Tower where Kelley and Dee had worked away pretending to make an elixir of eternal life. Dee was back in London, penniless, Kelley was dead, Brahe dead, and the golem just disappeared one day. The city seemed diminished, almost austere after all that had taken place. Indeed, some of the priceless relics surrounding St. Wenceslas's tomb in the St. Vitus Cathedral had been stripped from their places in the chaos, never recovered. The crucifix in Týn Church was still at the menders'.

The two friends entered the main square of the castle, where Petaka was being walked. The old cat, failing more and more, could only eat meat that was ground. The men were led to Vladislav Hall, which, no longer filled with butterflies, resembled a cavernous and cold barn and smelled of the stable. The emperor was already sitting on his throne, his best, the one he had used at that ill-fated birthday banquet.

"Your Highness." the rabbi bowed low.

"Rabbi. I am ready."

"I am afraid, Your Majesty, that we must reconvene on the banks of the river."

"In the mud?" The emperor did not remember precisely this part of the process. True, the rabbi had explained over the course of the summer, if not exactly, roughly, that to become immortal, the emperor not only needed to have words said over him, but must also, in some mysterious way, become bodily transformed. He was reminded how alchemists make base metal into gold. It was to be, if you will, a recombination of basic elements, and thus he must, in essence, become golemic, golemish, golemesque, transcend, or was it descend, the purely human state. Something or other, that was what the emperor was a trifle vague about. No matter. Eternity it was to be.

"Dust we are, Your Highness," the rabbi recalled for him on this, the day of all days.

"Next to worms, Judah?"

"Remember the silkworm, Your Majesty."

"I want to be a man, always a man, an extraordinary, exceptional, man of a man."

"Exactly," the rabbi answered.

"An eternal emperor is what I wish to be."

"To be sure, Your Highness."

"An immortal man." The emperor cleared his throat, looked again at Václav, as if his trusty valet would untangle this knot of logic. "Worms, Václav?"

"Remember butterflies start as caterpillars, Your Majesty," Václav offered. "It is a stage."

"A stage? Where are the butterflies?" The emperor looked around.

"They have been moved," Václav said.

"To a better place," Kepler added.

"You are not afraid, are you?" The rabbi was ever so solicitous. "'Yea, though I walk through the valley of the shadow of death, I will fear no evil: for Thou art with me; Thy rod and Thy staff they comfort me.'"

"I am not going to be walking through the valley of the shadow of death." The emperor began to fidget and peered toward the folds of the curtains. The devil did not have a shadow, that was one of the ways you could tell. And he lived in wells. Whelks were like leeches. He had a portrait by Arcimboldo of him as Vertumnus, the god of change and vegetation. Arcimboldo painted portraits made of fish, game, birds, roses, so if roses could become a face and stones could be made into roses, and he owned—nay, possessed—Dürer's *Garland of Roses*, then his collection, his castle, his things, his Empire . . . all was as it should be forevermore.

"You will not feel anything. Perhaps a little tingle as you dissolve," Václav said, "become one with the earth."

"How is it you know so much about it, Václav?"

"We are all here to help you, Your Majesty." Kepler stood with his hands behind his back, his legs open. He looked fatter. The emperor could not quite place it. He had not been paying him, so why did he look so self-assured, so well fed? Could the wretch be happy?

"Somebody fetch me some wine. You did not say this dissolving part before. It sounds too much like the alembic, like the laboratory, like Kelley and Dee, like the melting fires of hell."

"Mere details, Your Majesty."

"I feel tingling, plain and simple?"

"What comes to mind are tiny pinpricks. Little needles, bee stings, if you will. Surely nothing compared to battle or anything else that you, as our emperor, have had to withstand."

Václav, too, had changed in some way. He was as obedient as ever, perhaps too obedient. The emperor could not quite put a finger on it. A page returned with a goblet of wine. The emperor grabbed it from him and drank it down in one draught.

"Do you think that is wise?" the rabbi said. "Drinking wine at a time like this?"

"I just did, for God's sake. Let us be on our way. Call the carriage."

Václav backed out of the hall, told the captain of the guard in the hallway to call a carriage. Shortly, the second-best carriage with a little crown on top was brought around to the main square and the emperor, the rabbi, Václav, and Kepler got in. Another carriage followed with four pages, who held between them the canvas of a small imperial tent designed for camping during battles, and several shovels for digging. The guards, on Václav's direction, were left behind at the castle. The old cat, Pataka, also stayed at home. It was not yet light, but the texture of the sky was changing. Expectation of the day was palpable. As they crossed the bridge, they saw a lone horseman. He was hooded, rode stiffly, his back ramrod straight, his legs out at an angle. His white horse trotted slowly, the hoofbeats echoing on the empty bridge.

"Who could be out so early?" the emperor asked. "I am telling you, that scoundrel Dee is not going to get away this time. We will apprehend the rascal, lock him up in the jug."

"Now that you will be living forever, with all the time in the world, you will be able to pursue him properly, Your Majesty."

"And I will have more time even than that, Václav, because next month, before it snows, we will be making a little trip to Transylvania. And the Jewess, too, we will find. She loves me, you know."

"Here is the spot," the rabbi said. They were on the bank nearest Judenstadt, the same place where the golem had been made and where Rochel had fallen into the water. Fishermen's nets hanging between staffs of wood looked like giant spiderwebs. Seabirds were circling the sky.

"It must be here where it is so dirty?" the emperor asked, for today he felt fastidious and was, in fact, meticulously dressed. He did not like this . . . mud.

The pages, following close behind on the bank of the river, erected the little tent near the shoreline. It was of white and green stripes, with a little crown on top, and from it flew the Habsburg flag with the eagles pointing east and west, their claws and tongues extended. The pages then handed Kepler and Václav the shovels, returned to their carriage, and waited. Václav opened two flaps of the tent, pinned them to the sides so the light of the sun, when it rose, could shine inside.

"Allow me," he said, as he ushered in the emperor, whose shoes and hose were already spattered with mud.

"I must lie down there?"

"Your Majesty, it is the only way," Václav replied.

The three of them crowded around the emperor.

"I will not be in any tight confinement?" the emperor asked. "You realize that when I was born, I was a sickly child and was immediately plunged into the body of a freshly killed lamb. When the cavity of the carcass cooled, another newly slaughtered lamb was rushed from the butchery, one animal after another. It was only after the second day that I could be set to suckle at the wet nurse. All my life I have feared small spaces.

"You do still want to be immortal?" Václav said.

"Yes, of course I do."

"Lie down, then. We will be right back."

Václav, Kepler, and the rabbi moved a little a ways, huddled together in conference.

"Are you certain this will work?" the rabbi asked Václav.

"It will," Václav replied.

"So he will return to the castle convinced he is immortal? It will be firmly embedded in his mind?"

"Rabbi, perhaps the idea will not be firmly embedded, rather it will be part of the loose jumble," Václav replied. "But he will bother you no more, that I can assure you."

The rabbi looked at Václav. "You have become adept in sophistry, Václav."

"Kirakos, I learned from him."

"I see. And the wherewithal to go to Karlsbad?"

"I learned that from Kelley, God bless his soul; in point of fact, it started with a certain clock Kelley desired. It had a moor on it with a turban studded with pearls and other precious gems. We were going to bribe the guards at one time, but then everything happened so fast, and I was left with it, so what could I do? And there are other things from St. Wensaslas's tomb. . . . I am a Czech, Rabbi. These are national treasures."

"Say no more, Herr Kola. You are entitled. Indeed, there is something I must tell you, and now may be the very time."

"Rabbi," Václav said, "I know."

"You know?"

"It is all the more fitting that I should be here today, at the end of it."

"And nobody will be hurt?"

"I promise, Rabbi, nobody will feel pain, nobody innocent will be harmed."

"So I can go home?"

"Happy New Year, Rabbi."

The rabbi walked along the Vltava River toward Judenstadt, lost in thought, his caftan belted against the October chill. Kepler and Václav returned to the tent. The pages, who were hungry, cold, and tired, were sent back to the castle.

"As I said, Your Majesty," Václav began, "you will feel nothing."

"Look, I believe the sun will be rising soon," Kepler said. "So to speak."

"It is your bedtime, is it not?" Václav said to Kepler.

"Yes, it would be nice to sleep a little. My time, as you know, is very full these days, these nights."

"I will see you later," Václav said.

"At the Golden Ox."

"At the Golden Ox."

Kepler took himself off toward Old Town. His work was coming along well, or at least better. He felt so close to Mars these nights that he knew he was in tune with the secrets of the universe.

"Now, if you could just hold still," Václav said to the emperor. "Best to close your eyes. I will count to forty. Forty is the number of years the ancient Hebrews wandered in the wilderness. David and Solomon reigned for forty years. The Flood was for forty days and forty nights. A period of quarantine is forty days. Christ was in the desert for forty days," Václav continued. "You will hear me count some of the numbers, but then it will seem like gibberish to you. Then I will encircle you seven times one way—"

"Gibberish, what are you talking about?" The emperor opened his eyes in horror.

"Close your eyes, Your Majesty."

"But the words, what are the magic words, the words which will make me immortal?"

"The word, Your Majesty, is EMETH, one of God's names."

"So I am to be like God. Good, good. So simple, yet so profound. One word. *God*. It is fitting. I will be like God, very like God. What do I do? They did not swaddle me as a baby, as is the custom. My coverings were left loose so I could exercise my legs, strengthen my ankles, which is why I am such a fine figure of a man today. The word, Václav?"

"Just keep saying it, Your Majesty. EMETH."

"EMETH, EMETH, EMETH."

Václav took one of the shovels, began to dig a little trench around the emperor.

"So in your ceremony, your ritual, do not bind me tightly in any way. Where is everybody these days—the rabbi, Kepler, Brahe, Jepp, Dee, Kelley, Kirakos, the Jewess?"

"Jepp has joined the parade of fools. Keep your eyes closed, the sun is going to be up any minute, Your Highness. Say the word."

"EMETH, EMETH. Brahe foretold that I would be killed by my son, which is why, Václav, I never married, and now Brahe is in the grave himself, poor fellow. They say his bladder burst."

Václav began to sprinkle the dirt from the border of the little hills surrounding the emperor. "Before we proceed"—Václav paused—"I must ask you, Your Majesty, if you are absolutely certain you wish to be immortal."

"For God's sakes, man, get on with it. EMETH, EMETH."

"Very well."

The Stone Bridge was now lined with carts coming into market.

"The earth I am lying on is magic, is it not?"

There was the story that the whole of Prague was magic, for it had been formed long before Cech and Lech, the two Slavic farmers, came over the hill and claimed the land for their kind. A lonely meteor hurtling through the cold sky, a piece of debris from some astral body, homed itself a valley between the seven hills, and some said the city, still bearing the traces of its ancient visitor, was beacon to the stars. Prague in Czech was *Praha*, which meant threshold.

"If the earth is magic, Václav, pile it on."

"Your wish is my command, Your Majesty."

"EMETH, E-METH, METH. METH. METH, METH, METH."

Václav took a spadeful of earth, then another, then another, and soon the emperor's legs were completely covered, next his waist, then his chest.

Before the rabbi made the right turn which would take him to Judenstadt, he observed the fishermen pushing their boats to the water. It was hard work, he thought, and a good thing he was a rabbi at his age. More people were coming in from the country across the Stone Bridge. The rabbi watched them warily, as well he might, for Thaddaeus and his like were still about in Prague and the world beyond. All who were coming to town to set up their stalls and booths for market in the Square beneath the Astronomical Clock saw the emperor's coach crowned by the little gold crown, his favorite brown stallions, the little striped tent pitched on the bank of the river with the regal Habsburg flag at each pole.

In Judenstadt, Perl was saying her morning prayers, thanking God for not making her a man. It was Friday, much to do. She had to clean the house, fetch the challah from the bakery, roast the chickens. At the synagogue, the Sabbath would be welcomed by "Let us go, dear friends, to meet the bride, the Sabbath presence, let us greet her." It was her favorite song.

Karel had started his rounds, rags, bones, junk to buy and sell. On the other side of the world, across the turquoise sea, Kirakos and Sergey were taking a nap after saying their respective prayers, because in Brazil it was the high heat of afternoon, and to care for their little acre of coffee plants, they rose before light, worked hard all morning, had their supper at noon. After their nap they bathed and enjoyed their veranda, which was surrounded by jacaranda trees and pale lavender bougainvillea. Sergey had taken up chess. Kirakos was still champion. Sergey hunted large lizards. Kirakos became a teetotaler.

Zev and Rochel never had any children, but throughout their long life together, they remained a most devoted couple. He prospered by making boots for the rich Dutch merchants; Rochel learned to read Dutch, German, and Hebrew. Because of her learning and fluency, she was voted the leader in the women's section of their synagogue. In her old age, she was proud to wear spectacles like Perl, and her face, only a bud before, bloomed like a rose of Sharon. Every weekday night, sitting by the fire, wrapped warmly in her coverlet embroidered with blue and white threads, she wrote, in a steady and fine hand, tales, some fanciful, others all too true. On Shabbat, she would read them aloud to Zev and privileged guests.

Once upon a time in a golden city nested within seven hills. Was the proud prince evil or merely mad? Could we regard evil as a form of madness? Certainly, the people feared for their lives. One day, magicians came from across the sea. Meanwhile, on the bank of the river, a wise rabbi. Work of his hands, child of his mind. The love of her life rose up within Rochel in all his starry glory, and without showing it on her sweet face, she was stricken with regret and sorrow. How could she not know what was wrong? Why did somebody not tell her? Rochel, the rabbi spoke, if we are able in our youth to foresee the perils in our path, would we have the courage to set out on the journey? And for further comfort, she held in her mind beautiful images. During that time of hate and fear when she was hiding in the attic of the Altneu Synagogue, she tiptoed down and, in perfect peace, she examined the whole building and all the objects. She smoothed her hand lovingly over the ark where the Torah was resting, touched the bimah, the rabbi's chair, Elijah's chair, the cantor's platform, the wooden seats lining the walls, felt warmth from the Ner Tamid, the Eternal Light. What moved her most, however, was the sight of a silver candlestick holder in the shape of a heart with wings. It is written, "For ye shall go out with joy." That was what she wished.

Acknowledgments

Special thanks to Jill Bialosky, Lucy Childs, Morley Feinstein, Michael Kouroubetes, Ceres Madoo, Lark Madoo, Leander Madoo, Dierdre O'Dwyer, Margaret Scanlan, Linda Schultz, Frederick Slaski, Manuel Wally, Sandra Winicur, and the staff of the main branch of the South Bend Public Library.

The Book of Splendor is a historical fantasy using fictional and non-fictional characters. Most of the events are constructed by the author, some are historically documented, and in a few incidences, the official account has been altered. The book is set in 1601 in Prague, the capital at that time of the Habsburg Empire. The daily life as described in the book—food, furniture, occupations, clothing, court and city, political atmosphere and attitudes—is authentic. Rudolph II was Holy Roman Emperor from 1576 to 1612. His strange behavior, family history, passion for collecting, and interest in the elixir of eternal life are part of record and legend.

Tycho Brahe was appointed by Rudolph as imperial mathematician and astronomer in 1599 and his character, silver nose and all, and the manner of death described in *The Book of Splendor*, are in accord with testimony. Johannes Kepler, appointed as Brahe's assistant, became imperial mathematician after Brahe's death, and did his great work on the orbit of Mars in Prague in the early part of the seventeenth century.

John Dee and Edward Kelley were Englishmen invited by the emperor to Prague to make gold. Dee was a well-known figure, a learned man, bibliophile, translator of Euclid, and believer in a spirit world. Some of his biographers emphasize his mystical-magical side; others concentrate on his role in Her Majesty's Secret Service as code breaker and spy, and he is said, by a few, to be the original 007. Supposedly, he was also the model for Shakespeare's Prospero. Kelley did lose his ears as penalty for forgery. While in Prague, he was imprisoned by Rudolph when he was not successful in transmuting base metal to gold. He died of a broken leg in an escape attempt.

Rabbi Loew, born in Worms between 1512 and 1520, was a famous rabbi in Prague from 1573 to 1609. His ideas, as described in this book, are to be found in his published work, and his feats of magic, including the fashioning of a golem, are the subjects of many stories. He evaded the Angel of Death many times, only to be eventually outwitted when he turned one day from his reading to receive a beautiful rose offered by his favorite grandchild. Death nested within the petals.

Mordechai Maisel (1528–1601) was the mayor of Judenstadt and a noted philanthropist. The attack on Judenstadt and Rochel is fictional, as is the specific massacre in the Ukraine. However, the restrictions on land ownership, trade and guild membership, the requirement of the yellow circle, placement in a ghetto, and the daily threat of persecution were realities for Jews in Prague in 1601.

Black Tower
(Powder
Tower)

St.Vitus
Cathedral

Golden
Lane

Dalibor
Tower

Stag Moat

Castle

House
of Three
Ostriches

The Golde
Ox

HRADČANY

Master
Galliano's
Shop

Petřin
Woods

MALÁ STRANA
LITTLE QUARTER

Mill

Glass
Works

Emperor's
Brewery

Vltava River

Chazaud

PRAGUE
PRAHA